Elle Connel is the pseudonym of Lucy Ribchester, whose previous novels, *The Hourglass Factory* and *The Amber Shadows*, were historical thrillers. She has a first class degree in English from the University of St Andrews and a Masters in Shakespeare Studies from Kings College London. Her previous work has won her a Scottish Book Trust New Writers Award, a Robert Louis Stevenson Fellowship, and short-listings for the Costa Story Award and Manchester Fiction Prize. She lives in Edinburgh with her partner and two sons. *Down by the Water* is her first book as Elle Connel.

D0474932

DOWN
BY THE
WATER

ELLE CONNEL

WILDFIRE

First published in 2021 by
WILDFIRE
an imprint of HEADLINE PUBLISHING GROUP

First published in paperback in 2022 by
WILDFIRE
an imprint of HEADLINE PUBLISHING GROUP

1

Cataloguing in Publication Data is available from the British Library

ISBN 978 1 4722 7261 4

Typeset in Sabon by CC Book Production

Printed and bound in Great Britain by Clays Ltd, Elcograf S.p.A.

MIX
Paper from
responsible sources
FSC® C104740

Headline's policy is to use papers that are natural, renewable and
recyclable products and made from wood grown in well-managed forests
and other controlled sources. The logging and manufacturing processes are
expected to conform to the environmental regulations of the country of origin.

HEADLINE PUBLISHING GROUP
an Hachette UK Company
Carmelite House
50 Victoria Embankment
London EC4Y 0DZ

www.headline.co.uk
www.hachette.co.uk

For Bridget Gray

AUTHOR'S NOTE

Some of the stranger happenings portrayed in the book are inspired by true events, which were recounted to me as I began to write. All characters, locations and explanations however are entirely fictional and products of my imagination.

It is the dead, not the living, who make the longest demands

Sophocles, *Antigone*

PROLOGUE

26 September 2007

The water is rough but the light is calm.

A cool haar blows inland from the open sea. It seems to hang in lavender rolls above the sea loch, not touching it. A moment ago the loch was grey, bled of colour, but now it has turned a dark violet, blacker in the middle. This is one of its tricks – to change in a second by the lurch of a wave or the passing of a cloud across the sun.

Late summer, early autumn. On a day this beautiful, anything could happen.

She has untied the boat already, and the rope chafes her palm as she drags it towards the water's edge. A couple of hundred metres out, mussel ropes are marked by three white buoys. She watches them toss in the waves, the currents whipping their rope necks back and forth. Suddenly, she sees beneath the water: skeleton bodies flailing in despair against the undertow.

It is just the buoys, she tells herself. She kissed him goodbye this morning. She saw him sleep. He is still there, sleeping beneath his blankets. She turns her attention quickly to the boat.

As she launches it across the shoreline, she realises she is not wearing the right shoes. Ice water soaks through them, into her soles and up over her ankles. She climbs on board, making the old wood creak. The boat needs painting. She reaches for an oar and pushes off, blade scraping against shingle, the final chime of dry land echoing into the air.

She rows in the direction of the mountains on the other side of the loch. She has grown strong doing this so often and, though her arms still burn, the resistance feels good. Over there are forest-covered peaks where the trees grow so thick and wild that it's impossible to see where you could moor and enter. She always wanted to go there when she was little – both of them did, but they were always told no. It was too dangerous.

She wonders now what that danger was. Witches? Axemen? Getting lost and contracting hypothermia? Could any of it be as bad as all that she's seen since, in places she'd expected to feel safe? But she also understands now that desire to protect, to keep a child safe from anything, to never let them know – or even glimpse – danger.

Before she knows it, she is in the middle of the loch. The shore she came from, a sickle-shaped shingle beach backed by friendlier clusters of pine trees, looks strange and plain. She pushes towards the buoys, but despite throwing her body into each stroke, the currents keep heading her off. Her back is towards the horizon. Sea on one side, mountains on the other. Plain shoreline, ahead of her.

She keeps rowing, and rowing, pulling and sweating as the mauve haar continues to roll in.

The mussels will be fat now, after a summer left alone. As the boat comes alongside the three buoys, it twists, pulled by an undertow, but she has learned, and she uses the oar to hook herself into the right spot.

She leans over the ropes and comes face to face with her reflection in the shining dark surface of the sea loch. Her curls blend into the water's black ripples. Behind her eyes is something she can't describe.

TEN YEARS LATER

PART ONE

1

Tessa woke with a start, as if she had heard something or felt a sudden jolt. But the train was still moving smoothly along.

Light bled through the fringes of the doorframe. Her nose was pressed to a crisp, laundered pillowcase. In the first few moments of coming to, she thought she was in the on-call wing of the hospital and that her bleep had just gone off. Then she felt the rocking motion, and rolled over to see the reflection of the sleeper car's interior in the blank, black windowpane. She caught herself as she almost fell from the bunk. The blind was still up. They must have forgotten to lower it. Her eyes slowly focused and she made out the cabin's straight lines and compact, square furniture, the snoring body of Georgie on the berth below her.

She began to roll the other way, away from the glare, in the hope of returning quickly back to sleep, when she saw a more solid form take shape in the window's reflection. She tried to focus. The shape became columnal, tracing a path around a head and slim shoulders. And then her skin froze as she realised someone was in their cabin.

She tried to wake herself fully, to take in what she was looking at. Then from somewhere else, deep in memory, she recognised a scent. Agent Provocateur perfume. It was powdery sweet, a ghost of recognition, a scent she kept boxed in the past. But here it was in the cabin, now.

That was when she knew she must be dreaming. Charlie was not here in the sleeper cabin, standing over Georgie's slumbering body. She wasn't here on the hen party weekend; she hadn't been there at King's Cross station when they had all gathered, nor on the train earlier when they opened the first bottle of pink prosecco. When the shots were poured and when they had finally turned in – 'Nightcaps, girls! We're growing old, long weekend ahead!' – Charlie hadn't been there.

But now the shape was moving in the dark – and no, Tessa was not dreaming.

'Georgie,' she said sharply. And then again, summoning assertiveness to scare the intruder. 'Georgie, are you in your bed? There's someone in—'

'Shhhhh.'

Tessa saw the figure reach forward and clutch hold of her bedsheet for support as the train lurched, and then she recognised the shape of the head, taking form, the tone of voice.

'Harriet?'

'Tessa? Are you awake?'

Harriet's tall body stumbled into the berth with the motion of the train. Her bony hand gripped Tessa's pillow.

Tessa wriggled onto her elbows, banging her head on the shallow ceiling. 'Ouch!'

'Shhhh. I don't want to wake Georgie,' Harriet said.

'What are you doing in here?' Tessa hissed.

She saw Harriet's head, with its long sheet of blunt-cut hair, swing towards the cabin door. The door opened a crack, letting in a blade of light. Now a second, more petite figure – Melissa – crept forwards.

'You need to come now, Tessa,' Melissa whispered. 'Please.' There was a tight note in her voice.

'What's happened?' Tessa picked up her phone to check the time: 2.46 a.m. She slid from her berth, landing hard on the side of her foot. She felt the nausea of getting up too quickly, and was aware her breath was rancid and her curls were on end.

'Do you have your medical kit?'

She frowned. 'Yes. No. I have a small first aid kit.'

'I thought you'd have your doctor's bag with you.' Harriet's voice was starting to creep up a notch.

'No, I think – I assumed – there'd be a proper first aid kit up at the castle. What's going on?'

Harriet put two fingers to Tessa's lips. Tessa smelled herbal soap; underneath it, the sickliness of prosecco. 'Don't wake Georgie,' Harriet whispered, nodding towards the lower bunk.

'Bea's in a K-hole,' Melissa whispered. 'You have to come and sort her out or we'll be chucked off the train.'

'Bea's what?' Tessa swerved, knocking against Georgie's berth.

'Bea is off her box on ketamine,' Harriet whispered, slow and precise.

11

Tessa looked down at Georgie's sleeping form, the wisps of curled auburn hair across her cheek. Her breathing was soft. The train swayed.

Tessa followed Harriet and Melissa into the corridor. Even though the main light had been dimmed, the acidic tone of the strip lights felt painful to her waking eyes. There was a guard idling at the end of the row of cabins, in the space where the toilet was, looking at his phone.

Melissa opened the next door down.

The cabin was fully lit – a mess of toiletries, prosecco bottles knocking back and forth, scattered clothes, jewellery. The air had the warm, specific scent of caramelised onion humous and nacho-cheese chips. Beside the bottom berth, cowering under a silk scarf, Bea crouched on her haunches, dry retching. She peeled away a corner of the scarf, looked up, clocked Tessa. Before the reunion at the station earlier that evening, they had seen each other only a handful of times since university. Bea had changed a lot, grown heavier, and she looked more tired around her eyes and mouth. She wore no make-up except for kohl and mascara that had smeared. But she had the same tenderness in her face that Tessa remembered. At the station, with her slouchy cardigan and gaping leather overnight bag, she had looked homely. Bea had been the meal-cooker back in student days, feeding people with almost crazed fervour. Now, something like that same intensity was in her eyes: she looked unhinged, like she was not used to psychedelics.

Her eyes widened at Tessa.

Harriet lunged down to her, quickly taking her wrists.

'Don't panic, Bea, we're not here to hurt you. We're your friends, all right?'

Tessa reached out. 'Don't agitate her. How much has she had?' She tried not to let anger take over. She crouched close and looked into Bea's enormous pupils; took her pulse, measured the intervals between her breaths. She stroked Bea's lank brown hair and made the noises that they didn't teach in medical school, but that she'd had to learn, nonetheless. 'Who gave her the ketamine?' Tessa asked, although she thought she already knew the answer.

Georgie had asked Tessa if she could nick some from the dispensary or write a prescription. She'd said no, and so without a doubt, Georgie must have gone to Melissa and asked her instead. Melissa had easier access, as a vet, and she wouldn't have dared say no to Georgie. Melissa never refused Georgie anything; and anyway, she was baked herself most of the time these days. Why Bea had taken the ketamine now instead of waiting until they got to the castle – they hadn't even crossed into Scotland yet – was a different question.

No one had seen Bea for nearly four years, before they had all gathered, together once again, at King's Cross at half past six that evening. It hadn't been as strange as perhaps it ought to have been. Maybe it had been more than four years, more than five even? Had she been at Freddie and Harriet's wedding? Tessa couldn't remember, but she didn't think so. Harriet, Melissa and Georgie had stayed in touch and met up regularly. Harriet would organise gatherings over WhatsApp, inviting everyone with short, brisk messages – no punctuation, no kisses – that made them sound like a summons. Though Tessa rarely came along, she lurked on the threads and had observed that Melissa always obediently attended, driving the hundred or so miles from her Suffolk village to London, maybe because she missed them all, maybe because it felt mellower to party with old friends, or maybe just because she was loyal. Melissa had always been petite and bright and loyal, mellow more than meek, where Harriet was cool and demanding. The gatherings would take place at Georgie's, because she was a fabulous host. Not only did she have no children at all, she had lots of Le Creuset kitchenware and lived above a wine shop in West Hampstead, whose owner she had befriended and who sometimes came upstairs with a few free bottles of wine and hung around afterwards. Sometimes the trio posted pictures on Facebook, with the wine-shop owner, an old Frenchman, grinning in the background like he had won a prize. Bea sometimes sent an excuse on the thread. Alice rarely replied at all.

Tessa had never minded missing out. These days she was too tired. Her shifts were too long, and it felt as if she had drifted from her friends. She hadn't seen Mel in over a year now, and Harriet – about the same? Alice hadn't invited any of them to her wedding, which might have just been because it was small and low-key. To be honest, Tessa hadn't even registered that Alice was married, until she'd brought it up in the WhatsApp group for this weekend.

But out of the blue, Georgie had asked them all to be her bridesmaids – not just Harriet and Mel, but the whole old university gang. She had chosen them, and only them: not any of her London friends, not any of the folks she had met travelling, not her sisters-in-law or the small children of distant relatives. She had chosen them, and there must have been something in that, some pull, some old stubborn thread between them that had made them all unanimously say yes.

And then it seemed like the time they had spent apart just melted away as they'd met on the station concourse and climbed single file onto the train, dragging bags of clinking bottles and food for the weekend. The snacks had been opened; bunks chosen. Melissa had brought along a ukulele – *Some Like it Hot*! She couldn't play it. Alice had a go. It was just like the old days.

Bea and Harriet each had two children now. As soon as the prosecco was popped, Harriet had been excited to swap sleeping complaints and share tantrum notes. 'Are you back at work?' she had asked, blinking at Bea.

'Part-time. I work in the university library, so Mo and I get lunch dates.'

Since Bea had lain low for the past few years, it seemed their children had never actually met. 'We must get them together!' Harriet insisted.

Harriet had been pregnant at her own wedding, five years ago. Bea had four-year-old identical twin girls. When Tessa had first heard about the twins, she had sent two baby grows in the post, via Bea's husband's university lab, but she had never received a thank-you card.

'Enough about kiddies,' Melissa had interrupted, before regaling them with stories of her adopted menagerie. 'Two bearded dragons, a rescue chicken, a goat from the RSPCA,'

15

and a geriatric collie who spent more time with her elderly neighbour.

But Harriet was not interested in animals. 'I'm a mumpreneur now,' she confided to Bea. She had a blog and an Instagram, Mama in the City. 'If you ever want to know anything,' she said, placing a hand on Bea's arm, 'Anything at all about how to manage two children in London, just ask – because it's an absolute nightmare, you know. Whoever designed the buses should be shot.'

Bea had smiled politely and said something about twins being their own kind of fish. Tessa had learned to read those sorts of smiles, usually on patients who were being gracious, but weren't taken in.

'Sips. Very small ones.' Tessa held a bottle of water to Bea's lips, barely trusting her not to gulp. She looked up at the others, who were watching. 'Did you take some, too?'

Melissa shook her head. 'We only knew she had when I heard her scrabbling around outside the door. I honestly don't know where she found it. Maybe – Alice?'

Tessa shook her head. Alice had gone to bed early with Rachael. There had been something of an awkward moment early in the planning stage when Alice sent a WhatsApp message checking if it would be OK to bring her wife Rachael along. After half a day's pause, Harriet had started a new Alice-free WhatsApp thread and asked, 'What do you think? I mean it seems to me that, if that's the case, I could invite Freddie and Bea could bring Mohammed?'

They had all assumed – or hoped – that this issue wouldn't

surface, because Rachael, who worked for UCL and London Zoo, was usually off in South America studying pumas. But it seemed she had taken time off specially.

'Why don't we invite Jack along, make it a communal kind of gathering?' Melissa had replied, and it wasn't clear if she was being sarcastic or dippy.

'It will make us seven. Seven is a lucky number,' Bea had texted.

'Just so long as I don't hear them fucking,' Harriet replied, and the thread had gone silent.

But then there had been a collective guilt in the air when Rachael and Alice had arrived at King's Cross, their arms laden down with a Fortnum and Mason hamper for the train journey and a case of Pol Roger, and they had produced from a stiff boutique bag a cashmere snood, monogrammed 'Mrs Jack', and given it to Georgie 'Because Scotland is fucking cold, even in April, don't you know?' And then Alice had made a joke about the scarf being better than a ridiculous hen-night hoodie, and they'd all tried to laugh it off as Harriet had distributed the hen-night hoodies with their university nicknames on the back – BB, Locky, George, Hats, Ally, Mel D – which, by then, they all realised they had discussed getting printed on the Alice-free WhatsApp thread. There was not a hoodie for Rachael. She'd said she didn't mind.

'Is that real Fortnum's?' Harriet had stared at the wicker, eyes roving for the crest.

'Mmm hmm.' Alice nodded.

'Not TK Maxx?'

'Nope.'

After that, Georgie had seemed quite tame about Alice's new haircut, leaning over and stroking a palm up one of the shaved sides. The fringe was dyed pink and purple in pale streaks; the sides showed off Alice's piercings, which ran up the cartilage of one ear. 'When did you get this done? It's gorgeous.'

'A few weeks ago.'

They all knew then that she had cut her hair after the email guidelines for the wedding had come through: *Long hair, natural colours, all tattoos covered up, piercings taken out on the day, please.* These guidelines were implicitly for Alice only, since none of the rest of them had tattoos or multiple piercings, and they didn't colour their hair other than highlighting it.

But perhaps Georgie really meant it; perhaps she did think it was gorgeous, and perhaps she had mellowed now the wedding day was drawing closer and they were all there together again, and the anxiety of all of the little things that could go wrong were melting into perspective. Now they were all on the train, and the hen party was underway. Everyone had shown up. Everyone had shown that they cared. That was all that mattered. They were together. There was a whole weekend ahead to reconnect. It didn't matter that they hadn't all been in the same room for years, that the humous was warm, and the pitta bread chewy, or that they started off their drinking with prosecco straight from the supermarket shelf in glittery plastic cups. 'We should save the champagne for when we arrive,' Georgie had said. They were on a train heading to Scotland, where they'd all met.

They were heading back to the past, to the parties and the booze and the feet on each other's laps and splintery jokes and late-night confessions, and the casual comfort of being with people they had all seen in that vulnerable half-adult state as they crossed from school to university, and learned how to wash up properly and how to manage heartbreak. They would merge again, in Scotland again, before they all dispersed like pieces of meteorite, back into their own lives.

After their picnic tea, Alice and Rachael had turned in first, about eleven. They had been up since six, they said, for their final 10k run before the weekend. Besides, Alice hadn't been much for partying, even back in the day. She was more into staying up late behind a computer screen, cruising weird parts of the internet.

After that, it was a nip of whisky each for the five remaining – drunk from the bottle, the taste of one another's lipsticks and lip balms all melding into one on the rim – and then they had all gone off to their cabins.

'Just think, ladies. When we wake up, look out that window, there might be a stag,' Georgie said.

'Yes, and he'll be called Jack and he'll be wearing a sapphire merkin and be tied to an Edinburgh lamppost,' said Bea.

They all laughed, even Georgie, though she did not like jokes about Jack in general.

That had been four hours ago. Now, Bea was groaning, trying to get words out.

'You have to call an ambulance,' Melissa was saying, her voice rising.

'Do you think that's wise?' Harriet said. 'If she has to be evacuated, wouldn't we have to reschedule?' She softened her tone. 'Georgie would be devastated. You know she would. Tessa, is she that bad?'

Tessa tuned them out and pulled Bea into the centre of the cabin floor.

'Georgina,' Bea moaned.

'It was Georgie who asked for the K on the WhatsApp group.' Melissa sounded defensive.

'How did she take it?'

'I didn't see,' Melissa said.

Tessa lay Bea on her side and stroked her back. The balls on her spine protruded, her lungs swelling with each moan. Tessa felt a memory of panic, suddenly thinking of a time when she had stroked Charlie's back in the same way, the feeling of the skin and blood underneath her fingers, pulsing erratically upwards. But back then there had been no drugs, and now she was a doctor and she knew what to do.

She stroked Bea's back until the vomit came, tapping, patting, checking she wasn't choking, pulling her hair out of the firing line. She put her hand on Bea's chest, counted her breaths again, watched the pulse in her throat rippling like a purple snake. It was all regular.

Tessa took her phone out of her pyjama pocket and switched on the screen. It was approaching three. 'You'll have to take shifts staying up with her, just in case. If she vomits again, the biggest risk—'

'I know.' Melissa cut her off.

Tessa had the words in her mouth – *No, you don't. She's*

not a fucking sheep – but she swallowed them back down. It was Georgie's weekend, not hers. They didn't need arguments.

'What if she starts screaming?' Harriet asked. Her glance flicked towards the door. 'The guard?'

'Tell him she's having nightmares.'

'But if she does it again and again?'

'I don't know, Harriet. Make it up. You're a novelist, after all.'

In the glare of the full electric light, Tessa saw her words pierce. She hadn't intended them to: she was just not very good at controlling her tongue when she was tired. Harriet had been a novelist, it was true. Before the mama blog, she'd had one of those freak six-figure book deals straight out of university, for a coming-of-age story about a girl in nineteenth-century Ireland. And then, for eight years, she had been working on the follow-up, until eventually marriage, the children, and the blog had taken over.

Tessa did not make eye contact with any of them as she slipped, business-like, out of their cabin and back to her own, emergency over. The guard was still bent over his phone.

She crept in and climbed up to her bed, only then becoming aware that the sickness she had felt earlier had turned to a deeper anxiety. Or was it just the bubbles churning, prosecco residue? She had not eaten enough, again.

As she lay between the stiff sheets, she became more and more aware of Georgie's snoring. Gradually, it overtook the rumble of the train. There was, it seemed to Tessa in the dark, an arrogance to the snoring, and as she lay awake, her

21

mind spiralling in the adrenaline come-down of jumping in and out of work mode, she began to resent Georgie for what had happened. She would stake her life on it that Georgie had given Bea the drugs. Something to loosen her up. It was Georgie who had corralled them all together after all, she who had demanded a whole weekend from them, not just a night out. That was on top of her wedding, which was in Tuscany, of course, the invite arriving on thick paper with a note on one half requesting contributions towards a five-star honeymoon, the opposite leaf stating with eloquent bluntness that children would not be welcome.

Perhaps, Tessa thought uncharitably, it would have served Georgie right if they had been caught, if the police had been called, if they had been thrown off the train. And had Melissa or Harriet felt the same way? Had they all, somehow – maybe in a way they didn't even realise – been trying to sabotage the weekend before it had even begun?

Tessa tried to still her mind, using all the tricks she'd learned. Clenching her toes and releasing, imagining herself walking down a staircase into oblivion, step by careful step. She almost got there, but just as she was drifting back into sleep, she caught that scent again – the Agent Provocateur from her dreams. There it was, close by once more. With a jolt of sudden, cold awareness, she realised it was on her own skin.

2

The train had halted somewhere outside Edinburgh to wait for sunrise. The sky had begun to grow light, but they still weren't moving when Tessa heard laughter spill out of the cabin next door. She smelled coffee. A knock came at their door and she leaned down from her bunk to see Georgie – hair already straightened and tied back; her perfumed neck set off by a huge chunky jade necklace. Georgie paused in fixing flicks of eyeliner on her upper lids, and winked at the guard as she accepted the red tray of packaged croissants and little butter slabs. Two paper cups of black coffee wobbled, steaming.

'You have both croissants,' she said to Tessa, balancing the tray on the messed-up sheets of the lower bunk. 'I can't eat before ten any more.'

When they eventually rolled onto the platform, it was about half past six. It was lighter than it would have been in London at that time, but the light seemed foggier, or perhaps softer, hanging a depressing gauze over the air. Tessa had never liked this time of day, and coming into Scotland always held mixed memories. She had been to school near the border, and they had all met at university, near here in St Andrews. The London train passed through Edinburgh to get there. Anxiety and anticipation; relief. Maybe exams or a new term, a new flat; hangovers, dissertations. Now there was a castle and a relaxing weekend waiting for them, an hour or so away. But Tessa still felt anxious. It had fallen on her to find the accommodation for the weekend, and she had chosen to go to this castle, she had arranged the booking. What was there to be afraid of? They were here to relax, to enjoy themselves, to rediscover each other among old memories. Surely that wasn't such a herculean task?

She wondered how Bea was.

On the platform, they passed around the croissants and coffee and made noises about the hour.

'I can't even,' said Melissa.

'Don't you get up at this time to birth cows?' Harriet asked.

'Not on holiday.'

'No such thing as a holiday when you're a mum,' Harriet muttered.

From beneath hooded bloodshot eyes, Bea fired Harriet a warning look. Tessa saw it. Bea looked grim, and was alternating between coffee and water, laughing forcedly at jokes while looking like she wanted to vomit. She would be fine.

The castle was a taxi ride away. They wouldn't all fit into one, so split themselves into a three and a four, heaving their bags onto the spare seats: Bea's battered leather holdall,

Tessa's neat wheelie case and Melissa's sports bag. Georgie had three suitcases in mismatching vintage designer logos; Alice and Rachael had brought backpacks with a multitude of compartments. And there were the bags for life, too, overspilling with food.

The cabs rumbled off down Princes Street, and they gazed through smeared windows at the grey stone streets and Georgian houses, until the trees lining the pavements grew thicker and then gave way to hedges, private gardens, shrubs, sheds and garages. Then industrial buildings fanned out around flyovers and, before they knew it, they were on the motorway.

Tessa was in a car with Rachael, Georgie and Bea. She kept a wary eye on Bea, who had her head on Georgie's shoulder, dozing. But if Georgie had noticed Bea's drug hangover, she wasn't saying anything. She curled her fingers absent-mindedly in the tendrils of Bea's hair. Rachael made chit-chat with the taxi driver about Scotland. She was the only one out of them who had never been. He had plenty of tips: the Small Isles, not Skye. Stovies – forget haggis. Deep-fried Mars bars were a myth made up for the tourists; try tablet instead.

Tessa watched as they peeled off the motorway, onto and off the roundabout with the metal sculpture at its centre, and down to the B-road that ran along the coast. She watched it all as if for the first time.

They passed through the village of Gilmouth – a strip of eighteenth-century cottages and a market cross – then came out the other side, where the cab took a sharp turn down towards the shoreline. On the inland side, the cliffs crept up, clutched by shrubs and the twisted claws of half-formed Scots pines, rooted in crevices. The road dipped low until the sea lapped towards them from behind a flood wall; then they began to rise into forest again.

'Christ,' Georgie said. 'If there are any more twists on this rollercoaster I'm going to chunder. I'm used to Finchley Road, mate,' she called to the cabbie, laughing. The cabbie smiled at her in the mirror, saying nothing.

Bea murmured and shifted in her seat. Tessa looked over at her chest, saw she was breathing fine, and quickly looked back out of the window before Georgie could notice. They were further away from the sea now, gulls dipping to the hard crests beneath slate clouds. They turned left and passed through a pair of eroded stone pillars, past a lodge house with a neat vegetable garden and a refurbished camper van parked in front.

'Are we here?' Georgie whispered. 'You'd think he could stop the meter now.'

'I don't think it's too much further,' Tessa replied.

The road crackled as tarmac gave way to rocks and uneven dirt. They rucked over potholes. Rachael glanced behind to look at the second cab. The trees were thick now – Douglas firs, pines and at their base, blackthorn bushes and huge boulders of rhododendrons, spilling out of control, creeping up the inland banks of the road, sliding down the hill to where the sea peeped through gaps in the trees. They were in full bloom, their garish cornets reaching out, shocking red. The car pushed past them as the track made another sharp turn, then dipped suddenly down until it was level with a small burn sputtering under a home-made bridge of logs lashed together with chicken wire. The cab rocked from side to side. Georgie giggled uncertainly. 'Bit rustic,' she said.

Tessa tried to smile reassuringly. Her stomach lurched as the cab cleared the bridge and revved back up the other side of the slope, spitting stones beneath its wheels. The cabbie laughed, but they all heard him drop a curse as he cleared the ridge and the road began to plateau again. The path was still narrow and the car clipped bushes on both sides, severing sprays of petals in its wake.

Georgie turned to look behind her. 'Pretty,' she said, breathing out. 'What are they?'

'Rhododendrons,' Rachael said, twisting round. 'I read about them when I was boning up on coming here. They're a pest. Victorians brought them over and now they run rampant, killing the native species.'

Tessa caught the look that passed over Georgie's face: boredom, faintly masking amusement.

'I'm not sure I like them,' Tessa said. 'They're suffocating.'

'I like them.' Georgie stared out of the back window and exclaimed 'Whoosh,' as another bunch of petals fireworked into the air, spattering the bonnet of the cab behind.

'Is that it?' Bea had woken up and was staring straight ahead, leaning forward to see through the windscreen.

They all turned to look as the car slowed.

Tessa watched Georgie, feeling nervous. If it wasn't what Georgie expected, if it wasn't what she wanted – well, there were two Georgies. One would hold back, smile, but make sure you knew she was pretending. The other wouldn't.

Georgie had the same amused grin she had worn a moment ago. 'It's not what I expected.'

'What did you expect?' Tessa asked tentatively. She knew that what Georgie had expected was probably the same thing every English person thought of when they heard the words 'Scottish castle': Edinburgh, St Andrews, Tantallon. Ruined battlements, windswept gables, grey.

'It's an old tower house,' she said.

Georgie squinted up at the pink turrets. 'It looks like something from Disney.'

Tessa nodded. 'It is. They say it inspired Cinderella's castle—'

Georgie interrupted her. 'Did they paint it pink recently?'

Bea snorted. She said groggily, 'In honour of your hen weekend.'

They all laughed. It shattered the tension that was beginning to creep into the cab as the castle had come into view, and Tessa realised it wasn't just her; they had all been worried that Georgie wouldn't like it. The trouble was, having not seen one another for so long, they didn't really know what the others were like any more. They were still feeling their way.

They spilled out of the taxis, exchanged ten- and twenty-pound notes, paid the drivers.

Tessa decided it was too late now to give Georgie an explanation of the pink harl that covered the castle's walls, and instead they busied themselves hefting their luggage, the Fortnum's hamper and the case of champagne towards the front door. The castle was small-proportioned, three stories high, with sunken four-paned windows to the front, a clutch of which they could see had been blocked in and painted over. Turrets shot up from the highest floor, on all four corners, and another was tacked on in a narrower block which looked like a later addition to the original castle. There were several of these blocky additions, all moulded together and smothered over with the same pink harl to unify the cubist form into one, although it was clear from the different window sizes that they were from different eras. The castle was set on a slope; there was another level to the rear, where the basement nestled into the hillside. Tessa watched Bea wander round the side, taking in the overgrown vegetable garden with its picturesque arch leading through to a forest, where some scrappy targets for an archery range were pinned to trees. Beyond the clearing sat two further cottages, set back from the woody path. They were small with low eaves; more later additions. The website had also said there was an icehouse.

'Is there supposed to be someone here to let us in?' Melissa asked.

'I've been emailing Tom,' Tessa said.

'Who's Tom?'

'Estate manager.' She took out her mobile, then noticed the pair of shaggy lurchers approaching from down the main path.

From behind Tessa there came a bloodcurdling shriek.

'I can't – I can't – I can't—' Alice had crumpled onto the stone steps and was covering her face. 'Get them the fuck away from me. You didn't say there would be fucking dogs here.'

Rachael knelt and took Alice by the shoulders. She began counting her breathing out loud. 'Look at me, look at me; I'm here, you're fine. I'm holding you.'

The scream had made Tessa jump, and now her heart was pounding. The rest of the group were gathered around Alice, and so no one other than Tessa saw the man appear from round the thicket of red rhododendrons. He wore jeans tucked into wellies, and a quilted gilet over a pale checked shirt.

He raised his hand to his brow, shielding his eyes from the sun, and frowned.

'She'll be all right,' Tessa called over.

'No, I fucking won't!' came a cry from inside the scrum of bodies.

'Tom?' Tessa stretched out her hand. He clutched it. His palm was bone dry. His nails were bitten to the quick and the veins between his knuckles were bulging. He looked tired around the eyes, and his stubbly cheeks hung from his cheekbones. 'Sorry, I never think—' he began.

'Why would you?' Tessa collared one of the lurchers, and held on to it, stroking its wolfish muzzle, while Melissa extracted herself from the group around Alice, and bent down and nose-kissed the other. She laughed as it licked her.

'Stella, Bella,' Tom said, calling them.

The dog in Melissa's hands squirmed free. They both trotted over to Tom and sat at his feet. He kept his hand lightly in front of their noses, something concealed in his fingers – a treat, or maybe just a scent they liked – as Tessa made a loose introduction. 'That's Georgie, our bride-to-be.'

Georgie looked across. 'Hi.' In that quick moment, Tessa

saw her take him in – the full size and shape of him – pass him through a quick set of calculations and spit him out again: posh, not too posh, friendly, guarded, effete in the way country men sometimes are, handy, cooks well but probably has some poor hygiene habits; visits a traditional barber in the village, buys clothes once a year. Single?

He gave her a silent salute, two fingers to the temple, accompanied by a smirk.

'Is everything ready?' Tessa asked.

'Hmm? Oh, of course.' His hand still hovered by the dogs' noses. 'Got you some bacon and eggs, some steak mince from the butcher and bits and bobs from town this morning. Lovely potatoes, and the beans are freshly picked today. Menu items as requested. Local cheese and bread, and I thought you might be able to use a bit of the shortbread our village bakery's famous for. Aga's fired up and there's wood for it in a basket. It's pretty self-explanatory to use – the door with the glass is for the fuel.'

'A wood-fired Aga?' Harriet's eyes lit up.

Tom looked at her. 'It's still fairly chilly so I'm sure you'll make good use of it. Come on in.'

'Sorry,' Alice said, parting the shoulders of Rachael and Bea, who were still crouched in front of her. 'Can you take them away, please? I'm going to have a panic attack if you don't.' She waited. They all seemed frozen. 'I can't be around—'

Tom cut her off. 'Surely. Back in a minute.' He whistled sharply. 'Girls.' The dogs loped after him, as he turned and began to walk back down the path.

'You could just give us the keys,' Tessa called out.

He stopped walking and rummaged in his pocket. It seemed to Tessa in that moment that his hand lingered there, and she wondered if he was hesitant to hand the keys over. She took an impatient step forward. 'It's a bit cold out here.' It wasn't, but Georgie was only wearing a light London-ish blazer, and Tessa was aware her own wrists were goose-pimpled.

'It's only that . . .' he began, then hesitated. 'There are a few things I need to show you, appliances and things. They have a mind of their own.' He suddenly seemed to make his decision. 'Just don't touch anything. If that's not rude of me to say.'

Georgie blinked her large, painted eyes. 'Not rude at all. It's your – castle.' She was looking up slyly now at the pink turret that shot like a rocket directly above where she stood. She waved her hands as if she were modelling the castle for a prize on a gameshow.

Tom nodded and smiled at his boots. 'I suppose it is.' He tossed the keys at Tessa. She stumbled, but managed to catch them.

'Oh,' he said, dropping his voice so that Tessa had to step closer to hear. 'If you do go for a walk before I get back, watch your feet. It's adder mating season right now. They won't go for you, unless you accidentally step on one.' He stood for a second, considering whether he had said everything he needed to, decided he had, and turned back down the path, the dogs on his heels.

'What did he say?' Georgie asked.

'Nothing, just something about the boiler being gammy,' Tessa said quickly. She caught Melissa's eye and shook her head gently. Melissa nodded.

Harriet was leaning over Alice, one boot resting on the Fortnum's hamper. She stood up straight now as Alice got to her feet. 'Will you be all right?' Alice's hand was still clutched in Rachael's. She didn't answer.

Harriet stared curiously at her. 'Have you always been frightened of dogs? Didn't we used to go to that café by the library where they had the Labrador?'

Alice shook her head. 'That was different.'

'What about big cats?' Harriet said to Rachael. 'Have you ever introduced her to one of your lions?'

Rachael hesitated. She looked like she was deciding whether to unpick everything that was wrong with that question, or simply answer it. But Alice interrupted, snapping, 'They're pumas, Harriet, and they are not the same as dogs. It's like the difference between a ladybird and a spider.'

Harriet chewed that over. 'Which is which?' she asked. But Alice and Rachael had followed Tessa inside, and they were all now adjusting their eyes and ears to the dark and the echo of the castle's main hall.

'I think it must be . . .' Melissa paused for effect. 'Prosecco o'clock!' She reached into one of the bags for life and yanked free a bottle.

'Do we want to chill it first?' Georgie asked.

'I don't think it makes a difference with prosecco,' Harriet replied.

They were all standing in the sprawling basement kitchen, which took up nearly the whole lower floor of the castle. In the centre was a marble-topped island, now covered in bags and baskets and unopened food packets, around which they all crowded. All except Tessa, who was flitting about, opening drawers and cupboards. She pulled open a chest freezer in the corner, her head and shoulders disappearing into it as she investigated. 'There's ice, if anyone wants.'

'Should we wait for Tom before touching anything?' Georgie asked. Tessa continued rooting.

'You could hide a body in that,' Harriet said, as Tessa stood back up with a bag of ice in her hand.

'I'll have ice in mine,' Rachael said to Tessa. She turned to Alice. 'Do you want ice, love?'

'I'd like a cup of tea,' murmured Alice.

'What time is it?' asked Georgie. She pulled out her phone, and waved it around. 'No phone signal, and no Wi-Fi bars,' she muttered.

Harriet put down the bottle of prosecco. 'But I need to send out my newsletter. I was going to do one on weekends away from the family. And I need to call Freddie, and the kids.'

'There'll be Wi-Fi,' Melissa said. 'Isn't there a password in the handbook?'

'I didn't see a handbook.' Harriet looked at Tessa.

'I'm – I'm not sure,' Tessa admitted, feeling suddenly defensive. She felt her cheeks colour under their stares. 'I didn't check – sorry.'

'Ah,' Georgie said. She was thinking something through,

but Tessa couldn't tell what. Something to do with Facebook, probably. Georgie had clung doggedly to Facebook. Harriet was more into Instagram these days, and Alice used whatever the latest platform was.

'Balls,' Harriet said. 'I made a Spotify list for the music. Now we won't have any.'

But then Georgie took a sip of her drink, winced and said, 'Ah, never mind. We can croon drunkenly. It'll be like the olden days. Actually, I think I will have an ice cube in mine.'

Melissa laughed. 'It's your hen weekend. You're only having an ice cube if it's made of neat vodka.' They all laughed. 'Anyway, prosecco was made to be drunk warm, wasn't it?' They laughed again.

Leaving her own glass on the counter, Harriet distributed the rest of the tumblers. She had ignored Alice's request for tea. Tessa looked covertly at Bea, who was wetting her lips with the slightest touches of her drink. The tall glasses had the precise gleam of having been rubbed dry, or perhaps they were brand new. The whole kitchen, in fact, had the air of having been scrubbed scrupulously, and while the finishings were dated in style, they looked fastidiously maintained, as if they were seldom used. Everything had been wiped and cleared. Nineties IKEA and Habitat mismatches were lined up in the cupboards. The cooking pots were heavy and cast iron. Tessa had watched Georgie and Harriet in particular for first impressions when they arrived.

They all clinked again; even Alice reluctantly shoved her tumbler of prosecco into the centre. No one seemed to notice Tessa standing back, without a drink. She didn't mind.

In fact, she preferred them not to notice. All of a sudden, she was flooded with a feeling that she could only liken to homesickness, although it wasn't. It was similar, though. She had felt it before, many times. Boarding school, university, travelling. It was the feeling of being suddenly unmoored, as if a lifeline had been cut. It was not necessarily wanting to be somewhere, but wanting to be with someone; not with the friends around her, but with someone else.

'Tessa!'

She had been rumbled.

'Get that down you.' Melissa was passing her the bottle, and they all watched and clapped as she downed the dregs. 'Right, that's your thank-you prize for finding this place. Don't expect another. Now, what are we going to drink next?'

'We should explore!' Georgie said. 'Choose rooms!' A sudden burst of energy sent her spinning with her arms out into the centre of the flagstoned floor. Tessa caught her, with uncanny timing, reaching her arms out to clutch Georgie's waist just before she could smack into the corner of the Aga.

The darkness had a luxurious gloom to it, low lamps in puff-balls of bronze, their light absorbed by Jacobean panelling and jewel-coloured wallpaper in crimsons, peacock blues, emeralds and glossy browns. They'd climbed the stone spiral staircase back into the hallway, which led to the front door at the other end. In their haste to start drinking, they hadn't really taken it all in until now. There was a whole wall covered in relics of animals: antlers inlaid into shields, curled goat horns, waxy taxidermal salmon and pike. The smell was of polish and thick cloth. Tessa inhaled. It was as comforting as it was eerie. Everything was old: clean, but with a scent of the past, which spoke of a very slow and elegant decay. The patina of dust seemed even to sigh as they passed, as if it had been waiting for them, like Sleeping Beauty's castle.

The central staircase was tucked to one side of the hall. Tessa watched Georgie to see if she would say anything about the castle's lack of size and pomp, but her face was unreadable, smiling with what could have been wonder or amusement as she looked up and down and around her. While it gave off an air of opulence, it wasn't wide and high and sprawling like the stately homes of England. The walls were thick, with small, deep-set windows that let in miniature glimpses of the grounds outside, and it had the medieval feel of a keep, of a building built strong enough to shelter in from the snow, or from a siege.

Georgie held out her hand to brush her fingers along a swathe of forest-green curtain concertinaed back from the front door. She tapped the gilt frame of an oil painting.

'Who is it, I wonder?' Harriet murmured.

'Some old man from the past.' Alice laughed, then yelped slightly as her backpack collided with the protruding petals of an art deco wall lamp. They began climbing the stairs.

'It reminds me of the medical faculty museum, you know the one?' Bea said.

Tessa nodded. She remembered it, filled to the brim with taxidermy and organs in jars.

'Didn't they have a ball in there once, that we went to stoned?' Georgie said. 'Christ, that was frightening.'

The first landing they came to was small and square. The walls were cushioned in a textured silk paper of blue and purple fleur-de-lis. Harriet pushed open a door to the left and the strong smell of Jo Malone Pomegranate Noir wafted out, masking something older and mustier. Tessa peered over her friend's shoulder into the castle's lounge. More rich colours – blood red and fur browns – made the room inviting, but with all the textures, it was almost too much. It felt alive. The sofas were worn and huge. Deerskin rugs lay next to a slate hearth.

'Dining room,' Tessa heard Alice say behind her. She turned to see her coming back out of the room opposite. 'It's like a vampire's bordello in there.'

Melissa made an 'Oooooh' sound and they giggled.

'It's Jacobean,' Tessa said softly. 'They liked dark, heavy things.'

They continued up the stairs to another landing, and then across to one of the more modern wings. It was easy to see where the architectural styles spliced. Creeping under a thick lintel, they emerged into a high-ceilinged hallway, still gloomy, but with fussy Victorian cornicing and pale half-panelled walls. There were only two rooms on this upper portion of the extension – a ladies' drawing room, which was spartan and contained just two IKEA sofas and a hard chair, which almost served as a polite sign to guests not to bother using it – and a bedroom with an en suite attached. It was plainer than the other rooms, the décor yellow and beige, chintzy and bland.

Tessa saw Georgie wrinkle her nose. 'It's the only one with an en suite, I think,' she said.

'We'll take it,' Alice said quickly.

'Where's the master bedroom?' Georgie asked, looking around. Tessa noticed she had brought her tumbler of prosecco with her, while the others had left theirs downstairs in the kitchen.

'I saw a four-poster bed back that way,' Bea said.

Leaving Alice and Rachael unfolding clothes from their rucksacks, the others crammed back beneath the lintel. Up on a mezzanine next to the main bathroom was a further bedroom, a twin room, which Bea and Harriet claimed, scraping their suitcases over the threadbare rug to the two ebony beds.

The master bedroom was back down off the main landing, with a nursery next to it that Tessa said she wouldn't mind sleeping in. It was small and the beds were low camp beds, but the pale yellow walls made it feel airier than the other rooms, and she preferred that to the cloying feeling of the more sumptuous ones. Melissa left her case next to the other camp bed without opening it and then trotted off to follow Georgie into the master. When Tessa arrived, Georgie was lying spread-eagled across a dark green satin quilt on a four-poster bed. The bedposts had been shined down by centuries of polishing, and in the top four corners, faces were carved.

'Looks like you're going to get lucky tonight,' Melissa said, pointing to them.

'Are those gargoyles?' A faint gust of horror passed over Georgie's face before she laughed again. 'How clerical. I bet this castle belonged to a bishop who liked to look at them when he wanked.' She rolled onto her stomach. 'Is this all the rooms there are?'

Tessa hesitated. She was trying to think of what it said on the castle website. 'I think these are all the ones open to guests. It's a tower house,' she said again.

Melissa was wandering around the low-ceilinged, wide room, eyeing the painted beams above their heads. She began exploring the objects on display, touching things gently: a silver hand mirror, a candlestick in the shape of a deerhound, a miniature painting of a woman in a gauze shawl, who looked back at the viewer with a kind of unease, as if she might be about to faint. Tessa found herself mesmerised by Melissa's fascination, by the whimsical trace of her hands as she caressed all of the objects, tickling them and staring at them as if greedy to know the stories they contained, where they had come from and to whom they had belonged. Tessa was snapped out of her reverie by Georgie. 'All right. Rooms done,' she announced. 'Lovely jubbly. What's next on the slab?'

Back in the cool arches of the kitchen, they polished off a second bottle of prosecco, this one colder, while rooting through the bags of food on the island.

Watching them remove the items with delight, Tessa was reminded of one of their moving-in days back at university, when she had shared a house with Georgie, Harriet and Melissa. Third year, it would have been. It was a pretty house with high ceilings, overlooking the vast, stretching West Sands beach, a strip of sand meeting water that was so long it was almost overwhelming to look at. When they had gone to see the house, Tessa had told them she didn't like it – the view made her dizzy – but they had persuaded her somehow. What had made them choose a house for only the four of them, instead of for Bea and Alice too? Was it just that they – Georgie, anyway – had liked that house more than any of the others they had seen, so it didn't matter if there wasn't space for all of them? But then Tessa remembered Alice had stayed in halls because it was cheaper, and perhaps Bea had decided to live with one of her other friends that year. Tessa seemed to remember she had liked to live with just one other person. Maybe they had only ever been looking for a house for the four of them. Bea had lived with Melissa later, in fourth year.

'What's he got us?' Harriet said. 'Ooh, strawberry preserve. It has one of those wax wrappers – delish!' She removed the jar, followed by a packet of bacon, some vacuum-packed mince and two soft packages of butchers' paper, each shaped about the size of a fist.

'I'll put those in the fridge,' Tessa said quickly, taking the butchers' paper packages. Melissa poked into the second bag. 'Sourdough! Three types of cheese, eggs – and they're white as well. Butter, potatoes.'

'These should go in the fridge, too.' Rachael picked up the butter and eggs.

Tessa saw Alice shaking her head and mouthing a pronounced 'Noooo.'

Rachael looked confused.

'Posh people don't keep their butter and eggs in the fridge.' Alice grinned. 'I had to have that drummed into me at St Andrews. It's because they have kitchens big enough to have cool pantries.'

Rachael looked mildly amused, but put the butter and eggs back on the counter.

Harriet's lips were puckered. Tessa tried to laugh it off. 'I remember keeping milk on my windowsill because it was colder outside than in that crappy fridge we had in halls.'

'What are the spices like?' Harriet changed the subject. 'I thought I asked him to get ras el hanout.'

Bea laughed raucously. Harriet stared.

'It's a village in the Scottish Borders,' Bea said.

'They have Yotam Ottolenghi in the Scottish Borders,' Harriet protested. 'They've got the internet, at least,' she murmured.

'Apparently not,' said Alice, looking at her phone. 'Definitely no 4G and no Wi-Fi appearing.'

'I was going to make this recipe for tagine,' Harriet said. 'I should have written it down. It's Felicity Cloake. You always assume you can get the *Guardian* app wherever you go.'

'I've got some recipes,' Tessa said, taking the cheeses from Harriet's hands. She looked down at them: a small wheel of Brie, a block of hard cheese like Cheddar, and a blue.

'Don't put those in the fridge either,' Harriet called. 'I mean, if you don't mind.' She caught herself, softening her tone, flicking a glance at Rachael and Alice, who were leaning against the counter, fingers loosely interlinked. 'It's just that you should let cheese breathe. I would think there would be a cheese store in a place like this. Those look too yummy to fridge.' She topped up her glass, then began poking into the cupboards.

'Let's go outside!' Georgie said. Bea still looked drained

and was busy necking her second mug of tap water. Alice looked preoccupied. She put her phone down and tapped her fingers on the island.

'Georgie's right,' Tessa said. 'We have a busy schedule. There's the perfume testing, and we have to leave time to cook. We should at least try to see the water.'

'And we have to strip Georgie naked and throw her in the sea!' Melissa laughed. Georgie swiped at her playfully.

'Don't you want to wait for Tom to come back?' Harriet asked. 'He's taking his time. Did he say how long he would be?'

Tessa shrugged. 'I wasn't paying attention. There was a lot going on.' She glanced briefly at Alice.

'Not worth it,' Georgie said. 'Sorry if you were banking on him being our butler in the buff.'

'Oh no,' Tessa replied. 'The two cabbies have agreed to stick around for that.' They all laughed.

'Lucky ladies,' Melissa said. 'Come on, Harriet, where's the next bottle?' She raised her hand, snapped her fingers.

Harriet was over by the fridge. She had moved on to the hamper now, examining the contents as she took them out and stuffed them onto the shelves: pâté, olives, artichokes. 'Does anyone want a snack, or brunch? Maybe bacon and eggs?'

'Bugger bacon and eggs,' Georgie said. 'Come on, we're in bonnie Scotland. Let's go among yon pines and take a bottle of whisky and christen the hen party.'

'Or the sea?' Tessa said.

'The sea is a couple of miles away,' Harriet replied.

'I'm starving,' Melissa said.

'Bring crisps. There's plenty of them.'

'It's not miles away, you can see the sea through the trees.'

They squabbled good-naturedly for a bit before Alice said, 'It's the sea loch you mean, Tessa. I looked it up on Google Maps before we came, and made a PDF in case there wasn't Wi-Fi. It's an estuary. It goes down to the sea.'

'Ah, right.' Tessa stood corrected.

'Even better,' Georgie said. 'We can send a message in a bottle, maybe net some horny sailors.'

'Georgie!' Harriet exclaimed. 'You are about to be a married woman.'

'I know,' Georgie whispered. 'And since I've seen how dull that is from looking at you for the past five years, I'd better have my fun while I can.'

Harriet's mouth dropped open in a frozen smile and she looked as if she was searching for a retort – a stabbing one. None seemed to come to mind. Alice and Rachael exchanged a look.

'Shall we get boots on, then?' Rachael said, moving the subject on.

'I'm going in these.' Georgie pointed down to her heeled Mary Janes. She was wearing tailored cargo pants in a silky sort of linen, turned up just above the ankle, showing off her expensive spray tan. 'I want to look good in photos, I don't want to be wearing clodhoppers.' She waggled her phone.

'There's no signal,' Alice said.

'Facebook, unlike time or tide, waits for man – and woman.' She laughed.

'Georgie, you'll break an ankle,' Melissa admonished her, laughing.

'That's the reason we invited the doctor along, isn't it?'

For a second – Tessa could not be sure, but it felt like it – for a second there was a tiny pause, as if no one could believe Georgie had said such a thing out loud. But then it was obvious it was a joke. They were all bantering, like they used to, weren't they? Like that thing she had just said to Harriet, about being married. It was just that they were out of practice. It had been too long. It took time to stitch up the frayed seams in those friendships, and in the meantime they had to feel their way, testing what they could and couldn't say. Anything else would have been dull, polite, bland. Friends had to be able to test one another. And tease one another. And grow. And yet that silence, that tiny silence which Tessa could have imagined, told her that all of the others had been shocked, too – that they had read it not necessarily as a joke.

Alice started fitting the cashmere snood around Georgie's neck. Georgie, Tessa noticed, was not making eye contact with Alice. She had always been a little like that with Alice, wriggling out of shoulder massages from her, reluctant to hold her hand, only kissing her very lightly on the cheek when she greeted her.

'Whisky?' Georgie gestured to Bea. 'It's in the Oliver Bonas bag.'

'Hoodies on?' Melissa asked.

'Yes!' Georgie yelled. 'Hoodies on!'

Alice discreetly passed hers to Rachael. 'It's OK,' she whispered. 'You wear mine.'

They picked a path through the forest, guessing the direction of the loch from Alice's PDF. Every so often Harriet stopped, wafting her phone around and refreshing the home page.

'Marooned?' Bea said. She sighed. The fresh air and mugs of water had brightened her cheeks a bit.

Georgie grinned, looking back over her shoulder from where she was leading the charge.

Bea proved herself a capable scrambler when it came to the ridge of boulders they had to scale to get to the edge of the loch. She stood on a flat slab of stone and leaned to pull Harriet up after her. 'Twin arms,' she explained.

Harriet looked confused, then her face cleared as she realised Bea was talking about the weight-training advantages of carrying two children at the same time.

'Did you carry them in slings together?' Harriet asked. 'There's a page on my website all about that, tandem-wrapping, tandem-breastfeeding . . .' She broke off, tantalisingly, as if expecting Bea to spill the beans.

'It's funny how many times I get asked about my breasts and my vagina,' Bea said. 'By strangers. "Did you have a natural birth or a C-section? Did you breastfeed them?"'

Harriet, reaching the top of the slope, dusted the mud off the knees of her skinny jeans. She had a discreet mother-chic style these days, expensive shearling-lined boots and soft knitted jumpers. She was still thin as a rake. 'People are just curious,' she said. 'There's a whole page on my website about twins. Gets so many hits.'

Bea looked sidelong at her. 'Who wrote it?'

Harriet met her gaze. 'I did.'

Bea smothered a laugh. Tessa hovered behind them. She could see Georgie up ahead, stumbling over the roots of trees and rocks, the bag containing the bottle of whisky dangling from one hand. She looked drunk already.

'There's eighteen months between my two,' Harriet said. 'They're practically twins. Apart from all the psychic stuff. Are yours psychic?'

Tessa realised she was staring at Bea. She quickly looked away and began to walk again, feeling her cheeks colour. 'Yes,' she heard Bea say. 'Definitely.'

There came the sound of running footsteps as Bea caught up with Tessa. 'Listen, I'm sorry about the baby grows.'

Tessa felt Bea's hand on the crook of her elbow and stopped walking.

'The baby grows,' Bea said again. 'I never wrote you a thank-you card.' She sighed. 'I was in pretty bad shape at the time. After that I just lost – it seemed I lost contact with you guys. But they were so beautiful. I loved them. And I appreciated it.'

Tessa felt her cheeks burn. Bea had dropped her arm. 'I didn't mind,' she said quietly. 'I didn't expect anything. I understand.'

They scrambled on, cutting a path through more clusters of crimson rhododendrons. Then, suddenly, the bushes fell away and they stopped.

47

Even Georgie drew in her breath.

Tessa held hers. She expected one of them to say something pithy, something like, 'Well, beats Tallinn,' or 'Ah, seen better on a Friday night passing down Kings Road.' Something flippant. But they all fell silent before the shock of the beauty.

It was a silence that for a second gripped hold of Tessa's body and made her want to shake, but she stifled it.

They stood, forming a rough, ragged line along the whispering shore, so that they could all see the same view.

The loch was a slender, jagged-toothed maw that stretched to narrow points in both directions, like a witch's smile. It was rippling now, beaten pewter, but every so often the crests of the ripples would still and the colour would sink to a deep sea blue.

Trees and rocks obscured the narrow opening that led to the sea, making it appear as one single lonely and complete body of water. On the far bank, a thick pine forest grew close to the shore, with a small slate pebble beach shimmering as the sun hovered over it.

For a moment, Tessa could feel her breath quicken, as if the air was being slowly squeezed out of her. The sensation she had felt inside the castle kitchen came back, too potent to bear, a force that was almost supernatural. She ached for one of them to speak, to break the spell that was threatening to strangle her.

In the end, it was Rachael who said, 'Oh Scotland, you do scrub up well in your fur coat and lipstick.'

Harriet, still breathy from the climb said, 'It is wild, isn't it? Real wildness.'

Tessa pulled herself together. 'You sentimental lassies. You'll be waving your handkerchiefs and swooning over kilted local boys before the end of the week.'

Georgie turned, mischievous and drunk. 'Or dressing Tom up in a kilt, the traditional way.'

'I bet wherever Jack is can't be as beautiful,' Bea said.

'Yes, where is Jack?' Alice asked.

'The moon for all I care.' Georgie swung her arms out and tipped back her head. For a moment it looked as if she was going to whoop into the wilderness. Then she seemed to have a better idea and reached into her hoodie pocket. She took out her phone, held out a stretched arm and began angling a selfie with the shoreline behind her.

'Can't we all get in it?' Tessa said. 'Come on, we can get the loch in the background if we stand on that flat bit.'

Georgie looked, for a tiny second, a little put out, as if she was reluctant to share her beauty filter with the others; as if they might mar the harmony between herself and the wilderness. Then she had a better idea. 'OK, ladies, before and after photos. Photograph one – we stand before this beautiful wild and uncommon piece of prime Scottish landscape, like the winsome lost Londoners we are. Photograph two – we all take a swig of the whisky and see what it does to our Botox jobs. I'm joking! I know I'm the only one who's had it done.' She looked at each of them in turn. 'I'm joking about that, too, you know. Aloe vera and ten-step K-beauty. Tricks of the trade,' she murmured, then winked. 'Right, come on, look lively. Facebook doesn't have all day.'

She gathered her arms out, beckoning them all in. 'Beauty

49

faces!' Georgie puckered her lips. Tessa huddled into the centre of the group, between Melissa and Alice. It was comforting to share the warmth and the smell of the newly printed hoodies, all of them wearing the same – except Alice, who had on the jumper she had worn on the train.

Georgie stuck out her arm, holding the phone as far away as she could.

'You're decapitating Rachael,' Bea said.

Georgie tried again, slipping on the slime-covered rocks, stretching her arm out as far as possible.

'It's not going to work,' Tessa said. 'Look, I'll set the timer on my phone, we can put it over there. No point taking a picture if we're not going to get the loch in.' She scrambled over to the rocks and placed her phone in a nook between two stones. She leaned behind it, eyeballing the screen. They were clustered, almost to the very edges, but on the left you could still see a slice of silvery loch. It was nice. Asymmetric.

'OK. Nobody beyond that piece of driftwood, or past that rock with the barnacles. Those are our markers. Shit.' She picked the phone back up.

'What?'

'Battery.'

'Use mine.' Georgie held hers out.

'Oh, don't worry, use mine.' Alice stepped forward, holding out a sleek silver iPhone of the latest model.

Alice set up the shot and the timer. She peered at the screen and fiddled with the camera's manual settings.

'Hashtag no filter,' Georgie sang.

'No filter,' Alice replied. 'OK.' She snuck quickly to the side of the group and grabbed Harriet's waist.

They posed, held the pose for a few seconds to make sure. Alice went back to the phone.

'OK, girlies.' Georgie reached into her tote and held up the bottle of single malt. 'Here comes nanny's medicine. Bride's perk – I go first.' She pulled out the cork with her teeth and spat it behind her into the water.

'That's a Lagavulin, Georgie. You don't chug it like it's White Lightning,' Bea protested. Melissa and Harriet looked at her and burst into cackles.

'What?' Georgie frowned.

Harriet was holding her hand to her mouth. 'Nothing, it's just – Bea.' She stilled her laughter. 'You're such a connoisseur, Bea, you really do go for the finer things, when it comes to narcotics, don't you?'

Bea looked stubbornly at them, refusing to play along. 'If you couldn't afford things like Lagavulin then you might be a bit careful with it.'

Georgie hooked an arm about her neck. 'Well, I can. And we have plenty. It's my hen party, and you are my besties and I haven't seen you for about a hundred years.' She looked at them all in turn. 'So drink up, and let's get back in line for the next photo. Come on, the sun will be down before you've finished faffing with that camera, Alice.'

She continued passing the bottle around, directing them all to swig and doubling over with laughter at each of their faces when they winced at the alcohol's strength.

Tessa took a look at the bottle. 'Georgie, it's cask strength.'

'Present from Jack's parents,' Georgie said.

Tessa raised it to her lips. That smokiness, the wood-fire burn, the bitter cinder and the salt-seaweed sweetness. She loved the taste of Lagavulin. But they were all watching, waiting for her to make the same face they had done. So, she did, obligingly. She winced and pouted, holding the bottle out for someone else.

Georgie slapped her back. 'I love you, Tessy,' she said, pulling Tessa's face close to her own. Tessa flinched, then seeing the look on Georgie's face she pretended she was wrestling her into a hug.

'You guys,' Alice moaned.

They all lined up in the same order again. 'Three – two – one – smile!'

In the warmth of the open fire, Georgie went from sofa to sofa, pouring them more whisky, this time into short, fat glasses.

Harriet had cut some of the bread and cheese, as well as dolloping out the home-made chutney that had materialised in the kitchen while they were out, along with a note from Tom. He'd said he would be back later in the afternoon to go over the electrics, and had warned them to be careful if they wanted to walk to the village, because the path over the wood bridge was prone to flooding.

Now Harriet was passing the food platter around, insisting they all eat something. Melissa tried to make a joke about displaced mothering, but it seemed Harriet was not in the mood, since the lack of phone signal and Wi-Fi meant she couldn't send her newsletter, or reach Freddie and the children.

'Wait, I have a signal bar,' Rachael said. 'Does anyone need to make a quick call?' She held out her phone.

'Let's put the photos on Facebook,' Georgie said.

'Hen weekends don't exist unless they are on Facebook,' Alice said drily.

Harriet began to speak, then shut her mouth, and went back to passing around the bread.

'You'd better look at them first,' said Tessa. 'Make sure we don't look like hags.'

Alice leaned over to where Rachael stood beside the window. 'I'll Bluetooth them to you, love.'

They clustered round the sofa where Alice sat. She made room, bundling her feet up beneath her. Her phone was large, the screen unnaturally scratch-free. Georgie lounged behind, stretching one leg along the ridge of the sofa back like it was a barre. Tessa scrambled onto one of the arms; Bea onto another. Melissa and Harriet crouched either side of Alice.

Alice swiped and brought up the first photo.

The colours of the loch and the forest behind it were stronger than they had seemed in the cloudy noon light. The sun had been high above them, casting a dewy glow onto their faces as they squinted and smiled into the camera.

'Nice one, muchachas,' Georgie said. 'Now for the good bit.' She giggled with glee, eager to see their whiskied-up faces. This was what it was about, Tessa knew, when it was boiled down: not the weekend itself so much as the records of mirth and merriment, the gleam and sparkle of their old friendship, a mystical thing, lending its power to all of them, peddling the shine of their excellent lives to outsiders. They had more power as old friends than new, their value greater, like vintage fashion. If they did not know each other enough after all these years, if there was nothing else left in common, none of them could deny the glamour they gave together, as a pack.

Alice brought up the next photograph.

Georgie looked straight away at her own face, and snorted. She had hammed it up and she knew it, and there she was, looking beautifully, casually shocked by the cask-strength whisky, her eyes screwed up in glorious pain and delight. But the others were not looking at Georgie, or themselves.

Bea let out a low gasp. Harriet leaned forward; a shudder passed through her.

'What is that?' Tessa whispered.

Alice looked flustered. 'I don't – I didn't have a filter on.'

'That's not a filter,' said Bea.

Alice's hand began to shake.

The second photograph showed them all grimacing at the taste of the neat whisky. But behind them, emerging from the loch with frightened eyes pinned wide and an open mouth was the small, drenched figure of a young boy.

3

'There's no point going back now. He'll have run away,' Georgie said.

'If he was there at all – I didn't see him,' said Harriet.

'We were all drunk,' Bea cried. 'What if he's still out there? What if he's drowned?'

They had dispersed around the room, slowly, gradually. The photo had been like a bomb going off, pushing them apart. Tessa had only been able to look at it for a second. The sight of him choked her. His face was twisted with pain and cold. Everything she wanted to say now kept turning to wool in her mouth. She felt a sudden, sharp stab of guilt. She had brought them all here; it had all been her idea. She had offered to be the one to find a place, a special place for them to reconnect after all the years apart.

Bea was growing shrill. 'What if he's drowned?'

Tessa wished she would calm down.

'He will be a local scamp, some poacher's little shit who wanted to scare the rich bitches,' said Georgie. She looked irritated, sobered, but there was something dented about her bravado.

Alice continued staring at her phone. She had gone through stages of frowning, zooming in, puzzling, zooming out, playing with the settings.

'Doesn't Tom have a son?' Harriet asked.

'No,' Tessa said.

'How do you know?' Harriet had taken herself off to the window and was staring down at the unkempt vegetable garden below, playing on and off with one of the dark wood half-shutters, swinging it so it made a regular creak. Now the creaking stopped, and the silence was unnerving. Harriet stared at Tessa. Tessa could not work out why she found the look so aggressive. It was a simple question. But she couldn't answer it – not properly, anyway. 'I don't know. I suppose I must have asked him.'

'Over email?'

'We chatted on the phone a couple of times.'

'A couple of times?'

'Once, perhaps.'

'Once, or a couple of times?' Harriet asked.

'You sound like you're accusing me of something, but I'm not sure what.'

Melissa looked up from where she was crouching next to the fireplace. 'No one is accusing you of anything. Come on, Harriet. You think Tessa put up Tom's son to photobomb us from the lake? While they were discussing local cheeses and breads, it just came up as an idea?'

'It's a loch,' said Rachael.

There was a pause. 'We should go back out,' Bea said.

'I'm not sure we shouldn't just call it all quits,' Harriet said. She looked back out of the window.

'What?' Georgie's head snapped up.

'Do you mean go home?' Alice asked. She had shut down her phone. Now she slid it back into her jeans pocket. 'But we only just got here.'

Harriet began creaking the shutter back and forth again, then shook her head lightly.

'It was someone playing a prank,' Georgie said. 'My feet hurt. I'm not going back out. I was looking forward to getting shit-faced, then doing facemasks and choosing a wedding perfume before dinner.'

They looked around at each other.

'How about we all start cooking together?' Melissa said.

'I'm not cooking. It's my hen party.'

'You guys are . . .' Bea trailed off.

'We're what?' Georgie stared at her.

'I want to go back out there.'

'OK, then.'

'Is no one coming with me?'

Tessa was about to say something, but Harriet was still staring at her. 'I'm just not sure why you were talking about children with Tom,' she said. 'And how you can be so certain he doesn't have a son.'

Silence spread its roots again and Tessa could not figure out whether the others were mulling over what Harriet had said, and were waiting for Tessa to respond, or whether

Harriet had caused some kind of awkwardness which they were now wishing would go away.

'No,' Tessa said. 'I'm not certain. But we were chatting, about – I don't know, being single. Or, being child-free and going on holiday, and we agreed we are both in the same boat.' She waited for someone else to say something.

Bea was putting her hoodie back on.

'Take the snood if you're cold.' Georgie gestured to the cashmere snood Alice and Rachael had brought, which she had discarded over the arm of the sofa.

'Thank you.' Bea picked it up and settled it round her neck. 'Harriet?' she asked.

Harriet looked at her, then sighed. 'Yes, I'll come.'

'Anyone else?'

Melissa swung her legs down from the arm of the chair, and reached for her trainers.

'I was thinking of making cottage pie,' Tessa said. 'Soak up the booze. And it's quite chilly now, so just the sort of thing. Does that sound all right?' She turned to Rachael. 'You're not vegetarian, are you?'

Rachael looked at her with hooded eyes. 'No.'

'Anyone else coming?' Bea said.

Alice looked up sharply.

'No obligation,' Bea went on.

'It's just the dogs,' Alice explained.

Georgie gave a sudden cackle – too loud, too much, but it shattered the tension. 'I love your cottage pie, Tessy. I remember gobbling up huge troughs of it on Sundays after lacrosse nights out.' She looked over to Bea and Harriet, who were staring at her. 'What? Someone has to hold the fort. The champagne's not going to drink itself.' She pretended to examine her nails. 'You're not going to find anyone, you know.'

Bea marched out of the room, letting the door slam behind her as Harriet and Melissa scrambled to follow.

'Keep an eye out for mushrooms on your way,' Georgie called after them, still laughing.

'What time do you think Tom will come back?' Rachael asked, after a pause.

'I don't know,' Tessa said.

'You mean, even with your telepathic connection with Tom over your shared childlessness, you don't know his exact movements?' Georgie asked, her eyes twinkling. And then Tessa knew she was being defended; Good Georgie was set on making things right again. It seemed like permission to relax. An order, in fact. That was what Good Georgie did: as much as Bad Georgie loved fucking things up, Good Georgie liked making them right. One was almost as maddening as the other. Almost.

Tessa knew then that they wouldn't leave the castle. Not now they were finally together again after all this time, not when they were just beginning to relax and get to know each other again, to remember the feeling of being nestled together, making quips and teasing each other, just like in that first year of university. A tough year: an unforgettable year.

It would be churlish now, embarrassing even, for them to think about trying to go home without having eaten, or spent time in the castle, or chosen a wedding perfume.

Tessa heard the front door heave shut. She collapsed on

the sofa next to Georgie, shunting Georgie's legs out of the way, then lifting them into her lap. She wondered if she should have gone with the others, but the feel of Georgie's linen trousers against her fingers calmed her. The strange thing was that it did not feel strange to be touching in this way. It was as if their bodies had remembered the outline of their friendship, even after all those years apart. The shock was beginning to dissipate; they were all beginning to forget the little boy's face, terrible in its grimace.

'Crisps.' Georgie snapped her fingers.

Alice hurled an unopened bag of Kettle Chips at her, whacking her in the face with a crunch. She laughed and popped open the bag, then passed it round, chomping loudly.

Tessa asked, 'Shall I start cooking?'

'What time is it?' Rachael pulled out her phone. 'Jesus, half three already. Shall I give you a hand?'

'What about the perfume?' Georgie said. 'We need to pick a perfume, and we might as well do it before we all get completely hammered.'

Tessa stroked Georgie's shin with a fingertip. 'We can't really do anything until the others are back.'

Georgie looked at her warily. 'Do you think they'll find him?'

Tessa didn't know what to say. She sighed, but it came out more roughly than she had intended, and made her sound impatient.

'I'm sorry,' Georgie said. 'I'm not saying that anything's—it will all be fine. We're survivors. We're from London!' She laughed.

'I might need a hand actually, especially feeding that Aga,'

Tessa said, glancing over to Rachael. 'I'm not very good with fire.' Rachael had built the roaring fire in the lounge, which was now growing almost too hot, too stuffy.

Rachael looked up. 'Sure.'

'I'll come, too. There's a vegetable garden down there.' Alice pointed to the window. 'I'm sure Tom wouldn't mind if we nicked a few bits and pieces.'

'Good idea,' said Tessa.

'What was that about the mushrooms?' Rachael asked.

Georgie gave her wicked cackle again. Rachael looked blank.

'Oh God, I remember!' Long-forgotten images surfaced behind Tessa's eyes. 'Bea made magic-mushroom risotto. It was the end of first year. None of us could cook. But the rule in halls was that you had to cook for yourselves on Saturday nights. The catering staff had the night off. Most people got pizza from Tesco, but Bea wanted to show off her culinary skills and her foraging prowess. We thought it would be fun to indulge her.'

'Georgie nearly failed her exams because of it!' Alice said.

'No, I didn't. I just got a bit of a dicky tummy.'

'Dicky tummy? You were almost arrested for jumping naked off the pier.'

'That was the booze.'

Alice held out her arms and flapped her hands. '"I can fly, you guys, I'm like an angel."'

'Yes, well, I started a trend, didn't I, because we all graduated on to ket after that. You all wanted a turn at growing angel wings and unicorn horns, didn't you?'

'It was you that always had the ket, Georgie,' Alice said. 'And you were dishing it out long before the mushroom risotto.'

'Was I? Well, you never said no to it.'

Tessa shoved Georgie's legs aside and stood up. 'I'm going to make a start, then. Slow cooking. It'll sober me up a bit.' Rachael joined her, chucking another log at the fire as she passed, accidentally sending a flurry of sparks out at Georgie's calves, where her legs lolled off the sofa.

'Ouch!' Georgie snatched up her bare feet. Rachael followed Tessa out of the room with no apology.

Tessa was crushing garlic when Bea, Melissa and Harriet arrived back through the utility-room door in a flurry of cold air. They were ruddy cheeked and breathless. Bea's mood seemed to have lifted a little. Her arms were full of bobbled spinach leaves and long, waxy wild garlic.

Alice was standing at the kitchen island, gently dusting the skin of the mushrooms with a spare toothbrush she had brought, 'just in case anyone forgot theirs'. She'd cried, 'You can't wash mushrooms!', when Tessa had started to take them to the sink. 'They're porous. They absorb water. You'll ruin them.'

Reluctantly, Tessa had let Alice have her way with the toothbrush. Rachael, across the kitchen, was chopping an onion, pausing every so often to pop open the oven door to keep half an eye on the meat browning.

Tessa glanced at Harriet, Bea and Melissa, trying to judge the mood. 'Well?'

'Nothing.' Melissa shook her head. 'Not a trace. Harriet even got her magnifying glass out.' She laughed.

'What?' Alice said.

'It's an app. No, there were no footprints anywhere around,' Harriet said. 'Not even ours. Ground was too dry. Nothing to see.'

'But to be fair . . .' Bea was clearing space for the spinach on the counter next to the sink, '. . . the tide had come in. There was nothing else we could do.'

'You would have heard something, Bea,' Harriet said. 'Or seen something. There would have been something floating.' She quickly took off her scarf and turned away, but Tessa could still detect the irritation in her voice. 'People don't just disappear. He was never there to begin with. It's a trick of the light, the clouds, a reflection of a piece of driftwood that the camera picked up weirdly. Do you remember all that Slenderman nonsense that was all over the internet? Or what about those people who find Jesus in their toast?'

'Let's look at the photo again, then,' Bea said.

Harriet paused, then shook her head. 'No. I don't want to. And there's no need. If he was there, he went into the woods and not the loch; that's all you need to know. There's a couple of cottages there. Not Tom's cottage by the gate, but, like, a gardener's cottage or something, just off the path. He probably lives there.'

'You were all for packing up and going home earlier,' Bea said.

'And I still would be, if that was what Georgie wanted.

But either we decide to do that, or we just get on with it. There's no point dicking around fussing.'

'Did you go to see Tom?' Tessa asked. She had finished mashing the garlic and wiped her hands on a tea towel.

Tessa couldn't be certain, but it seemed to her that Bea hesitated. 'Yes.'

'There is so much lettuce in his garden,' Melissa said. 'I don't know how he does it. And herbs. He's like a witch. He's got everything, and he insisted we take some. He also said to raid the veg garden out the back, but to make sure we know what we are picking because it's a bit weedy.'

'Did you ask him about the boy?' Tessa said.

'He seemed distracted,' Harriet said curtly. 'An old woman was there.'

'I think he lives with his mother,' Melissa said.

'But you did ask,' Alice said.

'Yes, of course. I asked if he had a son. He said no. We asked –' Bea looked at Harriet, '– if there was anyone else living on the estate just now, and he said no to that too.' She dropped her head. 'I don't know, it seems weird. But I'm not going to start a fight about it.'

'Who's fighting?' Harriet said. 'I just think you're not thinking about the full picture. The way these people think. Come on, think about it. If there are squatters on the estate, family members or whatnot, that he doesn't want us to tell the owners about—'

'The way what people think?' Rachael asked. She finished chopping the onion and went to the sink to rinse her hands.

Harriet sighed. 'You know I'm tired, and I'm just vocalising what I'm thinking. We had a problem with something similar on Freddie's estate once. The gardener had his whole extended family staying in a caravan. They were – not gypsies – what are you supposed to call them now?'

'People?' Alice said, under her breath.

Tessa saw Harriet take her phone from her pocket, check it again for a signal and put it away.

'Signal not miraculously appeared in the two hours since we last checked?' Alice asked.

Harriet snatched up her scarf from the counter and twisted it briskly in her hands. 'Where's Georgie?'

'Upstairs. I think she wanted to choose the perfume when you guys got back.'

'I'll go and get the samples.' She left and they heard her footsteps heading upstairs towards the lounge.

'If you'd taken Alice's phone, you could have shown him the picture,' said Rachael.

Bea sighed. 'I don't know why I didn't think of that.' She put the wild garlic leaves down on the island. 'In Harriet's defence, I think if it was his son or someone he knew, and they had disappeared, he would have been freaking out about where he was and he just didn't seem . . . worried. Which is reassuring, isn't it?'

'Yes,' Tessa said quickly. She wanted the whole conversation to be over. The others joined in, placating.

'He did say again to be careful with the path if we want to go to the village. That dip that we came through – you know the bit with the wooden bridge? He said the stream, or the burn, or whatever he called it, sometimes floods and the trees there are all a bit unstable.'

'Unstable?' Alice said.

'That's what he said. On the banks.'

Alice wrinkled her nose. 'Glorious.'

Bea hung back, fiddling with her garlic leaves. 'I think he was just being cautious. You know the insurance for a place like this, with tourists and everything, must be insane. Don't really know how anyone can make a go of it, the running costs must be extortionate.'

No one said anything. They fell back to their silent tasks. Melissa picked through the bunch of leaves. 'He has so much veg for one person,' she said quietly. 'Suppose he gives it to the local church or something. A hobby.'

'Maybe he likes feeding the estate rabbits.' Tessa smiled, coming over to inspect the garlic leaves.

'Got them from the forest.' Bea saw Tessa's frown. 'Don't worry, I know what wild garlic looks like. I'm not going to poison us. I thought we could make fresh humous for a starter. Or just to snack.'

'If you can find a blender in here,' Alice muttered. 'Kitchen equipment is as old as the castle.'

'I'll pound it,' said Rachael. 'The traditional way.'

'Will you?' Alice whispered and they both erupted into giggles.

Bea began opening and closing drawers.

'What are you looking for?' Tessa asked.

'Chopping board.'

Tessa reached behind a vintage toaster on the side beside

the sink and pulled out a selection of plastic boards. They all had laminated labels: raw meat, cooked meat, vegetables.

Bea began searching again. Tessa watched her. 'Looking for a knife?' she asked, passing one to Bea. 'Here.'

'Christ, it's blunt. Is there another one?' Bea went back to rooting. 'You know blunt knives are more dangerous than sharp ones?'

Alice took over washing the spinach leaves in the sink while Rachael leaned against the other side of the counter, warming her hands on a mug of tea.

'You should wash those too.' Tessa pointed to the wild garlic fronds. 'Dogs probably pee in those woods.'

'Hmm.' Bea took the garlic leaves to the sink, then hesitated. 'It's just that washing makes them soggy, and if we want to use them in a salad, they're better crisp. I got them from high up a bank.'

Tessa went through the various soil pathogens in her head: *listeria, clostridium botulinum, salmonella, toxoplasma*. She decided she couldn't be bothered with another argument like the one about washing mushrooms.

They all hung around, pottering and loitering between tasks, like they didn't want to leave the cosiness of the kitchen. Tessa wished they would go upstairs and join the others. She didn't feel much like making chatter. Perhaps she was tired. She was used to her sleeping patterns being disturbed, but only in a way she expected. And if she did not expect to be disturbed – as she had not expected to be last night – it hit her hard. Her body had adjusted to the patterns of hospital shifts, so that when she gave it permission to sleep, she slept. She had thought that being here might help her rearrange, untangle the things in her head that she wanted to untangle. But it was not helping. It was making her feel more foggy. University memories and memories from before then were clouding together, and every time someone threw up a new memory – like the magic-mushroom risotto – it stopped her from clearly seeing the things she wanted to hold on to.

So had the boy's face. The thought came suddenly to her, as if placed there by someone else.

She heard a sudden hiss and smelled onions, and she turned to see Rachael stirring a giant cast-iron pot. Alice was rubbing her eyes. 'I think I am going to go and have myself a bonnie siesta before tea time.'

'Do you mind if I go upstairs as well?' Bea asked. 'Looks like you have everything under control. I might try and get a signal to say hello to Mo and the munchkins.'

'Try the very top floor,' Tessa said. She was relieved they were going. 'Might help.'

'Good shout.' Bea opened the fridge and helped herself to a half-opened bottle of bubbly with a teaspoon clanking around the top. Melissa took a bunch of glasses from one of the cupboards.

'Don't forget the perfume testing,' Tessa reminded them.

Bea frowned. 'I forgot. Well, I'll join you in a bit once I've checked in with my troops. That should be OK, shouldn't it?'

Alice looked slightly nonplussed about missing out on her nap, but she held the door open for Bea and Melissa.

Tessa listened to their footsteps recede and for a second there was quiet, just the cooking noises. The meat was starting to smell good. She tossed the crushed garlic into the pot, over Rachael's shoulder. She wished Rachael would go away, too, so she could make the surprise starter.

'Shall I make up a jug of stock?' Rachael asked.

'You don't have to.'

'It's no trouble.'

Tessa had the impression that Rachael might be avoiding the rest of the group too. She sympathised, but was puzzled, if that were the case, about why Rachael had bothered to come at all. Maybe Alice had wanted moral support.

Tessa wondered if she could get away with hovering down here until they had chosen the perfume. She would only worry about giving the wrong opinion. Even though she was an adult now, a doctor, there were still times when she was uncomfortable speaking her thoughts. It felt, she realised, like a regression coming here. She guessed only old friends could do that to you, strip away the years to make you feel as raw as a teenager. Family could do that, too, of course.

'So why pumas?' she asked Rachael. 'Was that your PhD?'

'No, my PhD was on llamas.'

'Seriously?'

Rachael gave a cautious smile. 'Yes. But I grew to find their predators more interesting, I suppose.'

Tessa fiddled with a wooden spoon, patting it against her palm. 'There is something glamorous about big cats, though, isn't there?'

There was that expression again: a flash of amusement. Rachael looked like she might be about to say something sarcastic, but then suddenly she softened. 'It's glamorous to outsiders, probably like your job seems. But there is a lot of – I was going to say dirt, but that's not the bad part, the tracking and the camping and the bugs. It's the tedium. It's waiting for hours in a concealed truck just to collect a few scraps of data that go into the whole pile. And you don't really see the big picture until you have all the data together, and then, well, it becomes data rather than pumas you are looking at, which isn't really so glamorous at all.'

'Right.' Tessa nodded. She was searching for a comparison in her own job. Probably there was one – the dosage of an anaesthetic drug against blood pressure and body mass turned into graphs and numbers, counts and estimates – but what sprung to mind instead was a jealousy for the tedium Rachael had described. Tessa had never been bored at work, not once. There wasn't time, between being buzzed to A & E, or having to administer the anaesthetics for a whole day of planned surgery, or running to the labour ward. There was too much reality, too many bodily fluids and too many emergencies most of the time. But she also liked dealing with patients, and the bustle, the chaos, kept her own mind anaesthetised. Sometimes she thought that might be why she had chosen to specialise in anaesthetics.

'Do you want me to wash the potatoes?' Rachael asked.

Tessa started to nod then changed her mind. 'No, it's fine. I'll do them.'

'I don't mind.'

'Go and have a drink upstairs.'

'I feel like I've drunk so much prosecco you could bottle my piss and sell it to hen parties.'

Tessa laughed. 'There's gin somewhere.'

'I didn't see any.'

'There should be some bottles of red and white in that bag.'

'What I really fancy is a beer,' Rachael muttered.

'Good luck,' Tessa said. She looked up and saw Rachael regarding her.

'What do you mean?'

'Oh, just – Georgie doesn't drink beer.'

'So, she doesn't let you drink beer?'

Tessa put a hand to her face. She smelled garlic on her fingernails. She felt as if she had been caught out at something, but she wasn't sure what – belittling Georgie or admitting an embarrassing truth. 'It's her hen party and I wanted to make sure we had the kind of drinks she likes.' She began gathering up the potatoes, placing them on the counter, cradling them to stop them tumbling off.

'Funny,' Rachael said. 'I would have thought she was the beer type. Didn't Alice say she met you all on the lacrosse team?'

'Not me.' Tessa shook her head. 'I know the rest of them through Georgie.' She paused. 'I knew her from before.'

'Before what?'

'Before – lacrosse. We were in halls,' Tessa said.

'But she was on the lacrosse team?'

'She was.'

Rachael was staring at her, frowning. 'Have I said something out of turn? You seem – I don't know – a bit unhappy.'

Tessa rubbed her head. 'I'm not unhappy, I'm just tired.

Shift work.' She turned her back and spilled the potatoes into the sink for washing. 'Anyway,' she said briskly. 'Yes, they were all on the lacrosse team except for me. I have two left hands and no stamina. And now you mention it, Georgie was fond of a pint. But – I suppose people change, don't they?'

Rachael chewed her lip. 'Yeah, guess so.'

Tessa turned the taps on to their fullest, coldest blast and watched the sink fill up, bubbles breaking on the surface. When she wrenched off the taps and turned round again, Rachael was gone.

She plunged her hands into the icy water and closed her eyes. She rummaged for the bony nubs of the potatoes. Four seconds passed, five, ten. Her fingers stretched until she found smooth, round hardness in her palm. Her skin numbed, then her veins went cold, then her wrists began to ache. She clutched. She opened her eyes and looked down then, she let out a small cry and stumbled backwards. In the disturbed, muddy water there was a face, and two out-stretched hands: tiny balled fists, reaching up on either side of a head, on either side of a slender neck which must have been beneath the water, still covered by the icy silt. Her own hands reached out, grasped. She felt skin, and pulled away, yelping. Water dripped from her hands onto the floor and she couldn't look back at the sink. But after a moment, she forced herself to look. The mud had settled and sunk. They were potatoes. Just potatoes – two small new potatoes and one larger one – tumbling in the sink.

But she had felt it, and she had seen it. Her hands, her own hands, had been beneath the water. They had held the two nubby fists down beneath the water, down where the head had been. Pressing down, drowning it all completely.

She took a measured, careful breath, then counted out two, three more. This would not beat her. She had things to do, special things to prepare for the hen party. That was why they were here, wasn't it? Georgie's hen party. The happy ending to her romance with teenage sweetheart, Jack. She went to the fridge and took out the two brown butchers' packets she had placed there earlier. She'd taken them out just in time; blood had begun to seep through the paper.

4

Tessa crept up the stairs, towards the muffled laughter coming from behind the door of the lounge. She had brought another bottle of champagne from the fridge, and had tracked down a box of flutes which rattled under her arm.

She pushed open the door, smelling a fug of mingling perfumes, vanilla and the savoury tang of lilies.

'Tessyyyyyyyy,' Georgie cooed, lingering on the sound until her breath ran out. There was something strained about her voice, doggedly maintaining the fun. Melissa was sitting where Tessa had been before, with Georgie's legs draped on top of her. Bea was perched in the window seat, while Harriet sat on the floor, facing the coffee table, with her back to the fire. Alice and Rachael were snuggled on one chair. Alice pointed to the other armchair as Tessa came in, but Georgie grabbed the hem of her jumper and pulled her down onto the sofa, budging Melissa out of the way.

Tessa struggled to keep hold of both champagne and glasses and the others laughed.

'It's like a beauty counter up here,' she commented.

In front of Harriet on the coffee table was a crisp black Selfridges bag. Next to it lay several anonymous clear plastic tubes, of the kind normally used for urine samples, and a printed spreadsheet. Harriet was fiddling a pen between her fingers and her teeth and she wore a similar expression to the one she'd had after the conversation about the photograph, annoyance and bewilderment, though she seemed mellower, or maybe just a bit more drunk.

'What do you think?' She slid the tubes towards Tessa, letting them tumble into each other.

'Is this what you wanted me to nick these for?' Tessa picked up one of the tubes. Each had been labelled with a plain white sticker and assigned a number.

'I went round the perfume counters and asked them to decant a sample. I know a few of them. I did a mummy perfume thing on Instagram a while ago: perfumes to calm your baby while giving birth, best for breastfeeding, that sort of thing. Lots and lots of likes. You'd be surprised. Smell,' she said, gesturing to the tube in Tessa's hands.

'It's not that one, Harriet, I can smell it from here. That's the Tom Ford,' Georgie said.

Tessa unscrewed the tube and dabbed her wrist gently. A strong aroma of amber and incense hit her straight away.

'Waaaay too much,' Georgie said. 'We're going to be in Italy. It'll be hot.'

'I wanted to get some variety,' Harriet replied.

'But that's not the one, anyway.'

'We've identified eight of them,' Alice said.

'Blind test,' Harriet continued. 'I have them all on the

spreadsheet but didn't want to tell her the names in case she was influenced by – you know—'

'Brand, boxes, trends, because that's exactly what I'm like,' Georgie said. She laughed, but there was a spiky edge to the laughter.

'But there is one perfume nobody can get,' Alice went on.

'The tubes are numbered,' Harriet said. 'It's got number nine on it. I'm sure I only got eight samples. I only have eight on the spreadsheet.'

'Oh,' Tessa said.

'You smell meaty,' Georgie said, leaning into her.

'Thanks,' Tessa winked.

'No, I mean in a nice way. Like it's making me excited for dinner.'

'Oh, good. It'll be about forty-five minutes.' Tessa picked up the tubes one after the other, looking at the numbers on the sides of each. She found her hands were trembling. Pressing hard as she unscrewed the caps helped to control them. There was a summery one, maybe Gucci Bloom. Then something light but sweet that she didn't know. But she knew straight away when she had come to the one they meant.

Alice was watching her carefully. 'I thought it was Jean Paul Gaultier Classique.'

'Definitely not. I have that,' Georgie said. 'It's too powdery for JPG.'

'Chanel Coco Noir, I thought,' Harriet said. 'It's the only thing I can think of, but I definitely didn't go to the Chanel counter because I would have remembered. It's run by a very handsome Danish man.'

Tessa didn't even need to dab it on her skin. The waft of the open tube was potent enough, and it was a scent she could recognise immediately. She looked up at Georgie. Georgie was watching her anxiously. Tessa knew then that she knew what it was, too.

Tessa's hand hovered with the tube at an angle, poised to tip it up and onto her wrist. Was it possible that with one movement of her arm she could unleash a genie? Did she want to? Scent could make a person present again in a way nothing else could.

'Why don't you try it again, Georgie?' Harriet said. 'Just see. You're obviously drawn to it.'

Tessa tried to pass her the vial.

Georgie sprang back as if she had been stung. She landed half on top of Melissa, who yelped, then tried to laugh it off.

'I don't like it,' Georgie said, squirming.

'You can't really get the sense of it until it's been on you for a couple of hours,' Tessa said.

'But I know I don't want that one.' Georgie hesitated. 'It's too sweet.'

'It's not as sweet as Jean Paul Classique,' Harriet said.

'You guys know too much about perfume.' Melissa sighed and leaned forwards to top up her champagne glass.

Tessa held the tube to her nose, and paused before she breathed it in. She hesitated, then said, 'It's Agent Provocateur.'

Bea snapped her fingers. 'Thank you. I bloody knew it. It was on the tip of my tongue.' Tessa watched as Harriet shot Bea a look.

'Are you sure?' Harriet paused, her pen hovering over the spreadsheet. 'I don't remember getting that one. It's got quite a distinctive bottle. I think I would have remembered.'

'I'm certain,' Tessa said. She watched Harriet hum to herself as she wrote it down. She didn't look at Georgie. In that moment she didn't want to know if Georgie was looking at her.

The shimmering sound of a gong echoed up the castle staircase. Dinner time already. Tessa wondered who had taken the cottage pie out of the oven. She hoped they hadn't poked about with her starter.

She was lying on one of the camp beds in the nursery, staring at the ceiling rose. The lampshade hanging from it was cobwebby and she kept having the urge to leap up onto a chair and swipe it with her hand. The sheets were clean, but old, and she wondered if this room was ever used as part of the holiday accommodation, or if it was only the larger groups that took it. She hadn't minded. It had felt right to her that she should have this room. She didn't need the en suite, and she was used to roughing it at the hospital. She wasn't yet sure whether Melissa was going to take the other camp bed in the nursery alongside her, or share the enormous four-poster bed with Georgie.

When the perfume samples had been cleared away and the sheet masks brought out, she had excused herself for a short nap, citing tiredness from her shift work. Now she felt groggy, as if she had slept for too long and had been interrupted in the middle of a sleep cycle. She had been dreaming, she was sure. She had the cold unease of a story half-finished in her head, and the feeling that her hands had been doing something against her will. But she couldn't remember exactly what it was.

Georgie's cackle came floating up on the tails of the gong. Of course, she probably found it hilarious – a gong for dinner. *Bong.* It sounded out again. Then again and again. Bong, bong, bong-bong-bong, a calamitous tattoo. Someone called 'Dinner is served!' and there was a peal of laughter.

Tessa realised she hadn't yet dressed and shunted herself out of bed.

The plan had been to dress for dinner, drink wine, savour food, perhaps smoke – they could go outside, wrapped up, looking at the stars – and reminisce, as if to exorcise all the bad or unfortunate memories from that era of their lives; to fix those narratives that needed fixing, now they were so far in the distant past that they could be fixed without worrying about the details. In the peace of the castle they would transform the messy truths of their pasts from poor, shambolic anecdotes into sparkling legends to be passed down.

She zipped herself into her black velvet jumpsuit and put on a string of multicoloured plastic beads she had bought for the trip on a whim, from an advert posted on the sidebar of her Facebook page.

She crept down the stairs, all the way to the kitchen. It was empty, and the surfaces looked disturbed but tidy. The loaf of sourdough Tom had brought them was half cut, the remainder left on a chopping board. Tessa checked the oven and was alarmed for a second when she saw that both casserole dishes had been removed. But then she saw on the counter beside the sink, the small, round black dish, resting on a coiled-wire pot stand. The lid was still on. Her heart beating heavily, she took a tea towel to protect her hands and picked it up. She heard footsteps. The kitchen door swung back and Rachael came in. She had made up her face with mascara and a deep blue lipstick that glowed against her dark skin. She smiled when she saw Tessa. 'Good nap?'

Tessa was aware of the pot beginning to burn her hands through the tea towel. 'I didn't mean to sleep for so long.'

'It's all right. You obviously needed it.' Her glance dropped to the black pot. 'We didn't know what that was, so we just left it.'

'I'll bring it up now.'

The dining room, formerly the castle's great hall, sat directly above the entrance, and would have been the original top floor until the turn of the eighteenth century, when the extra bedrooms above were added.

Tessa pushed the huge oak door open with her hips, hefting it against the draft excluder on the other side. At the slow gothic creak, the gathering fell silent. Then one by one, they began to join in with the creak, imitating the noise at the back of their throats, like a murder of crows, then bursting into laughter as Tessa stood framed in the doorway. She saw that apart from Rachael, who was still downstairs, she was the last of them to appear. She wanted to do something playful and dramatic – affect a scream or breathe, 'Now I've got you!' or raise her hand as if she held a knife. Something

80

to do justice to the way they were all staring expectantly. But she froze and couldn't think of anything, so she just nodded at the pot in her hands. 'Starter,' she said.

They all laughed as though she had made a joke after all. Melissa said 'Yummy!' and Bea helped her deposit the dish on the table, clearing a space near Georgie. Rachael brought in another bottle of wine and the oil and vinegar and sat next to Alice. Tessa felt a fist of nerves in her guts. She almost whipped the lid off then and there, but they were still arranging the side dishes. She surveyed the table. There was a thick white twill cloth, and mismatching cutlery and crockery. The room looked pleasingly opulent, and smelled of meat and tomatoes. Slabs of sourdough drenched in butter and shards of wild garlic lay on wooden boards, with the huge cauldron of cottage pie as the centrepiece.

They were all made up to the nines, dressed with the aplomb their drunkenness had instilled in them. Georgie had on a fire-coloured sheath dress and jade jewellery. Her face was garishly contoured to look flushed, and she had painted on some light brown freckles and a beauty spot. Bea was wearing a black bodycon dress with a scoop neck, straining tight at her belly and chest, with the sloppy cardigan she'd worn the night before draping off one shoulder. Harriet looked inexplicably pressed to perfection, and had changed into a blouse and tailored trousers, while Alice had on thick black lipstick and a backless silvery drape top with long sleeves that showed off the elaborate gryphon tattooed on her shoulder blade. Rachael's jumper was pale pink and she wore a long skirt in khaki silk, and trainers with an inch-high sole. She had piled her braids into a giant knot on top of her head, but some of them had strayed loose down the back of her neck. It was hard to see what Melissa was wearing because she was slumping on one hand, close to the table, but Melissa had always had a windbitten sort of village-woman beauty that let her get away with looking made-up when she might only have thrown on a cotton dress that was ten years old. Tessa observed them all, now so collectively confident and eclectic, sort of like the room they were in. They were passing condiments and wine bottles back and forth, admiring each other's adornments. But apart from the clothes and the confidence, they looked not dissimilar to the way they had at university when it had been somebody's birthday or an end-of-term dinner out. There was the same glee, the same fizzing, overlapping conversation, the same smell of wine and make-up in the air. Tessa felt jolted into her twenty-year-old self, looking at them all and wondering who they had become. Collectively, they were a beautiful, powerful forcefield of women, ploughing into their thirties, unstoppably brilliant, nothing to hold back their happiness: no darkness, no shameful secrets, no bitterness, nothing but shimmering smiles and light.

Someone passed Tessa a champagne glass. The stem was sticky, as if froth had spilled over the bulb.

'I'm so sorry,' Tessa said. She took a seat halfway down the table, in front of the black cookpot with the scent of the starter wafting from it.

'What for?' Bea asked.

82

'I meant to do all of this.'

Alice smiled. 'We're all here to do it, not just you. Anyway, kept me busy. Those sheet masks give me the horrors.'

'We got to play house. Castle, even,' Rachael said.

'So many yummy things,' Melissa was saying. She had reached across, helped herself to a piece of garlic bread. As she bit into it, butter dripped down her chin and her tongue shot out to mop it up. Already she was very drunk.

Georgie had her hands in the salad bowl, mixing in the dressing with a sensuous, massaging motion. She grabbed a handful, and holding her hands up high, sprinkled it like snow onto her plate, where it formed a messy pile. 'Mmm, I am starving,' she said.

'Shall I play mum?' Bea asked, reaching for the spoon to serve the cottage pie.

Tessa's hand hovered above the cast-iron pot.

Harriet noticed, and said, 'I think there is a special starter first. Tessa made it.'

Tessa looked bashfully down at the tablecloth. She smiled. She found it tricky, all of a sudden, to make eye contact with any of them, as she said, 'It's an old Scottish tradition. Something I came across—'

Georgie interrupted. 'Uh-oh! "Scottish tradition" rings St Andrews flashback alarm bells!' She giggled, licking salad dressing from her fingers. 'You're not going to make me walk around the castle naked carrying a sword?' She laughed.

Tessa didn't want to meet her eye. 'You can if you want,' she said. 'We're not judging. But this is something for weddings – to celebrate the meeting of two souls.'

'Come on,' Alice goaded. 'Just open the dish. It's haggis, isn't it? Smells like haggis.'

'It's like haggis. It's more symbolic than haggis.'

'You mean,' Harriet said, 'you found something more symbolic than a sheep's stomach?' She leaned over the dish, peering nosily, sipping her champagne.

Tessa paused. She looked up at Georgie. She wanted to see Georgie's face when she removed the lid. She had put a lot of effort into preparing the dish, picking the seasonings from the castle's spice rack, battering the meat to tenderise it, stuffing it with oatmeal, dousing it with wine, and setting it in the Aga's coolest oven so that the blood and juices would not boil off. And it spoke, in some way, of their past, marking and uniting memory and ritual. It was the perfect dish to serve in the perfect room. She took off the lid. The aroma was pungent, meatier and richer than the cottage pie.

'It's two goats' hearts,' she said. She had taken them carefully from the stained butchers' paper, placed them on the granite counter, and sprinkled them with salt before striking them with the end of a rolling pin, for there was no meat hammer in the castle.

'What the fuck!' Alice exploded.

Tessa kept talking, her eyes fixed on Georgie. 'Two goats' hearts. Tradition. Scottish tradition. Before a wedding.' Georgie stared at the dish, eyes wide and alight with amusement.

'I've never heard of that,' Alice said.

'Well, you're not Scottish, are you?' Harriet said. 'None of us are – except, Tessa, don't half of your family come from up here or something?'

Tessa ignored her. 'It symbolises the merging of two hearts.'

'What, they merge in your stomach?' Georgie asked. She had plucked up a fork and paused, toying with it close to her lips.

'It's pagan,' Tessa said.

'God, of course it is,' Alice said. 'Anything weird and bloody has to be pagan.'

There was silence. Harriet peered into the dish. It had come out perfectly, the two hearts still holding on to their red gloss, slicked with wine, and lying in a steaming bath.

'All right, you fucker. I'll do it.' Georgie took a large swig of champagne and raised her fork in her fist, as if it were a dagger. Tessa was curious, though not surprised, to see her approach it as a dare rather than a ritual. She brought the fork down in a peal of laughter, spearing, then sawing with the edge of the fork as she wrenched off a chunk of the first heart. She blew on it. The others fell to murmuring as she popped it into her mouth. 'Come on, Jack. Come tend on my mortal thoughts or something like that.' Then she chewed indulgently and swallowed with flourish. 'It's actually quite nice, but it's a bit like eating pâté. It's so rich. Mind you, so's foie gras.' To a chorus of melodramatic gasps and giggles, she helped herself to another bite. 'Now to eat my own heart. God, how poetic.'

'Make sure to have a bit of each,' Tessa said.

'I like it,' Georgie said, with her mouth full. She washed

it down with more champagne and belched lightly. 'Good seasoning. Pink peppercorns?'

'Black cardamom. Thanks,' Tessa said.

'Can I try some?' Bea leaned curiously over. 'It sounds quite like a Moroccan kebab thing that we had at our wedding.'

Tessa caught her hand as she leaned in. Bea looked startled at the speed of her reaction. 'It's supposed to be just for the bride,' she said. Then she heard her voice sounding too stern. 'But I suppose if anyone wants to try a little . . .'

Bea leaned back. 'No, no, far be it for me to deprive.' She smiled awkwardly and put her fork down.

'You can if you want,' Tessa said, aware of Bea trying to paper over her surprise.

'How about we all dig into this?' Bea was saying, beginning to dish out the cottage pie. Plates were passed in rotation and the bread and wild garlic was handed out. They all made appreciative noises and their jewellery clinked as they exchanged plates.

Tessa watched as Georgie continued to pick at the hearts. 'Did you find a signal?' Tessa asked Bea.

Bea looked at her for a second. 'Oh, yes,' she said. 'Right at the top.'

Tessa took a mouthful of cottage pie, then turned to her again. 'Which part? I might try later myself,' she explained.

'Do you have a boyfriend to call back home, secret Tessy?' Georgie asked, and Tessa was relieved when the spluttering mouthful she took of her drink blanketed out any answer she had to give to that. Harriet leaned over to pat her on the back.

'This is so delicious,' Alice said. 'Thanks to you all, fine chefs. We should raise a toast. To . . .' She pushed back her chair and stood up. 'The castle cooks.'

'The castle cooks,' came the slurry response, and there was a pause while everyone took a slug.

Alice sat back down. 'You know, it's interesting to think about the women who would have kept this place running in the previous centuries. It must have been back-breaking carrying buckets of hot water up and down all those stairs, and butchering all the animals and tending the kitchen garden – and the laundry, Christ—'

'Oh Alice, no one wants to talk about feminism,' Georgie said, through a mouthful of food.

'It's not feminism, it's just history,' Alice said. Rachael had already placed a hand on top of Alice's.

'I have a story about the castle's history,' Tessa interrupted. Melissa was busy whispering something to Georgie. Tessa had noticed Melissa slouching lower and lower until Georgie had had to rescue her chin from ending up in her plate. Harriet reached to pour her a glass of water and place it in her hand. Between them, they steadied Melissa's head. Harriet brushed her hair out of her face, while Georgie gave her small sips of water. They both did it with such unassuming tenderness for the state she was in. Once again, Tessa felt herself jolted into the past, and it caused her unbearable pain to see them be so tender and caring.

'Just sit back for a second,' Georgie said. 'You'll be fine.' Melissa said something in protest.

'No,' said Georgie. 'No kets till coffee.'

There was a small pause.

'What were you saying?' asked Bea. She was blushing, changing the subject deliberately. Was she chastened after her indulgence on the train, Tessa wondered? Or embarrassed for Melissa? It had been a long time since they had seen each another so vulnerable.

'I'm listening,' said Alice, a little haughtily. She crunched her garlic toast.

Tessa looked up at the carved panelling on the ceiling, at the frieze depicting ships and armoured medieval men on horseback in flaking paintwork. 'This room was part of the original castle. It says so on the website,' she added. 'It was where the Laird would meet his tenants and resolve legal issues: "So-and-so stole my corn; so-and-so stole my wife."'

Georgie snorted. 'Go on.'

'And, of course, any time a crime took place locally, here was where justice would be decided.'

'But not – meted out, surely?' Rachael frowned.

'I don't know if they did executions in the castle. There would probably be a gallows somewhere in a public place for that. Maybe on the grounds, I don't know.' Tessa paused to take a mouthful of wine – she had switched to red now, a juicy, acidic Malbec, and it was improving her mood. 'But what I do know – what it does say – is this: at the time of the Jacobite rebellion, long after the hall was in use as a court, this room was the site of the murder of a maid and her son, who both refused to give up the hiding place of her Catholic mistress.'

There was a small pause. Tessa saw Bea and Harriet cast

glances around the room, as if a gruesome bloodstain still remained.

Georgie was less subtle. 'Where?'

'What do you mean?'

'Where did they murder them?'

'I don't know.'

'You mean they didn't mark it – like at Holyrood,' she went on.

'What's at Holyrood?' Rachael asked.

'Stains on the floor where the Italian lover of Mary Queen of Scots was stabbed to death.'

'They didn't mark it, it just happened. Anyway, they're fake,' said Alice. 'It's just the colour of the wood.'

'I don't think they marked it here,' said Tessa.

'Perhaps we should.' Georgie began to tip her glass of red wine towards the floorboards.

'Georgie!' Tessa cried.

'Kidding!'

Silence rippled down the table.

Tessa felt a shock of nausea as she realised how admonishing her tone had been. She had not meant to cause this silence. It came to her again how anxious she was about this trip, always trying to second-guess Georgie. It was exhausting. But Georgie had eaten the hearts without question or fuss. At that, Tessa could relax.

Tessa smiled warmly and said, 'I think she was probably strangled anyway. Or drowned in a bucket.' She took a sip of wine and laughed. 'That's what they did to women back then.'

Georgie thrust her glass into the air. 'To the maid!' A few

drips spilled onto the cream fringes of the rug. 'Oops,' she said.

Rachael and Harriet leapt up. Harriet grabbed a salt pot and they set about with napkins and a bottle of white wine, arguing over the best way to lift the stain. Tessa stared at Georgie. After a second, Georgie crouched and helped with the clean-up.

Bea had stayed in her chair. 'What happened to the boy? Her son?'

There was too much commotion for anyone to answer. When the others finally sat back down, she tried another question. 'So they were Jacobites, the castle owners?'

'So it says,' said Tessa.

'Is that why there's a priest hole in the attic?'

'Ooh,' Georgie said. 'A priest hole. Sardines later, ladies? Does it come with a hot priest?'

Tessa looked at Bea. Her face was blank, expectant. 'A priest hole?' Tessa asked.

'What were you doing up there?' Harriet asked.

'Looking for a phone signal.'

'And did you find one?'

Bea paused. 'No.' She drank some of her wine. 'I poked around a bit, but I . . .' She hesitated. 'I was a scaredy cat and I sort of didn't dare go in.'

'Oh Bea,' said Georgie. 'You missed your chance to frighten us out of our wits. You might have found a secret corridor and emerged from it carrying a candlestick and a severed head.'

'I would have, but I couldn't find a candlestick.'

For a moment they all laughed along, and then the laughter faded quite suddenly. Tessa caught Bea's eyes, then Alice's. They looked chastened. She didn't know if it was the guilt of poking around the castle, or the complacency of laughing at its gory history, or the memory of the boy at the loch earlier gradually dawning. The mood grew sober for a minute, though no one seemed to want to say anything. Georgie was the first to look blithe again. She tossed her hair and kept drinking. Harriet covertly checked her phone. It was quick, and mechanical, like she couldn't help it: a tic.

Melissa sighed loudly. 'There is something, though.'

Harriet turned and giggled at her. 'What do you mean?'

Melissa balanced her chin in one hand. 'Something sad happened here. In this castle. You can tell. It's like it's seen something wither and die.'

There was a pause. Tessa swallowed a large gulp of wine. It had just been a vision, back in the kitchen, in the sink, she told herself; a weird vision, a trick of tiredness and dim light and perception. She was an NHS doctor. She had never hurt anyone in her life. She would never hurt anyone, hold them beneath the water. But she also knew, in some deeply pressed-down part of herself, that the hands in her imagination had not really been her hands. They had belonged to someone else.

Rachael said, 'Well, from what I know about Scottish history, this place has probably seen a lot of people die over the years: witches burning and Jacobites hanging and maids drowning and women bleeding to death in childbirth.'

Silence crept back over the table. Georgie flicked her eyes up and around, and then, with comic aplomb, dived back into the goats' hearts, loudly clinking her fork against the cast-iron rim of the pot. The rich aroma coming from it was making Tessa feel sick. She drank more wine.

'Did I hear Tom come by just an hour or so ago?' Bea asked.

'Yes,' Rachael said. 'I let him in. He fiddled with some of the fuses down in that utility room off the kitchen and told me not to run too many electrics at once. They have a generator. It's not on the mains. I left him to it, so he must have let himself back out.'

'Such a strange existence.' Melissa seemed to have sobered up a bit. She blew sweaty fronds of blonde hair out of her eyes. 'I mean, living on his own in a cottage, with no one for company but those two dogs. Doesn't he have a girlfriend?'

'Doesn't say on the website,' Tessa said, and they all laughed. She felt her stomach soften with relief.

Georgie looked slyly at Bea. 'Did you see any woman signs in his cottage?'

Alice guffawed. 'Woman signs? What, do you mean pink feather mules by the door?'

'I thought he lived with his mum,' Harriet said. 'There was that old woman there. She didn't say much.'

Bea looked a little confounded. 'The cottage was definitely – it wasn't that it was missing a woman's touch. But it seemed too small for more than one person.'

'Did you go inside?' Tessa asked.

'I stuck my head in,' said Bea. 'It was all very bland, very plain. He had a games console hooked up to the television.'

Georgie rolled her eyes. 'You can take the man-child out of – wherever it was he came from, but – oh, I don't know the rest.' She drank some more wine.

'Weird,' Melissa said softly.

'Is gaming weird?' Rachael asked. She turned to Alice, grinning. 'That means we're weird, too.'

Melissa waved her hand. 'I don't know, it's just weird. Where does he come from? Not here.'

Tessa couldn't help but snort and a spray of red wine came out uncomfortably through her nose.

Harriet laughed. 'Do you mean like, Mars, or do you mean England?'

'You know what I mean. What's he doing here?'

'I don't know what you mean,' Tessa said. 'It's beautiful here. It's wild. Maybe he likes it. Maybe he's from here.'

'Sounded English,' Melissa said.

'He's just posh. And it's the borders, anyway. Folk come from both sides.'

Melissa reached across for the half-drunk bottle of champagne on the table. Georgie intercepted her hand. 'You're saving yourself, remember.' She tapped the back of Melissa's knuckles and gently confiscated the bottle. Tessa watched her place it down close to the edge of the table. She caught Tessa's glance and smiled, then pushed it a few inches in, to safety.

'You're such a bully, Georgie,' Melissa chided. She was laughing, but she went on. 'She always calls me drunk. She tells me when I've had enough.' Her eyes fell on Rachael, as if searching for an ally who was not in their web.

Rachael smiled diplomatically, blankly. 'I think it's good to have friends who can tell you when to stop.'

Alice tipped her head back. 'Oh, is that why you do it?'

'I never tell you you're drunk. Mainly because you never are.'

'Yeah, I've always been the dullard,' Alice said. 'Mind you, Tessy never drinks too much, do you? I don't think I've ever seen you really hammered. I don't remember you coming drinking with us in first year.'

'You were never there at the weekends, were you?' Harriet said. 'You used to go home a lot in first year.'

'Was that just because of the workload?' Bea said. 'Us bloody lazy arts undergrads, and you were the only medic.'

Georgie nodded towards Melissa. 'Didn't stop you boozing, did it, Mel?'

Melissa began to say something, but ended up rolling her eyes.

Tessa paused, then raised her glass. 'Well. Good time for me to start, then, isn't it?' She took a huge gulp of the wine, a much bigger one than she had intended to. She felt the choke reflex in her throat, but for some reason she became absolutely determined that she would not choke, that the gesture would be slick and not clumsy, not something they could laugh at. The acid, the tannins caked her throat, but still she swallowed elegantly.

Rachael was helping herself to seconds, leaning across the table and asking Georgie what it was, precisely, that she did.

'Oh no, don't,' Harriet grinned. 'She'll give you the Meryl Streep speech.'

Georgie smiled until her eyes shimmered. 'Do you see that jumper you're wearing?'

'Yes.'

'Don't, Georgie, you're not the fucking Devil wearing Prada, you're a fashion buyer.'

Georgie poured herself more wine, taking her time. She was holding Rachael's eye, comfortable, the distance safe enough for her to flirt. 'Well, what do I do? I decide what people are going to wear.'

'People who shop for their clothes on the Senorita.com website, not all people.' Harriet laughed. 'And even then, a small minority of them might rebel and send their clothes back, or not click on them in the first place.'

But Georgie was smiling thinly, eyes like a leopard's. 'That jumper has the slight beginnings of epaulettes – Commes des Garçon, 2009. It's in a variation of Stella McCartney millennial pink and it has the shortened sleeve rib of Balenciaga, two winter seasons ago. That was based on the old naval sleeve.' She sat back triumphantly. 'It's high street, because it's a wool–acrylic mix, not pure wool. If I am not mistaken, – and I rarely am – I'd say Zara Basic range. This season.'

Rachael smiled. 'Very good. But . . . ' She looked almost sheepish. 'This jumper, I'm afraid, was bought by my mother. In C&A, probably in about 1986.'

There was a clamour. Explosions of exclamations. 'Georgie the guru!' 'On point, fashionista!' 'The Anna Wintour of a teeny tiny bit of North London!' Cackling. Fingers pointed in the air.

'Are you being serious?' Georgie was still smiling.

'You can look at the label.' Rachael leaned across the table, proffering the nape of her neck. Georgie declined with a flick of her fingers.

'Well,' Georgie said. 'What goes around jolly well comes around, doesn't it?'

'I'll say it does,' said Alice, but she said it a little too loudly, and they all turned to stare.

Tessa reached for the champagne bottle Georgie had taken from Melissa, and poured the remains of it into her own glass. She closed her eyes, tipped it back and swallowed.

5

The neatly laid table had disappeared beneath a chaos of dirty plates, streaky glasses and a cottage pie dish that had been scraped clean. The pot of goats' hearts sat forgotten beside Georgie's place as the party retreated to the lounge.

Harriet had popped open an old suitcase to discover a built-in gramophone hidden inside, and began raiding a nearby cupboard for records. 'Who needs Spotify?' she said in a rhythmic, sing-song, mischievous way. She flicked through old LPs and forty-fives, smacking them against one another. Her back was turned, and they couldn't see what she'd found when she paused, cackled, and then withdrew a shiny black disc from its sleeve.

Big-band brass sounded, authentically tinny and flat, streaming out of the old cone of the player. The crooning voice swam up.

'Strangers in the night . . .' Harriet sang along, indulging the long vowels.

They listened for a few moments, then Alice said, 'Do you think we are strangers now?'

Georgie laughed and said, 'It feels like we only just graduated. I don't think I could feel strange around you guys, even if it was twenty years.'

The music poured over them. Georgie was flopped across the three-seater sofa, with Melissa curled in a ball at her feet. Harriet sat on the floor beside the gramophone, her feet pressed together, knees splayed outwards. Alice was in one of the armchairs, while Rachael knelt at her feet, cradling and fiddling with one foot or the other. Bea sat on the other armchair, arms spread out, head tipped back.

Tessa stood by the window, looking out. She could see the silvery purple leaves of the broccoli in the vegetable patch swaying in a persistent breeze. The sage and the rosemary bushes, hard and woody, moved back and forth, pushed firmly by an invisible hand, lit by the moon.

Each of them stayed frozen in place for the duration of the song, sipping their drinks.

The tune ended and the record began tripping and hissing. Harriet removed the stylus and looked for another. She put on some Edith Piaf.

Georgie patted her throat. 'Those goats' hearts are repeating on me.'

Bea asked Alice, 'Have you ever been out to South America?'

Alice was peering at her phone, while Rachael fiddled with her feet. She shook her head. 'No interest. Oh no, that's not true. We honeymooned in Patagonia. But that's not what you meant, was it? You meant, have I been on safari with this one?' She kicked lightly.

'It's not safari,' Rachael said.

'*I* know that,' Alice said – the implication: *they* don't. 'I wouldn't have anything to do while she hacked through the undergrowth looking for puma poo.'

'She-puma poo,' corrected Rachael.

Harriet sat forwards. 'Do you get to feed them, at the zoo? Do you go into their cages?'

'I'm not a zookeeper,' Rachael said.

'She just watches them from outside, like a creep,' Alice said. 'Then she writes down what they do. Sticks it all in her scrapbook and on Post-it notes all over her wall.'

'And what can we learn from the pumas?' Georgie said lazily.

Tessa turned from the window. Georgie's hand was draped over her brow. She looked beautiful in an affected way. Her slim, fire-toned sheath dress poured down her body in a dramatic ombre. Her giant jewellery shone at her wrists and throat.

Rachael was studying her too Tessa noticed. 'Well,' she said, as if they were all about to be in it for the long haul. 'I study the mothers. That's the first hurdle, distinguishing them from the males and the juvenile females.'

'Do they look different?' asked Harriet.

'No. They're difficult to tell apart, unless you are up close or tracking them. The first difference is that you'll see the mothers live in groups with their young, while all the other pumas are solitary. Then, the second – well, the males wee-wee on their territory. The females shit.'

'What?' Harriet said, her face a frown. 'They shit on their territory? What makes them decide to do that?'

Rachael tipped back her head as if she might be about to indulge in a laugh, but she controlled herself. 'They don't decide. It's evolutionary.'

'Why?' asked Bea. 'And why is it just the mothers who do that?'

'In answer to your second question, we don't know exactly; that's what I investigate. But to answer your first – it helps them to defend their territory. We think. It also,' she said, smiling, 'it also attracts their mates.'

'Nooooo. Shut up,' said Harriet. 'Male pumas like the smell of lady shit?'

'Some human males do, too,' Alice said.

'What do you know about that?' Harriet laughed.

Alice looked at her with a mixture of scorn and disbelief. 'We've all had sex with weirdos. When we were starting out.'

Harriet raised her eyebrows. 'Have we?'

'The mothers are the most brutal,' Rachael went on, ignoring them. 'I once saw a mother drag a llama carcass for over a mile to feed her cubs.'

'Gosh,' Harriet said. 'I should put that on the blog.' She laughed uncertainly.

There was quiet for a moment. Then Georgie said, 'You talk just like an academic. Doesn't she? "To answer your first question . . ." Christ, we're becoming those dullards that we had to sit and listen to for four years. Four fucking years. Why did we all decide to study in Scotland? We could have been out in three in England.'

'What did you study?' Rachael asked her. She seemed, to Tessa, impervious to any kind of baiting from Georgie.

'English.' Georgie hoisted herself upright and pointed to Bea and Harriet. 'English, English.' Then she pointed to Melissa. 'Vet medicine.' To Tessa. 'Medicine.' To Alice. 'Computer science.'

'It was maths and chemistry,' Alice corrected her. 'My masters was computer science.'

'We always thought you were going to be the academic, Alice. You were such a try-hard. Always burrowing away.'

'I was hiding, not studying. I didn't come out until the end of second year.'

Georgie snorted. 'Yes, I remember.'

Harriet quietly interjected. 'Are we ever going to find out what it is you do for a living, Alice?'

Alice looked at her for a second, thinking about it. 'You could look me up on LinkedIn.' She went back to fiddling with her phone.

'You're not on LinkedIn,' Harriet replied.

'So you tried?' Alice smiled, then looked back down at her phone. 'I'm sure there must be a way to tap into one network's 4G, and then we can all tether for Wi-Fi.'

'It's GCHQ, is it?' Bea probed.

Harriet gave Bea a look, unseen by Alice, but clear to the rest of them. *Don't feed her ego.* Harriet said, in a breathy mocking voice, 'I could tell you, Bea, but then I'd have to kill you.'

Alice looked up. 'Something like that,' she said, hooding her eyelids in a slow blink.

Melissa stirred. 'Well ladies, did we ever think back then that in ten years' time we would be sitting in a castle like this, with proper jobs and everything?'

101

'It's been eleven years,' Tessa said. 'Eleven since we started university.'

'Eleven years – has it been that long? Really?' Georgie asked.

Tessa held her gaze for a moment.

Georgie turned to Harriet. 'You got married so young.'

Harriet rolled her eyes. 'So did Bea.'

'But that was different. Bea was marrying . . .' she trailed off.

'A Muslim?' Bea smiled wryly.

Georgie shook her head. 'You know what I meant.'

'Do I?' Bea said softly.

'Listen, ladies,' Melissa said, sitting up. 'I've got a little surprise.' She paused for effect, then leaned over and fumbled in the small handbag on the floor. But she was too drunk and couldn't manage the clasp, and her hair kept falling in her face.

'I thought we were going to have coffee with the kets,' said Tessa.

'Spoil the surprise, go on.' Georgie said.

'It's hardly a surprise, is it?' Tessa looked back down at the garden.

'It was a joke, Tessa. What's the matter with you, anyway? Standing there looking out that window as if you're about to jump.'

A sharp, immediate ball of fury welled in Tessa's stomach. She felt rage flash – unbridled rage. It took all of her practised control to swallow it back down. It reminded her of a time when once, during her training, a woman giving birth had punched her across the jaw after having a bad reaction to the epidural Tessa had inserted into her spine. She had been on the tail end of a fourteen-hour shift and the woman had hammered Tessa with her knuckles, catching her across the chin with a diamond cluster ring. Tessa had wanted to punch the woman back. But she couldn't, because she was a junior anaesthetist and the woman was in labour. Now, she used a similar logic. Georgie was the bride-to-be, and this was her hen party.

But Georgie had scented a wound. 'You'll be lucky if we let you have any, since you refused to harvest some for us from the NHS's burgeoning supply.'

'I'll make coffee,' Bea said, but she didn't move.

The others were laughing nervously. Melissa was being clumsy with the drug, setting up lines of fine white crystals with her fingers on a compact mirror. 'I'll do it,' Georgie nudged her. She wiped a few stray granules from the coffee table and licked her finger.

'No, I'll do it. I was the one that had to cook it,' Melissa protested. 'You had it easy when you used to buy it from that bloke with the smelly hair. I have to fill out forms, evaporate the stuff. The nurses think there's an epidemic of horses with tumours down our way now.' She took a train ticket from her handbag, rolled it into a tight straw and snorted a line. Alice took the proffered mirror and train ticket and snorted, then offered it to Rachael. Rachael rolled her eyes and passed it on.

'Why haven't we brought Charlie anyway?' Harriet said, as the mirror was passed to her.

Tessa's spine turned to ice. Her guts knotted. For a second she couldn't process the question, the tactlessness of it. Then she realised quickly what Harriet had meant.

'Because coke turns me into a nutter,' Georgie replied.

Alice cackled. The icy rush departed from Tessa, but she was left with the ghost of a shiver under her skin.

'Anyway,' Georgie went on. 'Old times' sake.'

Harriet took a line. 'Ugh, snot. It's supposed to go up, not down. What's the matter with me? Yuck.'

Tessa was still trembling slightly as she was passed the mirror. She looked at it for a second. She had gone easy on the drugs since she started her clinical training and she didn't know what effect they would have now. Way back, Georgie would hand ketamine out at parties, nestled, Tessa recalled, in the open half-cups of flying saucer sweeties, replacing the sherbet she had tipped out – a creepy little joke Tessa had always been a bit repelled by. She had been frightened the first time, terrified of what she would see in the void of her own mind. But it had lifted her instead, moving her an inch or two forwards from her body. Her fascination with the new world presented to her had made her forget everything else. She had taken it again, and again, and again. They had all sat night after night, long into the small hours, comparing extraordinary worlds. It meant she could avoid the immediate one. But sometimes she had taken dark trips, too.

Tessa hesitated, then put the mirror and the rolled ticket down on the windowsill and went over to the record player. Edith Piaf had finished, and the record was jumping in a little hiccupping sound. She flicked through the selection of sleeves, took one out and set it spinning. The needle caught; a sound like a striking match. Then measured piano chords, and a low, soulful voice. Tessa closed her eyes.

'Is this Mariah Carey? Are you kidding, Tessa?' Alice said, laughing.

'It's Harry Nilsson.' Tessa went back to the window. Now she dabbed out a stubby line of the powdered ketamine and snorted it quickly through the makeshift straw. After she had taken its bitter flavour to her sinuses and passed the mirror on, she heard Georgie say, 'Oh, apothecary, thy drugs are quick.'

She looked up to see Georgie smiling, running her tongue round her mouth and up to her palette to cleanse the snotty dregs.

'This isn't really a wedding song, is it?' Harriet muttered.

Tessa couldn't speak. The drugs had hit her brain and the first thing she saw was the network of vessels inside her eyelids each time she blinked. Very clean, long vessels, like they were made of blown glass and sculpted hollow. The blinks took a long time, time enough to see her hands again, her hands materialising through – no, behind – the vessels, the glass vessels, behind in the cavity that led to her mind. This time, the hands were hers and they were very clearly clutching a child's neck underwater. Crystal liquid lapped over the blue face; the fronds of weeds melted into hair. Harry Nilsson burst into the chorus.

Other voices in the room joined in, warbling, laughing.

Inside the glass underwater maze of her head, Tessa choked. She reeled and tried to climb back out again into the room, away from the child's face, and the eyes that were staring at her as they began to close. Catching her breath, she looked around at them all. Just as quickly as the haze had come on, it vanished, and the drugs now threw her into a sudden lucidity, like the lens focusing on a camera.

She saw in close-up, Harriet examining the paraffin lamp on the sideboard by the gramophone. She was humming along; she began rooting again through the records, not really looking at them, just enjoying the snap as each flicked from one side of the pile to the other. Melissa and Alice were singing at the top of their voices, in semi-hysterics, belting the notes off-key. Rachael looked pensive. She had not taken any of the ketamine. Melissa gave up singing. Alice looked, to Tessa in her sudden frightening clarity, as though she was trying too hard to have a good time. She was still singing.

Melissa said, lazily, 'Now that we have partaken of the truth serum, I think it's time to play truth or dare.'

Georgie squealed. 'Hahaha.'

Harriet looked up sharply. 'I'm not doing any dares. I'm a mother, you know.' But as she said it, she collapsed into a heap of sensual laughter, letting the records spill over onto her lap and stomach.

'Truth or dare is shit if no one does a dare,' said Alice.

'How about, then,' Melissa sat up and looked groggily, wickedly at the room, 'Never have I ever. Only truths, no dares.'

Georgie cackled again and clapped her hands. 'This is the hen party I came for.'

'Regression, regression,' Alice muttered.

'It has been,' Georgie counted on her fingers. 'Six years since we all saw Bea.'

Bea stayed still, but her eyes flicked onto Georgie's. 'Four,' she said, softly.

'There must be plenty of things Bea has done in that time which we should all know about. Not to mention Tessa. You can spill the beans on the crumbling NHS.'

Tessa blinked, but the words didn't pierce. The ket was shielding her.

Georgie leaned forwards. 'I'll start. Has everyone got a drink?'

The others looked blankly about.

'Well, get a sodding drink,' said Georgie, with sudden, vicious ebullience. 'It's not like we're running dry. Drink up, ladies. Pretend it's freshers' week again.' She stopped suddenly and her eyes flashed up to Tessa.

Bottles were passed messily across the table, knocking candles and ornaments. 'Whoops,' said Harriet, catching a lit candle, laughing as the hot red wax dripped onto her wrist.

Tessa centred her balance against the window ledge. The glass veins behind her eyelids were back again. It took concentration to see past them.

'Never have I ever,' said Georgie, sitting up, her back straight, one hard orange-nailed finger pointed to the ceiling. 'Never have I ever knowingly killed a patient just cos I was having a shit day.'

'Georgie,' Melissa chided.

Tessa regarded her for a second before deciding, without

too much trouble, to play her part. 'Pass me the whole bottle,' she said, and it made them all laugh, which was a relief.

But Georgie wouldn't let up. 'Never have I ever, in that case, killed a patient by mistake.'

Alice began to protest that she'd had her turn and someone else had to ask now, but they were all distracted by Melissa taking a swig.

Georgie turned her attention on her. 'Did you mean to do that?'

Melissa nodded. She was smiling, but she wouldn't meet their eyes. 'I gave a tortoise methadone by mistake once,' she said quietly, still smiling into her drink.

'Are you serious?' Rachael said.

'Yes,' she said, slurring, her drugged balance swaying her forwards. 'It was some fucking – tortoise. It had a stomach tumour. I didn't – I hadn't operated on a tortoise before. We had to tell the owner it had died under the anaesthetic. Which was true.' She looked pained for a second, as if she was trying to control a smile, then all of a sudden she was giggling into the bubbles of her champagne.

'Christ almighty,' said Georgie. 'Melissa!'

'I can't,' Melissa squealed. She calmed herself. 'At least it was just a tortoise.'

Rachael sat forward, open-mouthed, laughing in shock.

'Oh, get off your high horse.' Melissa waved her hand. The drugs had made her acidic, had sharpened up her mellowness. 'For goodness' sake. You're not out in Brazil researching tortoises, are you? No, so. If they were as important as pumas or dogs, or perhaps children . . .' She waved a hand towards Harriet, then let the sentence fade.

'Let's not argue about tortoises,' said Georgie.

'Next,' said Harriet, ignoring her.

'OK, you go,' Bea said to her.

'Never have I ever.' Harriet paused, thinking. 'Kissed someone else's husband.'

'Boring.' Georgie drank proudly, then looked around at them all to watch if anyone else was.

Both Rachael and Alice took a sip.

'The lesbians!' Harriet's hand flew to her mouth a little late.

'Yes, the lesbians,' said Alice.

'Both of you?' Georgie asked.

'At the same time.' Rachael grinned, licking the drizzle of whisky that had trailed down the rim of her glass.

Harriet was still open-mouthed.

'Cosplay,' Alice said. 'His wife was in the room at the time, if that makes it any better.'

Harriet was staring at them, from one to the next, like they were creatures behind glass. 'Is it like—' she began to say.

'Is it like we're really straight deep down?' Rachael interrupted. 'That we're just pretending, and this is our perverse way of letting our true selves out?' She shook her head. 'No.'

'That's not what I – if you—'

'Oh, fucking hell! Next time, we'll just cheat at the game and keep it to ourselves,' Alice said.

'OK, enough!' Melissa waved her hands. 'Hang on, Georgie, who was yours?'

Georgie wrinkled her nose. 'University. Remember that fighter pilot? Used to put his fingers up my arse. He was married, but I didn't find out until after he'd given me thrush. I was on a break from Jack.' She took another sip, and looked into the pool of her champagne, as if re-watching the memory there.

'I have never,' Melissa began, 'cheated on my own partner.'

They all looked around at each other. Tessa noticed that their eyes all lingered on Georgie before skimming off her. She didn't know if it was the drugs, but Georgie looked brighter, like she had been given a lustre that was singling her out, making her untouchable. No one drank.

'Well, you pair just admitted you did,' said Harriet.

'It's not cheating if the other one's there. Like, a three-some's not cheating. If your partner is one of the three.'

'I have never had a threesome,' Melissa said, then giggled and downed the rest of her drink.

The others ignored her. Harriet was staring at Georgie again. 'Georgie, have you really never cheated on Jack?'

Georgie looked at her for a second, her own soft, incredulous stare turning hard at the edges. 'No.' She shook her head. 'No. I haven't.' She paused. 'What? I'm a little bit offended by your surprise.'

Tessa went to laugh, but it would have been a cruel laugh, and she caught herself.

Harriet seemed to accept this, shrugged, then turned to Tessa. 'You now.'

Tessa fortified herself with a sip of whisky. It was fiery, undiluted.

110

'You can't drink,' Georgie said. 'Until you've – said the thing.'

'Never have I ever—' Tessa thought. *Never have I ever – never have I ever.* She had fantasised about this moment for years, but when it was offered to her on a plate, she couldn't find the right words. 'Never have I ever stolen anything from someone else.'

Harriet looked at her. 'Like what? Stolen property?'

'Yeah. Anything.'

'Like someone's husband?'

'We've had that.'

'No,' Alice interrupted. 'It's different.'

They fell silent. Tessa wouldn't look at any of them. She leaned back against the windowpane and looked across at the coffee table, at the red wax spilled on the lace runners, leaking through into the wood.

Alice said, quietly, 'Drink up, Georgie.'

Georgie looked up sharply. Her pointy features turned on Alice and she looked genuinely bewildered.

Melissa leaned forward. 'I used to shoplift from Tesco, but that's like, not really a person and it was only because the flippin' – you know what, the automated tills were shit, and I couldn't be bothered waiting for an assistant. It was like a bell pepper and maybe some porridge.'

'You took lipsticks from Boots as well,' Georgie said, inclining her head to Melissa, but still looking at Alice.

'Yeah, I think I did. Ugh, oh well.' She poured herself more champagne. 'Is no one else starting to feel sleepy?'

'We haven't had the midnight walk to the loch yet,' Tessa said. They all stared at her.

111

'What did you mean by *steal*?' Georgie asked.

'I know what she meant,' Alice said.

The hairs on the back of Tessa's neck prickled.

Alice went on. 'Just before I came out, I told you all when I was drunk that I liked that girl on the lacrosse team, the horsey one. I don't know what I was thinking, telling you, looking back.'

'You called her the princess,' said Georgie.

'Oh, so you do remember? Well, whatever, and you knew that she had said she wanted to kiss a girl, and I told her that I wanted to kiss a girl, and that night . . .' Alice paused, confused by her own story. 'Well, anyway, that night, I was planning to kiss her, but you sat on her lap and flirted and I couldn't believe it when I saw *you* kissing her. I couldn't do it then, because it would seem like I was just copying you, and I didn't want to be her second best.'

Tessa remembered the evening. She had not been there, but she remembered it because Alice had knocked on the door to their flat later in floods of tears, and it had taken all of her powers of composure just to sit in the strip-lit kitchen and listen and absorb Alice's rage, her repeated howling about how terrible Georgie was, how cruel, while Tessa made her tea and said nothing.

'It wasn't that exciting,' Georgie said sleepily.

'Not for you, it wasn't. It was just another game, but—' Alice broke off, noticing Rachael's hand planted on her thigh, squeezing. 'All right,' she said, nodding. 'But you should drink, Georgie. Drink up.'

Georgie took a large slug of champagne. She patted her

décolletage, working a crack out of her neck. 'Well,' she said. 'I have never touched the royal buttocks.'

'It's not your turn, Georgie.'

'It's my hen night. *Every* turn is my turn, and I have never – *never have I ever*,' she corrected herself, punctuating each word, 'touched royal buttocks. And you have, so we're even. Touché!'

'Shut up Georgie,' Alice said.

Rachael looked sidelong at Alice, smiling, her hand still clamping her wife's leg. 'I don't believe I know this story.'

Georgie leaned forward, boozily. Tessa had another sudden flashback, watching the gesture. It was indeed like the old days: Georgie drunk and poking with her stick; Alice angry and hurt. It was just like no time had passed – but not in a good way. 'I'll tell the story,' Georgie said. 'Because you are going to sugar-coat it and you'll get it wrong. You were too drunk to remember properly. We were in The West Port, and that prince from Thailand came in with his – you know, his bunch of not-very-well-disguised bodyguards, and you were pissed and you said – and I quote – "I am going to touch the royal buttocks." And we tried – Melissa was there – and me and Mel tried valiantly to stop you, but you were determined. Absolutely determined. Nothing was going to stop you.'

'It was me,' Tessa said quietly. 'I was there. Not Mel.'

Georgie ignored her. 'And there was only so much we could do. There was no holding you back. You were like a mustang.'

'As I remember, Georgie, you were encouraging her,' Tessa said.

'You were like a wild thing.' Georgie steamrollered on. '"I will touch the prince's arse," you said, and then you pretended to go to the toilet, and on the way past, you just, just went for it!' She threw both her hands in the air, spilling champagne on the sofa.

'No, that's not what happened. I wedged past him very discreetly.' Alice wagged her finger.

'I remember it!' said Georgie.

'So do I.'

'I bet you do!'

'I brushed past him. If I had grabbed his arse, I would have been arrested.'

'You sexually assaulted a prince?' Rachael said, smirking.

'Are you making light of sexual assault? Alice? The feminist? You're so . . .' Georgie searched for the word. 'Oh God, I don't know. I love you, Alice, we had so much fun back then.' She leaned back into the cushions and downed the rest of her drink, spilling more of it down the side of her neck.

'We all remember things differently, don't we?' Tessa said. She thought nobody had heard, but they fell quiet and she realised she must have sounded stern or sour.

'Does anyone want any more?' Melissa was holding out the mirror. Three little lines of ketamine had been neatly cut.

'Yeah, go on.' Harriet took it.

'I'll make coffee,' Bea said again, and this time she did get up and leave.

The mirror was passed round quietly. It functioned like a sort of peace pipe. Melissa cut some more and they all took a line, even Rachael this time. Tessa watched them all flop back against the plump upholstery as they let the drugs creep into their tired, drunk brains.

'Can we look at it again?' Georgie said. Her eyes seemed to shine, diamond-polished, her little pointy nose sharp and keen, her rosebud lips smiling in delirious pleasure. It was an unpredictable kind of glee. 'I want to look at it again, you know the one, the one with – you know the one.'

'The what?' Alice asked, aware Georgie was looking at her.

'The photograph.'

There was silence.

'Now we're baked, it's not so scary, yes?' Harriet said.

Melissa laughed, a shrill, impulsive laugh.

Alice took a few more moments to defrost from Georgie's anecdote, then began laughing as she tried to unlock her phone. With some effort, she managed to press the correct finger down for fingerprint recognition and passed it to Georgie. 'You look for it.' Then she seemed to think better of this. 'No, actually, I'll get you to the right spot.'

They scrolled through the phone together. 'Here,' Alice said. 'Here's the before one.' Georgie stared for a few seconds, a loving look softening her face. It wasn't pure narcissism. She wasn't just looking at herself. In that moment, it seemed that she was besotted with all of their faces, with their love-liness as a group, and how it had been captured. She made a small 'N'awww' sound, and pushed her thumb across the screen. Then she tried again, and again.

'That's the last picture – you deleted it?'

'No,' Alice said. 'No, I didn't.'

'It's not there. Take it.' Georgie thrust the phone at Alice.

115

Alice scrolled. 'You must have deleted it,' she said.

'I haven't touched it.'

'You touched it just now. You were scrolling.'

'I know how a phone works. It wasn't there. You must have deleted it.'

'I didn't.' Alice looked puzzled.

'Someone else must have, then,' Georgie said.

'Don't be a fucking idiot,' Alice snapped, and for a second Georgie looked back at her, a vicious, violent expression slamming onto her features. Alice stood her ground. 'Nobody, nobody can hack *my* phone.'

'I didn't say they *hacked* it,' Georgie spat. 'I said they picked it up and deleted it, like normal people do when they want to delete something, not your creepy spooks and their weird techy-techy witchcraft.'

'Techy-techy? You work for a website, Georgie.'

Georgie looked at her blankly, clearly not seeing the connection.

'Anyway, it's fingerprint locked. They'd have to cut my finger off to unlock it.'

'I didn't stitch it back on without you knowing,' Tessa said. 'Not even I'm that good.' And she laughed loudly, finding somewhere within herself the will to try and lighten the tone again.

There was a pause, the grisly image of Tessa stitching Alice's finger sinking in, then they all laughed.

'Maybe,' said Harriet. 'Maybe it didn't even happen?' She shrugged. 'The photo's gone. It's been deleted. Or *maybe* it was never there in the first place.'

Georgie threw back her head and moaned, a small sound. 'It's such a creepy castle,' she slurred. 'Ten points, Tessa, for finding the creepy castle.'

She leaned back again, sinking into the soft, worn velvet of the sofa. She rolled her tongue round her mouth. She suddenly seemed very high or very drunk, or both. 'I feel really, really horny, all of a sudden,' she said, and then she was breathing irregularly and running her hands across her throat, down towards the low neckline of her dress. 'I fucking feel it,' she said, and then, in a sudden sea change, she moaned. 'Oh God, I feel sick. Too much, too much, too quick. Get it out of me.'

'Jesus,' Tessa muttered. 'Get her outside.'

'No, I don't want to,' Georgie said. 'Scratch me. The room's moving.'

'Fresh air,' said Tessa. She began yanking at the sash. The window had guards on it to stop it from opening more than a couple of inches.

'Scratch me, scratch me, I feel dizzy.'

'Water,' Melissa said, shoving a mug of it towards Georgie. Georgie batted it out of her hand and the mug went tumbling over the gramophone, splashing it with water and hitting the horn with a clang.

'Georgie, fucking hell,' Harriet said, jumping up, floundering for the pile of paper napkins on the coffee table.

'Oh, we paid a damage deposit, get over it.'

'Get her to the kitchen,' Harriet said.

'I don't want the kitchen,' Georgie said. 'I want to go outside and see the stars.'

'We need to do the washing-up, anyway,' Harriet continued.

Georgie slurred at her. 'I'm not washing up at my hen party.'

'Come down to the kitchen, you can have a cup of tea,' Rachael said.

'Scratch me.' She appealed with her eyes to Rachael. She tugged on her necklace and opened her lips, breathing heavily in a crass performance of desire. Alice rolled her eyes bitterly, then got up and pinned open the door.

Tessa waited for someone else to do it, then realised they were all waiting for her, so she hooked her arms underneath Georgie's armpits and began supporting her in a waving, stumbling walk to the door. Melissa and Rachael cleared the way of cushions and bottles.

'Jesus, I'm drunk,' Melissa murmured, on her knees.

Tessa heard Harriet at her back, a breathy, almost silent voice. 'Sometimes I just don't know,' she said. She breathed out heavily, contemplating her next phrase, whether to say it, and then seemed to decide. 'I don't know why we are still friends with her.'

6

Rachael and Alice cleared the dining room in rounds, clattering down the stairs, slipping in and out of the kitchen with all the discretion of servants.

It was cold in the basement. There might have been a draught coming through one of the rickety windows. The Aga stove had burned down to silvery ashes and the flagstones sucked out the remainder of the heat. With the sun sunk and the natural light gone, the strip light overhead felt harsh and institutional, like the kitchens in the university halls from years ago. In the window's reflection, Tessa watched her friends file into the room. They all looked gruesome, the glaze of the window picking out each sunken shadow and line in their faces, ageing them on the spot, giving them a frightening vision of their future selves. Their eye make-up looked smeared in the light. Lipstick bled into the lines around their mouths. Her own cheeks looked clownishly red, flushed with wine and drugs.

Georgie's face had set in a scowl. She gathered her arms around herself and shivered. Forcibly unmooring herself from Tessa's grasp, she leaned on the kitchen island, reaching for the leftover sourdough bread and an abandoned tub of humous.

'That humous has a brown crust, I wouldn't touch it,' Harriet said.

Georgie ignored her and scooped some into her mouth with a chunk of bread. 'God, that's what I needed.'

'Fine,' Harriet whispered. 'Poison yourself.'

Georgie heard her. 'Haven't you got some washing-up to do?'

Tessa watched Harriet as her face calcified. Harriet went to the sink, and very slowly dribbled out a glass of tap water. She walked back over to the island, her heels cutting a clang on the flagstones, and handed it to Georgie. Georgie drank it in one, gulping. She placed the glass down with a smack.

'Feel better?' Harriet asked.

Tessa felt as if she ought to do something, so began to stroke Georgie's back. Rachael came back in, balancing on her forearm the wooden board with the remains of the garlic bread. Her hand braced a pile of side plates.

'She just needs to ride it out. Like Bea last night,' Tessa said. Harriet shot her a look. But Georgie either hadn't noticed, or perhaps, as Tessa had suspected, she knew anyway. She began looking around. 'Where is Bea? Wasn't she getting coffee?'

'Maybe she went back upstairs,' said Harriet.

Rachael had gravitated towards the back door that led into the utility room in the porch. 'Did you leave this open for a reason?'

'Is that why it's so flipping cold?' said Melissa. 'No.'

Rachael went through the utility room and they heard her shut the outer door with some effort.

'Wait a minute,' Harriet said. 'Maybe Bea nipped out? Shouldn't we leave it open?'

'In the dark?'

'It's only nine o'clock,' Rachael said.

'Jesus, is it only nine?' Georgie said, through a mouthful of bread. 'I forgot how savage this country is. Cross a border and they steal half the daylight.'

Rachael had begun to say, 'Actually, you'll find that in summer . . .'

But no one was listening.

'Leave it on the latch,' Harriet said. 'Don't lock it, just in case.'

Alice emerged with another pile of greasy plates. 'Shall I put these straight in the sink?' she asked Rachael.

'Ugh, that's better already,' said Georgie, shivering again, shaking off the cold. It wasn't clear if she meant the temperature, or the bread soaking up the drugs.

'Let's rinse the larger things first,' Rachael said.

'I can't believe they don't have a dishwasher,' Harriet said. 'Who owns this place anyway, Tessa? You found it on the web? Is it National Trust?'

'Jacobites,' Georgie said, and cackled. 'They are so last century.' She pursed her lips and looked around. 'Is there any cheese left?'

'It's privately owned,' murmured Tessa.

Alice passed Georgie a board with a net cloche on top.

Tessa moved over to where Georgie sat and hovered over her shoulder, taking a little nub of the Cheddar they'd had earlier and nibbling on it. Georgie took a lump of what looked like Brie, squashing it with her fingers before smashing it into her mouth in one.

'Go on, shift change. You've done the heavy lifting,' Harriet said to Rachael.

'I don't mind,' said Rachael.

But Harriet reached for a tea towel to tie around her waist in lieu of an apron, then she budged Rachael with her hips, taking from her hands the cast-iron casserole dish with its smeared remnants of goats' hearts. She dumped it into the empty sink with a clang and switched the taps on to full spraying blast.

'How are you feeling?' Tessa said to Georgie over the noise of the water.

'Fine. Just need to wait for the comedown.'

'Keep drinking water. Not too fast.'

Georgie swallowed the second lump of cheese she was working on. 'Did you take some?'

'Yes,' Tessa said.

Georgie ran her tongue across her teeth. 'Any good?'

Tessa shrugged. 'I didn't take much.'

'Wouldn't do to get caught, right? Doctor taking ket.'

'I'm sure I'm not the only one. What about you?'

Now Georgie shrugged. 'Don't suppose my CEO gives a shit. But they'd probably have to fire me.' She looked at Tessa plainly, as if trying to focus. 'Tessa, how are you? I mean how are you, really? I feel like I haven't seen you for so long. And

122

you've gone to all this – this trouble.' She reached out and took Tessa's hand. Alice had come over and was leaning on the third side of the island now, picking at the leftover cheese with her tattooed hand, Celtic designs on her ring finger and a single word on her thumb that Tessa couldn't make out.

'I'm – tired,' said Tessa. 'Yeah, just tired. Shifts are a bitch. We're understaffed. Obviously. I mean, it's not the time to have a political rant.' She smiled weakly.

'Do they work you to exhaustion?'

Tessa surprised herself by feeling very suddenly like she might cry. Perhaps it was the strange sincerity that had come suddenly over Georgie, a widening of her pupils as if with real love, a crest of narcotic blissful pure love, as if she were truly seeing Tessa as a friend for the first time. Tessa felt her own body surge in response, relax and dilate with the intensity of the look, and though she was absolutely resolute that she would not cry in front of Georgie, at the same time she had the feeling, just then, that in that moment, perhaps it wouldn't matter if she did; that it would be safe to cry and to lean on her friend.

She said, softly, 'They do I guess.' She looked down at the counter, the white and grey pattern of the granite. 'It's a bit shit sometimes.'

Georgie said, with the same sincerity, 'I know, Tessa. It's brutal at my work, too. I know exactly how you feel.' She went on. 'They call me at all times of day and night. I mean, a company smartphone is not a perk, it's a leash. It wouldn't surprise me if they used Google location data to keep tabs on us. They check our Facebooks, they follow us on Twitter

123

and Instagram. And this whole shitshow about having beds in the office and a nap room. I hate it. I really, really hate it sometimes.'

Tessa buttoned shut her mouth. She didn't want to martyr herself or start a silly competition. She was aware that she might look as if she wanted to hit Georgie. She fought the surging waves of the drugs; back and forth, they mashed with her emotions. Alice ate some more cheese.

Georgie ploughed on, oblivious. 'You have beds at work, too, don't you?'

'We have beds at work,' Tessa said. 'For when you're on call. Or work a double shift. But we have to pay to use them.'

She became dimly aware that, behind them, Harriet and Rachael were wrestling with the sink.

'And your sister, how is she? It's been ages.'

Georgie could not have failed to see Tessa's face freeze.

Melissa looked blurrily at her. 'Sasha?' she murmured. 'I remember Sasha. She was so pretty.'

'Sasha,' said Georgie. 'Didn't she move to the Emirates?'

Tessa shook her head. 'No, she runs a business in the Midlands, just a little cottage farm.' She turned quickly to look at Harriet. 'Are you OK?'

The sleeves of Harriet's patterned silk blouse were rolled up to the elbows, her hands sunk into the basin. Rachael had opened the cupboard underneath the sink and was peering among the pipework.

'It appears to be blocked,' she said.

'Let me look at it.' Alice lifted her head in a resigned, slightly bored way and ambled over. She pushed Rachael out of the way and bent down. 'If you can unscrew the plug, I can just poke about with a knife for whatever is down there.'

'It's probably just a build-up of food bits from previous guests,' Rachael said. 'Yuck.'

'Holy fuck, this place is actually a bit of a dump,' Georgie said, turning her attention on them.

Tessa stayed at the island while Georgie stumbled over, rather like someone on a luxury safari, keeping a safe distance but eager and curious to see what was happening nonetheless. She peered over Harriet's shoulder. 'Let me,' she said.

'We're fine,' Harriet sighed.

'But I've got thinner wrists than you.'

'Oh, well done you. What are you going to do, put your whole hand down there?'

'I have to do all of our plumbing stuff,' Georgie went on. 'Because Jack is such a titty; he's a real girl about it all.'

Alice stopped what she was doing and leaned back on her haunches. Rachael nudged her as though to encourage her to ignore the comment, and she began working again.

'Give me a butter knife and I'll unscrew the plughole,' Georgie said.

'I think it needs the U-bend taking out,' Alice grunted from inside the cupboard.

Rachael had gone to the utility room and returned with a bucket.

'How much are you guys paying for this?' Georgie said. 'We should go and rouse Tom from his Netflix binge.' She crouched down and butted Alice out of the way with her hips.

Alice looked at her, but moved aside. 'There's no internet signal, so he's not watching—'

'Fine, his computer games for one, and his – his shit books about rhododendrons.' Georgie stood back up and fiddled with a butter knife at the central screw of the plug. 'This is gross,' she said, but there was a sort of relish to her voice, as if the grubbiness of the task had sobered her up a bit. She grunted and twiddled away, removing the metal plughole cover with a clatter, then wiped her wet hands on her coloured dress. 'It's no good,' she said, standing back. 'I think the U-bend needs to be taken out.'

Alice opened her mouth, then caught Rachael's look.

'Oh no, hold on,' Georgie said. 'The water's draining, something's moving. Let me just wiggle this out.' She put her index finger down the plughole, then recoiled swiftly. She stumbled backwards in her heels, scraping the flagstones. 'Fuck,' she whispered. 'I dunno what I just touched.'

Tessa leaned forwards.

Out of the open plughole rose the keen, kite-shaped head of a snake. At first, just a couple of inches were visible; then, slowly it rose, swaying, flicking its forked tongue, staring with small, lidless black eyes. It seemed for a second as if it was dancing to some pipe tune that the rest of them could not hear. But its movements took on a sudden swiftness, and its body curled in S-shaped repeats as it propelled itself efficiently up through the plughole and into the sink.

A silent, white-hot terror spread across the kitchen. They all seemed struck dumb with revulsion. Harriet shuffled backwards, still staring, unable to take her eyes off it.

126

'It's an adder,' whispered Melissa. 'Look at the pattern. Don't touch it.'

It was writhing in and up and over the draining water in the sink, bewildered by the washing-up bubbles, the cast-iron pots, the lids, the sudden bright light that was not daylight.

Harriet was still stumbling backwards, reaching for the island.

Georgie had frozen on the spot. She was staring in disbelief, as if the whole thing might be a trick, a hallucination from the ketamine.

'How did it get into the pipes?' Alice said.

'Probably looking for somewhere to hide. They can get through tiny holes,' said Rachael. She was inching over to it, holding open her hands, fingers splayed, just watching.

'Georgie.' Melissa went over to where Georgie had begun to sway on the spot. Georgie's eyes were suddenly very bright. She edged away from Melissa and sprang towards the knife block on the island.

'Don't touch it,' said Rachael.

'Georgie, what are you doing?' Melissa said.

Georgie was fumbling over the knife block. She knocked it over into the leftover cheese, her hands shaking, then she pulled open the drawer below.

'Georgie, they're protected.' Melissa went to slam the drawer shut, but she was too late. She caught at Georgie's hand as it emerged holding a meat cleaver.

'Georgie,' Melissa said sharply.

Alice and Rachael were deep in a discussion over the bucket. Rachael was saying, in a calm voice, that she had caught snakes before during her research trips. In fact, she'd had a bushmaster in her sleeping bag once. She kept up a calm, breezy patter as they fumbled with meat tongs and the bucket and large plates, deciding which way to scoop and which way to tip, while Tessa looked on dumbly, repulsed. She had seen them before many times in the wild, on hikes, but the thing about adders was that they seemed able to change their pattern and shape, to shape-shift. They were not like cats or dogs or mice or spiders. The shapes they could form were endless, throwing the brain off course, so that you sort of recognised it as a snake, but had never before seen one in that configuration. They always looked unnatural to her. And her family's spaniel had once been bitten by one and died. She kept her distance. She felt, suddenly, very badly drugged.

It was about two feet long, zig-zag-patterned, hooking and uncurling, reaching up for the edge of the sink. Slow, then fast. With a sudden lick of movement, it slithered up onto the dish drainer and began tasting the air up and around the wooden rack perched there.

Alice yelped at its speed, then giggled as Rachael hovered the plate upside down above it, trying to guide its movements. 'Keep the bucket still,' she said.

Then, with a roar and a blur from behind them, Georgie came charging forwards, bearing at axe height, the meat cleaver. She slammed it down into the edge of the metal counter.

'Georgie,' Melissa yelled.

'Hold her back!' Rachael said. 'If she takes my fingers off, I'll fucking scar her.'

'Georgie, you can't do it,' Melissa said. But she was drunk herself, and she couldn't seem to muster enough strength or speed to grab Georgie.

Georgie was preparing for another swing, warrior-oblivious, Boudicca in heels and a dress, wildness in her eyes. She tracked the snake with her quavering gaze.

Rachael tried to place her body in the way, to catch Georgie's eye, but she ended up ducking as the cleaver swung towards her. 'Are you listening? They are protected. I'm serious. You can get six months in prison. Can you hear me?'

The cleaver came down again.

'You fuckwit!' shrieked Rachael. 'You fucking arsehole. You nearly got me in the shoulder. Put that meat cleaver down!'

'It's getting onto the counter,' Alice called. 'Quickly. If it goes AWOL in the castle, I'm never going to sleep.'

Tessa took a frightened step back. The snake had made its way onto the granite counter now, and was weaving towards the back of the toaster.

'Rachael,' Alice said. 'Rachael.'

'No, she needs to understand.' Rachael was still standing in front of Georgie, her brow creased in fury. But Georgie lunged to the side, flinging the cleaver, and this time she caught the snake in the head. The speed with which it leapt to strike her was alarming, but Georgie was quicker. She brought the cleaver down again, chopping off its tail. It made a repulsive sound, a hissing, whistling shriek. It began twisting on the counter, a strangled dance that made Georgie laugh a strange, unreal laugh.

Rachael shook her head. 'That was not cool.'

'Just get out of the way,' said Alice. 'I don't want you losing a finger, or worse.' She pulled Rachael's arm.

Georgie took another, smaller, more calculated swing. This time the snake stopped writhing, twitched a few times, then rolled, white belly up, and was still.

Georgie whooped. 'I killed a fucking serpent. On my hen night. I killed a serpent. Ha! That's got to be a metaphor. Can you imagine what Professor – fucking – what's his name – would say? Can you?'

She turned to the group. They were all a few feet away from her, huddled into a loose semicircle, at a safe distance.

'It's like slaying a dick,' she said.

Tessa shivered. The kitchen felt very cold again. She looked at the body of the adder, ridged underside up, scaly back down, twisted body. Alive, it had been horrid, but dead, it was hideous. That same biological grip, that protective revulsion that came on her when she saw a fresh corpse at work, came over her now.

'Georgie,' Melissa said gently. 'If Tom finds out, he might have to report you.'

Georgie was still holding the cleaver's chunky handle in her manicured hand, her orange Shellac nails smeared with lines of a very dark blood. The squat blade had a few brownish scales clinging to it, and there were a few spurts of blood on her dress. Her eyeballs were sunk into their shadowy sockets, but the irises were still bright, brimming.

'Can you put the cleaver down, please, Georgie,' said Alice.

Georgie looked around, then at the snake, as if coming

back to herself from somewhere far away. She did as she was told, placing the cleaver at a distance from the curled body.

'You guys,' she said. She broke into a wide, wild grin. 'Your faces. It's just an adder,' she added casually, as if she had squashed a spider with her toe.

'What should we do with it?' Alice asked.

Rachael was looking over at it. 'Not sure,' she said slowly. 'I think you should probably bury it.'

'Nonsense,' said Georgie. 'Just chuck it in the bin. That's what we used to do with the rats at the Camden flat.'

'Georgie, were you listening?' Melissa said. 'Six months in prison if Tom finds out.'

'Oh, for fuck's sake, I bet it's not the first time a guest has killed a snake.' Georgie seemed to realise what she had said, and burst out laughing. 'You guys, I killed a snake. That is mental. Aaaaaah!' She clutched her face with the orange, blood-smeared nails, pulling them down her cheeks, dragging the flesh and leaving streaks.

'You have to bury it,' Rachael said.

Georgie took a second to realise she was being spoken to. She looked back at the snake. 'I'm not touching it.'

'You killed it, Georgie. You bury it,' Alice said.

'What? Just chuck it in the bin.'

'Which bin?' said Rachael. 'The recycling? The compost? There's half a dozen bins, Georgie, and in any of them I think Tom is going to notice a dead fucking protected species from his estate. You killed it. You bury it.'

'It's my hen party,' Georgie started to say. Then she cast her eye over them all in turn. 'Tessa?' she said, appealing.

Tessa chose to pretend she was feeling very spaced and stoned. She just shrugged. 'I don't know, Georgie, I'm not a wildlife expert.'

Georgie looked around at the detritus: the dirty dishes and plates, the half-drunk glasses, the cheeseboard and the abandoned quarter of a loaf; then at the bloodied cleaver, the adder. She looked towards the sink, but it seemed she couldn't face washing her hands yet in case there was anything else down there, so she wiped the blood off on her dress. Her voice came out very small. 'What am I going to bury it with?'

'Your Shellac nails,' said Alice.

Rachael went into the utility room and they heard her rummaging and clanking.

Georgie stared at Alice, then, with a smile, she broke off a chunk of bread and threw it at her. Alice dodged as it hit her, then laughed, then dodged again as she veered too close to the dead snake.

Melissa was craning over it, examining it with a drunken veterinary curiosity as Rachael came back in holding a gardening trowel. There was a William Morris pattern on the handle. She held it out to Georgie.

Georgie stared at it, then laughed wildly, throwing back her head. 'Where's my hoodie?' She looked around, then grabbed the nearest one she could see, which was Alice's, abandoned on a chair by the Aga. 'You all have to come with me so you can conduct a voodoo séance while I bury this *monster*.' She rolled up the hoodie sleeves and crept over to it. Grimacing, she turned from the counter and shuddered. 'Aren't there gloves to go with the trowel?'

Tessa pointed to the Aga. 'Oven gloves.'

Hanging on the oven door rail was a folded pair of linked oven gloves, with a stag design on each of the mits. Georgie fiddled them onto her hands. Her eyes were gleaming and gleeful again. She made a hissing 'He, he, he' through her teeth as she picked up the main intact body of the snake, draping it between the mits. 'Ooh, it's much heavier than I thought.'

'All muscle,' Melissa said. With finger and thumb, she picked up the amputated tail and held it away from her, peeling up her sleeve with the other hand. A few drips landed on the flagstones.

Tessa grabbed the utility-room door, and pinned it open with her foot. Rachael still held the trowel. 'Careful, it's dripping,' she said.

Georgie staunched the end with one of the oven gloves. A red smear grew swiftly into her mitted palm. 'Can you get a bottle of champagne out of the fridge?' she said over her shoulder to Alice.

Alice frowned, but did as she was told. They grabbed discarded scarves and jumpers and jackets – anything they could find – and threw them on over their dinner clothes. Tessa placed an old Barbour jacket that had been in the utility room around Melissa's shoulders, carefully avoiding the hand carrying the adder's tail.

7

The night air was brisk but not biting, and the sky a dreamy mauve, pierced by many fine stars. There was a lacy, misty rain that came in bursts whenever the wind changed direction. Giggling, Georgie led the procession, clattering down the cobbles and onto the mulchy grass to an area beside the vegetable patch. 'We should drink its blood or something,' she muttered, then went over on her ankle, the stiletto of her shoe catching in the mud. 'Oops, nearly dropped it. This is so disgusting.'

'What if there's more out there?' said Alice.

'That's what the champagne is for.'

'You're going to bottle them?'

'No, we're just going to drink ourselves brave. Isn't that what the old highlanders used to *dooooo*?' Georgie feigned a Scottish accent.

'We're not in the Highlands,' said Alice.

'Oh, shut up, Miss Know-it-all. Sorry – *Ms* Know-it-all.' Georgie turned back to Tessa, who was last out. 'Hold the door open, we need the light.'

'I've got a torch,' Tessa said, letting the door fall back ajar and coming forwards with the thin beam of light from her phone.

Georgie dropped to her knees, yelping at the wet and the cold. Tessa held the beam in a shaky hand and they all laughed and shrieked a little in horror as Georgie flung the snake to the ground. It landed on its stomach, its camouflage pattern blending into the grass with terrible precision. It was hard to see one minute, and then the next, the whole shape of it jumped out.

'You know,' Georgie said, looking suddenly up at them all. 'My hands didn't feel like my hands as I was killing it. It was – like I became someone else.' Her voice was cool. 'I never knew I had it in me. You never know, do you?'

Tessa swallowed as she watched Georgie scrape the earth out of the way. Georgie attempted to tuck the snake into a coil, but it kept springing free. She tried a few more times, then gave up. As she was scraping damp earth over it, she looked up at them.

'I just realised,' she said. 'We have bags full of ketamine on us, and you guys are worried in case Tom finds out I killed an adder.'

'It's different,' Melissa said. 'K doesn't hurt anyone.'

'What about the animals missing out on their doses because you nicked it?'

'You asked me to nick it.'

'I'm joking. Joking. Pass the fizz.'

Alice gave her the bottle. Georgie wrenched the cork out with a misty pop and gobbled the overspill. She passed it

135

around and they all took a gulp. Tessa looked up at the stars, as the rain kissed her cheeks. There were so many more than she was used to seeing, even outside London, and they were all so tiny that it was difficult to pick out any of the constellations. Raindrops flicked into her eyes, and she blinked and looked down again.

Georgie stood up, satisfied, and stamped mud down on the adder grave. She brushed her hands off briskly. 'I think that exonerates me from any washing-up.'

Rachael's face was caught by the side of the torch's beam. There was a very vivid, unguarded and bitter disapproval in her expression as she watched Georgie.

But still, she took a swig of the champagne when it was passed.

'Stars,' Melissa said, looking up, 'make me want a fella.'

'Don't you have a fella, love?' Georgie said, slipping her arm through Melissa's. 'You always have a fella. You're just going through a dip.' She poked her hand into the pocket of the borrowed Barbour jacket and pulled out a tube of lozenges. 'I think these are Tom's. Maybe you need to return them to him. Maybe we should all go and call on him and tell him the sink is blocked and we need a man to fix it.'

'I don't always have a fella. I never have one,' Melissa said.

'It isn't blocked any more,' said Harriet curtly.

'He won't know that until he comes. And then we will have him. We can do whatever we want with him. Is that a good idea? Or will we lose our deposit? Tessa? Tessa, where are you?' She seemed only just aware that the beam of Tessa's torch had cast itself elsewhere, and Tessa had climbed up onto the small wall that bordered one side of the vegetable patch.

'What are you doing?'

'I was looking to see if you can see the loch from here, and as it happens, you can. Just the edge of it, past the trees.'

Rachael climbed up next to her and held out her hand for Alice. Georgie swooped up alongside them, wobbling in her heels. Tessa could feel Georgie's warm breath next to her, a sour mix of cheese and bread and champagne and the chemicals that had dripped from her nasal passages onto her tongue.

They rubbed their hands together and passed the champagne and looked at the stars, and Tessa felt like the bubbles on her tongue were perhaps connected to the stars overhead. The rain had begun to fall harder, and it seemed to Tessa as if it was there to nourish them. She was about to speak – perhaps to tell them all how much she loved them, how beautiful it was to all be friends tonight – when Alice said, suddenly, 'Where *is* Bea? She never came back down – if she went back up. Or came back in, if she went out.'

'She's probably in bed,' Georgie said.

'Do you think someone ought to go and check?' asked Melissa.

'I'll go,' said Harriet. She was on the edge of the group, and now she took a brisk step away.

'No, let me,' said Tessa, hopping down off the wall.

'No, Tess, you've got the torch,' Harriet replied. 'Just stay put and drink up, and don't kill any more snakes, any of you.' She called out behind her. 'And keep an eye out for ghosts.'

She disappeared out of the beam of the torch and they saw a slice of misty light as the kitchen door opened and then closed.

'Do you think that boy was a ghost?' Melissa asked.

The torch beam caught Georgie's face. She was frowning at Melissa. 'Melissa, you are a vet. I'm not being funny, but sometimes – I mean – no, really, don't take this the wrong way, but I do wonder how you got through those vet exams.'

Rachael sucked in a breath.

'Bitch,' Melissa said. She laughed and slapped Georgie on her arm.

'No, but really,' Georgie said. 'A ghost? Are you being serious?'

'Do you know what?' said Alice. 'We were probably all just imagining it because we had drunk quite a lot of whisky, and we're all a bit sleep-deprived from a night on the train, and it was probably a bit of driftwood. And now it's deleted and we can never tell anyway, so who gives a shit?'

'Who, indeed?' Georgie said, and swigged the champagne.

The quiet of the castle grounds enveloped them. Something shuffled in the bushes. Soft noises came swimming through the trees, over the rhododendrons, air skating off the choppy night loch.

'I'm really impressed,' Georgie began, letting her breath out in a small whooshing sound. Her breathing sounded from left to right; she was whipping her head back and forth. 'I'm really impressed,' she said again, 'that no one has vomited yet.'

'Oh, Georgie,' said Melissa. She took the champagne bottle and swigged heartily.

'Well, you know—' Georgie cut herself off as they heard footsteps. Tessa shifted the torch beam and caught Harriet coming back out, a little breathless, walking fast.

'I can't find her. She's not in any of the rooms, not in the lounge, not in the dining room.'

They looked at each other in the weak torchlight, searching for signs for how to react.

'Do you think she went for a walk and got lost?' Rachael asked.

'Her hoodie and coat are on her bed,' Harriet said.

'She might have taken someone else's,' Melissa said.

'How light was it when we were all upstairs after dinner? If she was drunk she might not have taken a coat.' Rachael hopped down off the wall.

'She said she was going to make coffee,' Alice said.

'That was ages ago. It was probably still light.'

'Well, she has to be somewhere,' said Georgie. 'Bea!' she yelled, to nowhere. 'Bea!'

'Shh,' Harriet said.

'Who's going to hear us? The owls? Tom?' Georgie parked the bottle against the wall and clambered down. 'Bea! Come back,' she cried. 'Bea! You fucking tit. You're missing champagne.' She laughed.

Harriet looked from Tessa to Alice, her frown deepening. She seemed very sober. 'I just don't know where she would have gone.'

'Did you try every room?' Tessa asked.

'I think so.'

'Bathrooms?'

'Both doors were open; she wasn't in them.' Harriet thought for a second. 'I mean, she wouldn't have been hiding, would she? For a prank? The cupboards are the only places I didn't look.'

'She didn't seem that drunk,' Alice said.

Tessa looked from Melissa to Harriet. They were the only ones she could be certain had known about the ketamine on the train the night before.

'I don't think she even took any tonight,' Harriet said quietly.

'What are you talking about?' Alice interrupted. She switched her own phone torch on and glanced over to where Rachael was standing. Rachael had followed Georgie to the edge of the forest path. Georgie was now stumbling forwards into the huge, hulking boulders of the rhododendrons.

Harriet coughed, then said slowly, 'Bea took ket last night on the train. We weren't going to say anything, but she got into a bit of a pickle.'

'On the train?' said Alice.

'I think she was overexcited to be away from her kids,' Harriet said.

'Who does that when they get away from their kids?'

'Oh, don't be so pious, Alice,' Harriet snapped.

'So, you think—' Alice began.

'I've no idea,' said Harriet.

'But what if she . . .' The others knew what Alice was thinking, as her head tilted in the direction of the forest path, the one that led into the woods, over the rocks, and down to the sea loch.

'She really wasn't that drunk,' Tessa said. 'I don't think she was. She didn't seem that drunk.'

'You don't have to be drunk to go for a walk,' Harriet said.

'And it gets dark very quickly here.' Melissa stuck her hands into her hoodie pocket. She shivered and swayed in a blundering way towards the champagne bottle. The temperature had dropped and the wind was whipping up sudden cold blasts.

Harriet looked around her, tangling her hand through her hair. Her fringe had blown aside and her brow was puckered into deep furrows. She looked weary in the torchlight.

'I don't know what she was wearing on her feet,' she said. 'But that path was uneven. And I don't know about you, but I don't think any of us are going to get any sleep if we haven't at least tried heading down to see if she's there.'

'You checked all of the castle?' said Tessa.

Harriet stared her down. 'Yes, I did. All of the rooms.'

Tessa paused, opened her mouth, then closed it again. Then she said, 'Did you check the attic?'

Harriet looked impatient. 'Why would she be in the fucking attic?'

'Exploring?' Melissa said. 'The priest hole?'

'She's not going to be hiding from us in a fucking priest hole, Mel.'

'I don't know!' Melissa protested. 'Before last night, I would have said she wasn't going to chug a load of K as soon as we got on the train.'

'Look,' Alice interrupted, swinging the beam of her phone torch around, suddenly illuminating a huge, wet

141

rhododendron bush, 'If she's in the attic, she's less likely to come to any harm than if she is down by the loch. So, I think first priority should be the loch. Then if we really can't find her, we'll need to get Tom out.'

'Why Tom?' Rachael snapped.

'He's the estate manager.'

'So? You don't think we're capable of searching the whole castle for her?'

Georgie laughed heartily, enjoying the squabble. She swigged from the champagne bottle, then passed it back to Melissa, who sank the last drops and let the bottle fall to the soft earth.

'No, I didn't say that.' Alice was looking peevishly at Rachael. 'But he knows the castle, and the estate, and we don't. And like Tessa says, there could be rooms that we don't – or haven't – seen. Or paths – and isn't there supposed to be an ice house somewhere?'

'Come on,' Harriet said briskly, taking the lead.

The wind was beginning to blast gusts of midnight spray and rain towards them from the loch. Tessa followed quickly as Harriet stepped beyond the torch's beam, and then she heard the crunch and slide of the footsteps of the others behind her on the wet path as they all pushed past the rhododendrons.

The loch was restless, lapping in glossy tremors that oozed up onto the bank and back down into the pool, where they collided in cross currents. The wind had picked up as they walked and now it was blowing trumpets of salty rain directly into their faces. There was more than half a moon, and that was just enough to see the black fingers of the trees, the budding shapes of leaves and blossom, gnarled in pure velvet shadow, moving with the motions of slow laughter as the wind pushed them back and forth.

The bank on which they had stood earlier and taken pictures was silver and brittle, rocky and crusted with fronds of dead bladderwrack that crunched underfoot. The tide had gone out a little and the shores were drier and felt more desolate, the water seeming further away, as if it had receded into another world.

No one spoke, but the silence fizzed with the noises of water and pebbles, sand and twigs, and the rounded hoots of owls. Tessa felt her skin twitch with the grim dread of anything she might see. Every turn, every time she cast her eyes on a new focus point, she braced herself. Her wet hair stuck to her brow and her spine felt electric, about to be shocked. She had been lost more than once, as a child, somewhere not far from here, on one of her many family holidays, and there was something distinctive about the landscape and the light in this part of the world that could plant her back in that memory. Although she had always had the feeling of trespassing here, in this landscape, back then she did not know what it was she was afraid of encountering. Now, she would not name it, even to herself.

'Bea,' Harriet called. Then, louder: 'Bea? Bea? Are you out here?'

Melissa was staring across at the forest on the other side of the bank as if bewitched.

'Was that boat there before?' Alice pointed to a wreck of a rowboat, a grisly, scuffed old thing with paint eroded along its sides, lying idle, half in and half out of the water.

Before they had the chance to creep closer, Georgie was striding towards it. She climbed over the rim, laughing, exclaiming 'Fuck,' as her dress snagged. 'Got a splinter in my cunt,' she squealed.

'It was there,' Rachael said. 'I remember thinking it was pretty, but that we couldn't use it.'

'Are you sure?' Harriet asked. 'I don't remember it from the pictures.'

'We were slightly further up,' Rachael said. 'It was there.'

Tessa had them both in the beam of her torch. She was hanging back, dread and terror preventing her from stepping closer to the loch. The stars seemed to be blinking. The dread clenched, and she wondered if she was starting the comedown from the drugs, full of fear and doubt and blinking stars. That was probably it, she told herself.

'Shit-sticks, it's cold!' Georgie screamed. 'There's a hole in the bottom.'

'Get out of there.' Harriet strode over the shingle towards the boat, yanking Georgie's arm. Tessa moved with them, holding them in the torch beam. Rachael helped Harriet to haul Georgie out of the boat.

Behind them all, Melissa made a small animal sound. 'Yeep,' she said, and it was a noise so strange it sent a chill to the back of Tessa's neck. She did it again. 'Yeeeep.' The sound was wolfish, moon-shrill. It didn't seem to disappear in the dark of the sky, but swirled around them, echoing.

They scrambled over the pebbles. Tessa hadn't changed her shoes since dinner, and tiny stones made their way into her sandals. Georgie scrambled, laughing, still holding hands with Harriet and Rachael, enjoying being held up.

Melissa had something in her hand. There was a whistling bitterness to the wind now. It blew firmly, and it picked up and danced with the thing she was holding, a pale thing whipping back and forth.

It was Georgie's cashmere snood. Georgie stared at it, and seemed to catch a sudden wave of sobriety. She snatched it from Melissa.

'She took it when she went back to the loch,' said Alice.

'Who did?' Harriet asked sharply.

With dread certainty, Tessa guessed the answer before Alice spoke.

'Bea. Georgie gave it to her when we went back to look for the boy, because it was getting colder.'

'I thought she'd be cold,' Georgie said.

'Maybe she took it off when we were on our way back?' Melissa ventured.

'Why would she do that?' Harriet asked.

'She might have tried to give it to me,' Melissa said softly, in a questioning, frightened voice. 'Maybe *I* dropped it. Maybe it was me. I don't know. I've drunk too much.'

'We all have,' Georgie said. 'Jesus fuck.' She clutched her head as if she could pull out the narcotics and separate their influence from reality.

Tessa had begun to feel sick, very sick.

In front of her, she saw Melissa recede from the torch beam.

Melissa was hitching her dress up. She was taking her heeled Chelsea boots off and wading into the loch. 'Bea!' she shouted. 'Bea, come back.' Her voice was drunken, desperate, guilty.

'What are you doing?' Harriet, Alice and Rachael were on her in a moment, but she had sunk to her knees in the silt. 'Bea.' Her arms thrashed against them.

'Melissa, calm down, calm down.'

'It was me who gave her the ketamine,' Melissa said. 'On the train. I just thought she was uptight and it would help her relax. I wish I could just get it out of my brain, I wish I could—'

'You don't know what's happened to her – just stop. Stop thinking until you've sobered up.' Alice was trying to get a grip on Melissa, but her arms kept slipping. Melissa reached up and slapped Rachael in the face, then plunged her body under the water's surface.

Alice reached beneath the water in a lick of movement so quick Tessa barely saw it, folding Melissa's arms behind her and hauling her out of the water, dragging her by her wrists. It was too quick to be anything other than professional, something she'd been taught to do. Tessa glanced round, to see if anyone else had noticed, but no one said anything.

Melissa spluttered and rolled and Alice tucked her on her side and slapped her back, keeping her hands pinned the whole time. Water vomited out of Melissa's mouth. The wet wind pulled her hair into wild serpents. Rachael and Harriet sat on her thrashing legs.

'What the fuck were you doing?' asked Harriet.

'I don't know. I just don't know what's happening.'

'You're drugged and drunk off your box, that's what's happening,' Harriet said.

Tessa stood, frozen, a voyeur who could not bring herself to participate. They were all breathing heavily.

Georgie dragged her hands down her face. 'Oh God, this party.'

'I don't think we should be outside any more,' Rachael said. 'This is turning into a storm.' She hesitated. 'We have to get Tom.'

'No,' Tessa murmured. 'The ketamine.'

'We could call the police?' Harriet offered.

Georgie, with her head in her hands, said something, very weakly, that sounded like 'Yum yum.'

Alice, still pinning Melissa, her thighs straddling her, said, 'The police won't come out for a missing adult until it's been twenty-four hours. Unless she's classed as vulnerable.'

'Even in this weather?' Harriet said.

'In any weather.'

'She's off her box. She's vulnerable.'

'No police,' Georgie said, taking her hands from her face. 'No police, no way. No fucking ketamine admissions. I don't want to spend my wedding night in Holloway.'

'Holloway's closed,' Alice said quietly.

'Yes, all right, pedant. Holloway's closed, ten points for you. Do you understand? No police.' She was slurring. She sat on the shingle and bent over Melissa, picking at the cold, wet hair on her face. Melissa had calmed down but she was still panting, her left cheek rammed into the stony ground.

'We are all very drunk,' Alice said calmly. 'And it's hard to think in the pissing rain. In the morning, all of this is going to seem very strange – and hopefully very funny. Drunky stuff.'

'Drunk shit,' said Georgie weakly. She blew out her breath and stood up, grunting. In some parallel comic world of vanity, she adjusted her bloodied dress, which was beginning to stick to her, and picked the waxy crusts out of the corners of her lipstick, as if freshening herself in a club toilet mirror. It looked very weird to see her do it with the loch behind her, and that made Tessa's neck freeze in dread again. *It's just the Special K*, she told herself. *Paranoia*. Her brain felt as if it was operating in two halves now, the cognitive processes on one side and her raw senses on the other.

Hauling themselves and each other, they made their way back, scrambling along the boulder ridge, pulling one another through the whips of wind. They inched along the path between the colossal rhododendrons.

The castle kitchen spilled golden light from its small windows. Back inside, it was a relief to shut out the weather. The room fell suddenly quiet as the door closed, and it felt hot and stuffy even though the Aga had gone out hours before.

Every surface was strewn with the debris of snake-catching: caked residue and drying blood. Everywhere the adder had moved now had the look of something frightening, as if the surfaces themselves would begin to slither, or something else horrifying could erupt at any moment.

They quietly cleared up and then made tea, passed out mugs and shared milk.

'There's not much left,' Harriet said, shaking the milk carton upside down.

'We'll get some more in the morning,' said Alice. 'Wander down to the village or something.'

'We can't go to bed without Bea,' Harriet said.

Melissa's head fell forward onto the island where she'd collapsed on a stool, and Tessa could see Georgie was trying not to smirk.

'It's not practical,' Harriet insisted. 'None of us will sleep.'

'I'll sleep,' whispered Georgie.

'It might be because I'm—'

'Because you're a mother,' Georgie muttered viciously. 'And don't we know it? Well, yes, it might. Look. She's fucking passed out somewhere in a cupboard, we all know that.' She looked round at the friends all watching her. 'OK, I'll go up to the top floor – but only if someone comes with me. Tessy?'

Tessa flinched as Georgie took her hand from the table. But she let herself be pulled to standing.

'We can do the downstairs bathrooms.' Rachael tousled Alice's hair and they moved sluggishly to the door.

Harriet rapped her nails across the marble top of the island. She gestured to Melissa, whose head was being cushioned by a piece of bread. 'Someone's got to get *her* to bed. Maybe that should be you, Tessa. So you can make sure she's not going to choke on her puke or anything.'

Tessa muttered under her breath, 'It's not rocket science,'

but she went to help Melissa off the bar stool. She hooked Melissa's wet arm around her neck and stood, propping her up.

'I'll go with you,' Harriet said to Georgie. Georgie didn't seem to notice. She slipped her hand into Harriet's as if the change hadn't registered.

Tessa hauled Melissa to the stairs. It was, all of a sudden, far too much like work, the feeling of being sprung to responsibility from drowsiness. Even though she was only dealing with a drunk friend, the weight of the task made her feel leaden and depressed. If she stopped to think too carefully about where the compulsion to care and heal had come from, she would crumple into a heap. She was sticks held together. They were strong, oaken sticks, but they were without glue or string, balanced carefully.

She helped Melissa hold on to the bannister. There was no sign now of Alice and Rachael, and Georgie and Harriet had gone on ahead.

It took forever to get Melissa up the stairs. She kept stopping, forgetting how to use her legs and clinging to the slippery wooden bannister. Up on the ground-floor hallway, she spied a sofa covered in velvet cushions and made towards it.

'Nope, up to bed.' Tessa listened for the others as they made it onto the landing of the second floor, where the bedrooms were. She heard the scrabbling of bags in the room Alice and Rachael had claimed, and assumed they had given up searching. She wriggled Melissa through the nursery door and eased her down onto the camp bed by the window, pushing her onto her side as she had done with Bea the night before. She headed back out onto the landing, intending to go back down to the kitchen and fetch her a glass of water. Harriet's voice up on the mezzanine made her stop. It was rising. She sounded bitter. 'We looked everywhere. How couldn't you have heard us?'

There was a pause that went on too long.

Then she heard the mezzo rumble of Bea, followed by Georgie protesting in a low drawl.

Tessa abandoned the mission for water and went carefully up to the mezzanine. Georgie's voice was forceful now. And then came the crash of glass shattering.

'Look what you've done! It doesn't even belong to us. You're so bloody tripped.'

The door was ajar. Tessa pushed it all the way open.

Bea was sitting on the single bed on the far side of the room. Her face was white, sickly. She was still wearing the black dress she had worn at dinner, and her hands were in her lap, poised around the ghost of an empty shape, as if something had very quickly been snatched from them, leaving its invisible imprint between her palms.

'Georgie, you shouldn't have smashed it,' Bea said. 'He's only a boy. Someone's son.'

'He's a fucking ghoul,' Georgie cried. She put her hand to her brow as if her brain was aching. 'I'm sick of this. People have photos all the time. Children play in the woods all the time. Doesn't mean a thing.'

Harriet had stooped to her knees and was picking up shards of glass.

Tessa stood mute. She saw the photograph then, which had floated out from the smashed, lead-rimmed frame. She sucked in her breath as her skin turned cold. It was a colour photograph, bleached by light. A middle-aged woman crouched, squinting into the sun, obscured partly by the shadow of the person taking the photograph. Her arm was held out and she clutched the hand of a boy. He was a good few years younger, but everything else about him was the same – hair, eyes, spirit. He was the boy from the loch.

'Where did you find this?' Tessa stared at the picture.

Bea jumped at the sound of her voice. 'It was in that bathroom. The main one. It was on the wall behind the toilet.' She watched Tessa examine the picture.

'I still don't see why that stopped you from hearing us shouting for you,' Harriet said. 'We went everywhere, right up to the top floor. Even out to the sea loch.' She waved towards the window.

Bea shook her head gently.

Tessa became aware Georgie was staring at her, a scrutiny dulled by drugs and her headache, but still oppressive. She let the photo fall back to the floor. 'Thank God you're safe.' She crossed over to Bea and sat on the bed next to her. Bea looked faintly embarrassed.

'Of course I'm safe. I'm sorry you were so worried,' she muttered. 'It's just an old house.' She wouldn't look at any of them.

Harriet finished picking up the shards of glass, ran her hand lightly over the floor, then grabbed the photograph and stood up. 'Christ. It makes you feel chilly,' she said. 'I mean what if he is—' But clearly, she didn't want to say what she was thinking. She ran her hand over the boy's face. His smile was shy and forced. He had one missing tooth. Tessa watched the maternal gaze, unfocused but impossible to hide, gleaming out of Harriet's eyes and onto him. It made her heart jolt. She suddenly grabbed the photograph from Harriet.

'It belongs to the castle, and now that we've smashed the frame the least we can do is take care of the picture.'

She dusted it off and put it into the pocket of her hoodie. The other three stared. 'You and your damage-deposit paranoia,' Georgie said. Her voice was slurry but her gaze – that oppressive scrutiny – still made Tessa queasy.

Tessa glanced over her shoulder towards the door. 'I was getting water for Mel.'

'Is she OK?' Bea asked.

'Long story.'

Harriet hugged her arms across her chest, then pulled out her phone, checked it, and put it back again. She had been doing this throughout the evening, Tessa had noticed. Harriet laughed at herself. 'Idiot. I don't believe in ghosts. Or at least I don't believe they can hurt you.'

'No,' Tessa said. 'They can't.'

Georgie smiled, baring her teeth. 'I'm tired.'

Bea said nothing. She seemed to disappear into herself and began tidying up the space around her, putting cream on her face, then lip balm. Then she fluffed her pillow and sat back on the bed. She made it clear she was waiting for them to leave.

'I'll go and get that water,' Tessa said. 'Night, night.'

As she traipsed down the stairs, she heard Harriet and Georgie hugging, the clink of their jewellery tangling as they squeezed, then parted.

Her finger flicked back and forth over the sharp corner of the photograph in her pocket. She stabbed the corner of it under her nail, and pressed hard until it stung.

She delivered the glass of water to Melissa and was crossing the landing towards the mezzanine bathroom when a hand shot out of the shadows and grasped her wrist.

'Did you say you can get a signal up there?' Georgie pointed with her phone at the ceiling. Tessa breathed out. Her heart was hammering. She looked to where Georgie was pointing, at the winding stairs that led to the landing above them, where a small wooden door opened onto a narrower staircase to the attic.

Tessa shook her head. 'I don't think so. No. Maybe try tomorrow.' She paused. Then she took a step towards Georgie. A lock of Georgie's warm auburn hair had fallen into her eye. Tessa tucked it behind her ear. She was still aware of the feeling of her heart. She felt certain it was making a sound.

'Thank God we found Bea, eh?'

'Tessy-Tess-Tess, you've gone to so much effort and here is me wanting a phone signal. I am a silly Londoner and you are – what are you, Tessa?'

'I'm a silly Londoner, too,' Tessa said.

'That's right.' Georgie smiled faintly. 'You are, aren't you?'

154

They looked into each other's eyes and for a second Tessa felt the number of years between them cram together, piling on top of each other, memories both sour and loving all jostling for prominence. The years did not melt away when they looked at each other, they just snowballed. She thought she could see each year, in the flecks of Georgie's blue irises.

'How did you find this castle?'

Tessa shrugged. 'Google.'

Georgie smiled. 'It's perfect.'

'Good.' Tessa smiled back. 'Glad I found the right place.' She exhaled. 'I'm gonna do my teeth.'

Georgie turned and slunk into the master bedroom, snaking her hips, singing a little song to herself, very faintly, like it was a tune buried deep in her memory. Tessa breathed in a huge gulp of the castle's ancient air. It was stale, mothy, familiar; like incense, wood and mould.

She went up the two stairs to the mezzanine bathroom. Then she kept going. Up and up she went to the next landing. There were no more bedrooms up there, just a maid's cupboard, a tapestry hanging on the stone wall, and the door to the attic. She opened this door and climbed up the chilly staircase, steep as a ladder, until she reached the top. The slate roof acted as an amplifier to the pummelling rain and the scream of the wind outside.

She walked straight over to the priest hole Bea had talked about at dinner. It was painted to look like the inside of a shutter on a window, and the way the turret was crafted, it looked as if it would open directly through the wall, into the open air. But it didn't. Instead, a high step led up into a small crouching corridor, which in turn led along the eaves of the main roof of the castle, and then to a secret staircase that led directly down beyond the vegetable patch and out into the gardens.

Tessa opened the small cast-iron latch on the shutter and reached up and around the first corner of the hole. The sound of the storm outside grew louder. Dust, the velvet of old cobwebs, crumbs of grit, splinters. Nothing more. Craning her head around, she could just make out the shape of a plainer patch of stone among the dirt: clean, rectangular, untouched by the dust, the floor protected by what had lain there until very recently. But now there was nothing there.

She already knew what had happened to the photograph. It was in her pocket. But, as she'd suspected, the book had been taken as well.

PART TWO

8

I don't know how to begin. This feels awkward, because I have never kept a diary before. Hi Diary.

If our introduction is awkward, it is because I don't know quite who I am just now. Perhaps you can help. Perhaps we can only ever exist in relation to others, so by relating to you it will be something like having a coffee or a glass of wine with a friend, or listening to music together on our beds, and I will see bits of myself in how I am to you. I hope I am courteous. I hope you are a good listener.

But this is silly because you are paper, and I am a person.

I am not myself, that is all I know. I knew it as soon as I walked through the hospital lobby and realised I had been there before. I had walked in that way, but I didn't recognise it − I didn't know it at all. And when I did recognise it, I realised very suddenly, like a bone snapping in my brain, that it was myself I did not recognise. It was as if I had stepped through a looking glass, but instead of seeing strange creatures, it was me who was strange. I was the one who was wrong. Everything else was as it should be.

There are things I don't know any more. I don't know what is going to happen tomorrow, or tonight. I don't know what I would seize if the house around me was burning.

Diary, you know nothing of me. And I am not yet ready to talk more about who I am now. I think a therapist would say – I think most of the blogs I have read would say – that I should start with what I remember from before: start with when it began. And I guess that would be with Jack.

Bea had stopped reading then, realising she was holding her breath. She could hear the noises from the lounge: murmurs, pierced by shrieks of laughter, and the clinking of crystal tumblers. She knew it was wrong. But they wouldn't notice her absence, and they wouldn't miss the coffee she had gone to get. They were too drunk and high.

She hadn't been deliberately nosy when she was exploring the castle earlier; she hadn't been looking to pry. But the priest hole had been inviting. Its painted door begged to be opened. Then, when she had seen the plain brown book, she had thought it might be a relic from the castle's past. Her librarian's heart tingled at that, and she had eagerly prised the moulded brown leather endplate away from the first page, expecting to see a fascinating hand, made more fascinating by age and strangeness, exotic in its forgotten detail: bushels of something or other, a debt, a judgement, oats.

Then she had seen the photograph in its slim glass frame tucked inside the cover. It had sent chills through her. But the sunshine squint in the older woman's eye, the missing-tooth smile on the dark-haired little boy's face made it hard to be frightened. It was so unlike the shock they'd had seeing him in the photograph by the loch.

She had opened the book.

It was a diary. The handwriting was modern: it was a hand Bea recognised, even though she had never seen it before. They'd all had that handwriting once, as girls in their late teens. Bubble letters, slow crafting of Latin 'a's. Ampersands instead of 'and's.

Who was she? For she was certainly a she. The writing was she. Bea knew it.

Bea had waited until she could slip away after dinner, then crept back up to the attic and taken the photograph and book down to the landing. There, she had curled into a curtained alcove that had once been a box bed for a maid. There were cushions there now. She had drawn the quilted curtain, and started to read.

Diary, if I had begun writing you when I first met Jack, there would be screeds of bad poetry that would have made your pages blush. My pen would have blushed. I realise now he was just a friend, a person. If what happened wasn't fate, it was some mingling of our hopes and dreams rubbing up against each other, and it just happens that some dreams have a stronger pull than others. Some lives bend more easily.

Let's pretend you are my therapist. What shall I say?

I can't yet draw one of those cognitive therapy grids Tom has told me about. I'm not ready. What I want to do is remember, because this feeling right now is like an amnesia of the soul, and I want to relive a time when I was happy and when I felt like myself. Tom says if I'm not ready to think of what's happening now, I can start in the past.

So, Jack.

It must have been about 2006 when I first met Jack. He was friends with Tessa more than me. They both played clarinet in youth orchestra, and I played viola, so we sat in different sections.

Jack was not very good at the clarinet and we used to tease him that he had slept with the woodwind teacher to get his place, because there were only two places for clarinets and Tessa was very, very good. He went to a different school, and he was a boarder too.

Tess and I had boarded since senior school began, and we always said we could spot another boarder, like they had a tattoo or a scar. There was a mystery of bravado and loneliness that you saw reflected back, and also a bit of grown-upness, like a pack animal, strange and survivalist. Tess once shouted at Mum that sending kids to boarding school was middle-class child abuse, but really we didn't know any other way to be, and so it had become a part of us, and in that sense we – or I, anyway – could recognise someone with that same soft brittleness. And that was, I suppose, what made Jack – among all the other people from all the other schools in the four counties that made up the youth orchestra – that was what made him more attractive. A poor, rich boy.

He was messy, skinny. He had cheekbones. He carried Sartre's Nausea *in his pocket, though I never saw him read it. He talked in a bright, brilliant, self-assured way about the grimness of the world. It was a grimness I now understand would never touch him, and that was why he could be so passionate about it. He taught me the word 'nihilism'. He had a lovely long nape and broad, bony shoulders. He laughed at himself. He always had weed. He was messianic. He was a rotten cliché.*

I'm exaggerating. I must be. But that was what I thought love was back then. Worship and devastation.

Tessa didn't always want to hang around with me at youth orchestra. Did that hurt? I don't know. It wasn't something we talked about. After sectional rehearsals, she would hang around the back of the dormitory building, shivering, waiting for someone to come along with smokes. And because I danced back then, I didn't smoke, so I would go to the pool table and mooch around with friends from the strings section.

I wanted to know him. I burned to know him. One day, I was given a pack of Rizlas by a girl in the second

163

violins who'd had her dorm searched. And so that afternoon, between sectional and full rehearsals, in the cold purple sunset, I walked around the damp grass to the back of the dorm building and waved hello to Tess and gave her the Rizlas. I don't remember what shit chat I had with them all, but after that Jack friended me on Facebook, and I wrote on his wall, a silly message about one of the pieces we were playing in the orchestra, and he wrote back on my wall, probably something about the food being shitty, and that was that. We were friends.

When I think back, all of our friendship was like this. All of our conversation was in little cryptic private-joke wall messages, or quotes from books, or YouTube videos I would email him. I spent hours looking for YouTubes to send him. Songs from the fifties that made me ache. Clips from old movies I loved. I used to lurk on Skype when I was doing my homework, in the hope he would start a conversation. Sometimes he took the bait.

I read Camus for him. I discovered Simone de Beauvoir for him. I started confrontational Facebook threads about how bad Beckett was, about how much I hated Nabokov, just to see what he would say.

I used to root around Google for these quotes. Most of the time, I hadn't read the books. But he didn't know, and it wasn't important. The important thing was that he thought I was clever and well-read, even though I knew deep down I was neither.

On the night of the last concert, I knew he'd kiss me. I would not kiss him first; the thought of initiating intimacy terrified me. The concert was in Carlisle, and he was going to Kuala Lumpur after that concert because his father was a diplomat and had been posted there. So, Jack would spend the summer in Malaysia. He was stylishly downbeat about this. It would be too hot, and he hated having servants run around after him: it went against his communist principles. When I think now of the things he said then.

But they made sense to me at the time. He made sense. He dropped these things into our MSN messenger or Skype chats and followed them up with screenshots of himself pulling stupid faces, of shock horror or boredom, slumped on the keyboard asleep, or with two fingers pushed to his temple, like a gun.

I would kiss him that night and he would have that kiss all summer, and we would send one another teasing messages and I would quote to him from Sappho and Shakespeare.

That was how it was going to be.

After the interval, when we were settling back on stage, I took my phone out and sent him a Google image I'd found of Munch's Scream blowing smoke rings.

He sent me a hands-to-the-face emoji; the question, 'Where?'

I waited until the end of the first movement of Rachmaninov's second symphony, and sent him a screenshot of a Google image I'd taken: Hopper's café on the *corner. There was a chippy that looked sort of like it across the road from the concert hall.*

He sent me an image of two black-and-white people from a film I didn't recognise, smoking sexily. Then a picture of the white rabbit in Alice in Wonderland *taking out his watch.*

Sometimes now, I look at this thread archived on my old phone. It has been more than a year since the last message he sent me, but he is still one of the first people I see on my Skype home screen, with the green bauble to say he is there, alive, somewhere, 'available' – Daisy Buchanan on the other side of the water (another of the books I read for him).

I waited until the end of the symphony, when the audience were clapping. While we stood for the applause, I slipped my phone back out and sent him an image of the clock tower in Back to the Future. *I saw him break from bowing to pick up his phone. The concert would finish around ten. The buses to take us back to our schools would leave at around half past. If we both packed up quickly, we could meet.*

I had butterflies in my stomach. We still had to murder our way through Sibelius's Finlandia. *What would he taste like? Where would he touch me? How did a boy like him kiss?*

And then the doubts began. I imagined his tongue like a snake's, forked and flicking in and out between my teeth, too small for my mouth. Once I had the image in my mind, I couldn't shake it. I imagined him holding me too tightly. I imagined him tasting of the Johnny Walker that he and some of the others had in a hipflask and were drinking before the concert.

The doubts shifted to me. My small, flat breasts; the stale spaghetti on my tongue, sour tomato. I imagined the women in the books he read, the films he saw. I was like none of them. He wanted to smoke with me, that was all. I should not expect anything more. I was a skinny pipe cleaner of a girl, hair too big for my body. I was the sort of girl people took advantage of. In films or TV shows, the girl seduced by the man she does not like. I was not a seducer: even I knew that back then.

After the concert, I went and saw him outside the café, rolling a cigarette between his fingers, standing with his clarinet case hooked over his shoulder, the same shoulder as his rucksack, his shirt sleeves rolled up, his bow tie in his pocket. I wanted to cross the street and run away. He was hideously beautiful, beautiful the way a boy in a teen film or a soap opera is beautiful. He was perfume advert beautiful, aggressively beautiful. He made me recoil, but I didn't run away. Some instinct stopped me. I spotted Tessa, heading towards the bus to climb on board and try to bag the back seat.

I told her, 'Give me your clarinet.'

She was bewildered, but I think she knew what I was up to because she gave it to me, and I tossed my viola case in exchange. I made a decision. I hooked her clarinet case on to my shoulder, and strode towards him.

'Charlie's not coming,' I said. 'She's tired, she wanted

to get on the bus. Don't give me that look, what can I say? She's capricious. You'll have to make do with me instead. Now give me a toke.'

He looked at me. He looked at Tessa's clarinet case on my shoulder. I remember that look. Amused, hurt. I relive that look sometimes as if it was the pivot my life turned on. When insomnia hits, when I'm awake, I try to fix my memories. I bend them like iron to see if I can change them. In the morning they have pinged back into their old shape.

He wasn't fooled. He knew it was me, not Tessa.

He could always tell the difference between Tessa and me. Even when we were dressed the same, hair the same, jewellery the same. Some of our closest friends struggled, even our older sister sometimes struggled, but he didn't. It was a skill of his from the very start.

Harriet's voice came echoing up the stairs. Bea closed the book.

She sucked in her breath. It felt as if something inside her chest had slid a few millimetres. It was like this now. There wasn't any logical explanation for it. But ever since her girls were born, every time she came across twins – identical twins, anything about identical twins, anyone *with* twins, anyone who *was* a twin – a bell chimed in her heart. It was irrational, the expectation that someone who had the same quirk of experience she'd had could possibly feel closer to her than anyone else: crazy. But it happened. Every double buggy she passed in the park, she smiled at the mother or

168

father or grandmother. Every set of identical pigtails or pairs of children who were the same size, with one parent. Half the time, she got it wrong, the chime was false. It wasn't twins she had spotted – there were eighteen months between them, and they looked ridiculously different. Couldn't you tell? Or they weren't identical, they were fraternal. They had different-coloured eyes.

But how long had she known Tessa? Bea wondered if she was being spectacularly dense, or blinkered, or was there something she ought to have known? She remembered the look Tessa had given her when they were walking to the loch that morning and Harriet had been quizzing her about her twins. Tessa had been staring as though she was thinking of something she couldn't shake and didn't want to share, and she had blushed when Bea caught her gaze.

Downstairs, the back door slammed. Suddenly there was laughter outside, a commotion, a scream. They were probably looking at the stars, Bea thought. They would forget about her under the ketamine stars, burning bright. She felt weird, duplicitous, but weighed down, forced to stay where she was. She looked at the photograph, wondered about the boy.

She didn't want to go back to the party now. She was tired, but more than that, now the stealthy magnet of a story loomed over her.

She looked around at the three pine-clad walls of the box bed. It was a nook now, a quirky historical feature. But once a maid had slept here, and now she was reading the private thoughts of someone else who was not there.

She wondered what she would do if she were caught?

Some time later, she heard footsteps again on the landing: Harriet's heels clipping the stone, muffled by the carpet runners. Then she heard her own name. Over and over.

Bea pressed the closed book between her hands. Harriet called again. She sounded hoarse, weary. Then she heard Tessa and Melissa talking, and Georgie's slurry call: 'Beaaaaaaa.'

Bea had thought she would ignore them. She lay down and clasped the book between folded, knotted hands. She closed her eyes, but the calls were persistent. She opened her eyes again, and they fell on the photograph.

That she could give them, that she did not mind surrendering. But for now, the book was hers. She buried it under a mothy pillow and crept down to the mezzanine room, clutching the photograph of the older woman and the boy.

9

Tessa had thought she would be first into the kitchen the next morning, but Rachael had beaten her to it.

She was sitting on one of the high stools by the island, sipping a green tea with the bag still in the mug. The kitchen was strewn with remnants of the previous night's mess, scraps of food and piled plates, the sink full of pots. The drain cover for the plughole had not been put back and the plughole gaped, mouldy black.

Tessa fiddled it back into place, then wiped her hands and went to investigate the remains of the bags for life they had brought.

'Did you hear the rain last night?' Rachael asked. 'Crazy wild.'

'I slept like the dead,' Tessa murmured. Memories of holiday storms had swum around her dreams, but she hadn't woken up. Maybe it had been the drugs or the interrupted sleep the night before, or maybe the air from the sea loch had helped her sleep soundly, although she had always thought that was an old wives' tale. In the morning light, she'd had those foggy hallucinations that come in half-sleep: blurred creatures crawling along the vessels of her brain. She had woken slowly, with a sense of dread and the feeling that there was something she ought to remember, but didn't. Relief took over when she realised she did not have to go to work today.

Rachael was watching her pick slowly through the bag. 'I don't know what's left in there,' she said. 'I haven't touched anything.'

Tessa glanced up. 'I didn't say anything.'

She rooted through cellophane cheese wrappers with half-eaten lumps inside, half-full foil crisp packets with the tops folded down, the cardboard sleeves of humous tubs dislocated from their contents. She found an opened packet of duck pâté, crisping at the edges. It should have been put in the fridge. There was a small box of teabags and a couple of bags of gourmet salt-and-dill mixed nuts.

'There's bacon and eggs,' Tessa said, reaching for the counter. 'And there should be coffee somewhere, too.'

'The coffee's there.' Rachael pointed at a bag of pre-ground coffee sitting next to a cafetière.

Harriet appeared in the doorway. She was wearing a linen dressing gown and bootie slippers buttoned with bamboo toggles, sheepskin poking over the ankle cuffs.

'Did someone say coffee?' Her hair was pinned back in a band, the fringe secured with kirby grips, and she had taken her make-up off. 'That wind was mental last night. I kept dreaming ravens were coming through the roof.' Her skin was greasy and bright. 'Is there another carton of oat milk, by the way? I thought I saw some.'

'There's just one.' Rachael pointed to the carton on the counter.

Harriet went to pick it up, rattled it, and poured the rest into her coffee, shaking out the drips. 'That was an oversight, wasn't it? How did everyone sleep?'

Rachael nodded, sleepy but content. 'Pretty well.'

Harriet seemed to take exception to that languorous smile and turned back to the coffee. She stood back from the sink as she filled the kettle. 'No slithery dreams, no K-holes?'

'I wouldn't have been awake long enough to know,' Tessa said. 'Slept so deeply.' She had located the bacon and the eggs, and laid them out on the counter, then began slicing bread into thick slabs.

There was a rustle behind them and the slap of bare feet on flagstones. Tessa looked up to see Bea wafting into the room in draped layers; loose harem joggers, multiple sweaters and scarves. 'Ooof, it's freezing.' She rubbed her hands together and looked at each of them in turn.

Rachael stared. 'We looked for you last night.'

'I was asleep.' Bea frowned. 'I was drunk, and I wandered off to – Harriet came and found me.'

'Only after we'd just about given you up for dead,' Harriet said quietly.

'Are you offended?' Bea hesitated. 'There's a maid's nook, a sort of box bed. It's soft as feathers and covered in cushions.' She arched her back, cracked it. 'I dozed there for a bit. But it's not wonderful for the spine. I wish I had just gone straight to bed.' She laughed, then breezed further into the kitchen, doggedly ignoring their stares. She began her own audit of the leftovers. 'Harriet, you know some good yoga, don't you?' She cracked her back again.

Harriet turned back to the kettle, watching the steam. 'It's not the sort of thing you can just do once,' she said.

Rachael hopped off her stool and reached for Bea's shoulders. 'Where's it stiff?' Bea wriggled and Rachael pulled and cracked.

'Wow,' said Bea. 'Feels amazing.'

Harriet poured more hot water into the cafetière and stirred, watching them. Tessa looked at them, trying to imagine Harriet and Bea back as their old selves, their university selves, some time in Freshers' week. Their faces had not changed much, but the way they stood, the way they set their mouths, had. It was odd to her that you could change inside and that those changes should paint themselves on the body. And it was a mystical kind of a painting to her. You didn't really know quite what traumas or events it reflected inside.

She felt suddenly the danger of her thoughts turning dreadful, and she ran her palm over the smooth eggs to calm herself. Twelve eggs, nestled in their crate. It was the kind of tray that didn't have a lid, that you found on farms and re-used.

'What did I miss last night?' Bea said, looking again at each of them, her huge brown eyes wide.

Tessa looked to Harriet. Harriet gave a sort of noncommittal shrug, as if Bea did not deserve to enjoy the 'fun' second-hand if she had not troubled herself to experience it first-hand.

Rachael burst out laughing. 'There was a snake in the plumbing.'

Bea blinked. 'What?'

Rachael sat back down and picked up her mug. 'There was a snake,' she said again. 'In the plumbing. In the sink. Georgie killed it with a meat cleaver.'

They were all quiet. Bea looked to Tessa and Harriet. Then she began to laugh. 'You are joking.' She looked around her for any signs of the murder. 'This is why I always went home to bed when Georgie hit the witching hour. Did you have some collective ketamine trip?'

'No. It was there,' Rachael said, pointing to the sink.

'That's disgusting,' Bea said quietly.

'It was pretty grim,' said Tessa.

'What was grim?' Alice had come in via the back door. Her cheeks were rosy, and she was wearing leggings and a long-sleeved top with thumb holes. Her hair was slicked back.

'Alice, Alice, Alice,' said Harriet. 'You've got a ketamine hangover and you're at a hen party, lovie. Even Goop says you don't have to jog at hen parties.'

'I told her she was mental,' said Rachael.

'I only went to the loch and back, it's not far. You managed it in heels last night,' she said to Harriet.

'I did no such thing. Don't confuse me with Georgie. She was in heels. I had wellies on.'

'You said you went to the loch last night. Was that . . . were you looking for me?' Bea asked suddenly. There was a note in her voice. It wasn't guilt or incredulity, but it was more than curiosity.

'Yes,' said Harriet. 'You missed it. Melissa went wading into the loch, looking for you. She was really rather valiant. Until she fell over.'

Bea fell silent.

Alice went to the tap and shoved the detritus out of the way. She blasted cold water into a dirty mug and gulped it down.

Harriet watched her. 'How is it,' she said, 'that you are not squeamish at all about snakes, and yet you're afraid of dogs?'

Alice caught her breath after the gulped water. 'They're different species, Harriet.'

'But they are creepy.'

'You might think dogs were creepy if you'd been mauled by one.'

There were hushed giggles from behind them. In the doorway to the hall, Georgie and Melissa appeared with a flourish.

'Hellooooooooo!' Georgie sang.

Melissa had her arm draped about Georgie's neck. They were both dressed and polished, faces made up with wing-tip eyeliner, hair straightened with an artful twist to the front strands. Melissa had a linen hairband across her brow; Georgie wore earrings and a thin pearl necklace, a pale pink cardigan and tailored jeans with turn-ups.

'Bright as buttons, you pair!' Harriet said.

Georgie ignored her and patted Rachael on the back. 'Budge up.'

Rachael made room at the island.

'How come you two are so fresh? Have you been doing

a master cleanse in your sleep?' Harriet handed out mugs of coffee.

'Is there almond milk?' Georgie asked.

'No,' Harriet said.

'Oat?'

'There was,' replied Harriet.

'Hmm, OK,' Georgie said. 'Yeah, it's amazing what a night of rocking lesbian sex will do for a hangover.' She pinched Melissa's neck. Melissa squealed.

Tessa stole a glance at Alice and Rachael, but they were ignoring it. Georgie breezed on. 'Breakfast, ladies. We need a hearty meal for a day of yomping around ye highlands.'

'So there was a snake last night?' Bea said to Georgie. But, at the same, Tessa said, flatly, 'There's eggs and bacon,' and Georgie chose to look at Tessa. She cast her eyes around Tessa's face, as if she found something new or strange about it, or was looking for something in particular.

'You're up early,' she said. 'That's not like you.'

'I always get up early. These days. You got dressed.'

Georgie shook her head. 'Can't stand not being dressed for breakfast.'

Come to think of it, Tessa had rarely seen Georgie in pyjamas. Artful leisure wear, joggers and hairspray, lipstick and cut-off sweatshirts and leggings and Converse trainers, and maybe a silk dressing gown when they lived together in halls, but not real pyjamas. And she could not recall ever seeing her without mascara. 'Georgie has short lashes,' Charlie had once said, full of spite, on one occasion when Georgie had gone to the toilet to 'freshen up'.

'What's in here?' Bea was rooting around the bags for life, bringing out potatoes and cans of chickpeas.

'Bea!' Melissa shrieked, noticing her for the first time.

'Mel!' Bea shrieked back in mock delight.

'Where were you last night? God.' Melissa creased her brow, remembering. 'I swam in the lake, didn't I? Looking for you.' She looked down at herself. She was wearing only a little bit of light-reflective concealer and some subtle contouring, but she looked luminous. Sluggishly, gorgeously tired.

Bea had a meek smile on her face. 'That was a bit silly, wasn't it?' She opened the cupboard under the sink, and briskly tossed into the bin a couple of humous pots with browning leftovers in them.

'Gross,' Georgie muttered, looking at the mess. 'I'm starving.'

'Bacon and eggs?' Tessa said.

Georgie made a vomitous face. 'I sort of feel like avocado.'

'Well, there aren't any.'

'Nobody brought avocados! W to the T to the F. A Bloody Mary?'

'Oh God, yes,' Melissa said.

Rachael looked up from her green tea. Alice laughed and ran her fingers down Rachael's braids. 'I'm in. I'm on holiday.'

Melissa disappeared upstairs to rummage in the lounge for cocktail spirits. Tessa opened cupboards in the kitchen, and they cobbled together a selection, some old and belonging to the castle. There was a quarter bottle of gin, about half the Lagavulin, some port, some vermouth and half a litre or so of Grey Goose vodka.

'Oh no, we don't have any tomatoes,' Alice said.

'Fuck,' said Georgie. 'First hurdle.'

'Yes, we do. There might be some left over from last night's salad,' Rachael said.

'Are you serious?' Georgie looked at her. Not for the first time, an air of faux-disgust seemed to mask her real disgust.

'You could have a – toxic spirit mix and orange instead?'

'There's orange juice,' Melissa said. 'I had some in the night.'

'Not quite the same as a Bloody Mary. OK, it will make for a memorable anecdote. Makeshift Hen Party Bloody Mary with leftover salad. I'm game if you all are.'

Rachael had retrieved a Tupperware from the fridge and was busy picking out the quartered vine tomatoes, while Alice rooted around for a blender. 'I completely thought there was another pack of tomatoes,' she mused. 'Sorry. I wouldn't have used them all in the salad if I'd known.'

Georgie had already begun mixing the spirits.

Tessa, looking on, felt a bit sick. She busied herself counting the slices of bacon and the eggs. There were twelve eggs and thirteen slices of back bacon, wrapped in greased paper, the old-fashioned way.

She began feeding wood into the Aga, piling up the kindling. Opening the blackened door, she was momentarily afraid of what she might find. But there was nothing but large flakes of ash, dancing about with the breeze of the opened door.

'I can make green shakshuka,' Bea announced. She was standing on tiptoe, looking over the sink and out of the window to the kitchen garden. 'There's leeks there from last autumn. They might be a bit woody, but they'll soften down.' Her glance ranged over the plants. 'There's spinach, or chard, or something. And I think I spy some herbs.'

'I thought we were having bacon and eggs,' Melissa said.

'We can have both. A breakfast feast,' Bea replied. 'Something green for the side.'

'There is so much foooood here,' Georgie cried. 'I love it. Hen Party: the Gluttony Diaries. I have time to Soul Cycle it all off, anyway.'

'Ottolenghi recipe?' Harriet asked, looking at Bea.

'No,' Bea said. 'Mo's mother.'

'I forgot you had live-in help,' Harriet muttered.

Bea nonchalantly slammed the cupboard door, cutting off Harriet's final word. She went out to the garden, and Tessa watched through the window as she gathered the vegetables, yanking out a leek with two hands, snipping the spinach from its woody stems with a pair of scissors she had taken from the kitchen.

For a moment, Tessa felt inexplicably blissful watching her, so much so that she wanted to laugh. And then it hit her why she felt blissful, watching Bea. She realised who Bea reminded her of, in that garden, and she felt queasy again. Suddenly, it looked like Bea was pillaging, raiding the estate garden, helping herself to what she wanted, without even knowing who had planted it.

Tessa looked away.

Harriet took a sip of her Bloody Mary and winced. Then she said to them all, 'Green shakshuka isn't a real thing, by the way. It was made up by the *Guardian*. I have a link to it on my blog.'

Georgie cried over her, 'Put hairs on your chest!' She took a gulp and made grunting noises at the taste. 'We, ladies, are fucking geniuses. Bitches, we could actually survive in the wild. Look at that!' She raised her glass. 'We just foraged a Bloody Mary in an ancient castle. What can't we do?' She laughed and took a larger gulp. 'It's not that bad, actually. The vinegar from the salad tomatoes is like the vinegar float they do at Pegasus in Chelsea.'

They had all gathered loosely around the island as they drank the recycled drinks. Tessa slid the empty bottles of spirits out of the way and put down a wooden board covered in the rough slabs of farmhouse loaf she'd sliced. Georgie eyed them for a second, then grabbed one and dug into the fluffy inside, ripping off a cloud. She ate the soft centre between sips of her drink, discarding the crust on the counter. Rachael took a piece of the crust and split it with Alice.

The kitchen filled with steam and metallic allium as Bea cooked the spinach and leeks. She made little wells in the pan, dropped in the eggs, then put the two cast-iron frying pans into the twin ovens and hopped onto a stool. 'Oh, you've eaten all the bread.'

'There's more.' Georgie gestured vaguely behind her. 'A baguette, somewhere.'

'I can't find it,' Tessa said gently. She had dodged the Bloody Mary handouts and now she was keeping an eye on the spitting bacon on the Aga hob as she nursed her coffee, black with a drop of cold water to loosen its tarry strength.

'I think a trip into the village is in order,' Georgie said. 'To fetch more bread and poke about. See whatever it is the people spend their Saturdays up here doing, anyway.' She looked across at Tessa. 'What about those taxi drivers?'

'They came from Edinburgh. They won't come up here to take us to the village.'

'There must be a local firm,' Melissa said.

Tessa shook her head. 'I don't think so. I don't know.'

'Don't you want to go to the village?' Melissa asked.

'It's not that,' Tessa said quickly. 'I'm just not sure how we would all get there.'

'Maybe Tom has a Land Rover,' Georgie said. 'We can all pile in. Cling on as we hurtle through yon bonny glens.' She drained her Bloody Mary and shouted. 'Hoo-ya!'

Bea got up to check on the eggs, then closed the oven door again. She leaned her back against the Aga.

'What is on the slab today?' Alice asked, to no one in particular. Melissa and Harriet looked at Tessa.

Tessa said, tentatively, 'There are some lovely walks. I think?'

'You mean you haven't booked a pole-dancing lesson?' Alice teased.

'No,' Tessa laughed. 'Or cake decorating, or pottery or wine tasting.'

'Didn't you already have a wine-tasting hen do for your London friends?' Harriet asked.

Georgie ignored her. 'Archery!' she said suddenly. 'There

is an archery range. I saw it on the way to the loch. We can make our own bows and arrows. Out of wood. Jesus Christ, that is the best photo op I've thought of yet. Stripped to the knickers, forest a go-go.'

Bea took the pans out of the oven and dished out piles of shakshuka.

'Tessa, I thought you said there was a baguette,' Harriet said.

'I can't find it,' Tessa said again. She put the plate of bacon in the centre of the island and they helped themselves.

Harriet sat down and poked her eggs with a spoon. 'Bit runny still. You're not trying to give us salmonella?' She laughed briskly.

'It's the countryside, Harriet,' Bea said. 'They're fresh eggs.'

Harriet took a bite. 'Mmm. Domestic goddess, aren't you?'

Georgie began gobbling her eggs, scooping huge, stringy forkfuls of the wilted leeks and spinach into her mouth. The others made appreciative noises and swapped condiments.

Harriet ate her food in neatly cut bites. 'Are your children fussy eaters?' she asked Bea across the island.

Bea shrugged. 'They have their days.'

'Would they eat something like this?'

'Probably. If their Jida had made it. Granny,' she said.

They all kept eating.

'Would yours?' Bea went on.

Harriet gave a short shake of her head. 'No idea. Probably. They like anything with lashings of butter in it. That's what I always say on the blog. If in doubt, chuck in butter. Tell them they like butter. Then they will.' Tessa noticed Harriet check her phone again, furtively, as she had done the previous day. She looked down, quickly took it out, checked it, then put it back. Her face fell a bit.

'It's not butter, it's oil,' Bea said. 'I only used a bit. Jida would drown it.'

Harriet kept eating. 'You're so lucky to have so much help around,' she murmured.

'Don't you have an au pair, Harriet?' Georgie asked. Harriet appeared not to have heard.

Bea stared at her food as she kept eating.

'Shame about the baguette,' said Melissa. 'Anyway, never mind.' She got up and began poking in the Fortnum and Mason hamper, as if Tessa might have been lying, or been careless and missed something. 'Yippee, a packet of crackers.' She pulled out a sleeve of poppy seed biscuits, then lifted the cardboard tube and looked through it like a telescope. Everyone's hands reached forward for a cracker.

'We should think about what to cook later,' Harriet said. 'Because if we don't do it now, then we'll have to do it when we're actually hungry, and it's never a good idea to decide what to cook when you are actually hungry. Didn't anyone make a menu for the weekend?'

'There's plenty to snack on in the hamper,' Alice said. She got up and went for another glass of water, swigged it down. 'I'm going for a shower,' she announced, and left the kitchen.

'Did you make a list of recipes and ingredients?' Harriet asked Tessa. 'So we know what we have?'

'No. Did you?'

'Don't be defensive. I didn't volunteer because you—'

'My job was finding the castle.'

Harriet paused. 'It's all right. I just thought that there would be rice. It would be good if we had asked Tom for some, or brought some.' She trailed off, but then she added quietly, 'If you'd asked me to, I would have.'

Georgie snapped to her feet. 'It doesn't matter. We are going into the village, and there is probably a pub where we can buy a bonny Scottish pint of someone's barn ale or something and then get some cheese and chips, so buck the fuck up, it's all absolutely A-OK. This is Scotland, not the arsing moon. We're not going to starve. And we're only a stone's throw from the border if the locals try to eat us.'

Rachael had got to her feet and was peering out of the window over the kitchen sink. 'It's sunny enough for a walk now.'

'I don't think we'll walk,' Harriet said.

'Suit yourself,' Rachael replied.

Harriet sank her head to her brow and placed her elbow on the counter. There was a scuffling in the utility room, two knocks and the sound of the boot scraper being used.

'Knock, knock,' a voice called. Tom didn't appear immediately. Melissa and Bea exchanged looks. Georgie stared, amused, as the door swung open.

'Hi.' Tom appeared, beaming and shiny-cheeked, slicking his damp hair back against his head with both hands. He was clean shaven, and in the artificial light, he looked a little older than he had done in the soft sunlight the previous day.

His brow was wrinkled; the veins on his cheeks threaded in places. He seemed weather-beaten and larger somehow in the confines of the kitchen.

There was a half-hearted effort at politeness. Plates were quickly stacked as they saw him sweep a quick, tidy glance around the filthy kitchen. Catching them catching him, he swiftly averted his eyes.

'Is it raining?' Rachael asked.

'No, I've just got out the shower,' he said.

Georgie looked away, smiling.

'Do you want a cup of tea?' Rachael asked politely.

'Sorry,' Tessa said, brushing her hands through her hair. 'I should have asked.'

Tom looked confused. 'No, it's fine. I just wanted to check the heating was OK for you, that you have hot water, that sort of thing. No bumps in the night?' He laughed. He was still breathing rather heavily from his walk. There was a pause as they all looked at one another. A short, sharp bark came from outside.

'They're tied up, don't worry,' he said, glancing around the room for Alice.

'It's fine,' Rachael reassured him. 'She's having a shower.'

'Ah.' Tom nodded. 'So everything OK? Nothing out of the ordinary?'

There was a general, stiff fluttering of consensus round the kitchen.

'What's ordinary here?' Georgie laughed.

'Do you need anything else?'

Melissa looked from Tessa to Georgie, and then to Bea. 'I mean,' she said gingerly. 'There's . . . the rice?'

Tom looked eagerly at her, waiting. She didn't venture further. 'Is all the food OK?'

'Oh, it's fine,' Georgie said. 'I think Harriet wants rice, though.' She laughed, deflecting her bluntness.

'I didn't. I mean it wasn't just me.' Harriet sighed.

A look passed over Tom's face. He glanced at Tessa.

'It's fine,' Tessa said. 'You got everything we asked for. I think we were just very hungry from the journey, so we might need a few more cupboard things.'

'There was the loaves of bread, bacon, veg. Tatties . . .' He trailed off.

Georgie suddenly amped up the charm. 'We are such greedy London girls, you know. Also,' she dropped her voice, 'we drank a bit too much last night. And I think Harriet –' she waved her arm, vaguely '– has a particular recipe she wants to do.'

Tom slicked back his hair with his palm again and glanced over his shoulder, back outside. 'I'll see what I can do. Now listen, did you hear the storm in the night?'

'I saw the mud this morning,' Bea said. 'I pulled up some leeks – I hope you don't mind.'

'Course not.' Tom shook his head. 'Well, listen. There's a tree down across the driveway down by the burn, so there's no getting out today. That was also what I came to say. You ladies are here until tomorrow, aren't you?'

'A tree down?' Harriet had lifted her head.

Tessa frowned. 'Actually, we have train tickets for the

sleeper tonight. I know we paid until Monday, but we weren't planning to stay the extra night.'

He sighed. 'The council should be able to be out early doors Monday, but I'm afraid until then . . .' He shrugged.

'We can walk around it, surely?' Rachael ventured. 'Isn't there another path? We can get a taxi from the main road?'

Tom tilted his head. 'Not really. Did you see the path when you were on the way in? It dips down to the lowest part of the estate, and the burn that runs through it has flooded up to the sea wall. It happens, from time to time.'

'Rotten timing,' Melissa said.

Georgie stared. 'Are we trapped?'

Tom made a conciliatory sort of grunt. Before he could speak though, Georgie said, with a note of delight, 'Oh, fuck.'

'You don't have a Land Rover that can get us round through the woods?' Rachael asked.

Tom shook his head. 'It's just not going to make it through the floodwater, I'm afraid. Look, it happens a couple of times a year. It's not the end of the world, and nothing really to worry about.'

'Not the end of the world?' Harriet asked. 'I've got kids to get back to. A blog to run.'

'Never mind the fact that Tessa's a doctor,' Melissa said.

'What about a boat?' Rachael asked.

'Nothing really?' Bea said at the same time.

Tom looked from one to the other. 'What do you mean?'

'You said there was "nothing really" to worry about. That means there *is* something to worry about.'

Tom sighed again. He seemed short with himself, rather

than with them. 'It's not a problem,' he said. 'You have everything you need.'

Harriet looked quietly agog, and it was true, Tessa thought, that he had spoken rather abruptly for a castle host. She looked around at the others. Harriet was checking her phone again, and Melissa looked slightly perturbed.

Georgie seemed to have taken the prospect of the extra night in her stride. 'We have everything. Apart from rice,' she said, laughing.

Harriet glared at her.

Tom tilted his head again. 'I can give you a bag of rice and maybe see what else I can dig up. Should keep you going for another day, at least.' He looked round them all again. 'I'm sorry.'

Tessa shrugged. 'It's the weather, isn't it? Not your fault.'

'I know, but with it being your hen party . . .' He tailed off, gesturing towards Georgie. She beamed at him.

Tom fidgeted a little, looking uncomfortable. He shook out his shoulders and pushed up his sleeves. Then immediately, as if he had forgotten himself, began to push the sleeves back down again. But it was too late. They had all seen the curious stream of fuzzed blue-green ink trailing up his arm: a crude tattoo, dark like a sailor's. It wasn't clear what it was supposed to depict; he was too quick rolling his sleeve back down.

There was a second or two of silence.

'Best be on my way,' Tom said, suddenly. 'Glad everything is, well, OK.' He stood for a moment. His rapport was better over email, Tessa thought. Friendlier and slicker.

He went back out into the utility room and they heard him pulling on his boots, then an excited scuffle as he opened the back door and appeared before the dogs. He whistled as he untied them, a tune like a lament, then he whistled again to call the dogs to heel.

When he had gone, Georgie clapped. She looked at the rest of them. Tessa had seen that glint before. She thought Georgie might be about to mention the tattoo they had all seen, but instead she said, 'What larks, ladies! We are trapped behind a fallen tree in little boy ghost mansion. Jesus, I never thought my hen party in a Scottish castle would come to this. Tessa, you are some kind of wicked genius. Here was me, thinking champagne and spas.' She gave a sharp laugh, then trotted out of the room.

Tessa knew, they all knew – all recognised – Georgie's disingenuousness, the way she sometimes hid her feelings behind humour. Was she cross? Upset? Concealing fury? Did it matter?

But no one said a word. They dispersed into a loose roster of chores. Melissa and Bea made a start on the washing-up. Harriet, still wearing a pained expression, began sorting the waste food packaging into recycling and landfill.

Tessa was wiping the island granite with a clean J-cloth she had unwrapped from a stash under the sink. Beside her, Rachael swept the floor, making little piles and stopping every so often to toggle between broom and dustpan and brush. She straightened up, shaking the detritus down into the dustpan. 'Georgie's like – what's the word for it? Teflon? No, that's not it.'

Tessa kept wiping. 'I don't know what you mean.'

'I think you do.' Rachael looked at her plainly. 'What would it take to knock her off her cloud?'

Tessa swallowed. 'Why would you want to?'

Rachael stared at her for a second more, and then walked off, with the dust and crumbs rattling in the pan.

10

Bea found Georgie snuggled up in one of the lounge arm-chairs. A bright ray of sunshine was streaking through the tiny castle window above her left shoulder and down onto her lap. She had picked a book off one of the shelves – an old paperback – and was turning the pages, engrossed with a light, nimble attention.

Bea watched her for a few seconds, as if she was an animal that she didn't want to get too close to. Georgie's forefinger slid under each of the thin pages then flicked it over with a tantalising scrape.

'You're a fast reader,' Bea commented.

Georgie looked up and smiled. 'English degree.'

Bea thought, but did not say, that she too had an English degree, and indeed now worked as a librarian. Yet she couldn't read at that speed. It occurred to her that Georgie had not asked her once about her life now. About what she did for a living, or what she did when she wasn't at work, where she had been all those years – where she hung out, how she enjoyed motherhood. But then she, Bea, had not asked

Georgie many questions, either. She already felt as though she knew a lot of the answers. What she really wanted to ask was why she had been invited on this hen weekend at all.

But that would have been rude.

'I think I'll go and have a read, too,' she said, after a while. Georgie looked up. 'Not coming for archery?'

Bea had forgotten. Or at least, she had perhaps thought that Georgie would forget. The idea tugged at her stomach in a heavy way. There were other things she would rather do, and she wanted some time to herself. 'I'm feeling a bit delicate.'

Georgie pulled a pout. Bea thought she might be about to castigate her, but instead she looked kindly. 'It's so nice to see you guys having fun this weekend,' Georgie said. 'I've missed that. I've missed you. I feel very lucky and very spoiled to have such friends. Thank you.'

Bea was caught off guard, and gave a short shrug. She didn't feel as if she could take credit for something that had been foisted on her. Inklings of university came back to her, wafts that made her feel unsettled. She decided she would go and grab the diary from the maid's nook, and then would go and explore the gardener's cottage before the others finished their kitchen cleaning and found her.

The book was still where she had left it, buried beneath the pillows.

Muck was smeared thickly on the stony path that led from the back of the walled garden up to the pair of semi-detached estate cottages. Moss had grown between the stones, making it slippery and more treacherous than the main paths or the grass on the lawns. But while the path had the feeling of having not been trodden recently, the little cottages were spruce and bright, and not lonely looking at all.

She chose the one on the right. Its garden was small, but better maintained, with tiny shrubs and rose bushes. Between pointed gables, a dormer window stuck out. Downstairs, there were two square windows deeply set in thick stone, quarter paned, on either side of a chunky wooden door that was painted a dark blue, just beginning to flake. There was no bell nor knocker nor letterbox, only an old round iron handle. Bea looked briefly through the windows. It was all cleaned up, but lifeless inside. It must have been another Airbnb. She wiped her feet on the soggy old doormat and felt its threads disintegrate beneath her soles.

She tried the round doorknob. It gave and turned smoothly. Inside, she was surprised by the sweet aroma: a scented-candle fragrance with a pungent fruity note, masking another, more chemical, smell – disinfectant, bleach. A pot plant stood sprightly in yellow and green fronds inside a terracotta pot in the hallway: a spider plant. It was cold and brisk, but not damp inside. On each side of the hall was a door and, ahead of her, a small wooden staircase, neatly swept.

Which way to go? On instinct, Bea chose the room on the left.

It was the old parlour, now tarted up in eclectic country boho style. The pictures on the walls were from a past era, but one of them – a Madonna and child – had been drizzled with modish splashes of pink and sea-green paint. A scratched painting of a bowl of roses leaned above the mantelpiece in a charity shop gilt frame. On the far wall, opposite the window, two more line drawings of flowers had been cut out of an old botanical book, their names etched below them: a type of yellow rose and an orchid. Behind the dining table, a Thai mandala throw was pinned to the widest wall.

She moved closer to the table and saw that there were embedded coffee-cup rings and watermarks spread across it. Propped up beside the empty fireplace was the incongruous sight of a plastic nappy-changing mat. It all looked pristine, but Bea felt it strangely cold, as if the cottage was cared for but not lived in.

She sat on one of the dining chairs, then thought she might find something more comfortable in the other room. She had her excuse ready: 'Sorry, we thought we had the whole castle – I'm so, so sorry. My mistake.'

This one was a plainer room, with modern furniture. An IKEA sofa sat about a metre from the left-hand wall, facing a stove that had been left ajar. The door swung in the current of air she had brought in with her, and she shrieked as a mouse ran out from under the black ironwork, scurrying in an impossibly straight, deliriously fast line beneath the sofa. Its brown body was different to the dark grey London mice Bea sometimes saw in her own kitchen, but its slick running had the same effect, sending white-hot shivers through her.

She was reluctant to sit on the sofa then, but the book was too much of a lure. Cautiously, not looking at anything else in the room in case she saw another creature, she crossed to the window where there was an old but freshly wiped electric heater still plugged in at the wall. She flicked it on. A red light glowed and the scent of burning dust rose up off it.

There was an armchair there, faded blue velvet with mismatching embroidered antimacassars. With a loud, mouse-repelling shout – 'Ah, get away, get away, get away, mouse!' – Bea shook out the cushion. She beat the chair with her hands and jumped back, waiting. Nothing scampered out. Satisfied, she gingerly sat down. Then, aware she could still be seen through the little deep-recessed window, she turned the chair around. The light was overcast, but good enough to read.

She opened the diary and flicked to the last page she had read. Turning the page, a couple of loose sheets fell out. They had been divided into grids, with headings written along the top, each box filled in in a messy, hasty hand. Bea put them to one side and started reading.

26 March 2007

Jack and I had been messaging, on and off. Sometimes, he would go for days without replying, then pick up the conversation without apology. Sometimes, I'd be able to see he was logged into Skype but not replying. The little green icon would be there with its white tick, solid pixels beside his name.

Back then, Tessa and I had plans to go to Thailand in the summer after we left school. That would have been nearly two years ago now. After that, we'd planned to spend the rest of the year traversing Asia, crossing into

196

Laos, then Vietnam, then heading to New Zealand in January, and then going back home via Kuala Lumpur to stay with Jack for a few days. Only, by the time we got to booking the tickets, Jack's dad had been reposted to Luxembourg and the family were living in the east of France.

We meant to take the Eurostar over to visit him. Mum and Dad were spending most of their time in London by that time, anyway. They had given up on the castle and Jenny was looking after it pretty much full-time, renting it out to tourists.

I missed it.

I missed the woodlands and the hiding places and I missed the village. But we had given up on the parties by then, and taking part in the summer fair. I don't know what had soured between Mum and Dad and the people in the village, or maybe nothing at all had, and they had just become bored of it all and wanted something else instead. But I felt sorry for the children we used to play with, who now – I presumed – could no longer play in the castle grounds.

Jack sometimes came to London for the weekend. Or so I heard. There were near misses we had at clubs and mutual friends' parties. But in the end, we didn't see each other before Tessa and I left.

I don't want to dwell too much on what happened in Thailand and Laos. I thought I was homesick. But now, I think I would have been miserable wherever we were.

Days in humid beach huts. Days deflecting men who

wanted to get high with us. Sweet, salty street food. Cocktails that made us puke. Moon parties, cold sand, bikinis. Why did I feel so anxious? Now, right now, in the middle of the night, in the bitter cold spring, I would trade any part of my body – my nipples, my teeth, a finger – to be on a warm beach. Just me, my blood, skin and the sand and heat.

Then an email came through one day. It was from Jack. He wrote to Tessa, not me.

I didn't mind.

How was our trip? he asked. What were we doing come winter, and could he interest us in jobs at a ski resort in Germany, owned by his uncle? It would just be waiting tables or working behind the bar. We wouldn't have to do outdoor work and we wouldn't have to ski, although – winky face – what would be the point if we didn't take advantage of the opportunity to learn?

By that point, my mood had spilled into Tessa and she was not having a very good time either. We had both been ill for a few days and we didn't know if it was the food, or if we'd had too much to drink, or even what we were drinking. Sometimes, you just didn't really know.

But we booked our tickets back home. We replied to Jack and said we would do it – we were sick of sunshine. You can be sick of sunshine, of course you can, when you know there's plenty more of it to come. We said we wanted to have a proper winter anyway. In a ski resort there would be snow, there would be bells and carols and hot chocolate – and Jack. We had planned to be in

New Zealand, so we wouldn't see our parents or Sasha anyway. I think I had given up caring about spending Christmas with family by then, or worrying that they didn't care enough about us to beg us to come home for it. I had told myself that was childish. They cared, whether or not they showed it. Anyway, Christmas was Christmas, so long as Tessa was there. And I had begun drawing up scenarios – only sketches at that point – of ending up under the mistletoe with Jack. How many people have used that ruse to get what they wanted without having to ask for it?

We packed up, flew back home, shoved our summer clothes and sarongs and sun cream, and the hats and beaded jewellery we had bought, into the bottom of our wardrobes. Mum told us we had been hasty, it was the flighty twins again, chopping and changing their minds. The June Geminis, unable to keep their brains on anything. I know she wanted us to get jobs in Namibia, or Madagascar – in conservation or building a school – but she didn't try hard enough, and I think we could see through that. The way I saw it, it didn't really make a jot of difference to her. She could always make it up anyway if she just wanted something to boast about to her friends. If we had grown up to be spoiled, and to want nice things, it was only because we had always seen her with those things, and she had taught us to want them.

It was a week before we were due to leave for Germany that Jack's email came. He wrote to Tessa again, the coward. He didn't know what had happened with his uncle, but he hadn't replied to his last few messages. Suddenly, the jobs were off, the vacancies all filled. I still don't know whether Jack was telling the truth, or if he knew something different that had caused his uncle's change of mind – a rift with his mum, maybe. Her exercising the only power she could, by making her brother withdraw something Jack wanted? It doesn't matter. It really doesn't.

But I was heartbroken.

I didn't want Mum to see me because I knew she would say I was being indulgent. When Sasha and Brian came to stay for a few days, I barely left my room.

Tessa became a go-between, between me and the world. She must have been wretched with frustration. She must, I thought, have wanted to desert me. I would have. That frightened me more than anything. That month, she went out more with the other girls from school, and came back with stories from some nightclub or other, someone's party, trashing a Knightsbridge flat, trying to lure me back outside with party drugs and designer clothes.

She emailed back and forth with Jack. He was still in France, but he had plans to come to London for New Year. Could he stay with us? The mistletoe materialised again in my mind. Room hopping, late nights in the kitchen. It never once occurred to me whether or not Tessa might have feelings for him, too. I just knew that, between Tessa and I, we knew the things we could share

– shoes, bags – and the things we could not – food, men.

Then, out of the blue, around mid-December 2005, Tessa said she had a Christmas present for me. She had found us ski resort jobs after all. It was all through one of our friends from school. Just for six weeks, working the chairlift, maybe a bit of bar work. And, drumroll . . . Jack was coming, too.

I remember her bursting into the room, waving a glitter eyeliner at me like it was a fairy godmother's wand. I remember the feeling of being lifted out of the fog, like I was being pulled from above by two heavy-winged birds. I shouldn't get too excited, she said. It was in Scotland, the Cairngorms. It wasn't France or Switzerland or even Germany. But there would be snow, and, more importantly, there would be Jack.

Mum made light complaints about having just finished making plans for Christmas dinner and Sasha and Brian having taken time off work to visit again so soon, when they could have gone to New York, or skiing themselves, or to stay with Brian's parents. (This was a lie, because Sasha couldn't stand Brian's parents.) Perhaps it was cruel of us, or selfish, to disappear so abruptly, to change our plans so whimsically. And maybe I misremember, because I want to forget how much Mum and Dad complained. But when I look back, I don't think of their protests being strong enough to keep us at home. There are few things that can interfere with the pull of what you think of as love.

We spent the next few days shopping for winter

jumpers and discount ski suits online. We chose our lipsticks carefully – deep colours; blood berry. On a whim, I had Tessa cut me a fringe, a thick, blunt one. I thought it would look cute poking out from a woollen hat. It was a pain in the arse in the end; I had to keep straightening it. But I think, maybe, it was a tiny bit of me saying I was ready to be drastically, almost permanently, different from her.

'What in God's name have you done?' That was Mum's reaction. I always had the impression she found it easier somehow for us to look the same.

We flew to Edinburgh. We lugged our skis around the airport, laughing while we struggled. We took a coach northwards through sparse, then thickening snow. I saw three stags on that journey.

Jack had arrived before us. I recognised his bag, dumped in the hall. He was sprawled across the scuffed pleather sofa in the lounge, watching sport on television, a book spread facedown across his crotch. I was not prepared for his smile. Now, I would say the feeling that came over me was something like taking poppers: a hit of a drug or downing a shot. Not romantic. Not animal. Dizzying, in a hard to define kind of way, and not altogether pleasant. I was not in control of my face, or my body, or what was happening inside my body, and I felt almost as sick as I had done in Thailand, pining for him. I wanted, at that minute, to be back safe under my duvet.

Jack rose and hugged me. I hugged him back, in a

202

*trance. Then, laughter in the doorway behind. I heard
Tessa hugging someone else.*

*'Here is who we have to thank for our jobs,' Tessa
said. It had registered with me, but only in a vague way,
that Tessa had arranged all of this through one of our
friends from school. I had forgotten that it would not
just be the three of us.*

*Georgie hugged me. 'You look fucking sexy,' she said,
tugging on my fringe, rearranging it to her liking. 'Oh
my God, I missed you so much. Tess said you weren't
well, but everyone was asking after you. I'm so glad
you're here.'*

*She said something like that. Something about high-
land air. She gestured to the air like she owned it.
Already, my mood slipped. She let go and nudged me
aside.*

*'I have heard so much about you, young man.' She
threw her arms around Jack.*

Bea heard noises outside. She closed the book hastily,
shoving the two loose pieces of paper back inside without
looking at them. Then she pushed the lot down the slim gap
between the chair's upholstery and its seat cushion, which,
thankfully, was nice and deep, and slipped out of the cottage,
back into the cool, damp air.

11

Tessa watched through the kitchen window, a cup of weak black tea in her hands, as her friends tested out the bow. They'd found it along with a quiver of filthy arrows in the utility-room cupboard, propped behind a bag of cat litter and a box of rat poison. The grip was mouldy, but the bowstring was still tense. They were taking it in turns to give it a ping, laughing and shaking their stinging fingers.

Rachael had her arms around Alice's waist. Harriet was standing with her arms folded. In the air, Georgie drew huge, extravagant gestures, using an arrow with red feathers at its roots and a rusty tip, probably telling an anecdote about something or other, or giving instructions for the game they were about to play.

They looked happy. Not Instagram-happy, not Facebook-happy – but carefree happy. That tugged at Tessa; that stung. Was it because she wasn't there? That was a sobering, embittering thought, but it was one that had hummed deep inside her for years. She'd always had the impression that her presence made people gloomy; that her misery was somehow as transferrable as lice or a wart. Georgie had even said it the night before: 'What's the matter with you? Standing there as if you're about to jump.'

Now, that misery twisted itself into a resentment, twined around her. It seemed to Tessa, watching, as if the happy scene playing out in front of her was a betrayal by Alice, who she knew must hate Georgie. And by Rachael, who hadn't so long ago talked about knocking Georgie off her cloud. And by Harriet, who just seemed to hate everyone. Was the secret to contentment, in fact, just to get on with people, to accept what was what, no matter what you were feeling deep down?

Or were her friends just better liars than she was?

Tessa had scrubbed the kitchen, collected together the food, swept the floor. She had stayed long after the others had gone to shower and dress and lounge with coffee, and after they had gone to find the archery range.

She heard a door scrape behind her, the door that led to the hall. Footsteps came down the stairs. Bea was there, wrapping her long cardigan around herself, hugging her arms close.

'Hi,' she said. She wasn't really looking at Tessa, just passing her in a quest for her own cup of tea.

Tessa felt invisible, and yet also as if she was in the way. She shifted aside and in a silent, obliging dance of passed spoons and flicked teabags, they made a cup of tea.

'What are they doing out there?' Bea asked, glancing out of the window.

'Gearing up for invasion.'

'Why are you in here? Keeping warm?'

They stood alongside each other now, both looking out of the window, sipping their tea. Tessa could feel the vibration shimmering between them; something that wanted to be said. She wanted to ask Bea something mundane, to break the electric charge, but every inane question in her mind was drowned by the feeling that there was something more potent in the air now.

'What do you want to do today?' Bea asked.

Tessa forced a laugh. 'Don't know. Just hang out, cook vegetables from the garden?'

Bea was watching her. Tessa continued to stare out of the window. Alice had the bow now, and was demonstrating something about posture, pulling her arms back, rolling her shoulders, pointing out details where the wire joined the wood. Then, with arms interlinking, they all turned and walked in a ragged line – Georgie skipping – towards the archery range they had spied yesterday behind the vege-table garden. Tessa could just see the fringes of it from the window. Along the garden's far wall, an arch led to a clearing where some trees had been felled into stumps. Into the remaining ones, old circle targets had been ham-mered into the trunks, cemented in with moss and lichen. The group of friends disappeared out of view. Tessa shook herself out of her trance.

'It must be tiring, what you do,' Bea said, unexpectedly.

Tessa took a gulp of tea, still hot enough to scald her palate. 'You try not to complain,' she said. 'It's a vocation.'

'Is it true, then? About the cuts, the long hours?'

Tessa nodded. She closed her eyes. Why guilt? Where did guilt come into it? She was entitled to a holiday. She had a vision of her colleagues rushing around the hospital, squeaking across bleached floors in rubber-soled shoes. The blur of decisions that had to be speedily made, all those regimented, swift tasks involving cannulas and masks, that had to be performed cleanly and at pace, like setting one foot in front of the other in a marathon. Sometimes, though, she liked A & E precisely because it was so fast, so pressurised. It was what kept her from looking down at the gaping valley of past and memory.

'You must be glad of the holiday,' Bea said. 'Fresh air and all that.' There was still something more she wanted to say, Tessa could tell. She was prolonging the conversation with soft openings. Tessa decided she was not going to be the one to deepen the conversation.

'You must be, too?' She looked at Bea now. It wasn't that she hadn't liked Bea at university. She just hadn't paid too much attention to her. She hadn't really had eyes for anyone at that time, and Bea had been someone without glamour, without pull. Just there, homely. Cooking, reading, always there. Never demanding, never insisting. And then she had disappeared for so long after having her children, just melted away into the world. Or melted out of it maybe. She never posted on Facebook or Instagram or Twitter. The others didn't even seem to know she'd had twins until much later on, when they were already about two.

Tessa's stomach clenched.

Bea took a breath. 'I suppose,' she began. 'I've got more of a balance now, than when they were first born.' She hesitated, then pushed on. 'It was hellish. I couldn't stand being away from them, but I hated being around them too. I thought being a mother would be a vocation. But then, with two, it was just too much – too much of everything. Feeding and sleep, splitting love down the middle. And knowing that however long they have known you, their mother, they have known each other longer. I think that was very strange. Twins are – gosh, well, you know, how can I put it . . .'

Tessa cut her off. 'I'm going outside to the others. Shall we take our teas out?'

If Bea felt irritated by the snub, she didn't show it. 'Sure.'

As they were leaving, Tessa said, quietly, holding open the utility-room door, 'I meant your job. Do you like having a holiday from your library job?'

'Oh,' Bea said. 'Yes. Yes, of course. Doesn't anyone?'

Georgie saw them first. She was holding the bow drawn back, poised to shoot.

She twisted to take aim towards Tessa as the pair advanced. Tessa flinched and cowered. Georgie erupted into laughter. She switched her body back round to face the target and let go. The arrow, hampered by its threadbare feathers, floated to the ground in front of her. She laughed again, with a harder edge. Georgie was competitive. Everyone knew that, despite playing the clown, she did not like to look foolish.

Alice took the bow and fiddled with it, adjusting the tension. She called over. 'Tessa, can you go and see if you can find a ball of string?'

'I don't know if string will help,' said Harriet. 'You need to fix those things professionally. Mind you, you have firearms training, though, don't you?' As she looked at Alice, a grin spread across her face.

Alice laughed. 'I'm not the one who lives on an estate.'

'I don't live on an estate!' Harriet hooted. 'I live in London, for Christ's sake. I mean, Freddie's family have a country house. They just rent it out for Airbnb now, though. *Estate*. Makes us sound like Downton Abbey. Just because I wrote about an estate in my novel.' At the mention of Harriet's novel, they all fell into an embarrassed silence.

Tessa looked down at her empty wrist. 'Anyone have the time?'

Alice took out her phone. 'Nearly two.'

'Funny. Tom hasn't been back yet with the rice,' Melissa said sleepily. She was sitting on the grass, propped back on her elbows, the Barbour jacket from the utility room spread out beneath her.

Tessa looked at them all. They had looked so relaxed through the window, but now Harriet seemed pinched and hungry, Alice and Rachael had drained faces, and Melissa looked knackered.

Georgie grabbed the bow back off Alice and, in some charade of professionalism, flicked the bend. She closed one eye and aimed, then released. This time she hit the black outer ring. Melissa and Bea squealed.

'That's better,' Georgie said, quietly.

Tessa looked at Alice, who was keeping her lips tight. Rachael clapped politely.

'There we go. I'm ready to take on the English now,' Georgie said.

'You should keep your voice down,' Harriet said. 'You don't know who's listening.'

Georgie blew a raspberry. 'It's a joke, Harriet. I am English.'

'Tom might not think it's a joke.'

'I don't think we need the string after all. Seems to be working fine,' Georgie said briskly, turning away from Harriet.

'So, what are the rules?' Melissa said.

'What do you mean, rules?' Georgie said. 'Just shoot at the target.'

'All right.' Melissa got to her feet slowly. She held out her hands for the bow and Harriet furnished her with an arrow. Melissa giggled as she pulled back the string. The arrow dropped sharply to the ground.

'It's because there isn't enough tension,' Alice began. 'Even though it feels like it's taut, you need to really . . .' She tailed off, seeing Georgie's face. 'I was just trying to be helpful.'

'Bea, you're up next.' Melissa passed Bea the bow. She stared down at it, looking awkwardly at the shape. It looked odd in her arms, too big and too menacing. She held it with her fingertips, trying to find a way for the weight of it to rest on her shoulder.

Alice helped Bea adjust her posture and balance the bow. 'It's not what you think. I just play a lot of Fortnite, that's all. Try here.' She pulled Bea's arm back and then showed her the motion of smoothly releasing the string.

'Oh, thanks,' Bea said distantly. She yanked the drawstring back and they all sprang away as the arrow flicked backwards, causing Bea to yelp before it bounced off the back of the bow and up into her face. Her hands rushed to cover her eyes, and she turned in a circle. When she lowered her hands, there was a small red mark on her brow, but no blood. She laughed, straining to lighten the mood. The others joined in tentatively. 'It's my own fault,' Bea said. 'I'm such a bloody klutz.'

'It's tricky. Are you all right?' Georgie asked.

'I'll just sit down for a second.' Bea squatted down on the grass.

Georgie said, 'Did anyone clock that other cottage? Behind the sea wall, on the way to the loch?'

Harriet murmured, 'That's the one I pointed out yesterday.'

Tessa said, 'Maybe it's a gardener's?'

'Didn't look very lived in,' Georgie said. 'Also, didn't you say Tom lived here alone?'

'I didn't say that,' said Tessa. 'Tom might have,' she added.

'Did anyone see his tattoo?' Melissa widened her eyes. 'On his wrist. Forearm.'

'I did,' Alice said. 'But I didn't see what it was. Did you?'

'It looked like he'd drawn it on with crayons,' Georgie said.

'Prison,' Alice said shortly.

Georgie made a face. 'Nooo,' she whispered. 'Do you think?'

'It was rough,' said Alice. 'Could be army.'

'What do you know about prison and army tattoos, Alice?' Harriet asked.

Alice shook her head, refusing to answer.

Tom's tattoo kept them buoyant for a few more minutes as they floated other ideas – Satanist ritual, self-harm cover – but then silence fell again, and with it, the realisation that it was now far past lunchtime and they were beginning to feel hungry. Tessa looked into the woods towards where the road dipped down to the flooded burn. A memory made her shudder.

She had never been able to grasp where exactly in the woods she had been, but she remembered being stuck in floodwater. She must have been about five, and a tree had come down; she had tried to scramble across it and had fallen. She was pulled out by her wrists by a man from the village who was walking his dog on the estate. Charlie had been screaming for help on the bank of the burn. The man had been with his own son – locals often walked in the woods – and he had called them 'the Shining Twins'. For a long time, Tessa had thought that had been a compliment, that it meant they sparkled together, like moonbeams. Later, when she was a teenager, she saw the film.

'What time is it?' Harriet asked. 'Tom must have been back with the rice by now. Kind of getting hungry.'

'We'll go back in a second,' Georgie said. 'Tessa hasn't taken her turn.'

'I'm fine.' Tessa waved a hand, dismissing the bow Bea held out to her.

'You have to have at least one shot. Come on.'

'I'm really – I wouldn't know where to start.' She raised a hand to her brow. The sun had come out from behind a cloud and was spiking down into the clearing.

'Just point and shoot. It's not rocket science.'

'I'll go,' Harriet said, standing up. She took the bow from Bea. There was a steeliness to Harriet's gaze as she selected the arrow she wanted, lined up the shot, faced the bleak thicket of impenetrable woodlands – and released.

The arrow slid through the air. Straight into the blue middle ring. Again, Rachael gave her polite clap.

'Hmmm,' Harriet said. 'Bit rusty.'

'Did you used to do this?' Alice asked.

'I've done it once or twice,' she said. 'You didn't tell me this would be here, Tessa.'

Tessa hesitated. 'I didn't know.'

Rachael took her turn next and scored a respectable yellow, left of the bullseye.

'Come on, Tessa,' Georgie said. 'You have to have a shot at it. Bride's orders.'

Tessa glanced at Georgie, standing between her and the target. Then she took the bow from Rachael, and tested the bowstring awkwardly with her fingertip. In one motion, she pulled back the arrow between two fingers, squinting. Then she let the tension loose and the bow hang down. She laughed. 'It just feels so camp,' she said.

'Come on, Diana,' Georgie egged. 'Huntress of the forest. Tess of the NHSvilles. Tes-sa, Tes-sa, Tes-sa.'

Suddenly, a bird flew out of a bush. Before she knew what was happening, Tessa pulled the bowstring taut again and released. There was a cool, sharp whistling sound, followed by a short scream. The arrow landed in the red ring of the target.

213

'You grazed me!' Georgie was yelling. 'Eeek! Ouch!'

Tessa dropped the bow.

Georgie was clutching her shoulder. 'Just here.' She was squeezing a patch below her collarbone. 'You could have taken my jugular out. Wow, fuck. Stings.'

'I told you I didn't know what I was doing,' Tessa said, rushing to pull Georgie's hands away. 'Let me look.'

There was a thin trail of very dark blood snaking through Georgie's fingers. 'I might have clipped a small vein,' Tessa admitted. 'I think it will be OK.'

'Do I need stitches?'

'Just sit down.' Tessa took hold of Georgie's shoulders and guided her towards a tree stump, pressing her to sit. The others had gathered around them. Tessa felt their eyes on her as she sanitised her hands with a bottle from her jeans pocket, then wiped the blood from the wound with a cautious thumb. 'I have gauze strips in the medical kit,' she said.

'It won't leave a scar, will it?' Georgie said. 'For the wedding? I've got an open-necked dress. I mean it's not strapless, it's Bardot-line – off-the-shoulder, sort of like Meghan Markle's, but a bit lower, more of a sixties version.' The words sounded absurd somehow, a fixation with her fashion choices even as blood dripped from her throat.

'It will be fine,' Tessa said, trying to sound certain. 'Come on. Let me know if you feel dizzy. I'm so sorry, Georgie.'

Georgie giggled. 'You're a shit shot.'

'I'd say she's rather a good shot,' Harriet murmured. She craned her neck over her shoulder quickly to make clear that she meant the fact that the arrow had landed in the red zone.

The herbs rustled in the breeze.

Then, as if Harriet's carelessly dropped words had stirred some dark summons, the wax leaves of the rhododendrons crackled, the huge blooms parted and the shaggy, panting forms of the two dogs, Bella and Stella, scraped through the bushes, mouths open, fur flying back against the wind.

Alice screamed and scrambled backwards. She plucked up the bow and began beating the air in front of her. Her own hair seemed to lurch into purple flames as she thrashed. Rachael immediately lunged and clamped her arms.

One of the dogs ran straight to Melissa, wagging its scruffy tail. She held the fur of its neck in a gentle grasp and let it pant against her face.

'Where's Tom?' Alice was screaming, her eyes feral as she strained against Rachael's grasp. 'Tom!' she screamed. 'Tom, get your fucking dogs away from me. I warned you!'

Tessa watched Georgie put her hand to her mouth. She thought at first that she was shocked, but then spotted the curl at the ends of her lips. She was hiding laughter.

Tessa left Georgie and grabbed the other dog. She held her arm around its shoulders, but she couldn't tame its fidgety excitement. It broke free and ran in circles around Alice and Rachael, leaping up and skittering around, going for the bow.

'Drop the bow, drop the bow,' Rachael was saying. Alice beat the wind and the dog jumped, like it was playing a game. The stink of its meaty teeth filled the air. It was as if the excited animals had brought with them a current, the blood of the chase.

Rachael tried to push Alice towards the castle, but she

was in a white-hot panic and it had poisoned her. She ripped her arms away, screeching in waves, a sound that made the dog bark, teasing and sharp, as it lunged again and again for the bow.

'Where's Tom?' Tessa peered through the bushes, but the kitchen-garden wall cut off the view.

She saw Alice pick an arrow from the ground, raise the bow and pull back the drawstring.

'Alice, don't!' Melissa leapt forward, pushing the dog out of the way as the arrow left the bow slickly, licking the air before hammering into the tuffet of earth where she had been crouching, clutching the dog. 'Alice, that's a weapon. Put it down.'

The lurcher in Melissa's arms was growing restless, howling in chatty, houndish bursts.

Rachael finally managed to wrestle the bow from Alice and threw it into the bushes. Alice's head was thrown back, stricken, fitting. She was panting now. Bea and Harriet helped Rachael get her across the lawn and through the stone arch. Melissa and Tessa hung back with the dogs, holding them by the collars at their throats until the others had crossed the kitchen garden and were back inside.

In the kitchen, Alice was given black tea with whisky in it. She was trembling.

Tessa went silently to the first aid kit she had brought and pulled out two gauze strips and a wipe. She cleaned Georgie's shoulder with the wipe, then carefully placed the two gauzes over the graze.

Georgie winced. 'God, it's like a lock hospital in here.' She looked up at Tessa. 'Is that what I mean?'

Tessa frowned. 'I don't think so.'

'Lock hospitals were for STDs,' Harriet said.

Georgie laughed, throaty, open-mouthed. Out of the corner of her eye, though, Tessa clocked her regarding Alice. It had been alarming to see Alice's reaction. In the few seconds after the dogs had appeared, the phobia had turned her into something else, something powerful in terror. It had stripped down her crafted bravado, exposed nerves that blazed with horror. Now, she drank her tea in tiny, girlish sips.

There was an embarrassed hum of small-talk chatter in the room, a clamping shut and shelving away of what they had just witnessed.

Melissa was the last to come back in.

'Did you chain them?' Bea asked.

'With what?' Melissa replied. 'Anyway, that's cruel. I left them outside. Tom will be along in a minute, no doubt.'

Tessa peered through the window. The two dogs were now sniffing around the vegetable patch. One of them squatted down to pee on the spinach bed. They were of a size with each other, but one had browner fur. Their mouths were lupine, but the tongues hanging out were a gentle pink, and through their feral panting there was an eagerness to please. Lurchers had been bred for estate tenants to hunt with; greyhounds being reserved for lords and ladies. Deerhounds were the hunting dog of choice for Scottish landowners. These ones had the same shaggy fur, but they were about the size of greyhounds, so they were probably deerhound-whippet crosses. They were beautiful, mythical. Watching them potter around together, sniffing in and out of each other's path, their twin beauty set off something in Tessa, and she had to turn back into the kitchen. She had to force herself to steady her breathing. She focused on Alice.

'Are you all right?' She put her hand on Alice's shoulder.

Alice shook her head. 'I just wish you'd said something when we booked.'

'I didn't know,' Tessa said.

'Didn't know what? About the dogs or about my phobia?'

Tessa shrugged. 'Either.'

Alice sighed. She was still shivering, as if the fear had climbed deep down into her bones. 'I suppose it's my fault.'

'Nothing's your fault, darling,' Harriet drawled, but her tone was cool. She was biting her cuticles. She had taken her phone out of her hoodie pocket once more, and then put it back. A few minutes later, she did it again.

'I need a drink,' Georgie said. 'And a snack.' She turned away to rummage in one of the bags on the counter.

'Stuck indoors now.' Tessa heard the words dropped behind her, but she didn't catch who had said them.

Rachael was holding Alice's head to her stomach, stroking her hair. They all stared into their own private spaces.

'It's started to rain, anyway.' Bea had gone to the kitchen window and was staring out.

'I can make us hot toddies with the whisky?' Melissa offered.

'What's a hot toddy?' Rachael asked.

'Oh, you'll love it! You haven't had one? I used to swear by them for getting rid of colds. There must be a lemon here. And some honey.' Melissa busied herself rooting around, searching for the whisky. In another corner of the kitchen, they heard the slap of the fridge door closing and the unceremonious pop of the final bottle of champagne.

Georgie, favouring the arm of her grazed shoulder, began slopping it indiscriminately into mugs and teacups and handing them out. It seemed no one really wanted champagne, but nor did they want to refuse it. Harriet muttered about what they would drink with lunch, but since there was no lunch, no one replied. She turned back to the counter and dumped half a bag of crisps and the remains of Bea's wild garlic humous on opposite halves of a ceramic dish.

'Can you grab the other bag as well?' Alice said.

'That's all there is,' replied Georgie.

'Surely, there were salt and vinegar as well?' Alice got up and looked in the Oliver Bonas bag. 'Must have eaten them.' She went over to the counter beside the fridge and brought back the half-eaten remains of the last two cheeses. 'What were we going to have for lunch, anyway?'

'I think the plan was to have a pub lunch,' Harriet said. 'And then – I believe it was thought churlish to make plans any further ahead than that. Seems we have plenty of time for planning, anyway, since we'll be here another night.' The remark was met with silence.

'At least the dogs have stopped whining,' Melissa said, glancing towards the window. 'Can't find honey or lemon;

shall we give up on the hot toddies?' She accepted a mug of champagne from Georgie.

Tessa went over to the sink, where Bea was still standing, staring out of the window, a cup cradled in her hands, as if its contents were warm and soft and comforting, and not chilled and fizzy and sharp. Even as Tessa drew close, she could feel the tension radiating from Bea. She stood directly behind Bea's shoulder, looking in the same direction as her, and so she knew that Bea had seen him, too, that Bea could see him, in fact, more clearly than she could. An electric chill ran through Tessa. They both silently watched the boy's form, his back turned, black hair falling down over his collar as he retreated down the path to the driveway, a dog lead in each hand, the two scraggy lurchers, Stella and Bella, trotting obediently at his heels.

12

By the time she looked round, Bea had made her face blank. But Tessa knew she'd seen him. She said nothing.

'Oh, fuckety fuck. Sorry, guys,' Georgie said. A few sips of the champagne had loosened her up, or brought her back. 'I feel as though it's my fault. Making everyone come away for the weekend.'

There was a pause, a stage laid bare for the inevitable protests. They did come, but they were forced.

'No, Georgie.'

'It's your hen party.'

'We haven't seen each other for ages.'

'We wanted to come. It was the excuse we had been waiting for.'

'It's you we feel sorry for.'

Tessa refused to look up until she was certain none of them were staring at her.

'I'll make us something delicious with every ingredient we have left in the fridge,' Bea said quickly.

Harriet had wandered over and yanked open the fridge

door, peering inside. 'You might be pushing it for imagination. There are some potatoes and a turnip, and I think one rasher of bacon left.'

'The garden, then,' Bea said. 'You can make a buttload of things with spinach and leftover cheese – and there are so many mushrooms around, and potatoes if we dig. And wild garlic. Who doesn't like garlic mushrooms and chips?'

Georgie looked like she might weep. Then her face changed. She seemed to be weighing it all up, calculating the value of the anecdote. 'A survivalist hen party,' she mused. 'Like the SAS programme.'

Alice gave a scoffing sound. Georgie glanced at her, but then reached for a handful of crisps.

'Tom must have come for the dogs,' said Melissa. 'They're gone now. But why didn't he knock on the door? He said he would bring us the rice about four hours ago.'

'We could have risotto if he did,' Bea said.

'Maybe he was embarrassed about the dogs,' Harriet said. 'I mean, letting them go like that when he knew he shouldn't. He knew Alice was scared.'

Alice squirmed at the word. She looked sheepish now. But when Melissa moved to open the utility-room door, her head shot up.

'Don't panic,' Melissa said. 'I'm just going to check he didn't leave it out there on the doorstep. Or he might have knocked when we were popping the champagne. Maybe we didn't hear him.' She left the room, humming lightly in a way Tessa recognised, because she did it herself when dealing with nervous or irrational patients.

'Close that door.' Alice pointed and Rachael obliged. 'I trusted him to keep them on the leads. To think I was just wandering around out there.'

Melissa didn't come back straight away. After a few moments of chatter, they realised she still hadn't come back.

'Christ, I'll go see where she's got to,' Georgie said. 'I don't want another fucking disappearing act.'

Bea's mouth dropped slightly as Georgie brushed past her. After a few moments, Georgie poked her head back around the door. 'Someone. Tessa. Can you get a tray?'

'A tray? What's happening?' Tessa asked.

'A Tupperware. Or a tray – something with sides.'

Alice and Rachael looked at Tessa as if she would be able to explain this. Without thinking about it, she took a baking tray from the bottom cupboard nearest the Aga and went out into the utility room.

In the back doorway, she could see the crouched and bent haunches of Georgie and Melissa. Georgie stood up and covered her eyes with her hands. 'Clusterfuck,' she whispered.

On the doorstep was a slaughtered hare, its fur still intact. Melissa was grunting as she decided the best way to pick it up. She tried grasping the ears first, but blood dripped from a wet gash at its throat. Then she tried draining it by holding it by its haunches. The guts had also perforated.

'Don't spoil the meat,' Tessa said.

'You sound like you do this all the time, Queen Tessa,' Georgie said. 'Oh, fetch me my yon dead rabbit that I must skin myself, but don't spoil the meat. The fucking *meat*. Jesus. Is this Tom's idea of a joke?'

'It's probably Tom's idea of a gift,' Tessa said calmly. 'They're scarce and very valued.'

'Oh, let's write him a thank-you card.'

'Don't forget the rice.' Tessa nodded to the bag, which had been tucked beside the boot scraper – a jumbo bag of Tesco Value basmati.

'Is *that* what he meant by rice?' Georgie said.

Suddenly Melissa squealed. They looked at her, then at the hare. 'Sorry, it just twitched. It's OK. It's just a reflex. It's dead.'

Georgie covered her eyes again and tipped her head towards the sky. She went back inside first, holding open the utility-room door. The others were craning now to see. Even Alice peered tentatively, though she stayed on her stool.

'Hold on, hold on, hold on, hold the door,' Melissa was saying. She had one hand on top of the hare, pinning it to the baking tray.

'It's completely illegal to course hares with dogs,' Rachael said, leaning over to take a look.

'And you were worried about me decapitating a snake?' Georgie gave a loud sigh.

'I've never cooked hare,' Bea said. 'But I can cook rabbit. I don't know how to skin it, though.'

'Well, isn't this marvellous? Lunch is sorted!' Georgie flourished her hands in the air. 'Forget cupcake decorating, it's skin-your-own-rabbit time! We've had creepy-boy time, snake time, a night of horrors down by the loch, storm, a tree down, and clusterfuck-over-the-fucking-food time.'

Tessa took a slow, deep breath.

'And yet you still seem to be enjoying yourself,' Harriet said, sarcastically bright. She took the knife from where Rachael had abandoned it and fetched a large chopping board.

'Now you get to show off your specialist skill, do you?' Georgie said. 'Have you written a blog post on that? Something to do with the kids on a wet Wednesday?'

Harriet ignored her and lumped the hare onto the board. 'I can't take the bones out,' she said to Bea.

'Doesn't matter. Skinned and butchered is good.'

'I'll try and get the organs as best I can, if you want to chuck them into the pot, too.'

Tessa placed the bag of basmati rice on the island.

Georgie got up and went over to the counter where Harriet was working. She peered over Harriet's shoulder, then reached down and gently stroked the dead hare's ear between her finger and thumb. The look on her face was miles away.

'What's his name again?' Rachael asked.

'Jack,' said Alice.

'What do you think Jack would do if he had to skin a hare?'

Georgie turned and stared at her. 'God, he'd probably get the maid to do it.'

'Maid?' Alice scoffed. 'The Jack I remember coming to visit used to prance around pretending he had communist principles. Didn't he carry a copy of *Das Kapital* around in that second-hand leather coat?'

'I'd forgotten about that.' Harriet laughed.

'Closer to his roots these days, then, is he?' Alice was still smirking. 'Civil service tends to do that to people.' She leaned back against the counter and picked at one of the tattoos on her forearm. 'I think I remember him saying he liked coming to visit because he thought St Andrews was egalitarian – didn't he say that? How absurd. I suppose, compared to his private school, it probably was.'

Rachael leaned back next to Alice and softly tweaked her neck. Tessa saw her mouth the words, 'Be nice.' Alice flinched, but fell silent.

'So,' Rachael said politely, 'What was it that brought you two together?'

Georgie shrugged. A smile spread. 'I suppose we were quite different at the start. Both party people, for sure, but he was a little emo goth who liked books and red wine, and I liked champagne and ket and dancing. Then you sort of blend into each other until you meet halfway really, don't you? Why did I go after him? I don't know. I suppose, when I met him, I just decided I wanted a bit of a challenge.'

There was an ear-splitting clatter.

Melissa and Georgie sprang to their feet, and Alice and Rachael stepped forward.

'Sorry, sorry.' Tessa dropped to her hands and knees. 'Butterfingers.' On the floor, still rattling to a halt in front of her, was a cast-iron saucepan lid.

'You could kill someone with that,' Alice chided, taking the lid from Tessa and replacing it on the counter.

Tessa had felt it happen, but been unable to do anything. The pan lid had just tumbled out of her hands, as if in slow motion. Still bent over on the kitchen floor, she felt nauseated, frozen. Bea crouched next to her and held out a hand, asking if she was all right. Tessa forced herself off her knees and back up to standing. They were all busy returning to their places: Georgie to the island, Harriet to the hare.

Georgie put her face in her hands. 'I'm actually starving,' she said.

Harriet looked sharply over her shoulder, as if to say, *Don't push it*. The knife's blade had collected a few threads of bloodied fur and they glistened as she gripped the handle. After a moment, she returned to her task, picking away at sinew, cartilage, fur.

Georgie rubbed the wound on her collarbone. 'How did we get on to Jack? Oh yes, the rabbit. Who knows how to skin rabbits, anyway?' she said.

'People who didn't grow up in London,' Harriet said, her eyes on her task. The knife came down with a crunch on the creature's pelvis, and Harriet slammed her spare hand on top of the handle to sever the joint.

'All of them. Every single one of them,' Georgie mused. Then she turned on Tessa with a strange, accusatory look that Tessa found hard to read. 'Do you know how to skin a hare?'

Tessa shook her head. 'I grew up in London, Georgie, remember?' She paused. 'I could probably have a go, though. I know how to skin a person. Can't be that different.'

Georgie didn't smile. 'What did you just say?'

Tessa laughed a little and looked down. 'Nothing. I said I'd never skinned a rabbit, but I could probably have a – go at it.' She thought, at first, that it must have just been a shock to Georgie, to hear someone other than herself say something inappropriate.

'No,' Georgie began. 'You said—'

Tessa looked around at all of the faces. They had all heard her. They were all staring. She glanced back at the flagstones. 'I took a pathology pathway. We had cadavers in first year,' she said, softly.

'Sometimes,' Georgie said. 'Sometimes, Tessa, I just don't know about you. Whether you did ever get over it properly?'

Alice and Rachael's heads snapped towards Georgie. Harriet, very deliberately, returned to chopping up the hare. Melissa and Bea began chatting about sauces. It had ceased to be a hare now. It was meat, lunch, it needed a sauce.

Tessa boiled inside. Those words, those casual words. *Get over it.* As if Charlie had been a boy she'd had a passing fancy for, or a distant friend who had snubbed her. It. Get over *it.*

Georgie sauntered out of the room. As she went up the stairs, she muttered something. Tessa thought she half-heard her words: 'You need counselling.' She looked around to see if the others had heard, too, but no one seemed to have noticed. She was being paranoid; Georgie could just as easily have said, 'I'll be in the castle lounge.' Perhaps.

Tessa could feel her heart banging against her chest. Bea murmured something about going to forage for wild garlic and moved towards the back door. Tessa, for want of something to occupy her hands, grabbed a J-cloth and began wiping the countertops, and then the floor, where the hare's blood had dripped.

13

A cool rain greeted Bea as she stepped outside. She breathed in, relieved to have escaped the toxic atmosphere choking the kitchen.

She had told them a white lie: that the wild garlic was some distance away, nearer Tom's cottage than the castle; that she would be more than twenty minutes or so, that there was no need to worry about her if it took a while. No one had questioned her going out in the rain. They had all been too absorbed in themselves, or their tasks, or their hunger pangs, which the champagne had turned from a background gnawing into a light-headedness. Bea could feel it now herself. She could have sworn that there had been more bread and more snacks and crackers in the Fortnum and Mason hamper, but then she had not been there last night when everyone had been very drunk and high. It seemed foolish for them not to have thought of how much food they would need.

She suddenly felt exposed, in woodlands that did not belong to her, a Londoner – not a rich one, but an outsider, anyway – making a playground of an old castle without knowing a thing about the people who owned it, or those who lived in the village nearby.

The rain poured down harder and she ducked off the path to shelter under a tree. As she waited for the shower to ease, she contemplated going further down the driveway to see if she could see where the boy had gone with the two dogs.

He would not be there, though. He would be indoors, in his house, for he must have a home that he could go to if it rained. Bea didn't believe in ghosts, but she believed in explanations. That diary she had found had been tucked away so carefully: its pages preserved, but hidden from prying eyes.

She spotted the long, green fronds of wild garlic beside the cottage path and picked some, then unlatched the cottage door and felt glad that she had left the electric heater on. The air was stuffy and smelled scorched, but it was warm. She tossed the garlic down on to the coffee table, pulled the book back out from between the cushions of the chair and sat down to read.

30 March 2007

If I say I had a terrible time working at the ski resort, I'd sound like a brat. Perhaps that's all I am. Maybe realising that I am nothing but a spoiled, whining brat who deserves everything that came to her is what hurts the most.

I didn't hate every moment of Christmas 2005. If I think I did, it's only because of what happened. But there were some good nights, and there was some kind of fun at the beginning, among the chaos.

Our chalet was a hovel – cheap staff accommodation. The ski lift felt as if it was always on the verge of sending a tourist to their death. The bar was clad with orange-stained pine, though it had sixty-seven different single malts – the sign told you this. It was decorated with beer mats and coins and notes from around the world. The beer mats had also been collated and made into a mural in the living room of the chalet we were in, covering the outer wall top to bottom, end to end. Jack called it 'Cairngorm insulation'.

Locals worked mainly in the restaurant and the bar; Spanish and Polish backpackers worked in the kitchens; Australians and Kiwis were instructors – which, looking back, seems strange, but didn't strike me as odd at the time – and a random selection of waifs and strays, travellers and people who knew someone who knew someone, filled in the other odd jobs, like the shop, the ticket counter, the lifts.

Georgie and I worked at the top of the chair lift to the main slopes, helping people disembark. She thought it was funny to spend all day telling me stories of the disaster television shows she had watched, where people got the straps of their rucksack caught in the giant cogs that shunted the chairs round, or caught their skis behind the safety bar and had their legs ripped off.

Georgie had this strange sort of violence in her. It wasn't a real violence, but more a way of planting

231

violence inside you, with thoughts and images, or just with the way she wound you up. She never knew when to stop. But again, I might be – what do you call it – doing the opposite of rose-tinting? Just remembering the bad bits, because I know she made me laugh, too.

Jack and Tessa alternated between the shop and the base of the lift, and sometimes we all had a rotate and worked on the nursery slope lift, which I liked, because it was nice to see old people and children and nervous first-time skiers shunting down the slopes, then the glee on their faces as they came for a second turn, more cocky.

I don't remember the first time we met Kenneth. He swore we had chatted in the bar, but I didn't remember that. I only remember him smiling at me as he came off the chair lift to the main slopes, and holding out his hand and grabbing mine and saying 'Whoops!', even though he was completely steady on his skis, then making a joke about wobbles and whisky.

'We should name a new shooter, the whisky wobble,' Georgie said. I wondered why he was smiling and acting as if he knew us. I wondered then if he knew Georgie.

There are lots of men who, since I met Kenneth, have reminded me of him. But even then, before I met any of them, Kenneth himself reminded me of someone, of a type I knew, or recognised.

He had something seasoned about him, about the way he held your eye when he talked to you, a charm that was the counterpoint of Georgie's. He treated you *as if he knew you intimately, holding your eye, touching your hand. But I think now it came from a sense of entitlement, whereas in Georgie it's insecurity. Yin and Yang. I honestly thought he was hitting on Georgie. She flirted back with him whenever he conversed in that twinkly, steady-eyed way that I grew to learn was his way of flirting.*

He wasn't unattractive. Not at all. He had wavy dirty blonde hair, fashionably flopping around his head, sometimes slicked back into wet marcel waves, sometimes left loose and wild. His skin had been damaged by too much sun, but in a cragged, handsome way. And he was stubbly, with a soft, wide mouth, good teeth. Everything very temperate, very symmetrical and classically handsome. But I didn't like his confidence. The way he touched you when he spoke – not only me, but everyone he conversed with – was absent-minded, the way you help yourself to sugar for your coffee while still keeping up a conversation. It wasn't inappropriate. It was always a shoulder, a wrist, the small of the back, sometimes the hip. Just a couple of fingers or the lightness of his palm. Once he brushed a fly away from my fringe; I was certain there was nothing there. But he did it mid-sentence, while he was telling me about a walk he had taken up one of the Munros, and it was over too quickly for me to flinch. Just the reverberations of the touch left, which didn't leave me, not for a while afterwards, like the memory of something someone has said that is a bit off, but not enough to comment on at the time, though it then hangs around your head, niggling.

He asked if we would join him and his friend, Ben, for drinks. I was certain he meant to make a move on Georgie, and since it would mean the chance to spend an evening around Jack, glammed up, drinking, on display, I jumped in and said yes straight away.

'Proper minx,' Georgie said, as we saw him place his goggles over his eyes and ski away down the only black run, slicker than James Bond: incongruous here, like he should have been in Switzerland or Liechtenstein.

I blushed – not in embarrassment, but a bit in anger, and I was sort of stunned Georgie would think that. Then it occurred to me that she didn't think that – she knew I was the opposite. She was winding me up.

But when we were finishing for the day, and fixing on our own skis to get back down, she nudged me in the ribs and said, 'Only a few hours to go till the hot date.'

'Whose hot date?'

'Whose do you think? Slut. You are all over each other. I should book you a room.'

'Georgie,' I said. 'He's greasy.' I knew it wasn't quite the right word for him, but I couldn't find a better one.

'Fit as fuck,' Georgie said. 'You look cute together.' She winked, and skied off. Georgie was a magnificent skier: elegant, coiled with tension, leaning at the right time into the turns. I was numb with cold by the end of the day and fuddled my way down after her. We met Jack and Tessa coming off their shifts in the main lodge.

I told Tessa about the drinks, avoiding Jack's eye,
terrified he could see how much I cared about him.

I don't remember too much about that drinks session,
because there were more to follow, but—

Bea caught sight of a shadow passing the window and
jammed the book back down behind the seat cushion. Then
she grabbed the wild garlic leaves.

She hid behind the front door. She could hear footsteps,
and she waited for them to die away before she quietly
twisted the latch and pulled back the door.

Tessa was standing on the doorstep.

Bea felt her face flush instantly with poisonous guilt.

'How did you get in here?' Tessa asked.

'It was unlocked.' Bea gestured pathetically at the door
handle.

'What are you doing?'

Bea felt a sort of electric tingling in her temples, the sign
of a lie brewing. She couldn't tell Tessa the truth. There was
no doubt in her mind that this Tessa was the same Tessa as
the one in the diary. But Bea had known her since university,
and she had never once mentioned a twin.

That stung. It hit Bea in the gut. There was nothing sadder,
she thought, thinking of her own two girls: nothing sadder at
all, to her, than to think of what they would feel if they were
estranged, or worse. Once, Lila, her younger twin by nineteen
minutes, had run on ahead in the park and hidden behind a
tree. It was a slim birch tree and Bea could see exactly where
she was, but to Noor, the first-born, Lila had vanished. Noor

had bawled her eyes out for a good ten minutes, even after they had reunited. Each second of Lila's disappearance had seemed like a lifetime of stabbing grief to the three-year-old.

'I was just exploring,' Bea said. She couldn't. She couldn't say anything else. It was too much of an imposition to tell Tessa she had found the diary. Even to think it felt like a violation. 'It's a really, really cute cottage. I could live here happily.'

Tessa regarded her.

They both knew.

Tessa said, 'I was looking for you.' She paused. Her lips hung open a fraction. 'I saw wild garlic here outside the cottage, so I wondered why you had gone as far as Tom's. Then I thought you might be in here.'

'I'm just nosy.' Bea laughed and looked away. 'There's a cute painting in there – the Virgin and baby one, with the paint dripping down it.' She closed the door of the cottage behind her and they began to walk, side by side, back down the path. At the bottom, where the castle turrets came into sight behind the wall of rhododendrons, Tessa made a faint gesture. 'I just want to get a bit more fresh air. It's hot in the kitchen. And the mustard stings my eyes.'

'Mustard?'

'Yes – wasn't it you that rubbed mustard onto the hare? Smells really strong.'

'I didn't put any on it. Must have been Harriet or one of the others.'

'Well,' Tessa said. Their eyes met.

Bea's mind swam. She blurted out, 'I miss my twins.' As

soon as she had said the word, she regretted it. But at the same time, she was watching to see if Tessa would give anything away. Perhaps Bea had misunderstood the whole thing. Tessa was looking at her with sudden concern and sympathy. Or was that her practised doctor's mask that Bea could see? Some means of keeping the power, rejecting all pity for herself, only deflecting it back out.

'Well, that's understandable,' Tessa said, nodding. 'But you'll see them soon. I wouldn't worry too much about the tree. Tom says it will be fixed on Monday.' She waved her arm towards the path again. Before she turned down it, she said to Bea, 'You know, I think the hare is going to be a little while longer cooking. I'm sure if you want to explore for a little longer, then it would be OK.' She looked as if she might say more, but then seemed to realise that was enough. She was giving Bea permission to go back to the cottage, to read more of the diary.

So she did.

14

Tessa let nothing of her face change until she was certain she was out of Bea's view. Even then, she kept her shoulders taut as the tears began to fall. She let them fall quietly, the way she would if Charlie was there watching her. She'd never wanted Charlie to see her cry, although she'd seen Charlie's tears plenty of times.

She was wearing jeans and a light jumper and had nothing to wipe her eyes or nose with, so bitterly, quickly, she grabbed a leaf from one of the rhododendron bushes and scrubbed beneath her nose and around her eyes. It didn't absorb much, but the action of the rubbing brought her round and made her feel a little calmer.

She picked up her pace, sure that getting the blood to flow would soothe her. Bea had not meant anything. She had not meant to upset Tessa. But it was out of the question to talk about it. Taboo didn't even come close. They were friends, a certain type of friends, and to talk about something like that would have felt, to Tessa, like pouring acid into that friendship. There were just no words to even begin.

She didn't knock on the door of Tom's cottage when she got to it. She just turned the handle and went in. Ethan was playing on the PlayStation inside, some game that had exploding pieces of aliens' brains and skulls all over the screen as he shot them down, one by one.

Tessa touched his head, just once, softly. His hand flew to the thick brown hair on his crown and brushed away her touch.

Often, she had wanted to be so much more to him than she was. Often, she told herself that she had tried. But she wasn't so sure she had now. She loved him, that was certain. And when they didn't see each other, which was for most of the year, she felt as if she missed him dreadfully, as if she ached to squeeze his skinny body. But whenever he was in front of her, flesh and blood and breath, there was something in her that always recoiled. It was a thing that would not let her get too close to him, in case – in case what? It felt like fear. Fear of collapsing.

She passed behind his back like a ghost. He kept playing the game. Another alien exploded.

'No more wandering near the castle,' she said.

He grunted, then fired with his controller and split the character in front of him lengthways with a samurai sword.

She reached into her pocket and passed Tom the sample tube half full of Agent Provocateur perfume. He blushed slightly and pocketed it.

'I'll get you a full bottle next time, but I thought this would do you for now.'

'Thanks,' he mumbled.

'Got all over my nightclothes on the train,' she said. She stood looking at him for a few moments. 'They saw your tattoos.'

He swallowed. She saw him staring at the tear tracks on her cheeks. She rubbed her eyes and straightened her face.

'Is your mum—'

'Jenny's gone to town,' he said. 'Won't be back for a couple of hours.'

Tessa passed by him and went upstairs. The bed in his room was made up neatly. His iPad was lying on the bedside table. She leaned down behind the table and flicked the router on at the wall.

Tom was in the doorway. He had climbed the stairs silently. 'I thought you said to keep that off.'

'I'll just be a minute.'

He had brought with him the smell of the outdoors, and a blood-like scent she always imagined she could smell on him after he had been hunting. She picked up the iPad. She had used it before and knew his password – Charl1£. But it still took her a few seconds to get used to the configuration of his screen. When she did this at home she was slicker, swifter. She could be done within a few minutes, in and out.

'If he gets wind you've switched the router on,' Tom said, pointing downstairs, laughing nervously, 'he'll be wanting to play shoot 'em with his friends halfway across the world.'

'I said I'd just be a minute.' She booted up Firefox and waited for the Wi-Fi to kick in.

Tom stood awkwardly in the doorframe, breathing

somewhat more heavily than was necessary, Tessa thought. What was it to him if she took five minutes to do this?

'I thought you said you weren't going to do that any more,' Tom said, after a couple of seconds.

'You don't know what I'm doing.'

Tom made a light scoffing sound. 'You didn't clear the history last time you were here.'

'I didn't know I was being watched.' She slid her finger around the predictive text function on the iPad and pulled up a picture of a man with bouncy blond curls, greased back to his head on one side, free-flowing on the other. His smile was frozen, looking into a sun glare that was two or three years old by now. She knew he looked much the same though, and she would have recognised him anywhere. He posted selfies frequently. She pulled up the other one in a different tab: the dark-haired one.

'Did you get the hare?' Tom asked.

'I thought you were going to leave it half-alive.'

'That's cruel and you know it.'

'We both know what's cruel,' Tessa said, quietly.

Tom stuck his hands in his pockets and looked at the ceiling. He blew his hair back from his brow. 'You will take care, though. Of yourself.'

Tessa looked up from the iPad. She had thought to give him a cool, firm stare, but it wouldn't form on her face. Instead, she smiled gently.

He blew his breath out again. 'She's not what I expected. From the photographs. I dunno what I thought, but not that.'

She wasn't listening any more. She'd gone back to scrolling

through the timelines. Facebook, then Instagram, then Twitter, all the while feeling the rising bile, the impotence turning to arsenic in her gut. She could not look away from their lives. Rage flamed, but there was nothing to do except stare. She pulled up Google Maps, typed in the name of a small town in California and stared at their office building, zooming in and clicking through to street view.

She did this every day, and if she didn't, then it began to hurt in the stomach and the head, like withdrawal from some slow-destroying drug.

There had been nights when she had visited here at the same time Ethan was visiting, and while Ethan blew apart and severed the heads of pixelated men downstairs, she drank whisky on Tom's bed, and together she and Tom cooked up schemes of revenge. Bombs sent to their workplace. Ricin in a jiffy bag, neurotoxins smeared on their computer keyboards. Then the plots became tamer, more realistic. Poison emails. Catfishing. Flaming. Telling the truth publicly.

In reality, she knew there was nothing she could do to spoil their lives. They were on the other side of the world, connected to her only through binary dots and code, made into images of their faces and hands and hair. Really, they were only pixels, like the men Ethan blew up.

Every time she logged out, her belly ached, like the aftermath of a monster period, like the muscle cramps that came after vomiting for hours. At the end of it all, she would feel a powerless masochistic catharsis, and she would be wretched. Tom would top up her glass and they would drink in silence and misery. Once they had made the mistake of having sex, thinking that would somehow salve a wound. It hadn't, and they had never tried it again.

'What's next?' Tom said. He was still there in the doorway.

She looked up at him, and now she did stare. 'I don't want you to lose your nerve. It's important that I talk to her, in the right place.'

'But what if in the moment—'

'You think I want to kill her.'

He was quiet and now he looked away, turning his head to glance downstairs, even though he could not see into the living room from there.

'You didn't answer my question,' Tessa said.

'It wasn't a question.'

'I'm not asking you to do anything illegal,' she said. 'I've never asked that. But if you're afraid, you could just ask me outright, couldn't you?'

He looked at her.

He didn't ask. Downstairs, they heard Ethan whoop as he pulverised the flesh of another digital enemy.

15

31 March 2007

Hogmanay is the night I do remember, because it splashes me in shame.

It plays over in my mind when I'm walking in the woods or if I can't sleep. I hope by writing it all down that I can fix it. I want to look that night in the face and accept that it happened.

Georgie's friend arrived that day. She was furious because the snow gates had closed and she had to be taken a roundabout route. She was a friend from the county lacrosse team. She didn't go to our school. She was called Harriet, and so I expected her to be a bit like Harriet in Jane Austen's Emma, *but she wasn't. She was sulky.*

We were getting ready to go out and Georgie was running in and out of the bunk room, screaming with laughter. She was drinking JD straight, and kept making puns on the word Jack. Jack pretended to find it all very dull, and he kept to himself and read a book in the living room. But I know he was watching us, because I was watching him. He made digs about what we were drinking. Why did I find him attractive? Maybe because, beneath his snotty digs, I saw something a bit desperate, a bit keen for a persona. And that was what I was looking for, too.

I contoured my cheekbones and Georgie painted my eyelids peacock blue with a delicate touch, smudging the edges with her fingers, going deep and ticklish with a brush between the lids and the sockets.

'God, she is so slutty in make-up. Tessa, don't you agree? We all know who the evil twin is, don't we?'

Tessa protested for me, but Georgie brushed it all off with mock offence. 'I was trying to be nice. She looks like Amy Winehouse. What's wrong with that? I'd kill for lashes like hers.'

'Nothing. I've got a headache.' And then Tessa retreated to the couch, saying she hated New Year's, anyway.

It occurs to me now that I was often spoken of, not just by Georgie but by other girls at school, as if I wasn't there, or was too simple to understand, or was just there to be looked at. People spoke to Tessa but not to me: teachers, boys. I suppose they think that, with twins, that was all you ever needed to do. We were one – we were telepathic.

'Little more, love.' Georgie rubbed her finger from the soft skin in the eye socket up to my temple. Her lips were parted as if she was enjoying the act of concentrating. She wet her finger and plastered the peacock blue up to my eyebrows until my made-up eyes were drag-queen huge. I didn't mind that I looked outlandish. I wanted Jack to see that I didn't take myself too seriously.

It sort of worked. Jack laughed.

'Do you want some?' Georgie asked. We got him to put on some eyeliner and glitter nail varnish and he looked like a younger, scrawnier Adam Ant. 'Let's give him lipliner.'

I will never forget the jealousy in my gut as Georgie leaned over him. She painted the outline of Jack's lips in bold vermillion, the same almost erotic concentration on her face she'd had when she painted my eyes. He pouted and fluttered his eyelashes. I expect he felt like a fop – like Byron or Jim Morrison or someone in Sartre's thirties Paris.

While they were busy staring into each others' eyes I spritzed myself liberally in Agent Provocateur, enough to make them both cough.

Harriet took a photograph of the four of us outside the lodge as the sun was setting, and Jack put his arm around me. Just as she was about to click, I had the sudden urge to put my head in close to his chest – in true Charlie fashion, it ended up in his armpit – and I felt him looking down into my face. You can feel the way someone looks at your face, like you feel their touch. It's a very unnerving sensation, and I feel it with Ethan now. Jack's gaze was like a peacock feather; it was like very soft pony hair being dragged across my cheek. Harriet didn't show us the photograph. For some reason, she kept it to herself and later on I felt too shy, or too ashamed, to ask for a copy. I would give anything to look at it now, because it was the last photograph taken of me before that night.

In the bar, we were the only people dressed up. It was still only tea-time. Everyone else was in après-ski jeans and joggers and woollens and scarves. Tessa was morose and, after we had all gorged ourselves on haggis, she said again that she had a headache and went back to the lodge. I still couldn't figure out what Kenneth and his friend Ben – who worked alongside Kenneth in one of the big tech companies, and was like Kenneth in almost every way except that he had slicked-back dark hair instead of slicked-back blond hair – made of Jack in his make-up. They kept sliding him sidelong looks and then looking at each other. How insecure they must have felt, to find Jack funny when he looked like that.

I think Georgie saw that, too.

I think she knew that on the arm of a man like Kenneth, you are only ever the prize, not the winner. The better prize is winning the man who can sit at a table wearing eyeliner and not care what others think. Georgie dressed Jack like her dolly and gave him that power, and in doing so, she made a bond between them that I don't think will ever go away.

Kenneth and Ben ordered us – Harriet, Jack, Georgie and me – round after round of cocktails. They bought whole bottles of single malt and explained the tastes we should discern in each mouthful. 'This one is peat-smoked, so you'll get a heavy taste of wood,' Ben said, sniggering.

'And in this you should get liquorice at the back of your mouth. Can you get anything that far back?' Kenneth asked.

'This one is like mushroom toast. And peppermint.'

Their suggestions got more and more elaborate, until I knew they were mocking me, although I couldn't quite make out in my foggy head what they got out of it. I think I know now.

When there was no champagne left in the bar, Kenneth asked us all if we would like to come back to their hotel room. And at that point in my drunk confusion, I thought the penny had dropped, and a sudden, serene cloud of relief washed over me. They were sharing a room; therefore they must be a couple. The relief of a man being gay is something I have felt again and again since then. It was, I recognise now, safety I felt in that sudden relief.

Looking back, everything that had happened that night should have told me exactly what was going to happen. This is what I cannot escape.

I don't want to frill this telling of the tale or draw it out for longer than it warrants. But I want to understand the order in which things happened. Tom says it's very important to tell yourself the truth before you can think about how to face it. He talks a lot of sense, but I often wonder if I am brave enough. And do I trust him enough to do as he says? Here goes.

What happened next grew very surreal, and I'm sure it was before I snorted the drugs. They were sharing a room in the resort's only fancy hotel, tarted up in silver and bronze.

Kenneth disappeared into the bathroom and came out in a vintage fighter pilot's jacket and goggles. He had a samurai sword in his room, God knows why – I think Ben had nicked it from the wall in the hotel – and he opened a magnum of champagne from their minibar fridge, using the sword. He just sliced the top right off, glass and all, and let the foam spill onto the carpet. I must have been drunk by then, because I could not stop fixating on that detail, and thinking that someone ought to mop it up. But no one did. They passed the cut glass bottle and Georgie made some comment about slicing her tongue into a fork, like the devil, and we talked about pierced tongues and piercings in general, and by the time I realised Kenneth had positioned himself behind me, where I was sitting on the floor, and he had his legs around me, and was very much not the gay man I had joyously envisaged, I didn't know what to do or say. I said nothing.

'She's too drunk, I'll get her home,' Jack said.

Georgie grabbed his wrist. Her mauve nails looked unnaturally beautiful against his white skin, with the smattering of hair on the back of his hand, and the black glitter varnish on his own nails. It is things like that that I remember in so much vivid detail, which makes me wonder if in fact I took the drugs much earlier in the evening, or if my drink was spiked.

'Yes, I should go.' I saw this chance to get away. And the thought of walking out into the icy sky with Jack and his glitter nails was like a shot of cold water in the face and woke me up.

'Nooooo,' Georgie began to protest in a wail.

'Noooo.' Kenneth and Ben took up the protest.

'You can stay,' I told Georgie. 'You guys stay.'

She and Harriet began some kind of conference with Ben. They looked like witches, huddled over their glasses, consulting. When I think now that it seemed like some business deal was being struck, my stomach turns.

'Just one drink more,' Georgie said. 'One.'

I said I felt sick.

'Come to the bathroom, come to the bathroom.' Harriet pulled me into the bathroom. Fuck knows what Jack talked about with them while we were gone. I would love to know.

'The thing is,' explained Georgie. 'If you go, then the champagne dries up, and I'm enjoying drinking the champagne.'

She and Harriet giggled.

Harriet said, 'It wouldn't be the first time someone had to take one for the team.'

I thought I knew what they meant, but they couldn't

250

possibly have meant that. And in my naivety, I thought that I must have misunderstood and they were simply asking me to stay. So, I stayed.

We finished the magnum. Kenneth brought out a bottle of vodka with gold leaf in it, floating hideously like glowing spittle chunks in a backwashed water glass. I couldn't drink any of it, and couldn't understand how Harriet and Georgie could drink so much. All those parties they had been to with Tessa while I was lying with my head under the duvet, eating bowls of sugar popcorn and moping for Jack, must have put them in training. I still don't know how they kept their wits about them, but they seemed to.

At one point, Georgie pulled me aside. 'Kenneth wants to know if you've been sexually abused. You haven't, have you?'

I was confused. 'No. Why?'

'He says you're being cold towards him. Like you're scared.'

'I just don't like him like that.'

We must have been in the bathroom or the hall. We were in the hall at one point because we stole packets of tea and shortbread from the trolley which had been parked there.

'They are both so hot,' Harriet said.

'You can have them.'

'They're not interested in us,' Harriet said. 'It's you they want.'

'Both of them?'

'Haven't you ever had a threesome?'

I'd never even had a twosome, but their faces, looking at me like that, made me not want to say so.

'Of course, sort of. If you count youth orchestra,' I muttered.

'Slut,' said Georgie. Then she laughed. Her teeth looked enormous; the wolf that ate Grandma. 'I'm only joking. You're wild. Jack said so.'

'Jack?'

She laughed then. A secret sort of laugh, and I remember a mad jealousy that she and Jack had been talking about me. As well as a sort of diminishing hope, like the Little Match Girl's last flame. I wanted Tessa then. I wanted the armour that came from having a twin, an identical twin at your side. I wanted her to speak for me, to think of something clever to say. 'I think I should check on Tess. She had a bad headache.'

'Tessa's fine.' Georgie grabbed my arm and steered me back into the hotel room. I couldn't stop thinking about that question: had I been sexually abused? Had I buried it, forgotten about it? Was there something wrong with me? With the way I was acting? What if I was an abnormal woman and they were right? I was only nineteen: what could I possibly know about myself? In the upside-down logic of the drunk mind, I felt some obligation to compensate for this sudden notion that I might be frigid, or damaged or that I hadn't woken up in that way yet, or wasn't paying

252

attention to the things that should arouse me. 'Three's your lucky number,' Georgie said. Her eyes twinkled.

I was drunk enough to try to sit on Jack's knee. He massaged my bare shoulders with his warm palms and it made me calm and sleepy.

Then they brought out the drugs. Lines of yellowish powder. Georgie said it was MDMA, but after we had all taken some – snorted it – someone said it was ketamine.

I don't even know how the rest unfolded. I was sitting cuddling Jack one minute, and the next I looked over and he and Georgie were lying on the bed, mouths clamped together like two molluscs fighting, and the narcotic hug I was in turned into a bad trip, and I began to cry. That made everything worse because I could not say – even if I had wanted to, and I didn't – what I was crying about. I didn't have the words. Kenneth took me in his arms, enfolded me, and Ben and Harriet sat in their own little worlds, staring peacefully into space, and I let what I saw as my ruined, damaged, dysfunctional little body be coaxed out of itself by Kenneth's slippery hands.

And then at some point, they all disappeared in a puff of smoke – Harriet, Jack and Georgie – and it was just me and Ben and Kenneth. And I knew somewhere, deep down, that I had been sold for champagne and ketamine. Though if ever I were to say so, I would be laughed at, and told I was making a drama out of something perfectly commonplace – people fucking on

Hogmanay. Threesomes. Hot rich men; expensive hotel rooms. What was I complaining about? I don't even know how to—

Bea did not read on. She looked away, down at the stained Persian rug on the bare floorboards. She felt queasy. She had her own memories of being around older men when she was that age, and knew – or thought she knew – what must be coming. She put the book down, but didn't stuff it behind the cushion. She put it on the coffee table, leaving it brazenly open – for a reason that burned furiously inside her, but which she couldn't articulate. She took the wild garlic leaves and went back to the castle.

16

The whisky bottle sat empty on the kitchen island between them all.

They all looked up as Bea came in.

'We got bored waiting,' Georgie said. 'Melissa put the hare in the oven. Blame her if it's burned.'

'We found some mustard,' Alice offered. 'Christ knows how old it is.'

'It would have been mouldy, if it was old,' Rachael said.

'Anyway, we've cooked the goodness knows what out of it,' Harriet said, 'So no listeria today. Hooray.' She planted her elbow on the counter.

'Smells nice,' Bea said quietly, going over to the oven to have a peek. A gust of hot, peppered air shot out. 'I'll put the rice on.'

'Done,' said Harriet.

'Are there any snacks?' Bea asked.

The others exchanged guilty looks.

She put the wild garlic on the counter and wandered over to the Fortnum's hamper. She found foil wrappers and cellophane, but no food. 'I thought there were crisps left.'

'There *were* crisps,' Alice said, tersely.

'Well, people have been snacking. What do you expect?' Georgie said. 'We don't keep tallies, do we?'

'It's all gone?' Bea asked. 'The nuts and the crackers?'

There was a cold silence. Bea stood back from the bag, trying to keep her face neutral.

'You were gone for ages,' said Alice.

'I got a bit lost in the forest.'

'We were worried, especially after last night.'

'I'm not drunk now.'

Georgie sighed. 'Yes, and there isn't much we can do to fix that.'

Bea was about to ask incredulously if there was no booze left, but their faces told her the answer.

'There must be a wine cellar,' Harriet said.

Georgie perked up. 'That is a very good point. We can go on a treasure hunt after lunch.'

'Why not before?' murmured Harriet.

'If we had something to drink, we could play another round of Never Have I Ever?' Alice suggested.

'What with? Tea?' Georgie's voice was caustic, but the others acquiesced so she sighed and flung teabags into cups. She put the carton of UHT milk they had dug out from one of the cupboards in the centre of the island, next to the empty Lagavulin bottle.

'Very civilised,' Rachael said.

Alice laughed, not kindly, and it seemed to Bea that the pair of them were taking a malicious sort of pleasure in it all. Seeing Georgie forcibly sober was like seeing other women forcibly drunk. It was embarrassing. Bea thought of the open diary.

Then she forced her mind away from it. She drank her hot tea.

Tessa got up and stirred the rice. Instead of coming back to the island she lingered against the Aga.

'Come on, Tess,' Melissa said. 'You're not getting out of it.'

Tessa reluctantly wandered back over.

'I'll start,' said Alice. 'Never have I ever –' She looked into her tea. '– Shat on a female colleague to get an easy promotion.'

'Of course *you* fucking haven't,' Georgie whispered. 'Sorry – did you say shat on or shagged?'

'Georgie,' Harriet warned.

'It's the tea, makes me a bit bitchy.'

'I said shat on,' Alice said. They all looked around at each other. No one drank. 'No one at all? Aren't we all good girls?'

'Alice.' Georgie stared at her. 'I don't know what you are getting at. You have no idea what kind of person I am at work.'

'It's true. We've never met any of your work friends, have we? Why aren't any of them here?'

An uncomfortable silence spread around the island. Alice looked contrite. 'I'm not getting at anything. We're just playing a game of honesty. It's aimed at everyone.'

'Well,' Georgie began. 'Since Harriet doesn't have a job, and Rachael and Mel work with animals, and Tessa's on the bloody saintly NHS—'

'Fuck you!' Harriet slammed down her mug of tea.

'It's a game,' Alice said. 'What do you want me to say? Never have I ever pulled my knickers down in front of a boy?'

'You haven't, have you?'

'I have one,' Rachael said, cutting them all off. The fractured silence was punctured by sips of tea. Behind them, the rice began to boil. Rachael looked around the room. 'Never have I ever shagged an animal.'

'Go on. Drink, Mel,' Georgie said.

'Does accidentally wanking your boyfriend's dog count?' Melissa said, laughing.

'How can you accidentally wank a dog?' Harriet asked.

'If you're lying next to them and – you know, you're stroking them and then it just sort of – pops out, you know.'

'*It?*' said Alice.

'I don't know,' Melissa said. 'You don't mean it to happen! It's just they're obviously turned on by you touching them. Does that count as wanking?'

'Just drink,' Alice sang.

Melissa took a swig of tea, and Bea exchanged a look with Tessa. Tessa looked away quickly.

'Tess – you're up,' Alice said.

'I'm gonna take the hare out of the oven.' She fiddled with the oven gloves.

'OK, I'll go,' Georgie said. She paused. 'Never have I ever slept with someone else's husband.'

'We had that last night,' Harriet complained.

'We had "kissed" last night, not slept with.'

'You're hardly going to have slept with someone without kissing them.'

258

Georgie sighed. 'All right. Never have I ever Facebook-stalked someone.' She cackled and threw back her head. They all drank.

'Tess?' Melissa called over.

'I'm doing the hare.'

'Come on, Tess.' Georgie had perked up. 'Tess, Tess, Tess.' She banged her mug on the counter.

'All right, all right.' Tessa put the casserole dish down and came back to the island. She thought for a second, cradling her tea. The smell of meat and mustard had grown stronger. Tessa tapped her nails against the side of her cup.

Bea felt her stomach slowly drop. She watched Tessa's face, the keen, concentrated expression in her dark eyes and suddenly, very suddenly, she did not want her to say anything at all. Her chest buzzed.

'All right. Never have I ever killed anyone.' Tessa laughed, a small, exploratory giggle.

Harriet joined in, then Melissa.

'We had that last night,' Alice said.

Tessa held up her hand. 'We had "killed a patient by mistake" last night.' She punctuated the words with her finger. 'That only applied to me and Mel.'

'So, like an animal?' Rachael asked. 'In which case.' She laughed. 'Sink 'em down.'

Melissa frowned at her. 'Really?'

'Come on,' Rachael replied. 'You've all killed a rat or a mouse. Or a snake. Or a *tortoise*.'

'I meant a person,' Tessa said.

There was a small silence.

'This isn't really the time to admit to a murder,' Harriet said.

'I didn't say murdered someone, I said killed someone.' Tessa took a sudden, small sip of her drink and then got up from the island. She took the rice off the hob.

'I'll get plates.' Bea stood up quickly.

'Was that an accident?' Georgie asked.

The others were silent. And now Harriet had taken a sip of her drink, too. 'You both just drank?' Georgie said. 'Tess, did you kill someone at work?'

Tessa turned around. 'No, I didn't kill someone at work. What the hell?'

'Sorry,' said Harriet. 'Sorry, I just drank because I wanted something to do with my hands, because you are all such weird witches.'

'Oh my god,' Tessa said, quietly, tasting the rabbit gravy with a teaspoon.

Alice got up to help serve, and Bea ripped the wild garlic leaves and scattered and stirred them into the sauce. They dished out plates of rice and stew. There was only a tiny portion of the meat each.

They all took little, polite bites.

No one spoke.

Harriet put her fork down, spluttering. 'I'm sorry. I know this sounds ungrateful, but . . .' She glanced around. 'Who put the mustard in?'

Alice mumbled, 'I told you that mustard was mouldy.'

'It wasn't mouldy,' Rachael said. 'Anyway, you could have put in just a little bit if you were worried.'

'Maybe if you put a bit more water in,' Bea suggested.

Tessa took another tentative bite, but it was inedible. A small bone cracked on her plate as she tried to peel off some meat.

'How much did you put in?' Harriet asked.

'Not that much,' Alice snapped. 'I don't know how it got this strong. Anyway, I thought we were talking about killing people. Maybe I was just getting in on the act.'

'OK.' Tessa seemed to have come back to herself. Her voice was a bit steadier. 'That was all a little weird before, I know. I think I'm hung-over. Look, what I meant was, has anyone ever killed someone, like in a novel or – or computer game or something? Harriet, you must have killed someone, for example?'

'If you put it like that.' Harriet sipped her tea.

'Ah-ha,' said Georgie. She put down her fork. 'Well, if you'd said that . . . Don't we all kill someone when we make them come? Or is it just men that have *la petite mort*?'

Alice picked up one of the tiny bones of the hare and gnawed the meat off it. 'It's all right nearest the bone.'

'Savage,' Harriet muttered.

'Whose turn is it?' Melissa said.

'I'll go again.' Alice was looking across the table at Harriet. 'Never have I ever had an abortion.'

Someone – Harriet – drew breath sharply.

'Come on, Alice,' Bea said quietly.

'It's a game,' Alice said firmly.

'That's not funny,' Melissa murmured.

'It's not funny when you hold someone's hand on the way

to the clinic and then they make fucking homophobic jokes about you constantly.'

'Who's making homophobic jokes?' Georgie said. 'You're being a cunt. Come on, it's my hen—'

Alice got up and left. Bea jumped as the door to the castle hall slammed.

They all looked at Rachael. She swallowed. 'I'll give her a minute.'

'I just said "savage",' Harriet said. 'It wasn't—'

'I don't think it was the "savage",' Rachael said. She got up. 'I'll make her a cup of tea.'

After Rachael had left, there was a pause. Bea willed Harriet to say something. She felt too cowardly to prompt her, and she wondered briefly if there had been other times at university when she had been too blinkered to notice when Alice was upset, or too weak to say anything. Then Harriet said, 'I'm not going to apologise.'

Georgie sighed. 'Ugh, let's just forget about it. This castle is cursed. This weekend is cursed.'

Tessa got up and began clearing plates away. Bea got up to help her.

'Do you think Tom would know about a wine cellar?' Georgie asked.

'I'm sure if we asked him nicely, he'd give us a bottle of wine,' Melissa suggested.

'One's not really going to cut it, is it? I mean, I'll pay for it,' Georgie said. 'Probably better to ask him, though?'

Tessa turned. 'Wouldn't it be more fun to hunt for it? I mean, there's not much else to do this afternoon.'

Bea couldn't be sure, but thought Tessa had glanced at her. Did she mean for Bea to go and read the rest of the diary?

Georgie checked her phone. 'Four o'clock. Not much left of the afternoon. Is that all the rice gone now?'

'Sorry, Georgie,' Bea said. 'I used the last of it.'

'I wasn't accusing. Just asking.'

'We can ask for another bag,' said Melissa.

'I thought there was some pasta and lentils. I'm sure I saw them in the bag. Tessa, didn't you see?' Harriet asked.

Tessa shook her head. 'I honestly don't remember what I brought. I should have kept a list, sorry.'

'There's more wild garlic,' Bea muttered.

'If I eat any more wild garlic, I'll be sick,' said Harriet.

'So, a treasure hunt?' said Georgie. 'Is anyone going to go and placate the lesbians?'

No one spoke.

Then Tessa said, 'Georgie.'

'Oh, Georgie this, Georgie that! I'm not going to apologise for being myself, you know.' She was quiet for a second. 'Anyway, I prefer Georgina these days. Everyone calls me that at work. Georgie makes me feel like I'm back at uni.'

'I thought that was the point of this weekend,' Harriet said.

'Are your work friends coming to the wedding?' Bea asked.

Georgie shrugged. 'Yes. We had a night out in London. They're not here because Tessa didn't invite them.'

Tessa looked as if she was about to say something, then closed her mouth.

'So, we aren't going to ask Tom about a wine cellar or whether the tree has been—'

263

'Ask me what?'

They had missed the scuffle at the utility door, but now Tom stood there. He had the rosy shine of a hot shower on his face again.

'We had in mind to play a game,' Georgie said quickly. 'Sort of hide and seek in the castle grounds. You don't mind, do you?'

Tom laughed. 'There's plenty of space, for sure. Don't get lost.'

Tessa said quietly, 'There's nothing like a hen party to make you feel five again. And now the sun's coming out.'

Tom let his gaze linger on her for a second. Then he looked away. 'Listen, I just came to update you on the tree. Council says they can definitely get someone out on Monday. No point even trying to find a private contractor.'

'Didn't know that was on the cards,' said Harriet.

He stared at her for a moment. It seemed as if he was trying to place her: as if he might have recognised her. Then he snapped out of it.

'Anyway, sorry about the dogs. They got a bit excited.' He gestured to the counter, where the remains of the hare casserole lay, a brown rim crusting the enamelled cast-iron pot. 'Smells like it was good.'

Georgie snorted.

Melissa cleared her throat. 'Do you think we could have another bag of rice?'

He feigned incredulity. 'Another?'

'There are . . .' Georgie counted on her fingers. 'Seven of us.'

'Eat me out of house and home,' he said. Then, as if he realised it had come out too sharply, he corrected himself. 'Sorry, I'll see what I have in, but I don't know if I have any left, even for me. Not until I get to the shops tomorrow.'

'You could come and have dinner with us? We could all share.' A grin spread across Georgie's face. Bea saw – felt – the room melt away around them until it was only Georgie and Tom left. It was witchcraft, this trick of Georgie's, to make you feel like you were the only one there. It needed to be seen to be believed.

Tom flicked a glance at Tessa. She was cleaning debris from the sink. 'Not much of a holiday, is it? Spending all your time cooking?'

'Oh, we love cooking,' said Georgie. 'Do join us. Don't know what we're going to eat, but the company will be fabulous.' She laughed.

'I'll see what I can do,' he said. 'Heating working? Hot water? Everything else OK?'

They all nodded.

'Sorry to keep bothering you.'

'It's no trouble,' Tessa said. 'I think we're all just glad you're here.'

17

Nobody mentioned the wine cellar to Tom.

When he was gone, Georgie pulled on her hoodie and grimly donned a pair of gloves as if she were about to dig another grave. 'Come on, then. Let's go and track down Tom's Lambrini stash.'

Tessa stayed behind to wash up, giving the promise that she'd follow. She gave them a few directions for the out-buildings she had seen between the castle and the loch, but suggested that they skirt the main building of the castle first to see if they could spot any store cupboards.

Bea, Melissa and Harriet went out with Georgie.

The mood had dipped. No one had eaten much of the ruined hare, and with the snacks and the booze having dried up, now everyone was tired, still hungry, hung-over or on a comedown. It seemed as if they were all just ready for it to be over, to get the extra night over with and to be on the train back to London in the morning, pretending to snooze so they didn't have to speak to each other until it was time for the wedding in a month.

The first thing Tessa did, when the kitchen was sparkling – her cleaning skills had improved since she joined the A & E roster – was to carefully replace the tea towels, hand towels and J-cloths. The ritual was soothing.

Then she went to the food waste bin and removed the biodegradable bag. Luckily, the bin was sloppy enough that no one had noticed the broken crackers, lumps of cheese, chocolates and the charcuterie from the Fortnum's hamper folded in slimy ribbons in among the vegetable peelings. No one had seen the quantity of dried pasta, the full bag of lentils and the three jars of pesto she had tipped into it. She had kept back some of the food in a high cupboard and had thought about snacking on some of these reserves herself, but it didn't seem fair under the circumstances.

Something monastic had overtaken her. Maybe it was the visions she'd had the night before: Ethan's face in the water. Maybe the visions had surfaced from guilt. And that guilt was there to remind her that she was not to enjoy even a second of this weekend, that she had so carefully arranged.

She felt a grim, sliding wetness in her underwear and went to the downstairs loo with her Mooncup – as if the stomach cramps caused by looking at Twitter and Google Maps at Tom's cottage had brought on her blood.

She heard Alice and Rachael talking as they came back down into the kitchen. She couldn't make out what they were saying, but Alice was complaining, Rachael placating. They were also – it was very clear from the pauses between their speaking – eating something. Crunching. They were sharing furtive food. They had waited, Tessa calculated, until there was no one there, and now they were snacking on some squirrelled-away sustenance, while everyone else squabbled over pieces of a caught hare soused in the mustard Tessa had chucked in herself with the purpose of spitefully ruining it.

Tessa waited, putting her elbows on her knees and her head in her hands. There was something comforting about people being in the house, in the castle, now. Seeing it full. Her parents refused to come here any more. Well, that wasn't quite true. They came for clear-outs. And left, having cleared out nothing. They kept on top of the holiday bookings and told themselves that they were keeping it because it was a useful business to have in their portfolio – especially now Airbnb made it easier to find guests – and not because it was, in some ways, a mausoleum, or a shrine.

They didn't take trips to the castle as a family any more. Sasha and Brian maybe came with Ethan and their own children, once or twice a year. She didn't know. And Ethan came by himself to stay with Tom and Jenny sometimes.

Tom had said he was teaching Ethan how to fish. But they didn't take the kind of trips that they had used to, boisterous and noisy, full of late nights and chaotic food and the lovely clean grime of the outdoors.

She had felt then not like they were interlopers to the area, but more like the adders who hibernated for winter and then came out and danced in spring. They had known people in the village back then. They'd had friends. They'd held ceilidhs in the grounds, used the castle for the local am-dram's open-air Shakespeare. Tessa still remembered being eight or nine and watching Puck and Titania, with dyed pheasant feathers all over themselves, using the kitchen as a dressing room.

Fuck knows what the locals thought of them now. She considered herself worldly enough not to deceive herself that anyone in any old village liked big-house owners to begin with, especially ones who came and went.

Now, she felt as if they must all be pariahs. Tessa had heard their names whispered in shops and from taxi drivers. The rich people got what they deserved, but at the expense of a stain left on the beautiful old castle. Tessa didn't blame the villagers for gossiping about them. They had become local lore now.

When she had received the message from Georgie, the plea for them all to be bridesmaids – sent via WhatsApp, but carefully worded, with emojis and hearts in the right places – when she had received that message and its accompanying appeal for a weekend hen party to rediscover those crazy, beautiful days, coming here had seemed to her like the only thing to do.

Here was the hidden part of Tessa's soul: the dark woodland on the other side of the water, the place that she had carried around with her for all of those university years.

It felt strange now, listening to Alice and Rachael, and knowing that Melissa and Bea and Harriet and Georgie, even, had gone off to hunt for wine. It felt strange that, inside Tessa, instead of bitterness or passion or fire or revenge, she felt in that moment only a nostalgic sort of peace. But at the same time, it made perfect sense. It made sense to her to feel the castle being inhabited once again, to feel it come alive.

18

I go over that night again and again.

Sometimes I even change what happened, so that at some point I pick up the samurai sword from the ottoman at the foot of the bed and slice into both of them. Sometimes, I split them down the middle, like a video-game murder. Sometimes, I cut cleanly through their veins and sit cross legged, watching them twitch and bleed. I imagine that, after their deaths, I will be handcuffed and taken to a police station, put in one of those white paper hooded suits and made to submit to an interview. At the very least, even if I accuse them both of rape, then I will be charged with manslaughter.

Sometimes, in my dreams, I cut off their heads or club their brains like they are wild wolves. I enact terrible violence on them.

And it's this which lets me know that now there is

*terrible violence in me. Violence I didn't know existed
before.*

*People talk about birth as if it is a very violent thing.
But there is a difference between violence and pain. I
think I know that now. Or maybe I'm just unable to
see past my own experience.*

*Mum doesn't like it when I talk about these things.
She says I am simply tired. Of course it is inevitable that
I will have 'some regrets'. 'Some regrets' is the phrase
she chooses. It sounds winsome and respectable to
have regrets. If I have regrets, though, they are neither
winsome nor respectable.*

*My regrets are the shape of human organs, pulpy and
crimson, red and wet and menacing. They are organs
with teeth growing in them. And while you can't see
their faces, they bite when you least expect it.*

Bea remembered the sheets of paper that had fallen out
of the diary when she'd first opened it in the cottage. They
had fluttered to the floor in her haste to close the book, and
were still lying face down where she had left them.

She had peeled off from the others once again, this time
less conspicuously, since Alice and Rachael had also disappeared. Georgie and Harriet had found a locked door
on the far side of the castle, near the old stable block, and
Melissa had gone back to the hall to see if she could find a
key. Bea had said that she would continue to look for the
old ice house that might now be used for wine.

It was warmer now. This afternoon's rain had given way

271

to a balmy afternoon damp. She listened to the sounds of the outdoors, filtered through the stone walls, and although she was listening for anyone coming to find her, the sounds that came through the closed door were also comforting.

She looked at the papers. They were printed with a grid, boxes scribbled in blue ink. Bea recognised it as a cognitive therapy table. The columns read: 'Situation', 'Immediate thought', 'Evidence or justification', 'Evidence against' and 'Alternative thought'. Onto this neat, clean template of order and reason, Charlie had scrawled her most intimate, self-loathing convictions. The first one read: *'Situation: he cries and I no longer care. Immediate thought: I am an abomination.'*

Bea placed them face down on the arm of the chair. She felt a strange and horrid conflation of feelings. She would not weep at this; she could not peer like a voyeur into someone else's life and then pretend she was touched and weep at what she saw – vulgar, hungry vulture that she was.

But the recognition, even in the hasty scrawl, was too much to bear.

Back then, when her babies were tiny and she was in her own purgatory, she'd had people to lean against, places to run and hide in. She'd had the entire female complement of Mohammed's family – his two sisters, his mother, his aunt, who was constantly making soup – and the baffled members of her own family. She had always known that, while she was inside her private shame, at least her babies were safe.

She picked up the diary again with a grim hunger, and a need now to reach the end, to know.

8 April 2007

I am struggling to remember now what I was like as a pregnant woman. Where was the fluttering warning, or the warm, spreading feeling, the thrum of life buzzing inside me and making me feel fecund, those things D. H. Lawrence or other poetic men who have written about pregnancy would have you believe?

I must have been pregnant by the time the ski season came to a close. Would I have been pregnant the very next day? If I go back to that day in my mind, and scrub myself thoroughly, what happens next? Does it all disappear?

We didn't see Kenneth and Ben the next day, but at some point during the wee hours of that night, I remember one or both of them had walked me back to my cabin.

When I saw them afterwards – at the bar, or around the resort, they did not try to touch or kiss me again, though they did acknowledge me.

Is that to their credit?

There is no way to know which of them is Ethan's father.

I tell myself it does not matter.

I didn't tell Tessa what happened. I had the impression that she had begun to sulk at me, and that maybe she was a bit jealous of our party that night. Looking back, I think that we both knew something had driven *a spear between us, but in one of those strange, horrid happenings of the soul, neither of us knew how to open a conversation about it.*

Georgie changed too, almost overnight. Once Harriet had gone home, and once it became clear she and Jack were now a couple – whatever happened that night cemented it – she lost, for a while, her steely edge. She was coy with me, but she never spoke about Kenneth or Ben; nor did she ever ask what had happened. She was beyond tight-lipped. And I had the impression that if I ever brought it up, something terrible would end up being said. And that seemed somehow the worst thing that could happen. The terror of that kept my mouth shut.

Better to forget, and to stay friends.

If we saw them in the resort, she was polite. But under her breath, she would say: 'Jesus Christ, that night.'

When we got back early in January 2006, Tessa and I found jobs in London. She was working in a shoe shop, where she got nice discounts and brought home lovely leather boots. I worked in a bar with a beach theme, which I liked because it had a student vibe and it was a safer form of travel than leaving London again.

I put my back out lifting a keg one day, and the next I felt sick from morning to night and couldn't eat a thing. Then it occurred to me that it had been five weeks since my last period, which had faded out some time around Christmas. I convinced myself I was only sick with anxiety, and the reason my period hadn't come was that I had not been eating healthily.

I told Tessa and Mum I had food poisoning, and after a couple of days moping in the house, I went back to work.

I was training myself to forget about Jack. I really think I would have succeeded if he hadn't come into the bar that day. He said he had messaged me and I hadn't replied. But when I checked my phone, there was nothing. We talked about nothing at all for a while – films and books, skirting anything real – and then suddenly he told me, quite abruptly, that he was glad it was all over with Georgie. She was so 'full on'; he felt as if he had shaken a second skin. I think maybe it was that phrase, the way he said it, appealing to me to collude with him, that put a splinter of doubt in me about him. I had a sudden wave of sympathy for Georgie.

'She's just a clown. She does it because it's her only way of being with people,' I said. 'She's harmless.'

Jack shook his head. His hands cradled his brow. 'Is she always off her head?'

This was a difficult question to answer. You see, the way I remember Georgie, she loved to see other people high. She was never quite as out of it as her friends were. Maybe she just liked to see others happy?

'I haven't had a sober day since we were together. I just feel like we're, like Wino and – whatshisname?'

I didn't remember his name, either. Jack offered me a smoke. That was the moment I admitted to myself

275

I was pregnant; instinct made me say no. And then, immediately, I was reminded of that other time when he had offered me weed and I had stood him up. I felt then as if I had crossed the bridge already. I didn't connect with him or his world any more.

That was the first grief I felt. Heartbreak, the feeling that the younger part of me who was brutally in love with Jack had died, and I could no longer access her. It's incredible to go through life to the age of nineteen without knowing what grief feels like. I did not know then that I was going to grieve again and again and again.

Did Jack come to see me in those moments as a last-ditch attempt to kindle something between us? Was he hedging his bets? Trying to backtrack? Is it arrogant of me to even dream that he liked me?

I'll never know. I could not touch him. We said goodbye for the first time without a hug.

10 April 2007

He chucked her later that day, and then a few weeks later she chucked him, and I lived vicariously through their battles, over text and Skype.

I brokered and nursed and mended their relationship in wee-hours texts and late-night video calls with both of them. All the while, the baby grew, and I ignored the bloating and disguised the sickness and told myself I was a fantasist, a catastrophist. I was not pregnant. And if I was, it would go away of its own accord.

At different times, I had extravagant fantasies of the mother I would be. It was real, all of it, and I, Charlie Lockwood, aged nineteen, would give birth, goddess-like and fertile as Angelina Jolie, carry my child in a bamboo fibre sling, nurse him – it was always him, even before I knew he was him – while I studied. Late-night feeding sessions, beautiful weariness, worldly knowledge, earth mother. I would be more than any girl in my class, because I had made the transition.

But when it came to telling Mum and Dad, I was a coward and asked Tess to do it for me. I had told her when it was no longer possible to cover myself up in slouchy jumpers, when the sun came out in April and we were gearing up for our last summer together, making travel plans, and debating the countries we could go to. I told her I could not have the vaccinations because ...

And, of course, she knew already. Because she is my twin.

It isn't – it wasn't – telepathy, the way they say twin telepathy is. But she knew my body, she knew the shape of it and the way we both put on weight. There was no difference between us. And so, when my waist mysteri-ously expanded and hers didn't, and my breasts grew a cup size bigger than hers ... She knew before I had admitted it to myself.

She didn't want to know anything about how the baby came about. Which was hurtful, but also a relief.

And I found I couldn't talk about it – I couldn't tell her, it always jammed in my mouth, even though I knew she sort of knew.

It was Georgie who offered to take me to the clinic.

It was a gloomy April day, warm but overcast, when we tried to cross the line of protesters. I had just about managed to walk the gauntlet when one of them shoved a fingerless glove clutching a picture of a foetus under my nose, and offered me 'help and salvation'. The only reason I didn't collapse was because Georgie caught me.

We went to a café instead. I was shaking, and she told me that she had chucked Jack once and for all. They were no good for each other. He was too poetic, too intense. He demanded too much love. He fucked weirdly. And he loved to take drugs now.

For God's sake, she only offered him ket once, and now he wouldn't shut up about it, was always pressuring her to get more and more and more, and she worried that it was because – because – if he wasn't high he couldn't stand to be around her.

I think that was the closest I came to some sort of understanding of Georgie, in the café round the corner from the clinic, drinking builders' tea.

Tessa goes on and on about how it should have been her who went with me, about how she never would have let the protester get anywhere near me with that flyer.

But the fact was, she didn't come with me and she wasn't there.

I don't know if I like the sentiment of her saying that now. Saying she feels guilty that I didn't not have my son. I know it pains her to see me like this, and yes, there is now someone who, by default, I ought to be closer to than my twin. But when my mind twists, I take this as her saying that it wasn't right for me to have Ethan. And despite everything, the thing that hurts the most is that it was right. I know it was right.

15 April 2007

Tessa says I have PTSD from the birth. She says that many women do. She says she had been researching it even before I gave birth, which to me sounds a bit fishy, as if she was waiting for it to happen.

I think by research she means googling, which doesn't really count, does it?

She was there with me. She saw that the birth wasn't traumatic. The midwife said so. She said that the teenage pregnancies like this always made the easiest births, and in fact that was the bit that shocked me the most; that she called me a teenage pregnancy.

I went into a bubble during labour and that protected me from thinking too much about it. It was something to focus on, like a brutal sprint, the hardest circuit class in the world. It stopped me from confronting what was coming next, which was the worst night of my life.

It was the shock of him that did it. Froze me like a deer. The very fact that he existed and breathed by himself, and was not just a part of my body, as I think I had always thought he would be. Mum was there, and I knew as soon as I saw her holding him that she was looking for signs of his father.

That moment was the first of the curtains dropping – or maybe it is better to say that the world turned half an inch. I seemed to have slipped outside myself, but only a very fractional amount, and I could see outwards from a different angle.

This feeling would come, and it would go, and then it would come again. Like when I saw the hospital reception, and instantly remembered not the frightened girl who had come in, in waves of pain, her jeans soaking because the sanitary towel could not keep pace with the waterfall of amniotic fluid, but the girl who had come last month for her final scan. Full of cockiness, a sort of practised optimism about the mother she would be. In all of these confident visits, it had never been about Ethan – it was always about me. I hadn't registered that he would be here; that, at the end of the labour, he would be the centre of all attention. Even mine, so that even I forgot myself.

Bea took a break. She could still hear the soft green noises through the door. There was no sign or sound of Georgie, Harriet and Melissa. They must have found something – if not the wine cellar, then something to take their attention.

She had stopped because it seemed to her too much of a violation to be reading another woman's birth story.

For her, the most brutal moment had been seeing the twins taken to the NICU. The first one couldn't breathe; the second couldn't feed. Noor's mouth was too small and Lila couldn't latch. Her sense of failure – of having failed them before she had even begun to mother them – took her breath away. She lay awake for most of the first night, breathless and gaping empty, and yet relieved on some guilty level that they were not there, because she was exhausted and all she wanted was for her body – stabbed and picked over, her vagina cut – to be left alone.

And yet, her body could not be left alone. The most important thing was to tick down the minutes before she could try to pump milk again, before the milk would invariably fail, the hospital-grade pump yanking her nipples into odd sucked shapes, the trickles to be ferried in surgical bottles to where her babies were being kept, looked after not by her, but by people whose bodies they had never touched or smelled before.

All of them, pulled apart like comets.

How easy, she had thought bitterly, how easy mothers of one baby have it.

That first night was only one of the many subsequent reasons she had not wanted to see Harriet again for a long time. She had ignored her emails and chatty, advice-filled messages; she had ignored all of them. She knew something about herself now that they didn't, that she didn't want them to know. And didn't, for that matter, want her old university self to know. It was safer to keep the two worlds apart.

Bea looked out of the cottage window at the crenelated ridges of the castle poking high above the trees, its beautiful geometry and its age, filled with antique trinkets. She thought about the diary lying there, in the cobwebs of the attic, for ten years, like a . . . She didn't want to think about what it was like. She stroked the pages of the diary, as if by stroking Charlie's handwriting she could touch her and find some way to cradle her in her hands.

19

'You found it!' Tessa crouched in the doorway to the castle cellar, her body silhouetted into a knot by the late afternoon sun. Behind her, the lawn was damp and dewy from the afternoon's rain.

She watched Georgie and Melissa on their hands and knees, picking over rolling dusty bottles, like pirates rummaging through treasure. Harriet stood coolly against the wall, smoking a cigarette, something Tessa had not seen her do since university.

Georgie looked up at Tessa, all malice gone, a huge grin on her face. 'The vintages! Tessa, my darling, you could not have planned this better. Treasure!'

Tessa laughed. 'True.'

The cellar was small, stretching back about six feet from the open door. It was damp. Green algae crept up the walls and the painted white ceiling was speckled with black mould. Once you crawled through the tiny entrance, the floor sloped away, and the cellar sunk down lower into the castle's foundations. There were three wooden wine racks, all rickety and rotting, looking as if they hadn't been touched for years, the bottles covered in dust. More bottles of wine were stuffed into half barrels, and a few rolled on the floor. Some were smashed, sticky red contents long absorbed by the dust. Others had labels gnawed off or faded.

Georgie was holding a bottle of red with gold writing on a cream label. 'This says 1987! Does old mean better?'

Harriet sucked her breath in and coughed out smoke.

Tessa shrugged. 'Does it matter?'

Georgie laughed, full throated. 'Could be rats' piss, right, so long as it's got booze in it. I honestly don't know how I could survive another night in this place without a drink. Hallelujah!' She thrust the wine bottle up above her head, misjudging the ceiling height and bumping the glass with a clang.

'Georgie,' Harriet warned.

'Oh my God, whoever suggested looking for a wine cellar is a genius. Was it my suggestion? I wonder when it was last raided, though. All of the bottles look old.'

'This one doesn't.' Melissa was holding up a champagne bottle, a *Grand Cru* with 2006 emblazed on the front of the label.

'The year we went to university,' Tessa said.

'Well,' Georgie said. 'We can put that in the fucking ancient pile. Feels like moons ago. Mind you, I think this hen weekend has taken years off my life. No offence, Tessa.'

Tessa shrugged again. She brushed a cobweb from the doorway and jumped back out of the cellar door onto the fresh grass.

'Do you think we're allowed?' she heard Melissa asking. 'I mean, they must belong to the family that owns the castle, surely?'

'Don't you think we should ask Tom?' Harriet agreed. 'I would have thought under the circumstances – I mean, he can't really say no. We could make out that we were on the verge of asking for a refund, because of the tree.'

'He can't really help the tree.' Melissa crawled back out onto the lawn and crouched next to Tessa.

'Do you know, ladies – or should I say lassies?' Georgie said, clambering out of the hole and strapping an arm about Tessa's neck, and another round Melissa's. 'Do you know, I think if one has 1987 plonk gathering dust in one's rat-dropping'd *wine cellar* I think one can afford to miss a couple of bottles, wouldn't you say?'

'It's theft,' Melissa said weakly.

'It's not really theft. More like redistribution. Or like, say, a chocolate on a hotel pillow.'

'Robin Hood, are you?' Harriet said, joining them. 'Steal from the Airbnb wine cellar to give to the—' She didn't finish her sentence. She flicked the cigarette into the grass, then thought better of it and picked it up, stubbing it against the wall before wrapping it in a tissue and putting it in her pocket. 'It's just that Freddie's family are so sick of people trashing their country house and nicking things.'

'Why do they put it on Airbnb, then?' Tessa watched her, but she just shrugged.

'It's what you do.'

Georgie had picked at random – one red, one sparkling

white. Not a champagne, though it was possible she hadn't noticed this.

'Where did Bea get to?' Melissa asked.

'She's been doing a vanishing act since we got here,' said Georgie. 'Possibly she has realised that, after four years of avoiding us, she doesn't actually like us?' She spoke without feeling, more amusement.

'I think she's enjoying being away from her children,' Harriet said drily.

'Speak for yourself.' Georgie laughed. 'Neither of you make motherhood sound very appealing, I have to say.' Her glance skipped past Harriet and landed on Tessa for a fleeting second.

Harriet looked down at her pockets, fiddled for her phone, took it out, and put it away again. She looked suddenly uncomfortable; restless, or perhaps just bored.

'What are you doing with that phone, Harriet?' Georgie said. 'You've been doing that all weekend. It's not like a signal is going to miraculously pop up after twenty-four hours. Or is it that you don't trust Freddie and the au pair?'

Harriet tutted gently, but Tessa noticed her cheeks reddening as she turned away. It was rare to see Harriet blush and Tessa had never, to her memory, seen her cry.

'Do you miss them?' Tessa asked.

Harriet gathered herself and looked back up, cool again. 'It's the first time I've been away from them overnight.'

'Really?' Georgie said. 'Five years. Jesus Christ. No dirty weekends while the grandparents pitched in?'

Harriet scoffed. 'It's not that simple.' Her eyes narrowed.

'You don't expect them to be everything, but suddenly they are. Perhaps one day you'll understand.' There was a small, stony pause. Tessa thought of the blog consuming Harriet's novel writing. The image that came to her was of a tiny wet mouth opening wide and gobbling up page after page after page of typewritten text.

'Just wait till Jack starts cooing about little Georgie-Jacks,' Melissa said, smiling and grasping hold of Georgie's hand, which was still dangling about her shoulder. The wine bottle swung dangerously between them.

Georgie looked as if she was searching for a riposte, then she changed her mind and just smiled. 'Yeah.'

'What are we going to have with our wine, then?' Tessa asked.

'I'm fine with a liquid dinner,' Georgie said, then laughed again. Melissa joined in. Harriet looked away. 'Two bottles,' Georgie continued. 'Do you think we should take some more now? Between seven of us, that's going to go in about ten minutes.'

'Speak for yourself,' Harriet muttered.

Georgie ignored the remark. Instead, she looked up at the castle and sighed. 'Gorgeous, isn't it? Did you say it was based on a Disney castle? That's why it's pink.'

'Other way round,' Tessa said.

Georgie cackled. 'Always the clever one, Tess.' She wagged her finger. They had rounded the corner, passed by the arch to the archery range and were approaching the vegetable garden. 'Alfresco tipple?'

'I'll go and get some glasses,' Harriet said, striding ahead.

'See if you can track down Alice,' Georgie began. 'Oh no, don't bother. Fuck them, more for us.'

Georgie studied the label of each of the bottles while Melissa trailed her hand among the herbs, breaking off leaves here and there, rubbing them between her fingers and sniffing them.

'I wonder how long these have grown here.' She breathed in a sprig of rosemary. Tessa bent down and sank her face into a clump of sage.

'Tess,' Georgie suddenly said. Tessa straightened up and looked across at her. Georgie was looking intently at her, and it took Tessa a few seconds to realise – or at least to think that she realised, with a shock – that Georgie was not in fact looking *at* her, but looking *into* her. Maybe for signs of someone else. It was as if she carried a ghost around with her, from time to time.

Georgie held out her arms. 'Hug.' The wind was blowing strands of her hair across her face. She put one of the bottles down to pick the hair from her mouth. She embraced Tessa and spoke into her hair. 'This is much better than anything I could have thought of, despite – you know. Me being a control freak and an Airbnb nut and all of that. You're all here and that's all that matters.'

Melissa laughed loudly. She had a kind sort of laugh, Tessa thought. Light and breezy. Melissa had always struck Tessa as kindly, but a little vapid. She had thought back at university that Melissa probably wouldn't finish vet school, but would end up downgrading to biomedical sciences or one of the components, chemistry or something. But there she was, sticking her hand up cows' bums and birthing lambs and driving a Range Rover round Suffolk. Perhaps, Tessa thought, maybe for the first time, Melissa wasn't vapid at all, she was only kind. She didn't really seem to dislike anyone, but then maybe that was because she was beautiful, or because she had no trauma to skew her.

'I'm having a really good time,' Melissa said, softly. 'I love the countryside, and we couldn't have asked for better weather – apart from the rainstorm. But that makes everything smell nice the next day, doesn't it?'

'Are you sure it's not just the dregs of the ket making everything smell nice?' Tessa laughed. She had always liked this herb garden. It had been there since the eighteenth century, her mum had told her; never changed.

Melissa suddenly gave a small cry, and Tessa and Georgie followed her gaze down to the edge of the flowerbed.

'Oh, crumbs,' Georgie said. There, on the edge of the spinach patch, where they had dug it over, the earth had been turned up and roughed into a mound. Poking out, its lifeless body lolling in an uncanny and horrible twist, was the adder they had buried the night before.

'One of the dogs must have dug it up,' Melissa said, going over.

Georgie looked suddenly queasy. 'It's horrible. I wish that whole thing hadn't happened.'

Tessa saw Georgie shudder. Harriet came striding back at that moment, bearing the glasses, followed by Alice and Rachael. They saw straight away where the others were looking.

'Yuck,' Alice said. 'How on earth did that get back up here?'

'One of the—' Melissa stopped herself.

'One of the dogs,' Rachael said. 'Disgusting.'

'See?' said Alice. 'They *are* disgusting. Digging up snakes.'

'They're just animals,' Melissa said. She nudged the adder gently with the toe of her boot, pushing some of the earth back over it. 'Same as us.'

Rachael snorted.

'What?' Melissa looked at her. 'Aren't we animals?'

'I think we're something else,' Rachael said quietly. 'Something worse.'

'Worse than that?' Georgie pointed with the toe of her shoe.

'I never saw a snake come after anyone with a meat cleaver,' Rachael said.

Georgie looked at her for a second, then laughed her raucous laugh. 'I can't believe that happened. It is one for the grandchildren,' she said, shaking her head, as if she had not, only minutes earlier, said quietly that she wished it had not happened. But perhaps, thought Tessa, she had not been referring to the snake at all – but to something else entirely.

Then she saw Bea emerging from the old gardener's cottage, and every other thought disappeared from her mind.

20

Bea had sat with the diary pressed to her chest for a few minutes, keeping the ghosts in its pages trapped. She wondered what time it was, and if the others were looking for her. And then a sabotaging selfishness kicked in. They would not miss her. She did not care if it was rude to disappear; they would not care. She was winded by what she had just read, and she wanted to read it again. She couldn't get the image of her own two girls out of her mind, sitting side by side, arguing over a pile of toys, then shrieking and refusing to eat because they were not wearing the same shoes. It all seemed so trivial to her now, so piss-boil irritating; things that Harriet, for instance, with her know-it-all blog on parenting, never had to deal with. But there was something her girls were knitting between them that Bea would never be able to grasp, something she could only watch and hope was never ripped apart.

She opened the book and turned back to the final few pages.

20 April 2007

They pushed me to come here. Mum said I was not doing well in London, and that it was probably the bustle of the streets, which she thinks aren't the place to wander with a buggy or a baby in a sling. She said that I would be closer to Tessa's university up here and that nature would be good for me.

But I knew she was ashamed of me. Sometimes when she took him for a cuddle it felt as though he was being torn from me, rather than taken off my hands for a minute.

When he cries, my lungs tighten. I know mothers are supposed to respond physically to their baby crying, but I thought it would be more bittersweet, with the pleasure you sometimes have when someone you love dearly cries and you are able to comfort them. Instead, his cries are alien and I flinch. In A-level biology, we learned that our bodies have automatic functions. They serve us like a team of staff, working behind the scenes. We are shackled to biology, unable to escape our instincts. I am terrified of what might be love but feels more like something suffocating, that I want to run from. I suppose it is a twisted mirror image of the love I wanted to run away from in Jack.

So, at the start of the spring, they finally said they wanted me to go to the castle, in the hope that the woods and the sea would become my natural habitats.

Mum said she would help me transfer doctor's surgery so I could still see a health visitor, and she would pay for all the help I needed. It would make a couple of jobs for people from the village, she said. Maybe Jenny, the housekeeper, could move in permanently. Who wouldn't want to live in a castle? I only found this out later, when I mentioned something about us all living there together again and she said, 'You don't expect me to commute to chambers in London from there? We'll get a groundsman and you can have paid help.'

Bea thought of the nights Mo had taken one baby from her arms, his mother another, when all three of them had been lying in an awkward, uncomfortable embrace, bloated with angry tears, no milk left in her, no chance of replenishing the milk without sleep.

Back then, she had strongly felt the pull of the pack, of the need to keep everyone close. Stepping out into Kentish Town High Road had felt so extraordinarily alien. And yet, the polluted air had been good for her. Its normality, its fullness of people and all of their pollution and grace was sometimes what had kept her from falling apart. She could not imagine being surrounded by nature. There was already too much nature, too much raw nature confined within her tiny flat.

Here there were forests and the sea loch; the whole estate dripped beauty, breathed peace. But it was a hoarded beauty, a selfish peace. She wondered if the ability to hold on to such wealth was rooted in the same trait that enabled you to send your daughter away with her newborn, to be looked after by strangers. There was cruelty in wealth; she had seen it at university and she saw it in Georgie. But she did not see it in Tessa.

She counted back over the years. Charlie must have been nineteen or twenty when the baby was born. That meant she, Bea, would just have met Tessa in first year. She couldn't remember where they had met, or the occasion, but their paths had crossed in the pub and at house parties, and she knew that Tessa was studying medicine. With a larger workload than the humanities students, she had only popped up every now and then, had disappeared for weeks at a time. It hadn't seemed odd, this disappearing act.

She'd known Tessa had an older sister, Sasha, and she had certainly mentioned a nephew – maybe two, in fact. But not a twin.

Tessa had never mentioned Charlie to Bea. Not once.

27 April 2007

I've moved into the old gardener's cottage. I couldn't bear the emptiness of the castle. It made me feel like Rapunzel.

Jenny stays most nights. Sometimes she sleeps over in the cottage, on the sofa. Sometimes she stays next door, but knowing she is there makes me feel safer for both of us. Tom comes over for his tea – I tease him that I hope Ethan will not be coming to his mum's for dinner at that age. But I think it is nice having more people around. He always asks how the diary is coming along; is it helping me to see things from a distance? And when I give him a one-or-two-word answer, he never probes further.

Tessa comes to visit as much as she can. Mum was right, it is easier for her to visit me here. And Georgie goes to St Andrews too. It's only about an hour and a half away, and because they have a break at the moment before their exams, Tess stayed a bit longer. The days before her visit were almost better; I spent the visit itself knowing she'd have to go back.

She is beautiful with Ethan. I feel no jealousy, seeing her sway him from side to side. She seems more natural at it than me, less anxious. But then, when I watch her, I also see how people might see me.

1 May 2007

I went down to London last week. Tessa helped me on to the train with him, and Georgie came by; a surprise visit. She is back with Jack. She talked about Virginia Woolf and Samuel Beckett and about Jack and I cried a lot.

I tried to reassure her that no, she was not upsetting me. It was 'just hormones'. But inside, I felt like an idiot for feeling something as base and unmaternal as jealousy. I can't put it in any more dignified terms than that.

Halfway through the visit, I think I was crying because Ethan had bitten me when he was feeding.

Georgie started to say, 'God, Charlie, I just feel so bad about what happened that day.' And at first, I was confused and wondered why she had said 'day' instead of 'night'. But then as I was about to correct her, I realised what she meant, the day at the clinic, and after that I could not get it out of my head, every time I looked at her for the rest of the trip. It sat in my mind like a spider lurking in a web, threads vibrating right down into my gut.

I have become determined to love him. My love for him will be a huge tempest of love. It will be my greatest revenge to the gods. All of my love, smothering and drowning everything else, as violent as the wind.

2 May 2007

Ethan continues his weaning. Tom brought vegetables he had grown in the garden, sprouting broccoli and last year's broad beans for me to puree. He is strange and lovely with Ethan and we were both excited to see Ethan taste them.

We are forming quite an odd little family, and sometimes I catch myself with how nice it can be. Tom has said that a man in the village is selling a boat, just a wooden rowing thing, but he says he can take me out on the sea loch, and in the summer there will be mackerel and, if I like, he can put down some mussel ropes.

He has a strange accent and tattoos on his arms, very

roughly drawn. He told me he worked in the merchant navy but his story doesn't add up, and I think he might have been in prison.

Anyway, he seems to like practical, quiet things. He is nice. He swears his accent is Scottish, but it's so mild it sounds more American sometimes, and other times I wonder if he is Irish. Jenny says they used to live in Dundee. I don't know what made them move. She is a very loving woman, but it seems odd for a man of his age, forty or so, maybe a bit younger, to follow his mother around. She isn't frail. Quite the opposite.

4 May 2007

Ethan loves carrot. He loves peas, apples, pears, rice and porridge. Jenny says the porridge will put hairs on his chest. I said I hope not, that would look weird, especially since he has none on his head yet. He is completely bald still. At the moment I feel quite optimistic and it is a bizarre feeling. It is very dependent on sleep. Mum came to see me and said, 'See, it was only sleep all along, that was all that was wrong.'

Then the health visitor came yesterday and when she gave me the questionnaire to fill in, I answered carefully and I passed with flying colours. I am officially not depressed, she said. So that is that.

But I think it is Ethan. He is so fucking cute right now.

I can't think of him as mine or anyone's; it's like he has been beamed down from outer space. But I am starting to love him as a human, as someone I am falling in love with because I have met them, and the more I get to know them, the more I realise how utterly intoxicating and beautiful they are. Actually, if anything, he looks like a chubby version of Jack.

5 May 2007

Tom took me out in the boat today. 'She' – he calls the boat 'she', which sounds both gallant and creepy – is painted white and blue. It is beautiful to be on the water. I want to take Ethan out, but Jenny says it is not a good idea.

We caught seven mackerel. They are precious as platinum. I will preserve them – he will show me how. Some days, Jenny goes to the village and I feel OK about that now. Some days, I go to the village on my own with Ethan and it is nice. I see Audrey, who owns the organic café, and Alistair, who works in the library. And there is a lady with multi-coloured hair at the Scotmid, whose name I don't know, but who is sort of my most confessional friend. She seems to understand that when I complain about this or that, I am not really complaining, but just loosening the things that are tied tight to my chest. We laugh, and she gives me tips on weaning. I entertain dreams sometimes on my walks back. Fantasies, that perhaps when Ethan is older, perhaps when I am feeling better, I could invite them round for a picnic lunch. I feel not so much like the girl who holidayed in the castle, but someone who lives here now.

Tom is becoming a good friend, too. I tease him that when he has Ethan in his arms, he looks like a natural.

8 May 2007

The visions have come back.

They were the reason Tom told me to write the journal in the first place, what seems like a long time ago now, when I had just arrived and he caught me on my knees in the vegetable garden in floods of tears, Ethan dumped in a patch of sprouting broccoli. At that time, I had no coherence in my head – I could not have strung a sentence together about how I feel now, let alone tried to explain it. He told me to start at the beginning, with the things I did know. And I've done that. But some days, I feel as if it hasn't made a difference at all. I don't know what is happening to my soul. Surely it is not just my mind. It is more consuming than that; it grasps my body.

I am part-monster, and I have seen my monstrous part. To tell Tessa this would be too much. To say anything to Mum would be out of the question; she would have me locked up, and I already feel exiled here. Jenny seems so naturally loving, I couldn't cope with the look on her face. There isn't a cat in hell's chance someone like her could ever possess such darkness in her, and I can't bear the thought that every time she looked at me she would see the darkness in me.

They are flashes; gone as quickly as they come. Just a short, bright photograph my mind creates, unbidden. But once I've seen it, it stays with me all day.

I can't help but think that my subconscious knows something about me that I don't. I have always felt assured that people who do horrid things are different to the rest of us, and that they must know they are different: marked. Maybe it is because I have been phys-ically weak all of my life. There was never the question of ever being able to overpower someone, or perform atrocities on their body – they would overpower me back before I had the chance.

But does anyone know they are a monster before the monster in them shows itself? Or are we all just time bombs, waiting for the right – or wrong – spark?

12 May 2007

His face is blurred by water. My hands are around his throat. His cheeks swell and he cries silently, the bubbles choking him – me choking him.

And then it is gone.

I am bathing him again, holding the sponge above his head, squeezing the water down his back. His mouth gapes open.

Laughing, not screaming.

15 May 2007

It's always the water.

This time I'm changing him. I take the water cup I keep for the cotton wool and throw it in his face. He chokes on the splashes, drips. The shock confuses him.

Then it's gone. He is smiling, locking his brown eyes on mine, his open toothless mouth.

I have thrown away the water cup now. We will use baby wipes from now on. I don't care about the environment any more, anyway.

'If you have a vision of throwing your baby over the bannister, don't panic,' Mo's mother had said to Bea while she was still pregnant, laughing, not unkindly.

Bea had laughed back because she felt it was the only sensible way to respond.

'It's OCD. I used to have intrusive thoughts, when I was chopping onions. I'd just see myself turning around and stabbing him in his high chair. Like this.' She'd made her hand into a fist and shoved it at Mo.

Mo had laughed, and batted her away, like it was the most natural family divulgence in the world, his mother's breezy

301

admission that she'd had thoughts of murdering him when he was a baby.

'It is your body's way of reminding you how fragile they are.'

It had happened to Bea when the hormone shifts took place, when she'd stopped breastfeeding. But Mo's mother had been a doctor for many years back in Fez, and she had reminded Bea to trust.

It will pass. Trust.

It didn't pass, or it didn't seem as if it would. In fact, it strung out into weeks of nebulous misery, and in the end went as mysteriously as it came.

But there had been no one there to tell Charlie that. To keep cheerleading her from the side of the road. To tell her, *Just keep going, trust your body. You're not morphing into a monster.*

16 May 2007

I have stopped bathing him. Jenny has noticed. She mentioned it gently the other day, and I think she is worried that I have grown slovenly. I am happy to pretend, if that is what she thinks.

18 May 2007

Weaning continues, but last night when I was boiling carrots, I saw myself throwing a pan of boiling water in his face. It took a few seconds for the scalds to fade to white, for me to realise I had not done it.

302

20 May 2007

Tom takes me out every day now in the boat, but I have stopped asking to bring Ethan along because I don't know what I might see. We put mussel ropes down a few weeks ago, and sometimes we check on them. Sometimes we fish, and sometimes we just talk. I told Tom I can't read at the moment, and he says he would be happy to read to me in the evenings, if I want. Then I can just fall asleep. It might be nice. Ethan likes to be read to, I tell him. And somehow this makes me feel as if I have compared myself to a baby, and that is probably not what Tom wants to hear.

One day, he pulls up the mussel ropes to check on the spawning and there, halfway down, in among the hard mussels, are two soft blue fists clutching the rope. I'm not shocked at first. It's like I knew all along he would be there, as if I put him there. I only feel a deep sadness to see him wanting desperately for someone to rescue him. Soon wrists appear, then the arms, and then the top of the head, small hairs growing.

It takes Tom some minutes to stop my screams, holding my hands crossed over my chest. I shake in his tattooed arms, and he thinks I have had some kind of fit.

22 May 2007

I will not change Ethan's nappy any more.

I can't cook for him. I won't do it. Just in case. I've asked Jenny to stock up on pouches for him to eat, but he will have to have them cold. I will not go near boiling water, or heat, or any kind of water, not while he is around me, and he is always around me.

23 May 2007

At least the milk from my breasts is safe. It cannot drown him.

Back when he was smaller, the visions would be of me falling asleep on him, crushing him, his mouth clutched to me, unable to roll away from my beached whale of a body. I was dangerous, dangerous and huge, and I could not sleep because of it. When I did sleep, I would wake up with that recurring dream: me crushing him. Me crushing him. Over and over. Now he is more robust, and he feeds less at night, my body has had to think of other ways to murder him.

But I will not let it win.

30 May 2007

I went to London for the May bank holiday. Georgie and Tessa came to stay. Tessa is tired. She says the workload is killing her. Georgie asks me, have I ever wanted to eat Ethan? She asks, is it true that mothers want to eat their babies? She asks it very casually. Because she has heard that, and she had a cat that ate its kittens once. I have to keep my face very steady, and work hard not to tell her, 'No, but I do have visions of drowning him.'

14 June 2007

Tom has asked if I'm still keeping up the diary. He says I must make sure to write it all down. Everything I'm feeling, even if it seems too frightening. He said this without prompting and it makes me afraid he might be able to read my soul. I don't know how he can tell that I'm not all right.

20 June 2007

I make sure Jenny is around now, as much as I can, to make sure that I don't hurt him. He is fatter and lovelier by the day, but if I am alone with him – dressing him, changing him, putting scoops of food into his trusting mouth – the visions still come. I poison him; I pour vodka into his puree. I watch him choke on his milk and do nothing to save him. In my own baths, I see his underwater face, and me, holding tight to his hands, binding them as they fight in animal instinct.

There is a witch in my soul.

I know this is my body's way of warning me: I am not exempt from darkness. I am cursed as much as any hidden murderer who walks in the night. I am swimming at night, swimming in the cold waters of dreams, and I am being pushed and drowned, not knowing what is happening to me, and the truth is – the truth is, when they were on me, holding me down, I should never have woken up again. When they were both on top of me, and I was struggling to breathe beneath them as they pushed, they should have crushed me to death, both of them. It wouldn't matter which one dealt the final blow. What matters is that none of this would ever have happened.

6 July 2007

Tonight, Tom came round to read to me. Ethan was asleep in the next room. I put on music, just gently, on the wind-up gramophone, and I even wore perfume, my old Agent Provocateur. It made me feel like myself again, like I was owning my own scent. That it did not belong to them.

It was bliss, and when Tom stopped, after a chapter of Ovid – Metamorphoses – I had the urge to ask him about his tattoos again. I thought he was going to lie and say the merchant navy and chide me for forgetting he had already told me. But he didn't. He looked down and said, 'Military prison.'

I didn't want to react, to show him I was shocked, or worse, not shocked. I asked, 'What are they?'

He offered me his forearm. 'One's supposed to be an Ouroboros – that's a snake eating its own tail, symbolising self-sufficiency; the other's a phoenix, though it's a bit shit and looks more like a pigeon. I did that one myself.' He laughed a little, but then he didn't say anything else, just stared at the floor.

I said, 'Do you know beforehand, if you are going to do something wrong?'

'What do you mean?'

'I mean, before whatever it was you did, did you have fair warning you might be about to do it?'

He still wouldn't look at me. 'No, not much. I could feel the rage coming, but I didn't know I was going to go that far. If I did, I couldn't have stopped it.'

'Where were you? Iraq?'

He took a heaving breath and looked into his mug of tea. It was only then that it occurred to me I had never once seen him drink. For a man like him – I mean . . .

what do I mean? A man his type, his character – out-doorsy, earthy – and yet he didn't touch a drop, not beer, wine, anything.

He said, 'I never made it to Iraq. I was kicked out shortly after passing out, that's to say graduating for folks in the forces. Felt like the biggest failure of my life at the time. Ah, but you learn what's for you won't go by you.' He nodded towards the window, at the castle. It looked very beautiful in the evening light, and the room felt unnaturally peaceful with Ethan gently snoring in the room behind us. I wondered if he really liked his life now, as a recluse in an idyll, living alongside his mother. Or if he had just learned to convince himself.

He looked at me. 'You have to face your demons head-on, or you won't get by them. Head down, deep breath, push through all the shit. You'll come out the other side.'

'Is he dead?'

'Who?'

'The man you hit – or shot, or what it was?'

Tom paused, and I was terribly fearful that he was about to tell me it was not a man he had hit, and I don't know what difference that would have made, but it would have made one. But he said, 'Hit. No, he was another marine. Ended up in hospital, but he bounced back.'

That night, I could not help thinking about all the mothers who had murdered their babies, wondering about how much warning they'd had, and whether they had tried to stop in time.

17 July 2007

Tom has given me cognitive therapy sheets. He says he learned it in the military prison, and that I need to write down all the thoughts that are bothering me, and write something to refute those thoughts, so that I can think more objectively.

So, I have done a bit of that today. And I feel better. I had cuddles with Ethan and took him on a walk in the sling to the village library. We saw Alistair. We brought back books about motherhood and some picture books for Ethan to look at.

10 Aug 2007

What exhausts me the most is not the darkness. Nor is it Ethan. It's the unpredictability of the darkness. Those woods on the other side of the loch, that we were never allowed to go to as children, because the trees were too dense and there was no path, and we would get lost – that is what the inside of my mind looks like now. The trees themselves are not dangerous, but it is what might jump out from behind them, when I can't see further ahead than my own outstretched hand, that terrifies me. Perhaps if I were to row there, and walk alone among them, I could find it, whatever it is, and look it in the face. But then, perhaps, it would be too *terrifying to look at. Perhaps, after looking at its face, I could never look at Ethan again. And that makes me unbearably sad. It cannot be healthy for him to live with a mother who lives half-in and half-out of this forest, and sometimes presses herself behind a tree to hide from him, so that she won't jump out and let him see her darkness. I know I need more help than Tom can give me, but I don't know how to go about asking for it.*

3 Sep 2007

Today was better, and that must be enough for now. Today I left Ethan with Tom for the first time. Am I insane? He just told me he was in prison for GBH. I am laughing, because I can imagine my mother's face. But I can make my own decisions about people now. If the decisions I made before were flawed, I will learn from my mistakes.

Anyway, it all went fine because Ethan is sleeping now, and Tom is snoozing on the couch and I am writing this and I did not have a single vision in that boat alone. Maybe that is the key; I need to sail alone instead of with Tom to hold my hand. Is there a metaphor there?

Bea turned the page. There was nothing left.

PART THREE

21

'Bea, you fucking skiver, get over here! We just dug up a
dead snake.'

Georgie had a stick in one hand and an arrow plucked
back from the archery target in the other, and she was using
them together to try and hook the snake up and into the air
like a puppet.

Bea recoiled.

Tessa was hanging back, a bottle of red wine dangling
from her hand. She swigged it, then looked at Bea and offered
her the bottle. Bea took it and drank, then passed it back.

'So we have to eat something tonight, girls,' Harriet was
saying. 'After the hare. I don't know if a liquid diet with
garden veg is going to cut it. I'm starving.'

'You don't know what starving is,' Alice said.

Harriet looked at her coolly. 'I doubt you do, either.'

'No, but I—'

'Mushrooms!' Tessa announced. 'Look, there's loads of
them. Bea, didn't you say you knew something about iden-
tifying mushrooms?'

'Bea? Mushrooms? Have you lost your mind, Tessa?' Harriet guffawed.

Tessa ploughed on. 'If we can find flour, I can make flatbreads, and then we can have mushroom and wild garlic toast. Hurrah!'

Even Melissa looked doubtful. 'I think I have an upset tummy from all the wild garlic,' she said.

'Have some wine.' Georgie gestured to Tessa to pass her the bottle. Melissa made a face, but took it and drank some anyway.

The sun had dipped a little, bringing a slanting rosy light onto the castle lawn. The leaf buds from the beech and oak trees overhead dappled shadows onto the veg patch. Sometimes a breeze sent a ripple through them, making the dark spots dance, and sometimes Tessa, catching these shadows, jumped, as if the shadows were another adder coming for her. She knew how many adders there were here in spring. On holidays, when she and Charlie were little, they dared one another to go into the patch of forest between the castle and the sea loch and count how many adders they could see. Once, when it was her turn, she had seen two mating – although, at the time, she didn't know what she was witnessing. They were standing upright, twisting in some awful tango. They looked like they were fighting, as if they would eat each other. It was more than the snakes that had disturbed her – it was something else, something about the urgency of their movements, the horror and the appetite of it.

'Is there a guide to mushrooms in the castle?' Harriet was saying. 'I think it's foolish to try and—'

'I'm pretty good these days,' Tessa said. 'We had to do a course on mushroom identification, for A & E.'

'In London?' Georgie asked, scrunching up her face.

'Yes.' Tessa held her gaze. 'You'd be amazed what people go picking on Hampstead Heath.'

Georgie snorted. 'I suppose so.'

'I mean, most mushrooms in the UK won't kill you,' Tessa said. 'They'll give you a dodgy tummy. There's only about four or five that will kill you.'

'Dodgy tummy is definitely what I want,' Alice said.

Tessa saw Rachael poke Alice in the ribs. Alice turned to Rachael and said something quietly. Rachael ignored her and said, 'I don't mind helping to make the flatbreads – but I'm not taking responsibility for the mushrooms.'

'Well,' Georgie said slowly, taking the wine bottle and gulping. 'I think, given past experience, Bea should be on bread duty as well, don't you?'

Bea shielded her eyes from the sun. 'I've learned my lesson. I think I'd rather go with Tessa.'

Tessa stared at her. 'No, you stay and make bread. I'll look out the flour for you.'

'How do you know there's flour?' Bea asked.

Tessa paused. 'Because I saw some when I was tidying the kitchen earlier.'

'But I'll need to collect the wild garlic anyway,' Bea said. 'So, I probably ought to come.'

'I know what wild garlic looks like,' Tessa said.

Tessa realised that Harriet was watching them. Harriet

seemed to have twigged something passing between her and Bea. Tessa forced herself to relax.

Alice yawned. 'I'm going to stay – I'll help you make bread. I don't want to bump into those dogs, and I don't trust Tom any more. But, to be honest, bread is probably enough for me. I don't really like mushrooms, anyway.'

A silence spread over the group.

'Come on then, Tess,' Georgie said. 'I can't remember what time the sun sets round here, so we should probably get on with it. Shall we take a knife?'

Tessa went back to the kitchen. Safely out of view, she inhaled a shaky breath. She would not cry. She would not think. If she began to think, then Ethan might come into her mind, and she could not think of Ethan. Not yet. The time for that could come, but not now. It was only the mustard fumes, anyway, irritating her eyes. And she would not feel remorse. Feeling was the enemy to all of her careful plans. This weekend, this opportunity, had taken years to come. She wouldn't waste it. She grabbed a knife, her hoodie, a Tupperware tub and the Oliver Bonas bag that had held the whisky.

Back out in the vegetable garden, they were chatting about the wine cellar.

'I wonder if Jack will have such stories to tell from his stag do,' Melissa said, looking up at Georgie in a flattering way. Georgie gave a weak smile. Tessa didn't know if that meant she missed Jack, or that she would be embarrassed to tell him how the hen party had turned out.

'Harriet,' Tessa said. Harriet snapped her head up at

316

Tessa's changed voice. She had on her hospital voice now, uncharacteristically commanding. 'Can you come with us?'

Harriet frowned. 'I'm useless at foraging.'

'Chance to learn,' Tessa said.

'I'll go.' Melissa tapped Georgie's arm.

Tessa hesitated then. 'Actually,' she said. 'There's hours still to sunset. Why don't we all just go? We can make bread together afterwards.'

Alice looked at Rachael. Harriet muttered something to Melissa. Tessa took in their faces. 'Are you really all frightened of a ghost?' She laughed, then realised her laugh was growing manic and stopped.

'Who said anything about a ghost?' said Harriet. 'I'm just tired and hungry.' She frowned. 'You don't think that little boy was real, then?'

'So what if he was?' Tessa said. 'What's he going to do to us?'

She could feel Bea staring at her. She fought hard the urge to stare back. Bea knew only a fraction of the whole story.

'I don't know, what could that boy do? Release the fucking dogs on us?' Alice said. Her voice was rising.

'The dogs are fine, Alice. They're not going to do anything,' Melissa told her.

'Oh go on, roll your eyes at me, Melissa. You spend all your life off your box, anyway. No wonder you're so chilled about everything.' Alice made a little hippy pageant with swooning arms.

Melissa blinked. 'Sorry. I was just trying to help.'

'You have no idea—' Alice began.

'I work with animals every day,' Melissa said firmly. 'And I know which ones are dangerous and which aren't.'

Rachael snorted.

'What is that supposed to mean?'

'Nothing,' Rachael said.

Melissa opened her mouth, shut it again, and then, in what seemed to be a fit of impulse brought on by exasperation and low blood sugar, said, 'I think people with doctorates like to believe their title means more than someone who practises.'

'Someone who practises?' cried Alice.

Tessa stood mesmerised by the squabble, then seized the bottle of wine from Georgie. 'I propose a toast.' The argument fell quiet as she raised the bottle. 'To Charlie and Jack.'

The blood drained from Georgie's cheeks.

'I mean, to Georgie and Jack,' Tessa calmly corrected herself.

'Who's Charlie?' Alice asked.

'To Georgie and Jack,' Tessa repeated, raising the bottle again.

Georgie was frozen, pale.

'It was a slip of the tongue,' Tessa said. She drank a swig of wine, poured another on the ground, where it splashed onto the tail of the dead snake. 'Oops,' she said. She passed the bottle to Harriet.

'Who's Charlie?' Alice asked again, looking between Georgie and Tessa.

'I meant Bonnie Prince Charlie, the Jacobite leader. God, I'm pissed.' Tessa laughed.

'No, you didn't,' Harriet whispered under her breath.

Tessa saw Bea look at Harriet, and then at her. She couldn't meet Bea's gaze, even though she felt it burning into her. It was as if Bea held Tessa's conscience in her hand, and Tessa would not have a conscience. She refused. She was sick of having a conscience.

The wine bottle continued to be passed around. The tension in the air held, but Tessa ploughed on with instructions about mushrooms: which ones were poisonous; details about gills and tips and bulbous stems.

'We shouldn't really put our hands into any dark spaces or under any logs, either,' Melissa said, indicating the snake's body.

'I feel light-headed,' Harriet sighed. 'Wine on an empty stomach.'

'Shall we just go?' Bea broke in.

'I'll protect you from the dogs,' Rachael told Alice, squeezing her shoulder. Alice gave her a knowing look, a sort of playful 'fuck off' which could have meant either *Fuck off, and stop playing along with them*, or *Fuck off, I can look after myself.*

Tessa reached into her hoodie pocket and pulled out the kitchen knife. 'Look, if the dogs come too close. Whoosh, whoosh.' She sliced the air in front of her.

Melissa looked appalled. 'Tessa.'

Tessa looked back at her. 'I know – and you know – it's not going to come to that,' she said.

There was another awkward pause, and then they began moving as one towards the rhododendrons between the castle and the woodland.

22

'So, were you all at Alice and Rachael's wedding?' Bea had fallen behind and had found herself walking in step with Melissa.

Up ahead, Tessa led the group with a strange, unnerving energy, cavorting from tree to tree and chatting about the flora and the cloud formations as if she was trekking them into wilderness. Georgie tagged just behind her, and seemed to have caught Tessa's enthusiasm as she, too, paused to point out this or that piece of wildlife. In the middle, Rachael looked as if she was dragging Alice by the hand. Harriet walked just ahead of Melissa and Bea, at eavesdropping distance. She turned around at the question. 'Nope, none of us were.'

'Is that right?' Melissa asked. 'Really?'

'Well, were you, Mel?' Harriet asked.

Bea caught the scorn in her voice and was about to say something to diffuse it, something about 'just being curious,' but then Harriet turned to her.

'Did you stay in touch with them, when – you know?' Harriet asked.

'When I wasn't in touch with you or the rest of the group, you mean?' Bea said bluntly.

Harriet was impervious. She didn't seem to register Bea's tone, and carried on walking, minding her feet as she passed a clot of tree roots.

Melissa glanced at Bea. 'Why did we lose touch?' she asked. 'I thought it was just me. I thought you didn't like me.'

Bea shook her head. 'No. I'm sorry you thought that. I lost touch with everyone. I mean, I just . . .' She hesitated. 'I just wasn't very happy after giving birth. I didn't think anyone would understand.'

'But I'm a mother,' Harriet said.

'I know,' Bea said. 'Like I say, I just didn't think anyone would understand.'

'What you mean is I only had one, back then. You were more worldly than me and I couldn't possibly . . .' Harriet waved her arm, but then seemed to lose the energy and trailed off.

Melissa laughed awkwardly. Harriet had fallen behind with them now, and they were walking three abreast.

'I wasn't very happy,' Bea said again, quietly.

They scrambled on for a bit. Alice helped pull Bea up a rocky bank, until they came to the crest that ran along the castle side of the loch. The shore level was a few feet below them, the water unnaturally still, a sheet of violet glass.

Harriet brushed her fringe out of her eyes and stood looking as if she had never seen it before.

'Did I miss much from those years?' Bea asked.

Harriet snapped her head round. 'What do you mean,

"miss much"? Yeah, I was out partying with them all every single night.'

Bea persisted. 'But you've always been closer to Georgie and Tessa, haven't you?'

'I knew Georgie from when we were little,' she said. 'We did county lacrosse together.'

Melissa tilted her head. 'Did you?'

'I thought you knew that.'

Melissa shrugged. 'Maybe I did. I forget who knows who, and how. It doesn't really matter, does it? It all blends into one after a while.'

'What does?' Bea asked.

'Friendship,' Melissa said. 'We all blend into one big gang. One pack. There's no "I knew so-and-so the longest," or, "I haven't seen you for longer than so-and-so." You know.'

Bea thought for a moment. Did she know? Maybe there was a good reason no one had ever spoken to her about Charlie. She couldn't be the one to break that taboo, especially not at a hen party, could she? She had done enough invading. There must be a good reason Charlie wasn't ever discussed. Besides, if Bea hadn't known about her, perhaps Melissa didn't know about her, either. Or Alice, and certainly not Rachael.

Up ahead, Tessa and Georgie had stopped. Georgie had her arm in the air, holding the wine bottle aloft. For a second, Bea's heart skipped. It looked as though Georgie was ready to bring the bottle down on Tessa's head. But then she heard Tessa's exclamation. 'Ah-ha! Mushrooms!'

They all gathered close.

Georgie and Tessa were squatting over a tuft of grass. Georgie, Bea noticed, had swapped yesterday's high-heeled Mary Janes for a pair of more sensible Converse trainers. Tessa was pointing something out. 'I think these ones are magic. Look, do you see the nipple on top?'

'Nipple?' Georgie squealed.

Tessa was pointing out a small patch of brown toadstools with peaked, pale tips. They were growing in a circle next to a tree stump. 'Actually, this could be where she was buried, you know?' Tessa went on.

Bea's heart took an ice shot of blood. Georgie giggled uncertainly and asked, 'What? Who?'

'The Jacobite woman,' Tessa said. 'This could be where she was buried. You know, mushrooms grow near bodies.'

'I didn't know that, actually,' Harriet said, turning away. 'But now you're really whetting my appetite. Did they teach you that in medical school?'

Tessa shrugged. 'I don't remember where I learned it.'

'Of all the woodlands, though,' Alice said, sceptically. 'I mean, she could be anywhere. If the story is true.'

'Happened so long ago, it's anyone's guess,' said Harriet. 'You can never tell what's true or not after a while, can you? Half of St Andrews is apparently a plague pit. And those letters on the ground where they burned the martyr. If you're talking about dead bodies from history . . .'

Tessa caught her eye. 'What other dead bodies would I be talking about?'

Harriet raised her hand to her brow again. It must have been a tic this time, for there was no glaring sun to shield herself from. The sun had sunk too low. She looked a little sickened, as if she was swallowing something, not wanting to bring it up.

Tessa picked one of the toadstools and licked the tip. 'Anyone?' She held it up.

'Well, now you've licked it. Makes it so tempting,' Alice said.

Tessa picked a second one. She looked around the group, from one to the other, her hand holding the mushroom outstretched, turning slowly. Then, as if it were the only logical conclusion, she stopped and held it out to Georgie.

Georgie watched her for a second. She took the mushroom between her orange nails. 'Are you serious, Tessa? You know exactly what this is?'

Tessa nodded. 'I'm going to eat one, too.'

Doubt crept into Georgie's expression.

'Don't you trust me?' Tessa said. 'Why wouldn't you trust me?' She waited. 'I'm going to eat it, too,' she repeated.

'Did I say I didn't trust you?'

'No.' Tessa shook her head. 'Shall we do it together?'

'Is this going to make me high?' Georgie asked.

Tessa laughed. 'I don't know what effect it will have on you. It's not like ket, where you can measure out the dose. Different ones are stronger than others. You have to let go a bit.'

Georgie still looked doubtful.

Bea caught Alice's expression. She was staring at them both with a kind of wondrous glee, anticipating.

'Trust her,' Melissa said, laughing. 'She's a doctor.'

'So was Harold Shipman,' Alice said.

'Is anyone else going to?' Georgie asked.

'I said I would,' Tessa said calmly. Georgie stared back at Tessa. There was something about her gaze that looked like she was accepting some kind of peace offering, some reconciliation.

Tessa nibbled the tip of her mushroom. She made a face. 'It's kind of bitter.'

'It's a raw mushroom,' Harriet said, folding her arms. 'What do you expect?'

'Tingly,' Tessa said.

'OK.' Georgie nipped the root off hers with a thumbnail and tossed it away, then ate the head whole. Tessa put hers slowly into her mouth. They swallowed at the same time.

'Now, what do the rest of us do?' Harriet asked. 'Wait for you two to go cuckoo?'

'Plenty more.' Georgie gestured to the rest of the ring. 'Think of it as an aperitif, before the main meal.'

She was already busy, taking the knife from Tessa's bag and slicing the mushroom roots from the ground, distributing them.

'I'd really rather not,' Alice said.

Melissa took one and gamely ate it.

'Bea?' Georgie held out her hand.

Bea shook her head.

Tessa glanced into the woods. It had definitely grown darker now. The sky was indigo where the trees reached up, and very still.

'Go on, Harriet,' Tessa said, turning back round. 'For Georgie.'

Harriet looked as if she was about to protest, but then she took the mushroom and with a wince, swallowed it.

'Woody,' Melissa said, and belched.

'Another.' Tessa held out a second mushroom to Georgie.

'Does pushing hallucinogens on people not go against the Hippocratic oath?' Harriet said, laughing nervously.

'She'll be fine. Come on, it's Georgie. You've got the narcotic tolerance of a horse,' Tessa said.

'Thanks. Should I be flattered by that?' Georgie took the mushroom.

'Once, you would have been,' Tessa said. She looked back into the forest again. The laughter died down. The air, despite its stillness, had a charge, a twilight energy. It had grown chilly.

'Another?' Tessa said. 'Three's your lucky number.'

Georgie flinched. She frowned for a second, seeming to wonder about the phrase. Then she looked up and grabbed the mushroom. 'Why not?' She looked around all of them, grinning, though her grin was skewed, the failing light bringing out shadows beneath her eyes. 'Bottoms up.' She washed it down with a swig of red wine. 'Euch, they are a bit manky. I wish we had crisps.'

Harriet cleared her throat. 'It's all very well to get high, but what are we going to eat?'

'Mushrooms,' said Tessa. She was still watching Georgie.

Bea had the sudden, panicky feeling that they were all waiting for something to happen to Georgie very quickly. But perhaps not. She wondered if Charlie had been so trusting. She tried to remember every time Georgie had offered her drugs at university. Mostly, Bea remembered taking them without question. Maybe Georgie only ever expected them to trust her because that was, after all, what she would have done too. There was nothing sinister in Georgie, she just wanted you to trust her, to have a good time. Perhaps.

'I'm feeling nothing yet,' Georgie was saying, sitting on the ground, hugging her knees. 'Bit drunk.'

Tessa stood up from the ravaged mushroom ring and looked out across the loch. 'Takes maybe half an hour to digest.'

'Well,' Melissa said. 'Shall we?' She pointed to the woodland, and said something about the fading sun. 'I think we're more likely to find something in there.'

Bea saw Tessa tuck the kitchen knife back into the bag and sling it over her shoulder. Alice and Rachael were first to follow her, walking parallel to the shore, away from the castle and towards the mouth of the loch. They traversed back into the woods, falling into single file where the bark-chip path narrowed between pine trees and ferns, keeping on their right-hand side the wavering reflections of light on the water. Tessa stopped every so often to examine the root of a tree. Sometimes Rachael had a small conference with her over a patch of fungi on a trunk, or Tessa would get out her knife and Alice her phone torch, and they would work together to scrape a little bit off.

'Starting to get really hungry,' Melissa murmured to Bea. The two of them were bringing up the rear. Georgie was ahead, Harriet lingering between, sometimes coming back to talk to them, at other times moving forwards and asking

Georgie if she was all right. Bea couldn't figure out whether Harriet was annoyed with them all or just fatigued. When had she become so brittle, so tired of everything? And what had been happening in their lives at university when the last part of the diary had happened? Tessa, she couldn't remember in much detail from first year, just flitting across each other at cafés and in the pub, always with mounds of work it seemed. She remembered Georgie though, from the lacrosse team and the parties afterwards. And Harriet had always been hovering in the shadows behind her, sulking. Yes, Harriet had always been something of a sulker, although now the sulkiness had hardened into something more bold.

God, it felt to Bea like ages since she had seen her children. She had a sudden rush of need to cuddle them. It was a physical urge, and came quickly and unexpectedly. She did not miss mothering them. She did not miss having to keep an eye on the clock for their timetable. She did not miss being in the middle of one task and being suddenly seized to a more urgent one. But she wanted to touch their skin and smell their fluffy black hair, to squeeze their fat. That was the hardest part, when she thought about it: the physical urge. It was like being separated from a lover. She had noticed Harriet looking at her phone for a signal for most of the weekend, as if the very touch of her phone was transportive to them, and it was touch she needed. Just then, as Bea was thinking of it, Harriet checked her phone again, but it was furtive now, as if she knew she was kidding herself. She looked almost embarrassed as she thrust it back into her pocket.

Up ahead, Tessa and Rachael were crouching down. Their voices carried. They were excited.

'St George's,' Rachael called up to Alice.

'St Georgie's?' Georgie echoed back, and laughed. 'Well, ladies, the gods have looked after us. I bless you all.' She threw open her arms. 'Goddesses,' she corrected herself. 'It must have been the snake I killed. The sacrifice brought us mushrooms.'

'Are you sure?' asked Bea, looking at Tessa. Tessa's face was obscured by the shadow of the tree she was hacking away at. 'I thought they only grew in fields.'

'I thought you knew sod-all about mushrooms,' Harriet said, but she cracked a smile and pinched Bea's arm in a friendly way.

'I did a bit of research after you guys all took the piss out of me for that risotto.'

'It's the edge of a clearing,' Rachael said, grinning. 'Near enough a field.' Bea looked past her. Sure enough, there was a sort of clearing up ahead, a patch of scrub, and what looked like an old shed further up the path. She trusted Rachael more than Tessa, but why was that? Was it purely because Rachael was a scientist? Was that ridiculous? Or was it something else? It seemed as if Tessa had changed in the last few hours. She felt uneasy, but she said nothing.

Tessa and Rachael gathered up a few handfuls of the puffy white mushrooms before they all moved on. The sun was setting over the sea end of the loch, in the direction they were heading, and some of the light filtered towards them. It seemed to Bea they had strayed quite far from the castle. They traipsed past the long, wooden building she had thought was a shed. Looking at it now, it seemed more like a boathouse, but it was all shut up.

They passed the hut in a quiet kind of chatter and were about to move into the thicket on the other side when a noise made Bea and Melissa – at the back of the group – turn. The trees on the loch-side of the path shivered. There came the sound of dragging, of something very heavy carving a path through the muck and shingle.

Bea shuddered and kept watching as the silhouette of a man emerged against the backdrop of the trees. He was dragging something on a rope. His shoulders were hunched with the exertion. The others up ahead stopped and turned now, too. Georgie flinched.

The man stopped as he saw them, and he straightened up, flexing back his shoulders until the bones cracked. Something about the way he stood – or the strange, quiet, furtive way he'd been concentrating on his task – chilled Bea.

'Hi.' His voice carried through the twilight. It was Tom. Relief. It was Tom and he was pulling, via a long rope, a small but sturdy wooden rowboat.

'Been fishing?' Harriet called over to him. She pointed towards the boat, from which a long rod protruded.

Bea thought this was a strange question, and couldn't figure out what sat wrongly in her mind about the idea. Then she realised they had walked the length of the loch and had not seen him at all. In fact, the whole loch had been flat as a millpond. There were no ripples from a boat, no frothing waves or the sounds of anyone fishing. But then, Bea told herself, she did not know what fishing sounded like. Surely the whole point of it was that it was a quiet pursuit.

Tessa was already wandering over to him. 'How's the tree?'

Tom laughed. 'Still there. Monday morning,' he said.

She touched her palm to her head in a little pantomime of self-reproach. 'Of course. You did tell us.'

He nodded to the bag slung over Tessa's forearm and creased his brow in a question.

Georgie stepped between them. 'Mushrooms for tea. Yum, yum.' She rubbed her stomach and laughed.

Cautiously, Harriet reached forward and took Georgie's sleeve. Bea saw her prepare to steady Georgie. 'We'd best be on our—' Harriet began.

'Did you catch any?' Alice interrupted. She wandered towards the boat. Tom had released the tension on the rope now and the boat lolled to one side in the dirt, leaning towards a huge bank of waxy rhododendrons, gaudy pink. Some of their petals had been lopped by the force of the boat's passing.

'See?' Rachael was saying. 'There was a boat on the shore yesterday. I told you.'

'Oh,' Tom turned to her, ignoring Alice's question. 'The one down there. No, that one has a cracked board. I keep meaning to get rid of it.'

Something nagged at Bea.

Georgie was staring at Harriet now, eyes glazed with a beatific calm. She attempted to take Harriet's face in her hands, but lost her balance, and ended up with a clump of hair instead, which she yanked towards her as she planted a clumsy kiss on Harriet's cheek.

'Ouch!' Harriet flinched backwards.

Tom looked at them both. The light behind him, even in the past few minutes, had dimmed another shade.

Alice asked again, 'Did you catch much?'

He shook his head. 'Couple of small trout was all I wanted.'

'You get trout in there?' Rachael asked. 'At this time of year?'

'Oh, aye. Sea trout. I should have thrown them back, really.' He slicked back his hair from where it had fallen down onto his forehead, revealing the uneven path of his hairline and the craggy brow. 'I gave away my hare,' he laughed. 'So, I needed something for tea.' He sounded like he was trying very hard to stop his words from seeming rehearsed.

Tessa took a step towards the boat. 'I mean, it might sound a little forward of us,' she said. Bea's ears perked up. There was a note in Tessa's voice: that rehearsed note again. She chided herself. She was imagining it. Then she remembered, suddenly, what it was that had disturbed her about the sight of Tom with the boat. In the diary – when the diary had suddenly stopped – Tom had been the last person left with Ethan. Charlie had gone out in the boat.

Bea felt a cold breeze stroke its finger across the back of her neck. Her shoulders froze.

She missed what Tom and Tessa, and now Rachael, were saying to each other. Rachael now had the rod in her hand and was examining it. Tom was looking uncertain, dismissive, telling her it was old and didn't work very well, but she looked more than capable as she pinged the hooks and tested the counterweights and tried winding the reel. She flung it away from them all, into the trees, then laughed as it caught on a bush, and went to untangle it.

'I mean,' Tom was saying. 'If it was daylight I'd say . . .'

Rachael had turned to him and was saying something dismissive, laughing. Probably something about camping and pumas and the Amazon. Bea was not listening properly. She was looking at Tom, trying to push him backwards through time into the story she had just read. What if Charlie had made it all up? What if someone else had written it? Harriet wrote novels – what if that was the twist? What if someone else had written the diary, like a sick joke for Georgie's hen party: a horror story, with real players, or half-real ones, like that boy.

Bea stopped herself, because she did not believe in ghosts. Mohammed did not believe in ghosts and – with some irony – like a ghost, she felt his presence next to her now, his voice of good, clear scientific sense in her ear. *It is the twilight*, she told herself, *taking away your wits*.

Tessa was laughing now, showing Tom the booty of mushrooms, and he looked impressed, raising his eyebrows.

'Look, girls, it's quite late, but I could take one or two of you out if you want a ride in the boat.'

'Girls?' Alice said.

Tom gave her a wolfish grin, which was the wrong response.

'Rach,' Alice said, hard brightness in her voice. 'Tell him about the time you counted alligators on that research trip in Louisiana.'

Rachael, still tampering with the fishing rod, laughed. Her braids had fallen across her face. 'Alice,' she said, sounding embarrassed. 'He didn't mean anything.' She came back over, trailing the rod. 'It's true, though. I don't think I'd be frightened of the Loch Ness monster.'

Tom grinned again. 'Well, you're an awful long way from Loch Ness,' he said. 'But I'd be more frightened of hypothermia. And I don't have enough life jackets for you all.'

'Fish,' Alice said. 'We do need to eat. Fish could be nice?'

'Who's going to go?' Harriet asked. 'I'd rather not, if it's all the same to you. And I don't think she should, either.' She pointed at Georgie, who was slumped against her, curiously quiet, enjoying it seemed, the first flush of the mushroom trip. 'She's, um, drunk.'

Tom gave Georgie a good, hard stare, looking at her for longer than necessary, as he had done in the kitchen earlier, taking her in in the way someone takes in a notorious person whose photograph has appeared in the paper. Bea told herself again that she was imagining things. Knowledge could skew you sometimes. It wasn't always good to know everything about people. And yet she burned to know more.

'I'll go, for sure.' Tessa was running her hand along the rim of the boat now, flaking the paint. 'I need some sea air.'

'Be careful with that.' Tom put his hand on top of hers. She quickly pulled away. There was a pause. A charge passed through the air. Bea knew this time she had not imagined it.

'You might get a splinter,' Tom said.

'I'm a doctor,' Tessa replied. 'Anyway, I should go, so that if we do get into any trouble, I might be of use.'

'I'll come with you,' Tom said.

'No.' Tessa waved her hand firmly. 'You won't. We'll be fine.'

'I'm staying here,' said Harriet. 'In fact, I'll go back to the kitchen.'

'I'll stay, too, to make the bread,' Alice said. 'But I think Rachael should go in the boat.'

'I know how to work a fishing rod,' Tessa laughed.

'I should make you sign a disclaimer.' Tom trailed off, the joke fizzling.

'Help us haul it back to the beach, then?' Tessa asked.

Tom, Tessa and Rachael took the stern of the boat, pushing it back along the ridges in the muck it had created when Tom had dragged it up. The mushrooms were forgotten. Tessa had left the bag up near the boathouse. Bea, for want of something to do, went and picked it up.

When she reached the shore, there was a conference taking place.

'It's her hen party,' Tessa was saying. 'Come on, you can't deny her the final experience.'

'Look at her,' Harriet argued. 'You gave her mushrooms. You shouldn't have done that if you wanted her to come fishing.'

Bea wondered why Tessa did not say the obvious – that they had not bumped into Tom and the fishing boat until a few minutes ago, and by that point they had already eaten the mushrooms. Instead, Tessa stared at Harriet. Then she said, somewhat coldly, 'I'm a doctor. I know what I'm doing.'

'I don't think she should go,' Bea called over.

But Georgie had come to her senses and was breaking free from Harriet, waddling towards the boat, her Converses slipping on the shingle. She whooped and pointed. A large full moon had materialised, low in the sky, over the other bank.

'It's a sign,' Georgie was saying. 'The moon wants me to go.'

'Georgie.' Melissa laughed. 'Remember what happened the last time you went near water when you were—'

'Drunk,' Harriet interrupted.

Bea realised they had already mentioned the mushrooms in front of Tom. But he hadn't said anything.

'I want to go,' Georgie said. 'Can I take your phone, Alice? I can get some lovely pictures from out in the loch.'

'Why mine?'

'Mine's got no battery and yours is better.'

'Why doesn't Alice go with you?' Melissa said.

Alice and Rachael exchanged a look.

'You're not frightened of water as well?' Harriet scoffed. 'You were on the swim team.'

'That's a pool, Harriet,' Alice said.

'You are?' Harriet asked. Her mouth hung open.

'Just open water.'

'Christ, what the hell do you two do? Lock the doors and turn on the internet at the end of each day? How do you function? Dogs, open water – any more neuroses? I don't know how you even manage to get through a day's work.'

Alice lunged for Harriet. It was a sudden, swift, nimble motion, the move of someone athletic, and she went for Harriet's throat, though not to grab her, just to knock her off balance. Harriet stumbled and took a couple of wobbly steps, then threw out her hand and grabbed the boat for support. Tom, standing in her path, caught her in an awkward embrace.

'Psychopath,' Harriet was shouting.

Rachael and Melissa were closest to Alice, and each grabbed an arm, while Alice tried to thrash free. 'How dare you, how very fucking dare you!' she screamed. 'If you knew what I did for a living, what I look at all day long, your guts would fall out of you. You'd be frightened of your own shadow. How the fuck dare you, you brutal, cold, spoiled bitch.'

It was the word *bitch* in Alice's mouth, of all people, the savagery of it, that caught Bea's breath. The rest of what she had said barely registered. Rachael was telling her to calm down.

'Take her back to the house,' Harriet directed, clutching her throat in some act of melodrama.

'I barely touched you,' Alice hissed.

'I could have you charged,' Harriet said.

Now it was Tessa who sucked in her breath. When she spoke, it was with a huge effort for calm. 'Can we please *try* to be nice to each other? Just for a few hours more of Georgie's hen party?'

Bea looked at Georgie then. She was watching with very wide, brimming eyes, as if the whole thing had been staged for her entertainment. She swayed from side to side, always catching her balance just in time.

After a moment, Tom said, 'I don't think you should go out in the boat.'

'Tom. It'll just be me and Georgie,' Tessa said. The firmness had crept back into her voice again.

'Rachael should go with you,' Melissa said.

Tessa looked at her, challenging her to say why. 'I think Rachael should stay with Alice,' she replied. There wasn't very much that could be argued with about that.

Georgie was already stepping into the boat, wobbling as it half-lapped between the shingle and the incoming waves.

'I'll come.' Bea stepped forward.

'Or me,' Melissa said, but her heart didn't sound in it.

'Just, go back and – won't we need to start packing for tomorrow?' Tessa called over to them. 'Look, this will be a time for Georgie and me to hang out. Feel like I've barely seen her all weekend. I just want you to myself.' She smiled at Georgie.

'You pair,' Melissa said indulgently.

Tessa was already settling a laughing Georgie into the boat. Tom stood up on the shore, hanging back with an uncomfortable frown on his face. Harriet was keeping her distance, arms folded. Alice clung on to Rachael's hand.

Bea marvelled at them all. How could none of them see what a strange and terrible idea it was, to let Tessa and Georgie, both of them high, out on the water in a rowing boat? Why were they not doing anything to stop them? But then something strange came over Bea, too. Maybe when people talked of ghosts, they were only ever talking about the eerie, miraculous urges and perceptions that came over people for no reason, that made them go against their senses, that made them lead their friends into traps or say nothing when words were needed.

Bea said again, 'I'll go.' But she knew then that if Tessa told her no again, she would heed it. She would not make a fuss.

'We'll be fine,' Tessa called back from the boat. 'I've been going out in boats like this since I was a child. Even at night.'

'Come on, leave them to their love-in,' Melissa laughed. 'Just bring us back some fish.'

'Are you sure?' Rachael dropped her voice. She passed the fishing rod to Tessa.

'Sure,' Tessa said airily. 'Keep the Aga warm and we'll have dinner on the table before you know it.'

Melissa laughed. 'Look at you pair, being the men.'

'Sometimes, Melissa,' Alice muttered.

'Be safe,' called Bea.

'You'll have to head a bit towards the sea,' Tom shouted over. 'But watch for the undertow. When the tide is changing, it can be strong.'

Just as Tessa was pushing off, she stopped. 'Nearly forgot,' she addressed Tom. 'Bait.'

'Ah.' He smiled. Laughing, he pushed the hair back out of his eyes. Then he reached into his pocket and tossed her something. Through the air flew a small, slimy bag, greased with dark stains. Tessa raised her hand and caught it in one movement.

Rachael helped push them off and the boat made a meditative sound as it glided into the water, further and further into the loch. They heard Georgie's laughter ringing out under the preternaturally large moon, as Tessa rowed towards the open sea.

Bea stood rooted to the spot, feeling her tiredness muddle her mind, as if she might be watching Charlie in the boat instead. She felt sick to her stomach. In her mind's eye, she saw a horrifying image; the boy in the photograph, rising from the deep.

'Bea, you coming?' Alice's voice drifted through the bushes behind her.

Why had she let them go? But she knew the answer, sort of.

The others had all reached the path now, and were heading back. As they walked quietly, in single and double file towards the boat shed, Tom parted ways from them to take a different route through the woods. Bea tried to keep sight of the boat on the loch, but it was dark now, and it flitted in and out of her view through the silhouettes of the pine trees and the bushes.

She opened the mushroom bag and peered in. It smelled muddy and satiating. She would concentrate on preparing the mushrooms. They did look like St George's. She was re-assured on that, at least. Contrary to what they all thought, she did know a bit about mushrooms. They would lose their size when they were sautéed down, but there would be enough to have some with flatbread, to fill their stomachs. She hoped – suddenly and passionately – that someone had liberated a few more wine bottles from the cellar.

The damp evening breeze made her feel better. It was mesmerising, the dusky sounds of the woods, the smell of the mud and the anticipation of going back to the castle: its stone, its comforting warmth and wealth. That was what you bought really, when you rented a place like that: the history and the illusion of wealth. It was there to be enjoyed. She might as well try to enjoy what was left of it. It might, after

all, have been a nice place to have come to after giving—
Bea stopped herself, because she knew she was telling herself
a lie. It might have been comforting, during the day, to be
surrounded with so much nature. But it would also have
been suffocatingly lonely, and she knew it.

Obviously, there was a reason Tessa had never mentioned
Charlie's name. Why none of them seemed to know she had
a twin, or at least didn't speak about it. Of course, Harriet
and Georgie had known. It must have been some pact, out of
respect, that they didn't talk about it. Other people's secrets;
other people's lives.

She stopped, flinching, as she saw something disappear
under a pile of ferns – a shadow moving, a crackle of wild
dewy vegetation – and she remembered what they had all
said about the adder last night, the horrid adder whose body
had been dug up by one of the dogs. Suddenly, she felt a
shiver at her shoulder and she began to imagine something
had crawled into the bag she was carrying.

She stopped, letting Melissa, directly ahead of her, wander
on. Bea peered into the bag, but of course there was nothing
there but the mushrooms. She jiggled them about a bit, the
shudders still creeping over her. She tried to laugh herself
unafraid. And then she realised that there was indeed something different about the bag. But it was not that something
had made its way into it; it was that something was missing
from it. She had thought it felt a little lighter than she'd
expected, despite the hoard of mushrooms.

She saw now. The Tupperware was still there. But the
knife was gone.

23

Tessa felt the temperature drop as the boat slid out into the centre of the loch. The further they went from shore, the damper the breeze, laced with spray. They were heading straight into the sunset.

Like lovers in a film, Tessa thought.

The peace of it was sending Georgie into mushroom bliss. 'I love this weekend, Tessa. It has been one of the best weekends of my life.'

Tessa smiled. The mushroom had had only a mild effect on her, and everything felt rather nice and as it should be. Georgie looked pretty against the rising moon. She had the kind of face Tessa had envied growing up: sharp and hard, a face that looked good in experimental make-up, large lined eyes, straight nose and solid cheekbones. Her mouth grew strange creases at the corners when she smiled. She was beautiful. It was no wonder Jack—

Tessa pulled the oars, felt the water drag, and her stomach lurched. All lochs were watery graves. She thought of all the dead things lying beneath the surface of the water, tangled in weeds. The mushrooms made it easier to imagine.

'That's good, Georgie.' She took her hand off one of the oars for a second, and placed it on Georgie's, on top of her extravagant engagement ring. They'd all had to admire it at the station, only two – no, one, no, two – days previously.

'Are the stars out, or is it my mind twinkling?'

Tessa laughed.

Georgie laughed too. Her huge mouth opened wide. 'Where can we live but days?' she quoted. She watched Tessa to see if she would guess the quote, then impatiently said, 'Philip Larkin.'

Tessa rowed towards the mouth of the sea. She was out of practice, but it was in her muscle memory to row the boat. *Row, row, row your boat.* She stared at Georgie, at her beautiful, shining hair. She could not get away from the beauty, the sight of Georgie lolling against the boat, almost tipping herself overboard. But it was a terrible, tragic beauty. Ophelia beauty. Snow White beauty. She thought about how Charlie might have looked, leaning back in the boat, and her heart felt such stabbing pain she thought the fibres would yank apart.

She felt sick. She needed to keep talking.

'Charlie used to come out here, when she was at her worst.' Tessa watched Georgie. She looked a fraction more lucid now. It was hard sometimes with Georgie, to see what was really in there. She so often hid behind a drug haze, or a hangover. It was how she got away with it, Tessa thought. But what did she get away with? What exactly? 'She liked the remoteness,' Tessa continued. 'It was like drifting away from her mind. Meditative.'

'I always thought it was strange she went away to bring up the baby,' Georgie murmured. 'Like being sent away in Victorian times. Mrs Rochester in *Jane Eyre*. It's not healthy.'

She hadn't realised the significance of what Tessa had said. This had been the danger of giving her too many mushrooms.

Tessa would have to be blunter. 'She liked it here,' she said. 'We used to come here all the time when we were little. This was our main home for a while, so I think it had good memories.'

Georgie dipped her hand over the side of the boat and trailed her fingers in the water. 'Freezing. Brrr.' She pulled it back out and flicked splashes from her fingertips.

Tessa couldn't figure out whether Georgie was listening to what she was saying and choosing to ignore her, or whether she was too drugged to care. That too was one of the hardest things to know about Georgie: how much was deliberate and how much was merely selfish.

Tessa remembered the day she told Georgie that Charlie had died, that they had pulled her body out of the sea. Her leg had become tangled in one of the mussel ropes in the middle of the loch, right around the place they were drifting now. After a while, she had bloated up and popped above the surface. By the time Tessa saw her, she was drained, but bruised. Charlie's was not the first dead body Tessa had seen; she had a cadaver that she had been assigned in first year medicine. But that cadaver had died of organ failure brought on by old age. It was withered and wise. Charlie's body, lying on mortuary steel, with flushed bruises, breasts still misshapen from lactating, was just terribly, bone-breakingly sad.

Tessa had told Georgie just before they went into the pub that night. It was on Market Street, the main street in the town, and it had been autumn. Term had just resumed. They were in their second year. Ethan was just over a year old. The streetlamps had come on. Tessa had wanted to tell her outside, so that her own sadness could filter away from her out into the open air. Inside the pub, she would have to reabsorb it, keep it in, tamp it down. This way, it was a little bit like scattering Charlie's ashes, her words and breath caught in the air to float above the town and vanish.

Georgie had said, 'Oh fuck, Tessa.' Tessa remembered her frozen look. Then she had hugged Tessa, which meant Tessa couldn't see the look in her eyes. But she could feel something between them, some hardening of both of their hearts towards each other.

Every time Georgie spoke about it – which was very little, and never in company – she always referred to 'the accident'. She kept calling it that, as if she could change history with her words. But it wasn't an accident; it had never been an accident. Tessa knew. She knew by the cold that ran in her marrow that her twin had taken her own life.

For all Tessa knew, most of their friends never had any idea she'd ever had a twin. Tessa was not going to bring it up. When was it ever the right time?

The wall around her heart had grown solid, oaken, while Georgie's had grown tall and flinty.

'I think this is the spot,' Tessa said.

Georgie's eyes flicked up, too quick to conceal what she was thinking. And then Tessa knew that Georgie knew exactly which spot she meant.

'Best spot for trout,' Tessa added quickly.

Georgie's face loosened in relief.

Tessa locked the oars and reached down to Georgie's feet, where the small anchor lay curled up in rope. Georgie followed Tessa's hands with her eyes and jumped at the sight of the rope.

Tessa grinned. 'I know what you're thinking. I see them everywhere, too.' She hauled the anchor towards her. 'It was worse after Charlie died. I think I had fallen into a bit of a depression myself, but it was blocked because of university and having no one to talk to about it. So, it just came out as strange things; neuroses. Black spots at the sides of my eyes. Snakes. Snakes everywhere. But being here, so many years later, feels like I can set it all free.'

Georgie was nodding. She was still watching Tessa's hands as she tossed the anchor overboard, as she tidied the rope, then hooked the rod into its holder.

'I wish I could have done something.'

'I think the tipping point was long before anyone realised,' Tessa said. She began knotting a length of twine to a fishhook. She opened the grubby bait bag and took out a thrashing worm, then speared it onto the hook.

Georgie stared at the worm. Her expression had changed. The trip had taken a turn. She looked as if she was trying to conceal panic.

'I really hope we catch some. I think the others are hungry,' said Tessa.

Georgie nodded dumbly.

Tessa cast back the rod, lobbed the line over both their heads. They saw the ripple, concentric circles pushing the water into silken waves.

'It was here?' Georgie said.

Tessa didn't look at her. 'Yeah, somewhere here.'

'How do you know?'

'It's near the mussel ropes.'

'No, but how do you know she was heading for the mussel ropes?'

'That's where she was found.' Tessa leaned back to allow room for the rod's full length in the boat. 'She kept a diary about it all.'

'About the baby?'

'About her misery.'

Georgie looked bluish pale. 'I wish you'd been there that night.'

Tessa fought the urge to spit, to make a scraping noise that would cleave the air. 'I've thought the same, lots of times,' she said.

The line suddenly twitched. 'Wow, quick,' Tessa muttered. Vibrations shivered up her arm. She became suddenly aware of the precarious rock of the boat, the chill of the air. She leaned back and began reeling, but then the tension slackened. 'Hmm, someone's nicked the bait.' She wound the line in. On the end, most of the worm had been eaten. The ragged stump of its body still wriggled. Tessa examined it, then dragged it off the hook and threw it overboard. She delved into the bait bag again. Georgie watched all the while. She looked revolted as well as fascinated.

'It's not why you became a doctor, though, is it?'

'Hmm?' Tessa looked up.

'Because of Charlie? You were studying medicine already, weren't you?'

'Yes,' Tessa said. She speared another worm, cast the line again. 'I thought, for a while, that I would end up in obstetrics. Or maternal psychiatry. As some kind of penance.'

'OK,' Georgie said. Tessa noticed Georgie's hands were clutching the bench. Her back was upright. It came to Tessa then, as it had done many times, of how it must have felt to Charlie, to have been drugged and left. Was she too out of it to notice? Or had she felt that rigid panic, the trip turning bad, the heartbeat increasing, the white-hot sweat that turned cold as soon as it burst on the skin?

She had never asked Charlie about this fear. Sometimes she regretted that; other times she was glad she did not know.

'Why didn't you?'

'Why didn't I what? Oh, go into obs?' She thought about it. 'I just couldn't get out of my head that all of these mothers were versions of Charlie. I don't mean empathy; it was more warped than that. Like they were possessed by her, like they were all doomed.' Tessa hesitated. How much did Georgie deserve to know? How much did she deserve *not* to know?

'I began to have visions,' she said. 'I saw myself stealing their babies. When they came to consultation, pregnant, I saw it. Quick as a flash. The snatch, just after birth. When they

348

were wheeled into labour or theatre for C-sections. I could have done it. I knew. I wouldn't have got away with it, but I could have got them out of the hospital, probably, and it would have ruined their lives after that. Even when they got the babies back, eventually, I don't think anyone would get over the terror of that having happened to them. Again, and again, I saw myself doing it. Snatching.'

Horror pinned open Georgie's eyes.

'I know,' Tessa said. 'Horrible, isn't it? It's a kind of OCD, intrusive thoughts. Snap visions. It's stress. You see yourself, in a snap moment, doing something vile.' She stopped, as the line twitched again. 'OK, maybe this time. Then we can go back.'

Georgie pushed her hands through her hair. She looked at the bank, which seemed very far away now.

As Tessa reeled the line, she looked around at the ancient landscape. The trees on the far side were darker, she decided. Not a trick of the mushrooms, just the sun vanishing. She tugged the line. 'Arse,' she said. 'It's caught.'

Gingerly, Georgie leaned over to Tessa's side of the boat and began to pull on the line. Tessa could detect the scent of her now, her perfume pretty much unchanged since school. Heavy and seductive. Sweet. And there was always something else about her scent, some other note that jarred. It wasn't body odour, the opposite. It was a sort of chemical smell.

'Ouch.' The line whizzed past Georgie's fingers, cutting her. She fell back. The boat rocked and a wave splashed over their legs. 'Fuck, my shoes,' she said. 'Oh, jeez, it's cold.' She climbed back onto the bench. The line pulled to a stop.

Georgie tugged at it. 'No, that's properly stuck,' she said. 'Probably snagged on a rock.' She seemed relieved to have something for them to focus on, to take them away from Charlie.

Tessa hooked the rod back into its holder, then rummaged at her feet. 'Don't worry,' she said, bending back up, clutching in her right hand the kitchen knife they had used to cut the mushrooms. 'I brought this.'

24

Bea scolded herself for being foolish. She was treating the diary like a horror novel. With an inevitable, catastrophic climax awaiting them all. When they emerged from the woods, onto the part of the shore where they had taken the photographs, she looked out and saw the boat, small but still close enough to see that Georgie was laughing, looking around her, and Tessa was rowing with a surprising, gallant strength. They looked fine.

Anyway, it was the tension between the rest of the group that you could cut with a knife, Bea thought, as they wove their way back through the woods, towards the castle.

Alice and Rachael had been quiet most of the way back. Melissa had dropped inane remarks about the sunset and the freshness of the air, and this or that bird, that she could identify from its call. Harriet had kept her arms folded, her mouth shut.

They neared the vegetable patch and Bea stopped to pick a few spinach leaves and some parsley. She suddenly spied the purple stems of some sprouting broccoli. When she got close enough, she realised they were too woody to pick, and she couldn't cut them because she didn't have the knife.

Alice came to help take the bundle of leaves from her, and Bea, without warning to herself, suddenly blurted out, 'Who's Charlie?'

Alice looked confused.

'Tessa,' Bea stumbled on. 'Made that toast. And Georgie seemed strange about it. Do you know who Charlie is?' She blushed and was thankful for the cold evening air. Probably the simple reason no one had mentioned Charlie when they were at university was because it was difficult to bring up the subject of your friend's twin, missing or dead or gone somehow. Or maybe not.

Alice looked blank and then thought. 'I've been wondering about that myself. I think Tessa had a little sister who died – of Hodgkin's, is that what I mean? A type of cancer. I don't really know,' she said quickly. 'It's just stuff you pick up, isn't it? She never talked about it to me.'

Bea fumbled for something to say. 'What a horrible thing to happen, poor Tess.' Her mind turned over. Alice didn't know about Charlie. And if Alice didn't, then the chances were that Melissa didn't either.

'Mel, did Tessa have a sister?' Alice called.

Melissa was up ahead, opening the kitchen door. She stopped and turned. The same vacant frown that Alice had worn came onto her face. It struck Bea then – how could any of them have been so cold and incurious as to not realise that Tessa was grieving? Not to ever ask what she was feeling if she seemed down, or distracted? If she didn't feel like coming for a drink, or if she seemed quiet or tired at lunch? Not to have asked questions about her family beyond, 'Do you have brothers and sisters?' to which, Bea supposed, she had probably answered yes and told them about her older sister, Sasha.

'She died in a car accident,' Melissa said.

'No, it was a boat accident,' Harriet called over.

'God.' Bea's head began spinning. The dusk made her weary and she just wanted, then and there, to be back home, to hide from them all again for another four years. She didn't want to go to Georgie's wedding – she had forgotten there was even to be a wedding. It seemed like some bizarre whim now. How could they possibly watch Georgie swear marriage vows, sip champagne, after all of this? And yet they would. She knew they would. They would have to, because there was no other way.

That was if they all made it out of there. The thought popped into her head, alarming. She almost laughed with the absurdity of it. Of course, they would all make it out. *This isn't a horror novel*, she reminded herself. The council were coming tomorrow to remove the tree.

And then, suddenly, she thought of the visions Charlie had seen. Her son underwater. Her, drowning him. Was it possible? Was it possible there hadn't been a boat accident, or a car accident, or cancer, but something worse? The boy in the photograph had not seemed real. On the path, with the dogs, there had been something wild or slight about him. And yet, again, Bea told herself firmly that she did not believe in ghosts. Besides, ghosts did not grow older; they stayed the age at which they had died, didn't they?

353

No, she was being utterly ridiculous.

'I only met her once,' Harriet was saying. 'They were identical twins.'

'What?' Alice frowned. 'Tessa had an identical twin? Who died?'

'Yes.'

'And you knew this?'

'An identical twin?' Melissa was asking. 'Really? Are you sure?'

'I met her,' Harriet said, forcefully. Irate, almost.

They were all in the kitchen now, and Rachael had begun a hunt for the flour. She was standing on a chair, opening cupboards and moving crockery.

'That's messed up,' Alice said.

'What do you mean?' Harriet said.

'I mean, it must mess you up. A lot. I don't think anyone can imagine that level of grief. I mean, a twin. Of all the siblings to lose.'

Harriet bristled. 'I don't see why being twins makes a difference. There's not a hierarchy of grief.'

'Maybe not.' Alice trailed to a halt.

Rachael continued searching, pulling out old spice packets and sticky bottles of half-used olive oil, a salt shaker and a cracked plastic pepper mill, a torn cardboard box of black peppercorns.

'Try that one, babe.' Alice pointed out a cupboard set apart from the rest, protruding above the door to the utility room.

'I'd have the willies searching through those after a snake got loose,' Harriet said.

'So weird,' Melissa mused. 'I've literally never heard of that happening with an adder before. Pet snakes, yes. They get in the plumbing all the time. Most of the time, they'll pop up in a neighbour's toilet, scare the shit out of them and end up in a rescue centre. Sometimes, a freaked-out householder has poured bleach down the pipes and we have to put them down. But an adder? They're usually really shy. There must be quite a colony here.'

'Or someone put it there,' Bea said. She had said it quietly, almost to herself, but now the others fell silent around her.

'What?' Alice asked. 'Like a practical joke?'

'Pretty shit joke,' Harriet scoffed. But Bea noticed she was busying herself extra hard, scrubbing the island with a dish sponge in preparation for the breadmaking.

Rachael scraped the chair across the flagstones. She climbed up. 'Bingo,' she said, her hand closing on an opened bag of extra-strong white flour. White powder puffed down onto their heads, making Melissa sneeze. Alice laughed and clapped her hands.

'Hold on,' Rachael was saying.

Harriet had already begun pouring the flour into a bowl when Rachael said, 'Aye aye,' and tossed down a full packet of crisps. They landed on the kitchen floor.

Alice picked them up. 'These are the same as the ones in the Fortnum's hamper.'

'Oh, you get all sorts of gourmet shops up in these weird, out-of-the-way places,' Harriet mused.

But then Rachael tossed another packet to the ground. They were Fortnum's crackers, sea salt and rosemary.

'How did they get there?' Alice said. 'Someone must have been very enthusiastic about tidying up.'

'There's more,' Rachael said. She pulled out a jar of anti-pasti, some more crisps, a small wheel of cheese. Then a bag of pasta emerged, some jars of sauce, olives and a full loaf of bread.

'Jesus Christ, get them open,' Melissa laughed. 'Treasure! Finally. Someone's head's going to roll for this.'

They lunged on the food as if they hadn't eaten for days. The bag of crisps was ripped open, the antipasti dug out, the breadmaking forgotten.

'Leave some for Georgie and Tess,' Harriet said.

'Oh, shit.' Alice wound the crisp packet back up. Melissa sheepishly folded the cardboard over the crackers. 'Such a weird place to put food.'

'It's where the flour was. Obviously, it's a food cupboard,' Rachael said.

'But who do you think tidied up?' Melissa replied. 'Harriet, were you doing the kitchen last night? I was completely out of it, so I have no idea what happened.'

'I thought we all were doing the clear up,' Harriet mused. 'But I can't say I was particularly sober either.'

'Whoever it was must have been drunk and forgotten about it,' Alice said. 'Otherwise, why not say anything when we had no food this afternoon?'

There was a small silence. Bea looked from Alice and Rachael to Harriet, and then to Melissa. No one seemed to want to say it.

Harriet tutted and got up from the table. 'I know Georgie's

a pain, but why put the rest of us through this to spite her? I think someone just tidied up drunk and then forgot about it.'

Bea said nothing. The relief of the food had hit her blood-stream. She realised she had been feeling queasy with hunger. The blood sugar shot had an almost narcotic effect, relaxing her. She did not feel quite so uneasy about everything. So what if Tessa had hidden the food as a nasty prank? Who was she to comment on her relationship with Georgie? She hadn't even seen either of them for four years. It was none of her business. And Tessa was a doctor. Doctors were trustworthy. Harold Shipman popped back into her head. She blinked, trying to take hold of her thoughts.

Alice drew in a breath.

'What's up?' Melissa gently tousled the purple strands of Alice's hair. Absently, Alice lifted her hand to brush away Melissa's fingers.

'Does anyone else think it's a bit weird?' Alice said. 'That we are all here, and not her friends from – I don't know – elsewhere.'

'She did have a London hen night,' Harriet said.

'Oh yes, she did, didn't she?' Alice said. She didn't sound hurt or put out, more curious. 'Yes, but to have us all here, when we haven't really kept in touch that much, on quite a fancy trip – which I assume she must have subsidised, because I wasn't asked for any money for the castle.'

'That's a good point,' Melissa said. 'I wasn't either. I just paid for my train fare.' She looked around at the others. They all shook their heads.

'Did you pay anything for the castle, Bea?'

'Nope.'

'Maybe Tessa forgot,' Harriet said.

'You wouldn't forget something like that,' Alice said. 'It must have been a thousand pounds or more. I mean, she's still a junior doctor, they're not known for being made of money.' She shrugged, then looked sidelong at Harriet. 'Maybe you wouldn't miss it. Who knows?'

'You've never liked me, Alice,' Harriet said. 'I don't know what I've done.'

Rachael caught Alice's eye.

'But why invite all of us to the fancier hen party,' Alice persisted. 'Why have us as bridesmaids?'

'Do you know, Alice,' Harriet began. 'I'm going to say this, even though it might offend you. Don't you think that perhaps some people value the old kinds of friendships? The ties that get you through your troubles?'

Alice paused. She looked like she was gathering her thoughts. 'Do you know, Harriet,' she echoed. 'I was just wondering if maybe she didn't have any other close friends she could ask to be bridesmaids, and that's why she chose us. That's all.' She went to the sink and poured herself a glass of water.

'You didn't invite any of us to your wedding,' Harriet said. 'Is that because you have so many new close friends with whom you share such wonderful ties?'

Rachael said, quietly, 'It was very small. We sort of eloped.' She laughed.

'And, to be honest,' Alice said, turning to face them. 'I couldn't trust you to behave.'

'What?' Harriet looked at her. 'Trust us?'

Alice winced. 'Well, it was sort of mainly Georgie.' She rubbed her hand against the stubbly side of her head. 'I didn't want you turning up in front of our families, making remarks.'

'What?' Melissa took a step back. 'Remarks?'

Alice continued. 'It's embarrassing, when your friends act like they don't understand your identity. Or that they think it's funny.'

'I have never—' Bea started to protest. She felt the reflex to defend herself, but she took a breath, seeing Alice's raised hand.

'Let me finish. You all come as one. If we invited you, Mel, or Bea or Tess, we would have to invite—'

'Harriet and Georgie,' Harriet finished for her. 'Oh, those villains.'

'Look, I don't have a problem with you,' Alice said.

'Could have fooled me.'

'But you don't get it. You just don't seem to get it.'

'What don't I get?' Harriet was almost squaring up to her now, her arms folded, her shoulders pushed back.

Alice looked flustered. 'I can't think of evidence off the top of my head, but there's the laughter. And your absolute fixation with my work.'

'Oh, for fuck's sake.' Harriet turned away.

'Listen, you don't get to decide what hurts me. Anyway, I said it's more Georgie really.'

'So,' Melissa said. 'You didn't invite any of us because you didn't want to invite Georgie?'

359

Alice lifted her hands and then dropped them. 'Basically.'

Harriet pursed her lips. 'You know, we're all adults. We can choose our friends.'

'Can we?' Alice said softly. 'Really? Don't we just fall into them, to some degree?'

'Do your other friends know what you do for a living?'

'Does that really bother you?' Alice asked. 'Does it hurt you?'

'You don't trust us.'

'I don't like talking about it.'

'Oh, really?'

'Do you really want to know? Really? You can't unhear it once you've heard it.'

'Oh Alice, please.'

'I'm just warning you.' Alice looked down. 'I track paedophile rings. I have to search for them, hack them, and then our unit goes after them.'

'Jesus,' Melissa said softly. 'You do work for GCHQ?'

'Police. I'm in cybercrime, but I had to do the basic training. And for a while, until recently, I was under confidentiality and not allowed to talk about it. Feels strange talking about it, even now.'

'That's why she's frightened of dogs,' Rachael said.

'Dogs?' Harriet asked. 'What's it got to do with dogs?'

'Don't push it,' Alice warned, but Harriet didn't take any notice.

'You can't say something like that and then not explain. I'm just trying to know you, know what you do.' Her voice tightened. 'It's what makes us friends.'

Alice sighed. 'I got bitten, a few years ago, when we were making arrests. It latched onto me, wouldn't let go.' She shuddered, and then began to roll up her left sleeve. Beyond the elbow, in the meatiest part of her bicep, sat two deep welts, whiter than the rest of her skin and knotted.

Harriet leaned over. At first, Alice flinched as she touched the scars. Then she relaxed and let Harriet examine them.

'Was it an Alsatian?' Harriet asked.

Alice hesitated again. 'Springer spaniel,' she said reluctantly.

'A springer spaniel?' Harriet looked very nearly like she might be about to laugh. Then, to Bea's surprise, it was Alice who laughed instead. She laughed and shook her head.

'I thought they were cuddly, too. But they are not. They are fucking mental.' She pushed out her breath. 'You can't trust animals, can you?'

Rachael lolled her arms around Alice's shoulders.

'Did you delete the photo of the boy by the loch?' Harriet asked.

Alice stared at her, then she nodded.

'Why?' Bea asked, her voice croaking.

'I don't like images of children on phones. You don't know what can be done with them. I don't know who he was or how he appeared, but I didn't like the idea of us obsessing over it, like he was a ghost or something thrilling. And Georgie was annoying me. I didn't want to have that conversation with her. Better to just shut it down. Make him go away, shut her up. If he was real, it was horrible and not something for us all to get creepy kicks out of. And if he wasn't – oh, it was just bothering me. Spur of the moment. I just did it.'

Harriet was quiet for a while, then said, 'If you really didn't want to keep ties with us, then why are you here?'

Alice slumped into a stool at the island, her head in her hands. 'Because Tessa asked. Tessa arranged the whole thing. That's probably why we're all here, I guess.'

'I'm going to make some tea,' Bea muttered. She felt cowardly as she fiddled with the teabags and kettle. She didn't know how to say, how to confess that she knew the reason they hadn't paid; the reason that Tessa had invited them instead of Georgie's London friends.

None of the London friends had been in Georgie's life at the time Charlie died. Bea had guessed that Tessa wanted to re-live that time by bringing everyone here. They hadn't paid because the castle belonged to Tessa's family. And the reason she knew all of this was because she had found and stolen a private diary, and read it indiscriminately.

25

Tessa tossed the anchor at their feet, then used the fishing rod to winch them towards where the line was tangled. She held the knife between her teeth. As they reached the place where the line pierced the water, she leaned over and cut it. It snapped back into the depths, rippling. The sudden, broken tension sent the boat rocking.

She clenched the knife between her teeth again, then wound up some fresh line and speared a new worm.

'Starting to get cold.' Georgie hugged herself. 'Do you think we should just go back?'

Tessa shook her head.

Georgie hesitated. 'It's probably good for our diets, this starvation. Bravo, again.'

Tessa watched her. Georgie was rubbing her arms, with a thin, chilly smile. Her eyes roamed the trees on the far bank.

Tessa leaned back and cast the line. She took the knife from between her teeth and placed it delicately beside her on the boat's bench. Looking back up, she saw Georgie focused on it, frozen.

'I wonder how Charlie felt,' Tessa said. 'I wonder how she felt when you guys left her there, drugged off her box.'

Georgie slowly met her gaze. 'I wish you'd been there that night, Tessa. You knew better than anyone what she was and wasn't up for.' She wriggled. 'Can we go back now?'

'Did Charlie ever ask to leave the party?'

'I don't remember.'

'Because she said Jack wanted to walk her back to the cabin.'

Georgie laughed at that, a scornful laugh. 'Is that what she told you? Jack was pissed. God, Jack back then, with his nail varnish and his Sartre.'

'You've done a good job with him,' Tessa said.

'Wasn't easy.'

Tessa tutted. 'He was always going to end up in the civil service. He had Foreign Office stamped on his arse from the moment he set foot in boarding school. People like Jack like to think they have choices.'

'I wouldn't cry for him,' Georgie said.

Tessa shook her head, laughing a little. 'Oh, I'm not.'

Georgie suddenly pressed her fingers onto her eyelids; then she laughed too. 'Tessa, I've missed you. Why do we never see each other?'

Tessa swallowed back the bile that rose in her throat.

'I know you're busy with work.'

'It's not that, Georgie.'

The fishing line twitched. Tessa gave it a tug, then re-cast gently.

'It took me a little while to think about it all.' She flicked her gaze up. Georgie was waiting for her to go on. 'It wasn't really until I read her diary.'

Georgie looked steadily at Tessa. 'You think I killed your sister, but I didn't. Tessa, I didn't. If anything, you should be chasing down those two men.'

'Oh, don't think I haven't tried.' Tessa's voice sliced through the quiet of the loch. 'The hotel wouldn't give me their names, but it doesn't take a genius to track down two tech bros like that. They were all over Facebook. Photos of them in yucky locations, drinking shitty cocktails. I think the worst thing about those kind of pictures is that they *do* show the truth – they show how a person wants the world to see them. Believe me, I would love to tell you that I cut out each of their hearts and fed them to you last night. I would love nothing more than to say they weren't goats' hearts. They were the hearts of devils.' She paused, tugging the line again. 'But the truth is, one of them is Ethan's father and I can't hate him for that.'

'Ethan,' Georgie whispered. 'He would be about nine now.'

'Ten,' Tessa corrected. She watched the realisation dawn on Georgie, the pieces slide together in her drugged mind. 'That boy,' she said. 'The boy on the shore, in the photo Bea found. Wasn't a ghost.'

Tessa shook her head. 'No, he wasn't a ghost. He lives with Sasha and Brian now, but he comes here to spend time with Tom. Tom and his mother took care of Charlie when she lived here. He likes them; he likes the woods and the loch. I told him it was a prank. Sneak up on us, make a scary face, run off. Make you see him, force you to look at him.'

She closed her eyes. 'For a while, I didn't want him to see Tom. I blamed Tom, because it was easy. But he loves him so much. They love each other. It's an instinctive love, you can see it. You can't fake that.' She stopped herself. Georgie did not need to know about Tom and Ethan. Or about Tom and her. She had a sudden feeling that they were her secrets, both of them. The only two people she trusted to have loved Charlie almost as much as she did. And she did not want to think about them now, either of them, any more. 'Then I blamed my parents, because they were too ashamed of her to look after her properly in London. Then I blamed myself.' She opened her eyes. 'Then I blamed you, Georgie.'

Tessa could see Georgie's mind working, attempting to say something coherent, to come up with some slick defence – but she was too drugged. Her gaze switched from knife to water, to shore and back to Tessa. 'She drowned here,' Georgie said, in a small, but still firm voice.

'She drowned herself here.'

Georgie's mouth opened slowly. 'It was an accident. You said, it was an accident. You let me think, all of those years, it was an accident.'

'I never said it was an accident. You decided that.'

'But the inquest?'

'It was an open verdict. I know my sister better than a coroner does.'

The slightest flash of scorn passed over Georgie's face before she corrected it. And that was when Tessa knew.

She'd made the right decision.

'You brought me here to punish me. Because I didn't

let her go back to the lodge with Jack. I know you always thought Jack had a thing for Charlie, but he didn't, Tessa. You're deluded. He didn't like her at all. Couldn't get away from her.'

'I didn't come here to fight for my sister over a stupid man,' Tessa suddenly shouted. Her voice echoed off the water. Georgie shrank back in the boat.

The fishing line twitched. Tessa grabbed it, as the rod arced towards the water, pulling them with it. She held the reel with both hands, trying to counterweight the pull with her body. Whatever was on the end was tough and large. Tessa grunted, bearing down on the side of the boat. The rod thrashed.

'Can you steer?' She gestured to one of the oars. 'Just paddle on the left – your left.'

Georgie fumbled, shaking, landing the paddle with a splash. She was still strong. She wrenched them in the direction the fish was dragging them. Tessa wound in the line and they swerved closer.

'Other way,' she ordered. 'Quickly.'

Georgie clunked the oar across the boat, plunging it into the water on the opposite side. They spun the other way.

'Stop!' Tessa cried. The line was cutting across her chest. The rod slipped from its lock, threatening to tip into the water. Tessa wound as fast as she could, as the boat spun, tangling her in the line. Eventually, a pair of shining silver mackerel breached the surface, thrashing.

Georgie fell back against the side of the boat. Tessa wound the fish all the way in. Hanging alongside was a medium-sized crab and a clot of weeds.

Georgie squealed as Tessa tried to untangle the crab. It made a pinch for her fingers. She flung it away hard, and its shell smacked the water, plummeting low beneath the surface. She got to work on the mackerel. Georgie watched as she pressed the barbs out of their mouths. They slipped from her hands and fell into the belly of the boat, still writhing. Georgie pulled a face. She twisted her feet out of the way, then leaned over them, watching the shimmering death dance.

'Georgie,' Tessa said, still working at the tangled weeds. 'Don't just watch them drown in the air. Kill them.'

'I'm not touching them,' Georgie said.

'You killed a snake last night.'

Georgie shuddered as she craned over the fish. Tessa could see she was reaching for the knife. 'No. Pick them up and hit their heads against the side of the boat,' she said.

'I can't.'

Tessa suddenly flung the rod, still barbed and dripping weeds, against the side of the boat. 'Yes, you can. Yes, you fucking can.' She could feel her eyes bulging in anger, the veins on her throat constricting. Georgie's neck was streaked blue with the shock, her eyes wide. 'You pick them up and you kill them with your bare hands.'

Georgie's pupils seemed to pop. She let out a tiny splutter, wriggling backwards on the bench.

'They're in pain, Georgie. Do it now.'

With a trembling hand, Georgie picked up the first fish. Her manicured acrylics tangled as she tried to get a hold. Eventually she found purchase, closed her eyes and, holding on to the tail, slammed the fish's head against the boat's rim. The mackerel twitched and fell limp. Georgie dropped it. Then, with a small, repelled whimper, she picked up the other fish, this time hooking her nails into its fins. She gave it two sharp whacks, then flung it into the bottom of the boat.

Georgie reached over the side of the boat and plunged her bloody hands into the freezing water. Whether it was the cold or the dark or the mushrooms or the task Georgie had just performed, Tessa did not know. But she felt something – not penance, but maybe absolution from Charlie – when she heard Georgie scream, then start to sob. She sobbed a few times, then, when it seemed she could no longer stand the cold, she pulled her dripping hands out of the salty water and dug the heels of her fists into her eyes.

Or maybe, thought Tessa, it was not absolution that she felt. Maybe it was just plain, crass, base, spiteful revenge.

By the time Georgie had righted herself in the boat and dropped her hands from her face, Tessa was holding the knife.

26

'You have to stay calm,' Tessa ordered.

Georgie had begun to shake, a freezing, panic-stricken shudder that rippled through her body. Her eyes stayed fixed on the blade pointed towards her.

'Stay calm,' Tessa repeated.

'Please don't hurt me,' Georgie whispered. 'I'm sorry, I'm sorry. I know I should have looked after her that night, and at the clinic. I should have let her go with Jack; I know.' She was speeding up. 'I was jealous. I was frightened she would take off with Jack. Please, I've said it. Tessa, please. Let that be enough.'

Tessa had thought many times about how to say what she was about to. 'I have lost a limb.' Her voice was calm. 'I have lost the right side of my brain. I have lost the friend who was in my heart since I was a baby. Since before I knew what love was, I loved Charlie. I loved her more than I loved our parents. I cannot relate to people without her. You started this, Georgie.'

'Please – Tessa, you're overworked, I know. I'll pay for therapy. I'll get you the best counsellor in London. Please.'

Tessa didn't respond. In her mind, there was no hate or

disbelief or even irritation left; she was already swimming, far out to sea.

'It wasn't – I didn't . . .' Georgie looked around, as if the trees and the loch and the rocks on the shore could help her. But they were impervious, ancient. They had seen the drowning of the Jacobite boy in the eighteenth century, and the death of Charlie ten years ago. They didn't care.

'When you have an illness like that,' Tessa said, 'your mind drowns very slowly, thrashing around until it can't breathe any more. Throwing herself into the loch only sped up what was happening to her anyway.'

'Nobody knew, though. She didn't tell – I mean, if you didn't know, then you couldn't help.' The boat began to rock. Georgie rocked back and forth with it, hugging herself.

Tessa, still holding the knife, had managed to pull off her hoodie. The hairs on her arms sprang up in the cold. Georgie had stopped rocking and was staring at her quietly with still, silent horror. She shook her head. 'I love you, Tessy. I loved Charlie. I love you both.'

'This is not about you, though, is it?'

'I love you,' Georgie said softly.

'You hijack people's lives. You push them and bend them to your will.'

'My will is not that strong. Don't put that responsibility on me.'

'You take that responsibility with friendship.'

'I know that, I know that. That's why I wanted everyone to get together. I wanted to show you all that I cared, that I've missed you. I miss you being in my life, Tessy.'

371

Tessa was cold. The adrenaline had kept her going, but now she was twitchy, afraid of what would happen, or what would not happen, of what she would see in the dark if she didn't move quickly enough. She closed her eyes again, swallowed.

'When you sent that message, asking me to be your bridesmaid, asking me to come up with ideas for your hen weekend, my first reaction was sickness. I don't know why, but I am still shocked by you. You wanted us all to come together not because you missed us, or you loved us, but because you needed us to serve your purpose. This was the only idea I could think of. I couldn't get it out of my mind, the thought of coming here, bringing everyone here. Because my heart has been here all this time. You didn't know it, because you never asked. Second year you were able to forget about it all, like it never happened. But ever since then, half of me has always been here.'

Georgie's eyes clarified. Her gaze was lucid, the drug glaze gone. 'I never forgot it all,' Georgie said. 'It was just too painful to talk about. The guilt. It was never the right time to say sorry. Just please, let it be enough now. I'm sorry, Tessa. I'm sorry I didn't look after her. I'm sorry I didn't help you when you were grieving.'

Tessa's fist gripped the knife, her knuckles stinging with the grasp. It had all started as vengeful catharsis. The goats' hearts, the photo of Ethan, the games. It had all been so poetic and symbolic, and she had savoured that power. But now it was gone. Her mind and heart were empty.

With sudden vigour, Tessa tipped her head forward, and

pulled at the front of her hair. She lifted the knife and began to slice, then saw. Locks fell about her feet. When she looked back up, Georgie's face was drained of blood, mesmerised, and she knew that Georgie was seeing the ghost she had created. Georgie was seeing Charlie again. Identical face, identical hair. Charlie's 'sexy as hell' fringe.

That was all Tessa had wanted.

She flung the knife out as far as she could. It spun through the air towards the sea, fell and sliced through the waves. Then Tessa hooked her thumbs together, tipped forward and dived after it.

Through the acid cold of the water, she heard the muffled sound of Georgie's scream.

27

'They should be back by now.' Bea had her hands wrapped round another cup of black tea, her second or third, she couldn't remember. The caffeine was making her twitchy. Tea-caffeine was different to coffee; it snuck up on you.

She ought to tell the others what she knew. But they would make her feel like a fool, or worse, a violator.

'It's pitch black out there,' she murmured.

Rachael, seeing her face, placed a hand over hers. 'They'll be fine. We're humans. We're very resourceful, especially in pairs.'

Bea looked away.

Alice had been kneading the bread, checking on it, kneading it again. Now she was testing a flat, round piece of it in a dry frying pan. 'Ooh, it's bubbling up!'

Melissa peered over her shoulder. Apart from Alice's enthusiasm, there was a listlessness in the air. And though none of them would have said it, they all knew that without Georgie to glue them together, their conversation was stilted, their rapport with one another forced.

'Tessa's savvy, she's a doctor,' Rachael was saying as Bea gazed into the depths of her tea, trying just to think about Mo and the children. She would see them tomorrow. She would hug them until they hurt. It was second time round on the tea bag – or third – and it was softer than the previous cups, but still bitter without milk. She became very aware of the smell of burning flour. The air was smoky. She looked up and saw the flash of a yellow flame catching in the pan. Alice's back was turned, as she rolled a ball of dough between her hands. She hadn't seen it. All of a sudden the fireball was huge; it puffed up in a violent cloud, swallowing the air above it. Before Alice could turn back to the pan, Bea had skidded over and wrenched it off the hob.

'What on earth are you doing?' Harriet said.

Bea looked at the pan.

There was no fire, no flame. Through the glaze of the Aga's fuel door the logs glowed, the flames swayed. Had she conflated the two images in her mind?

She was breathing hard.

'Are you all right?' Alice asked.

Bea was staring at her feet. Shame, mixed with something else, stirred up a poison of guilt and panic.

She whispered, 'Charlie died in that loch.'

'What?' Harriet came to her, taking hold of her shoulders. 'What did you say?'

The knot in Bea's belly was a snake. It told her she had always known that only one of them was coming back from the boat.

She said it again, louder this time. 'I think Charlie must

have died in that loch. Tessa's twin sister, Charlie. She died. It must have been on that loch. Where Tessa and Georgie are.'

She could feel the looks passing between the others, over her head. She couldn't care any more. One of them was not coming back. She was certain now.

She took off, suddenly lithe in her panic, ducking under Rachael's arm and out of Harriet's grasp. She flung open the door to the utility room and, leaving it swinging, burst out of the castle and into the damp, frozen air. The sky was a bleak pewter, drowning the trees and the rhododendron bushes, which seemed huger than ever now, splay-handed and trumpeting. Her ankles were splashed with icy mud. Tiny stones sprayed into her shoes and she thought of the adders but ploughed on, up banks and over rocks, through the small openings where the path narrowed and led to the shore. The moon was garish neon, but she couldn't yet see the loch through the lace of shrubs. She was aware of cries behind her.

'What the fuck are you doing, Bea? Have you lost your mind?'

She suddenly emerged on the ridge, the clear vista of slate water pinched at its two ends, a slash in the land. It was impossible to see any detail, but she knew she could hear cries. The sound skated over the still depths; it bounced like a skimming stone towards her. Alice had caught up to her. 'Bea, Bea.' Bea let her arms be grabbed. Alice's hands were cold and clammy.

'What's the matter? They'll be fine.'

'They're not fine.' She didn't have time to explain. She

pulled herself free and scrambled down onto the shingle. There was already another figure there. Bea's heart jumped as she recognised Tom. He was taking off his jacket and boots, extracting his keys and wallet from his pockets, dumping them among the stones. She could hear screaming in short, piercing bursts.

'Tessa! Georgie!' Bea cried. She could see the empty boat rocking on the water, behind it a frenzy of spray, like a whirlpool.

Tom waded into the water, breathing in sharply for a second before launching himself underneath the black surface. He swam like a python, twisting and fighting the currents. The shingle crunched and Bea turned. Alice and Rachael had arrived behind her.

Rachael was taking off her boots.

'You can't!' Alice was screaming at her. 'Just let him go in.'

Rachael peeled her wife away. She stripped to her under-wear and T-shirt.

Bea was panting. 'I can't, I can't. I wish I could, but I'll get into trouble, I know I will.'

'Don't you dare go in there.' Alice lunged in front of Rachael. Rachael suddenly took Alice by the shoulders, jerked her hard. 'Do you want to watch your friends die?'

She ran into the water. Her hips rose as she plunged beneath the surface with a short shriek, then worked her way to invisibility in the dark of the loch.

Alice turned on Bea. 'Why did you let her go? What's happening out there?'

Bea couldn't look Alice in the eye. She stared at the shingle.

'Tessa's family owns this castle, this estate. I found her sister's diary in the loft and I read it. I think she died – her twin sister died in the loch. Over there.' She pointed.

'What's it got to do with Georgie?'

Bea opened her mouth, but she couldn't say. It was something she couldn't simplify or explain.

Then came a moment when the sound dropped off and the world was calm. There was only the lapping of the water, the quiet thrashes of Tom and Rachael's limbs cutting into the freeze and the salt, the frosted crests picked out by the moon.

Melissa appeared beside them. 'What's happening?'

'Georgie's screaming,' Bea said. 'Tom and Rachael have gone in.'

Alice began to shake.

The last thing Tessa had seen was Charlie's face mixed with her own. Ravaged, although she couldn't name what they had each been ravaged by. Fear, guilt or hatred? She didn't know anything now. She was travelling back through the darkened cave.

She had seen many people die. She had watched their souls lurch forward or recede, and this had been one of the twin questions that had hovered over her life until now. How would she go? How did Charlie go?

She would see now, she would know.

She had taken her last look at the trees on the far bank. Neither of them had ever made it that far. The forest on the other side of the loch would remain a shared mystery to both of them.

And then she had seen their face; her eyes beneath Charlie's fringe. Now instead of plunging forwards into understanding, her mind was racing backwards, past the white mussel buoys that had long-since deflated into filthy brown lumps. Past the shingle beach, past the castle, right back to the cot where Charlie had placed the sleeping baby Ethan safely under his blankets and tucked him in while Tom read in the living room. It was such a prosaic, domestic tender vision, it tore her apart. Charlie had kissed Tom; he'd told her. She had kissed him on his lips for the very first time that morning, and she had gone out of the door, latching it quietly.

Weeds wrapped themselves around Tessa's cheeks. Her legs brushed against wood. Her heart burned.

Charlie was down here, somewhere. Something had to be left of her here. She would find it.

Silt and salt stung her eyes, the membranes of her nose, choked her throat. Her drowning had begun, and with it came the terrible peace of knowing she could feel something that Charlie had felt.

And then she felt the grasp of hands.

Wrapped around her ankles, two firm thumbs, the scratch of nails at their tips. Bliss took her. She was being pulled down. Charlie was there. She had been right: Charlie was there all along. Here was the spot, and now she wanted her here too. Tessa's heart burst. She choked inside the remnants of herself and all of a sudden, the grit in her lungs broke free and there was only clean black water and the sensation of the beautiful hands holding her feet.

But the hands were no longer pulling; now, they were

pushing. Tessa kicked and felt her toes touch rope. She was too far away to know where she was, but she was being pushed, not pulled; not pulled from the water, but pushed up by hands underneath her. Later, she would say that she had known the touch straight away, because it was the same position they had lain in once before, before life, submerged in fluid in a single amniotic sac: Charlie's unformed hands clasped around her feet.

She broke the surface and gasped.

They saw, very clearly under the glare of the white moon, Rachael ploughing back towards them. Georgie's head was locked under Rachael's armpit, clamped, struggling and grunting in her arms. It looked as if she was trying to free herself from Rachael's grip and swim back to where they had come from. Behind them, Tom was swimming backwards, weighted down by the bulk of a body writhing against his chest.

Melissa pulled off her jumper. Bea did the same.

When Rachael made it to shore, she collapsed. Alice fell on her, weeping and peppering her wet face with kisses. Melissa peeled Georgie's body from Rachael's arms and, together with Bea, covered her with the woollens. She stank of the sea and her hair was stiff with a brittle, frosted cold. She was still trying to thrash.

'Tessa,' she gasped. 'Tessa!'

'Tom's got her,' Bea said.

'What the fuck happened?' Melissa asked. She was scraping the hair from Georgie's face, squeezing the water out of it onto the stones. She rubbed vigorously at Georgie's arms. Bea, aware how useless she was, with no medical training, no outdoor experience, had begun peeling Georgie's wet jeans away from her legs. Suddenly, Georgie sprang up, rigid, a vampire rising.

Tom had come quietly back to shore, with Tessa's body heaved on top of his. His back was to them, leaning over her. They saw the shape of legs, more skinny jeans, sticky with seawater, rolling from side to side. Her shoes had come off and she had weeds between her toes. Tom had her turned half over and he was whacking the water out of her lungs, almost beating her. She was making inhuman retching noises.

Georgie stumbled away from Melissa and Bea. She hauled herself across the shingle to Tom, and leaned over him. He turned and blocked her with his chest before she could launch herself at Tessa.

'Wake up!' she screamed past his shoulder. 'You bitch, wake up!'

She scrabbled sideways past Tom and raised her hand to strike down on Tessa's head, but he caught her wrist. Rachael came up behind them and dragged Georgie backwards, pinning her arms to her chest.

'What about Ethan?' Georgie cried. 'What about all of us? Come on, you bitch, wake up!' She turned on Tom. 'Get her clothes off. Doesn't anyone know how to resuscitate someone?'

Tom held up his palms, backing away, showing her he wasn't about to touch her. 'Be calm, and shut up. That's the least you can do for her.'

He bent quietly back over Tessa. She was spluttering. He stuck his finger into her mouth and pulled out a clot of silted weeds.

'What happened?' Bea asked. 'What did she do?'

Georgie clutched her hair, shaking. 'She had a knife. I thought she was going to kill me. She threw herself overboard. I couldn't let her, I had to go over as well. I was trying to save her, I honestly was trying.' She looked suddenly, coldly at Tom. 'You knew what she was doing, didn't you? You can be as self-righteous as you like, but how the hell could you let us go? You knew everything. That boy, and the food and the fucking rabbit – you're sick.'

'Help me get her up to the house,' Tom said, hooking his hands under Tessa's armpits.

Rachael was shivering, Alice's hen-night hoodie hanging loose on her, her legs still bare. Along with Bea and Tom, she and Alice hefted Tessa semi-upright and began carrying her, ferrying her over the ridge and through the trees. She felt cold and leaden, and Bea was repelled a little by the feel of her drenched clothing sticking to her skin. She kept her head down and concentrated on breathing as the ache in her arms grew.

Bea was too busy to notice if Georgie and the others were following them. It was only when they heaved back the kitchen door and pulled Tessa into the warm stuffy kitchen, still smoked with burned flour, that she realised Harriet hadn't come at all.

Harriet's hand was over her mouth, as if she knew what was coming and had been waiting for it.

They threw jackets onto the floor in front of the Aga.

'Don't let her get too hot too quickly,' Melissa warned.

'Come on, Tessa, wake up.' Bea bent over her, rubbing her face.

'Someone call 999,' Tom was saying.

'I thought you couldn't get a signal,' Georgie said, through chattering teeth. They had got her onto a chair and covered her legs in Tom's Barbour jacket. She was holding herself, shivering. Harriet had given her a cup of warm water.

Tom hesitated. 'You can make emergency calls.'

'They won't be able to get through,' Rachael said. 'The tree.'

Tom didn't answer. He was already down on his knees beside Tessa. He felt for a pulse on her throat, then tipped her head back, pinching her nose. He started to give her mouth-to-mouth. Georgie let out a low moan as they all watched.

Rachael said, again, 'The ambulance won't get through. The tree?'

Tom stopped breathing into Tessa for a moment and looked over his shoulder at Rachael. 'There is no tree. There was never any tree. It was all part of her plan.'

Rachael looked about to reply, when suddenly Tessa jerked up to sitting, her hands around her throat, coughing, her wet hair hanging around her face. She was trembling, but she was breathing.

28

Bea knocked softly on the nursery door. There was no reply, and she hesitated, trying to think of a time when she had felt miserable and truly wanted to be left alone. She couldn't think of one – she had always wanted people around her.

Bea pushed open the door. Tessa was sitting on the camp bed nearest the window, wearing a Fair Isle jumper Alice had dug out of her rucksack, and a pair of pyjama bottoms. Her hair was dried and fluffy. She coughed, and then winced.

In the end, Tessa had insisted on no ambulance. Her vitals were all there, she said. There was no one else with the knowledge to argue. She looked disturbed, but contrite.

Tessa looked round. 'Where's Tom?'

'Harriet asked him to leave.' Bea chose not to mention that he had refused, and was sitting just outside the nursery door, on a hard dining chair, looking faintly ludicrous in one of the hen-night hoodies. She didn't want to have an argument with Tessa over whether he should be allowed to stay or not.

'I can go, if you want.'

Tessa looked up. 'Why didn't you say anything about the diary, when you gave them the photograph?'

Bea shook her head. She only half knew. 'I didn't know what it was.' She had felt protective of that mystery, but she didn't know herself whether it was a selfish, hoarding protectiveness, or if she'd felt something more instinctive about its unsettling first page. She sat down on the corner of the other camp bed.

'I wish I had been there when you had your children,' Tessa said.

Bea couldn't meet her gaze. She had to force herself not to think of one of her own twins sitting there on the bed, like Tessa, without the other. She couldn't bear it.

'I wish I had known Charlie,' Bea said.

There was a soft knock, then Alice and Rachael came into the room with Melissa behind them. They stared at Tessa in undisguised shock, none of them able to find the right words. Then there was more movement behind them, and Harriet and Georgie entered, the others making room for them. Harriet had Georgie's hand firmly in her own.

Alice and Rachael had brought a sprig of rosemary in some hot water and a plate of dry crackers. 'I swear by rosemary tea when I'm feeling like shit. Not that I've ever felt quite so shit, or anything.' Alice cut herself off. She touched Tessa's arm. 'I want you to know.' She hesitated. 'I don't know what to say. I'm sorry if I had any part in this. I'm sorry. I didn't know.'

Tessa managed a weak smile, and Alice gave a soft sigh.

She sat on the floor with her back against the wall. Rachael slid down next to her. Tessa drank the tea in polite sips.

Melissa crossed the floor in two bounds and enveloped Tessa in an enormous hug. Tessa went a little rigid, seeming to tolerate the hug rather than melt into it. After a while, Melissa pulled back. 'I love you and Georgie so much. I'm so sorry this happened.'

Bea watched Tessa give that polite smile again. She seemed to move backwards, back inside herself. It was the same introverted politeness that Bea had always felt so safe around when they were at university. Safe Tessa. Reliable Tessa. She realised now that the reason Tessa was safe was because she kept her secrets to herself, never burdened you with them. Was that really what they all wanted from a friend?

Melissa lay back on the bed behind Tessa and tried to lighten the mood. 'I'm bloody knackered. I need a holiday after this.' There was some weak, obligated laughter. Bea joined in.

Then quiet. Bea heard Tom shift outside the door and Melissa try to cover it up with unconvincing musing sounds.

Eventually, Rachael asked what they all wanted to know. 'Why?'

They watched Tessa, waiting for the answer. The silence made Bea dizzy, an absence of everything, even breath. The others were staring at Tessa with brutal fixation, violently demanding her answers, spreading out a canvas on which she could pour forth her story, with its gore and misery.

For the first time, Bea thought she might understand why Tessa had never talked about her twin with any of them.

How bald and how ugly truths were. Better to soften and sand down and stow away sometimes. Hadn't Bea herself run away from them all with her own – the words still snagged on her thoughts – post-natal depression? What were friends for, if not to be there for you? But then how did you go about changing a friendship from the shape of parties and hand-holding and beach walks, and a certain type of candid, bodily confession, to something else – to a confession darker than you ever cared to admit existed?

She watched Tessa, just like the others.

They all watched her.

And then Tessa said, 'The mushrooms. I don't know what came over me. I thought there was a snake in the boat. It must have been the snake in the sink last night, creeping into a hallucination. Fuck. Thanks for saving me, Georgie. That's a finale to a hen party to remember. You're a lifesaver.'

Georgie said nothing. She stared at Tessa, lips pressed together, eyes wide, and she shook her head as if she was still in shock.

Bea wondered if that would be the final word. But in the end, it was Harriet who cleared her throat and said, 'Well, what's done cannot be undone.'

Bea looked at her, wondering if there was some coded message of guilt in her words, or if she had just said them because she thought it would be ironic to quote Macbeth in a Scottish castle. They sounded pithy and final, words to help them all move on. And yet, Bea knew that by trying to forget everything, they would learn nothing.

Four weeks later

At eight, they were putting on facemasks and eating bruschetta with mashed avocados – 'a strange request,' said the manager of Castello Maggiore. At half past, the champagne was cracked open. The cold bubbles felt blissful in the languid heat.

'One glass only, ladies. Don't want you pissed when I walk up the aisle.'

At nine, the hairdresser came. Georgie was last into the chair. Her up-do was complicated. 'Medusa,' Alice whispered, out of earshot.

At ten, it seemed as though there was nothing left to do. Bea touched up a chip in her nails – pale pink – and began to roam the hallways of the *castello*, fanning herself with a spare order of service. It was a fourteenth-century villa, much the same period as the castle in Scotland. Nobody had spoken about the hen weekend since they'd arrived, two nights ago. The sun had cast its spell over them all, and it seemed, between the wedding preparations and lounging around in the heat, that thoughts of that weekend had been squeezed out, smothered.

When it came time to put on the dresses at eleven, they paired off. Harriet laced up Melissa. Alice laced Bea. Bea was careful to arrange the neckline of the bodice so that it didn't cut the claws off Alice's large gryphon tattoo. Georgie had relented in the end, and the body make-up Rachael had brought along was not needed. 'I like you as you are,' she had said on the first night, then quickly squeezed Alice and run away to fiddle about with the flowers or the menus.

On the bed, there lay an extra dress. The boned corset created a stiff outline of a female torso in the silk.

'Why doesn't Rachael wear it?' Harriet asked quietly.

Rachael gave a small, embarrassed laugh. 'It wouldn't fit. I'm taller than Tessa.'

They all fell silent.

Bea had messaged Tessa a couple of times late last week. She was back at work now. A busy shift was planned for this weekend. She wanted to make up the hours. They were short-staffed. She was sorry, but she just couldn't come.

Bea didn't know whether Tessa had realised how her absence would sit amongst the rest of the group, a ghostly presence more vivid than if she'd been here in person. The empty dress, the extra champagne glass, the hairdresser finishing half an hour ahead of schedule – all of these were a reminder of the hole she had left.

Bea walked downstairs, feeling a romantic delight at the way the silk dress brushed against her legs, cooling them. Immediately, the Tessa-shaped hole materialised in her mind and she felt a pinprick of shame at her delight.

The *castello* was exquisite, the opposite of the dark tower house Tessa's family owned. Vaulted pale-coloured ceilings in the original parts and high ones in the new extensions; an olive grove and a herb garden filled with pungent rosemary. There were oil paintings all over the walls, eyes watching from other centuries, lit by spotlights cut into a plaster ceiling. On one wall, running along the corridor that led to the back patio, a montage of photos from Georgie and Jack's lives had been arranged, polaroid-style printouts stuck at angles. Most of them were people Bea didn't recognise. Cousins, a sister – Georgie had never mentioned a sister, but you never knew, did you? – and then some childhood photos with her parents, who had remained friends since their divorce. Both were now sitting in the breakfast room.

Bea scoured the wall, peering into Georgie's past. She cringed as she saw the university pictures, how her own hair had been full of bleached highlights back then. She saw them, manic and drunk and eager to show the camera how much fun they were having, posing together. Water pistols. Wet T-shirts. Wine from the bottle. Cigarettes and joints. Hung-over, studying. Then the travel pictures – Bali, Uluru, Las Vegas, Cairngorm.

What she was really looking for, she knew, was Charlie. Evidence that Charlie existed. Evidence that Georgie would acknowledge Charlie existed. Because, although Bea felt she knew what he must look like, it felt nebulous without seeing it for herself. The opposite of the boy in the photograph. He'd been there; they'd all seen him. And yet they all knew almost nothing about him.

At noon, they were married. Georgie, in her Bardot-necked dress, stiff as sugar, seemed to carry a haze of serenity around her. She wore the veil as she walked the open-air aisle, and she looked demure, and almost – to Bea's eyes – humble. If the shadow of Tessa hung over her, it was only in this contrition, which served to make her look even more like the sacrificial, mythical bride. Her humility – Bea thought with a jolt – seemed to add to her beauty, but in a way that suggested she was wearing it, like it was couture.

Jack did not wear eyeliner or black nail varnish. He wore a three-piece morning suit, slate grey; a slightly unflattering cut and fussy for the heat. He would have disappeared in a crowd of civil servants. He was so unlike the boy Charlie had written about. Bea wondered if that Jack had ever existed at all.

At three came the speeches.

When they took their seats, there had been another awkward moment when they realised an extra place had been set with Tessa's name handwritten on the favours, but before Harriet could hiss at the event planner, or Georgie notice, Rachael took it and put it into her clutch bag.

Bea was sitting at the top table, away from Mo, who was on a table of Jack's colleagues. She knew he found this kind of wedding preposterous.

They had been poor when they married. He had been studying for his PhD; she was between library jobs. His family had insisted on funding the loud, elaborate and chaotic shindig – couscous, gilded fabrics, Chivas Regal in hipflasks – in Casablanca. And then they'd had a party in a pub in Islington when they got back. She couldn't even remember if Georgie had been there. She must have been invited. Tessa was there, and Alice and Melissa. Harriet had been on holiday.

Jack was making a speech. He started the toast by saying, 'Myself and my wife—' at which point the applause and cheers cut him off while the two of them kissed. After that, Bea switched off. That was all she needed to hear. She had a sudden snap vision of Georgie bending over Tessa, trying to slap her dying face and calling her a bitch.

At six, they cut the cake. There were photographs and brandies in the hotel grounds.

At seven, the band began.

At eight, Bea was dancing with Mo. She broke free of his arms and excused herself to go to the ladies'. But instead of turning into the cloakroom off the hallway, she went upstairs to the bedroom where they'd dressed. She sat on the bed and listened to the noises floating up from outside, laughter and chat. Then she retrieved from her handbag a brown paper package.

She had wrapped it already because she did not want to read it again. When they got back, she would post it to Tessa. She had thought of addressing it to Ethan or Tom, but decided that might be cruel. It had been important to her that Charlie be there at the wedding, even if Tessa wasn't. But now that it was over, she was passing it on.

Charlie had become her friend over the past month. In some ways, she had been more of a friend than Bea and Tessa had been to each other, because neither had ever been so candid as Charlie's diary. Bea had taken Charlie to the park, sat on the tube with her. They had watched mothers playing with their babies in Starbucks together.

As she let go of the book, she expected the weight of the secrets in her to shift. But they stayed, trapped under her skin. She still felt sad and morbid, with a mournful sense of inevitability about the wedding and the festivities.

Life went on. It would be rude to cry about it all at Georgie's wedding.

She hurried back downstairs, along the photo-lined corridor of past smiles. The bathroom door opened in front of her and she stood aside politely.

Jack stepped out. If he hadn't turned to smile at her, she might have let him pass by. But that smile went right through her.

'Jack, congratulations!' She hugged him.

'It's amazing, isn't it?' He swept his arm out along the stone corridor, towards the garden. The tables and chairs had been cleared away, and the scents of candles and the hot perfumes of the guests were wafting in on a dark breeze. 'Georgie found it on Mr and Mrs Something.com. Isn't she amazing that way?'

'You guys are very lucky,' Bea said.

Jack started to nod enthusiastically. 'Amazing,' he said. But the expression on his face froze as he cast his eyes past her shoulder. She twisted to see what he was looking at.

There was a photo in the centre of the collage. One she hadn't noticed earlier. It was so large and distinctive, she couldn't believe she hadn't noticed it before. It was impossible she hadn't. She had scoured all of the photographs. It hadn't been there.

It was in the centre of the board, overlapping pictures of Georgie and Jack in Mexico and Dubai. Bea recognised it straight away, although she had never seen it before: four people standing in front of a snow-covered mountain as the sun set. Georgie, Tessa, Jack, and next to Jack, the fourth person, an almost-mirror image of Tessa, but with some undefinable difference in her expression or her face – and a fringe, brushing her eyebrows.

Jack had his arms around both Tessa and Charlie, but it was Charlie he was looking at. The camera had caught his expression, a furtive, fleeting glance, eyes made huge with kohl. He was gazing down at her from his slightly taller height, an open-mouthed smile on his face, her head nestled into his chest. The photo had captured a candid moment, as revealing as it was intimate.

There, on both of their faces, was love.

Bea's heart sped up. She looked out into the gardens, knowing it could only have been Harriet who put it there. It was Harriet's photograph. She had taken it and refused to show it to Charlie. Bea remembered that from the diary. Now she had looked it out, printed it, packed it in her suitcase. Harriet had been more courageous than Bea. Bea had hidden

Charlie away in her handbag, while Harriet had placed her out in the open.

She turned back to Jack. The blood had drained from his face. In his paleness, Bea saw a glimmer of the boy Charlie had loved. His cheekbones seemed to mould into shadows, his eyes darken.

'Is that Charlie?' Bea asked.

Jack wouldn't look at her. He pressed his fingers into his eyelids. 'Yes. She was the person who introduced me to my wife. It's funny how things turn out. I don't mean funny, I mean awful. I don't know what I mean. '

'You look close – like brother and sister.' Bea stumbled over her words.

'No,' Jack said quickly. 'It wasn't like that.' His expression flushed in sudden, drunken candour.

Bea's heart quickened again.

'But she didn't like me in that way. Then, she died. Sorry, this is supposed to be fun.' He laughed, awkwardly. 'Grab some champagne. It's all open bar, make the most of it.' He turned away.

Bea made a flash decision. 'Can you wait here?'

Before Jack had time to answer, she had bolted back upstairs.

She felt the most fleeting sense of betrayal – towards Charlie or Tessa, or perhaps even towards the boy she didn't know, Ethan. But Tessa would understand – and Charlie would understand, too. She felt no malice, even though she knew what she was doing was thoroughly wrong. She grabbed the diary and tore off the brown paper. Then she hurried back downstairs.

Jack had managed to compose himself. He had a gin and tonic now, and was rattling the ice. He was peering intently at the other photographs, the pictures of him with his university friends.

'I'm a librarian,' Bea began, breathless. 'So I like to give people books.' She held out the diary.

'What is it?' He looked down at the brown leather binding. His brow creased.

'Just read it,' she urged him. 'On your own. In private. It might – just, read it.'

An amused smile began to spread, but when Jack saw Bea's expression, it faltered.

'Georgie always says what a kind person you are,' he said. 'You're a good friend to her, aren't you?'

Now Bea faltered. She was poised to answer when they heard a voice trumpeting, 'She's the best friend a girl could ever want!' Georgie whisked out of one of the corridor's open doors, veil blazing white flames behind her, nails spread like claws. She wrapped an arm around Bea's neck, yanking her into her elbow crease.

Then she spied the book in Jack's hands.

'What's that?'

Bea hesitated, but Jack moved swiftly, and she saw the transformation in him, the morphing back. 'Wedding present. I'll look after it.' He kissed Georgie on the cheek and disappeared up the stairs.

Georgie looked drunkenly into Bea's eyes. She pulled her into a hug. 'I love you, Busy-Bea.'

'I'm glad you're having the day you wanted,' Bea whispered into her hair.

As Georgie pulled back, Bea saw her eyes ping open. While Bea's face had been buried in Georgie's hair, Georgie had been staring over Bea's shoulder, at the picture of Jack and Charlie.

Bea felt the blood rush to her cheeks. She should not have given Jack the diary. Harriet should not have put up the picture. They should not have done any of it, not today. But Georgie's face only fell briefly before she fixed it, before she breezed towards the patio doors, where the scent of rosemary drifted in strong wafts, still clutching Bea's head in a sort of lock, pointing to the features of the *castello* and exclaiming how everything was 'Beautiful, happy, wonderful!'

Epilogue

It is around eight o'clock in the evening when Tessa feels her bleep go.

She looks at the time on her phone. She thinks, *They will be out in the gardens. Whiskies and cake. It will be balmy.*

It's warm in the hospital canteen, but it's far from balmy. London is shrouded under moody skies at the moment: a smothering, stormy summer. Tessa hasn't minded the rain, but she hates the darkness it brings with it.

She downs the dregs of her black coffee and pushes back her seat. As she stands, her foot snags on the metal chair leg. The sting chimes up her leg and she looks down and hitches the hem of her scrubs to check she has not broken the skin. But no, her ankle is fine, pristine. The brand new green-blue squiggle is intact. Still, it nips where she has caught it. It is a fresh tattoo, and the skin is still healing.

Tonight Tessa is the duty anaesthetist in A & E.

The band will probably be playing by now, classics from the university days.

Before her thoughts run away, she reaches the nearest telephone and dials the extension number on the bleep's screen.

This patient has had what the nurse is calling, 'An accident. Smashed wine bottle, deep laceration to forearm, with quite a big shard still lodged. She's been drinking so they can't put her under general anaesthetic.'

'Send her to theatre,' Tessa replies. 'I'll do a regional block and meet the surgeon there.'

They will be dancing in the warm, candle-scented air. Maybe Melissa has brought along some ket.

Tessa has other friends. Of sorts. Work friends. Neighbours.

Last weekend, Tom came to stay, picking up Ethan from Sasha's on the way. They drove for miles out of London, to the South Downs. He made Tessa and Ethan leave behind their mobile phones, iPads and laptops, and they camped in the middle of a forest. She had to trust that he knew where they were. He made terrible food in tin containers and Ethan stung his bottom on nettles when he was going to the toilet. But the sunset gave them a glimpse of the gods, and they all snuggled in the same tent, and for the first time in nearly ten years, for two nights in a row, she did not look at the timelines or the Twitter feeds of the men she cannot name.

But still, she can't shake the feeling when she meets someone new that they can see her disfigurement, her incompleteness. In every coffee date with a colleague, in every social gathering, she imagines them staring at her covertly, able to see the part of her that is so clearly missing.

400

It is brutal how much she still misses Charlie. She has dreamed several times about the underwater hands, pressing her up towards the surface.

The patient is lying on her side in the anaesthetic room, next door to the operating theatre. Tessa busies herself preparing the ultrasound probe and monitor so she can see exactly where the woman's nerves lie.

People don't realise, she thinks, how calm a hospital ward can be. They hear the words A & E or High Dependency Unit and imagine doctors rushing around and incessant beeps. It is not always like that. There are some quiet moments, some lulls. She asks a few questions about the woman's medical history, and passes her a clipboard to sign a form.

She sits down on the PVC-topped stool beside the bed and gently applies cold gel around the swelling in the bony arm. The entry point is ragged, about the size of a shark's tooth. Bruises are beginning to fan outwards.

'What is that?' The woman is staring over the edge of the bed. Tessa leans down and sees she is looking at the tattoo on Tessa's ankle.

'It's a whirlpool,' Tessa murmurs. 'It was the closest I could come to a drawing of pure water.'

'Looks fresh.' Her face is pasty; her voice croaks.

'It is.'

'Why would you want a picture of water on your foot?' The woman props herself up on her unhurt arm.

Tessa wonders how the shard of glass got into her. But she is not a psychiatrist. It is none of her business.

'My twin sister died,' she says, not meeting the woman's eyes. She roves the probe over the flesh, focusing on the images on the screen, searching for the nerve. How strange to be able to see the source of a person's pain, like a map, with roads leading to the nexus.

'How did she die?'

Tessa looks at her. She is young, only in her early twenties, Tessa guesses. Has nobody called her family yet?

'Look away,' Tessa instructs. She places the woman's arm flat beside her head, the elbow bent, palm facing up.

She had not even told the tattoo artist the truth. He thought she was a hippy who liked the idea of water signs. She has not opened her mouth and told anyone what she felt under the water that night, how she has felt since – not Tom, not Bea, certainly not her parents. She has not spoken about it yet, and she still does not know how the words will feel in her mouth.

The woman ignores the instruction to look away, and watches Tessa. She has something about her that is both alert and haunted. It's a look Tessa recognises in anxious depressives, because she has seen it before, was once very close to someone who bore that look – although other than being around the same age, this woman looks nothing like Charlie.

She tries again. 'Was it an accident?'

The surgeon will be here any minute to collect her and take her to theatre. Tessa brushes the long strands of overgrown fringe from her eyes. It almost tucks behind her ear now, but sometimes still makes a play for freedom.

'Take a deep breath, sharp scratch coming,' Tessa says, and she takes a breath, too. Slowly she injects anaesthetic into the tissue around the woman's armpit, numbing the wound, and as she does so, she begins to talk, starting with the sea loch.

ACKNOWLEDGEMENTS

Thank you first and foremost to Daisy Parente, skipper extraordinaire of my strange, wandering career, who brought me to this project. Many thanks to Kate Stephenson for being such an exceptional editor, challenging, open-minded and always considerate, and for putting together a brilliant team to work on the book. Thank you to Serena Arthur and Ella Gordon for their careful work on the MS, to Karen Ball for her insights and ideas, and to Tara O'Sullivan for her eagle copy-editing eye. Very many thanks to Jenny Hewson and the team at Lutyens & Rubinstein for taking good care of me during the writing and editing process.

I'm hugely grateful to Dr Sarah Davidson for taking the time to write to me about the role of an anaesthetist. Any mistakes on that front are mine alone. I have taken liberties with several things, not least the geography of Scotland, and the University of St Andrews degree structures, amending the degree in medicine from three to four academic years to enable Tessa to stay close to the group, and adding in a degree in veterinary medicine which doesn't exist. I hope this doesn't have too many of my fellow alumni reaching for the smelling salts. On that note, there are, to my knowledge, currently no pumas at London Zoo.

A very great thank you to Lindsay Morrison, without whose nannying work I wouldn't have been able to start writing this book. And above all, thank you to my mum for the hours and hours and hours of unpaid childcare she put in – always willing, never complaining – to enable me to work. Thank you to my dad for being her capable and enthusiastic sous-nanny. Thanks also to Buster for knowing when I needed to get outside for some fresh air even when I didn't (a bit like Stevens in *The Remains of the Day*). Last but very much not least, my endless gratitude, respect and love for my three boys. Thank you Alex for every kind of support and encouragement, and thank you Gabriel and Harry for just being you.